Hazardous Imaginings:

The Mondo Book of Politically Incorrect Science Fiction

Andrew Fox

MonstraCity Press
Manassas, Virginia

www.monstracitypress.com

Other Books by Andrew Fox

Fat White Vampire Series

Fat White Vampire Blues (Del Rey Books)

Bride of the Fat White Vampire (Del Rey Books)

The Bad Luck Spirits' Social Aid and Pleasure Club (tie-in; available February 2021)

Fat White Vampire Otaku (paperback available April 2021)

Hunt the Fat White Vampire (available June 2021)

The Good Humor Man, or, Calorie 3501 (Tachyon)

The August Micholson Chronicles

Fire on Iron

Hellfire and Damnation (available August 2021)

Edited by Andrew Fox

Again, Hazardous Imaginings: More Politically Incorrect Science Fiction (available December 2020)

For my children, Natalie, Levi, Asher, and Judah, and my grandchildren, Zoe and Matthew

May they grow up in a world where they aren't afraid to speak their minds.

Contents

Introduction:

The Night They Burned Uncle Hugo's Down

UNCLE Hugo's Science Fiction Bookstore was a landmark, both for America's science fiction community and for its home, Minneapolis, Minnesota. Founded in 1974, it was the nation's oldest independent science fiction specialty bookstore. Later joined by a sister store, Uncle Edgar's Mystery Bookstore, in 1980, the two stores stood side-by-side on Chicago Avenue, hosting book signings and readings in a culturally vibrant district of Minneapolis, a city long known for its "Minnesota Nice" vibe.

As of this date, July 2020, Uncle Hugo's is no more. It wasn't the economic precariousness of the book-selling industry that did the store in. Nihilists did. Depending on the legal vagaries of owner Don Blyly's insurance policy, with its civil insurrection carve-outs, Uncle Hugo's may never be rebuilt.

Rioters burned Uncle Hugo's and Uncle Edgar's Bookstores to the ground in the early morning of May 30, 2020, along with numerous other businesses on both sides of Chicago Avenue, supposedly in response to the police-involved death of George Floyd. On May 25, 2020, Floyd was arrested by four members of the Minneapolis Police Department for having allegedly passed a counterfeit $20 bill in a convenience store. When Floyd resisted being placed in a police car, a struggle between him and the officers resulted in one officer pinning Floyd to the sidewalk, face down, restraining Floyd by pressing his knee on Floyd's neck, a method of restraint approved by the MPD. The restraint, filmed by onlookers' cell phone cameras, lasted approximately eight minutes. The restraining officer, Derek Chauvin, did not relinquish the hold despite cries from Floyd that he could not breathe and was in distress; Floyd had also complained thus prior to attempts to place him in the police car, before he was in restraint. Floyd became non-responsive and was transported by ambulance to a local emergency room, where he was pronounced dead. The autopsy report later showed that Floyd's neck and esophagus had not suffered damage and that Floyd had ingested potentially fatal levels of fentanyl and methamphetamine, that he suffered from heart disease and hypertension, and that he tested positive for COVID-19.

Floyd was black; Chauvin is white; one of the other three officers is white and two are of Asian background. Minneapolis Police Chief Medaria Arradondo fired the four officers the following day. Massive protests against police brutality and racially discriminatory policing began in Minneapolis on May 26. These were initially peaceful, but late in the evening, violent members of the crowd began vandalizing police buildings and vehicles and physically clashing with police. Over the following three nights, several Minneapolis commercial corridors suffered severe damage from rioters, looters, vandals, and arsonists, the prelude to weeks of protests and riots in cities across America and the Western world.

The mob came for Uncle Hugo's during the early morning hours of Saturday, May 30. Owner Don Blyly received a call from his security company at 3:30 AM. Motion detectors had alerted the company Blyly's store had been broken into. He immediately threw on a set of clothes and headed for his business. When he was two blocks away, he received a second call. This one informed him that smoke detectors had been activated in the store. When he arrived, his two bookstores were ablaze. Arsonists had broken every window in the stores and had spilled accelerants through each window prior to setting the fires, ensuring the destruction would be total. Blyly ran to his back entrance, hoping to access his fire extinguisher, but choking black smoke billowed through the door as soon as he opened it. He then attempted to limit the damage to his neighbor's business, a dental clinic. That building also proved too far gone to be saved.

I doubt very much that the arsonists had a particular animus against science fiction, the mystery genre, or even books in general. Rather, I think they burned down Uncle Hugo's due to their love for destruction, an adrenaline-fueled high that came from their exercise of nihilistic power, and a savage joy in tearing down what they had not built up. Upon carrying out their arsons, the perpetrators, all young white men, did not evince anger, bereavement, or resentment. They acted as though this were a festive occasion. Blyly did not witness rioters screaming or crying or expressing rage. He saw arsonists and vandals dancing on Chicago Avenue, the uproarious flames on both sides of the street illuminating their exultant faces.

As of late, science fiction has accrued its own arsonists, vandals inside the field, both professionals and fans, who brandish a far more particularized sense of grievance than that displayed by the destroyers of Uncle Hugo's. So-called "progressive" elements within the science fiction community have successfully canceled a handful of "problematic" icons from science fiction's past. Their victims included the most influential editor in the history of the field, John W. Campbell, arguably the father of modern science fiction, a contrarian who inspired his stable of writers to new feats of extrapolation through speculative discussion sessions and editorials that did not steer clear of controversy, whether social, technological, or political. In 1973, Dell Magazines, publisher of *Analog Science Fiction/Science Fact* and *Asimov's Science Fiction Magazine*, began awarding the annual John W. Campbell Award for Best New Writer, meant to honor the worthiest author whose first science fiction had been published within the past two calendar years. In 2019, winner Jeanette Ng denounced John W. Campbell in her acceptance speech, calling him a "fascist"; Dell, the award's sponsor, immediately cowered and changed the name of their award to the Astounding Award for Best New Writer (thus defenestrating the most significant employee in the company's history).

This followed on the heels of the 2016 banishment of H. P. Lovecraft's visage from the World Fantasy Awards. Since its inception in 1975, the annual World Fantasy Awards trophies, presented by the World Fantasy Convention, had been stylized busts of H. P. Lovecraft, a founding master of dark fantasy and horror fiction. However, in 2016, the award committee bowed to pressure and changed the trophies to a tree in front of a full moon, due to concerns regarding evidence of racism and anti-Semitism found in Lovecraft's correspondence.

The science fiction community's iconoclasm has not been limited to dead white males. The late Alice Sheldon, who had written under the pen name James Tiptree, Jr. and had long been a feminist icon in the science fiction world, has been subjected to a similar posthumous cancellation. Sheldon and her husband Huntington had agreed to carry out a mutual suicide pact in the event that either of them should suffer a catastrophic decline in health. Huntington became blind late in his older age, and Sheldon, following a highly-praised late-life career in science fiction, found herself suffering from depression and heart disease. In 1987, she shot him, then killed herself. In 1991, the organizers of the feminist science fiction convention WisCon began awarding annual James Tiptree, Jr. Memorial Awards to honor works that advance the consideration of gender issues. In 2019, however, the awards committee, responding to complaints that Sheldon had shown herself problematically "ableist" by choosing to kill her disabled husband, decided to strip Alice Sheldon's pen name from their awards, renaming them the Otherwise Awards.

At least Campbell, Lovecraft, and Sheldon find themselves in good company. During June 2020, in a spate of monument destruction that began with the topplings and removals of memorials to Confederate generals and politicians but quickly extended to statues of virtually everyone held in high regard by traditionally patriotic Americans, vandals damaged or destroyed statues of Christopher Columbus, Andrew Jackson, Ulysses S. Grant, Theodore Roosevelt, Frederick Douglass, Thomas Jefferson, George Washington, and Abraham Lincoln. Even the Robert Gould Shaw and the 54th Regiment Memorial, honoring the Union Army's first all-volunteer black fighting force, did not escape the defacers' destructive attention. This either illustrates the vandals' breathtakingly arrogant ignorance of history, or their desire to emulate the Khmer Rouge's Year Zero in an American context, a violent erasure of everything that predates the onset of their revolutionary zeal.

The Jacobin wing of the science fiction community have not limited their cancellations and online shaming-and-shunning campaigns to deceased luminaries. They have also targeted a number of the field's elder statesmen, writers who have provided the conceptual and speculative scaffolding for all science fiction being currently written. Robert Silverberg is perhaps the most honored living science fiction author, a dominant force in the field since he burst onto the scene as a wildly talented teenager in the mid-1950s. In 2018, following the third consecutive Hugo Awards ceremony at which woman-of-color N. K. Jemisin was awarded the Hugo for Best Novel (she had published a trilogy), Silverberg commented in a private online chat room that he considered her acceptance speech to have been particularly graceless. Despite Jemisin having won an unprecedented three consecutive Best Novel Hugos, a triple honor that greatly boosted her earning power and prestige, the honoree had opted to deliver an angry, condemnatory speech focused mainly on the alleged racism and sexism rife within the science fiction and fantasy field. She mainly aimed her vitriol on a minor writer not in attendance, Vox Day, a provocateur who had called Jemisin some nasty names on his blog. Robert Silverberg has dedicated his entire life to science fiction; the annual Hugo Awards ceremony is one of the highlights of his calendar. So he was understandably perturbed when Jemisin chose to turn such an occasion into a Maoist reeducation session. Silverberg made his comments in a private forum; an unscrupulous member of that forum then leaked those comments — which focused entirely on Jemisin's gracelessness, not her sex or her race — to a public forum. Internet purity enforcers thenceforth tarred Silverberg, who has exemplified the best aspects of liberalism throughout his long career, as a racist and a sexist, branding him with the contemporary Scarlet Letters "R" and "S".

Silverberg's public humiliation followed a similar episode involving two nearly as prominent authors from the generation that followed his. In 2013, award-winning writers Barry N. Malzberg and Mike Resnick were fired from their quarterly gig of writing the "Resnick/Malzberg Dialogues" column for the Science Fiction and Fantasy Writers of America (SFFWA) *Bulletin*. Their "crime"? They wrote a series of articles celebrating the little-remembered women editors and assistant editors who had staffed the offices of several science fiction, fantasy, and horror pulp magazines of the field's Golden Age, including famed magazines such as *Weird Tales* and *Amazing Stories*. The articles praised these women in the most effusive and adoring terms and resurrected their names and reputations for a new generation. But Malzberg and Resnick stumbled into a "wokeness" trip wire when they used the term "lady editors" (certainly period appropriate for a remembrance of the 1930s and 1940s) and recounted an amusing anecdote from the 1950s during which the wives of some male fans fretted over their husbands' poolside socializing with one of the woman editors because of how striking she looked in a bikini. The resulting explosion — Resnick and Malzberg were variously excoriated online as "misogynistic, irrelevant dinosaurs," "old men yelling at clouds," "hideous, backwards, and strangely atavistic," "blithering nincompoops," "antiquated," "gross," "shitty," "prehistoric," and perhaps most colorfully, "giant space dicks" — provoked a six-month hiatus in the publication of the *Bulletin*, a panicked hunt for any signs of atavistic attitudes within SFFWA, and the end of what had been the magazine's most informative and entertaining feature. As collateral damage, Jean Rabe, the woman editor (ironically) of the *Bulletin*, was forced to resign, due to her having signed off on the Resnick/Malzberg articles and for having approved a cover that featured an illustration of a scantily-clothed female barbarian warrior, an homage to iconic fantasy pulp magazine and paperback cover art.

The science fiction community is not alone in possessing these neo-Puritanical tendencies. The community overlaps with and emerges from larger communities where cancel culture and obeisance to the tropes of wokeness are especially prevalent — academia (particularly the liberal arts and studies departments), media, government, and the non-profit sector. Unlike the early decades of the commercial science fiction genre, when many writers possessed backgrounds in the hard sciences or engineering, today's writers and editors tend to be graduates of MFA programs or academic programs in the soft sciences or liberal arts. Many have day jobs as college instructors.

Cancel culture has grown so severe and pervasive in academia, journalism, media, professional sports, and the arts that *Harper's Magazine* pushed back against the phenomenon by publishing "A Letter on Justice and Open Debate" on July 7, 2020. It read, in part:

> The free exchange of information and ideas, the lifeblood
> of a liberal society, is daily becoming more constricted.
> While we have come to expect this on the radical right,
> censoriousness is also spreading more widely in our
> culture: an intolerance of opposing views, a vogue for
> public shaming and ostracism, and the tendency to

dissolve complex policy issues in a blinding moral certainty. ... (I)t is now all too common to hear calls for swift and severe retribution in response to perceived transgressions of speech and thought. More troubling still, institutional leaders, in a spirit of panicked damage control, are delivering hasty and disproportionate punishments instead of considered reforms. Editors are fired for running controversial pieces; books are withdrawn for alleged inauthenticity; journalists are barred from writing on certain topics; professors are investigated for quoting works of literature in class; a researcher is fired for circulating a peer-reviewed academic study; and the heads of organizations are ousted for what are sometimes just clumsy mistakes. ... We are already paying the price in greater risk aversion among writers, artists, and journalists who fear for their livelihoods if they depart from the consensus, or even lack sufficient zeal in agreement.

The letter was signed by 153 prominent writers, journalists, and academicians, most of whom identify as political liberals, including J. K. Rowling, Margaret Atwood, Jeffrey Eugenides, Martin Amis, Francis Fukuyama, and Wynton Marsalis. Pundits from opposite sides of the political spectrum joined virtual hands on the list: David Frum and David Brooks on the right, Gloria Steinem, Noam Chomsky, and Matthew Yglesias on the left. Ironically, Yglesias, senior editor at *Vox*, was subjected to a Twitter shaming campaign by junior staffers at his own magazine due to his signing the letter, and several of the letter's signatories have since renounced their support, after learning that some of their co-signatories possess "unsavory" views. Cancel culture is the snake that swallows its own tail.

* * * * *

Science fiction cannot survive as an intellectual and artistic pursuit (as opposed to a flavor of adventure and suspense media) in an atmosphere of fear and pervasive self-censorship. Speculation and extrapolation — asking *what if?* and *why?* or *how?* — are the life's blood of science fiction. Its writers can't mentally wrap themselves in yellow CAUTION tape; if they do, they creatively cripple themselves and the field they profess to love. They need to be free to follow their *what ifs?* wherever those speculative rabbit-holes may lead... even if they lead to unpleasant, disturbing, or frightening places.

Traditionally, science fiction has prided itself on making room for contrarians, for heretics, for the unfashionable and unpopular, for dreamers at the fringe. This freedom of entry and freedom of thought has resulted in a rich, century-long conversation between generations of practitioners of extrapolation, a conversation that lies at the heart of science fiction. This ongoing dialogue has fueled the field's growth and inspired its greatest works. An environment of self-censorship kills the conversation. It results in work that is derivative, stale, and decadent, lazy fictions that reek of commonplace pieties and socially-enforced ideology.

More than fifty years ago, in 1967, at a time of cultural upheaval and social unrest not too dissimilar to that of our current season, writer and anthologist Harlan Ellison captured the attention of the science fiction community, as well as much of the larger literary world, by publishing the largest original anthology of science fiction printed to that time, *Dangerous Visions*. Ellison sought submissions that couldn't be printed in the science fiction magazines or anthologies of the day. He asked for taboo-shattering stories. And he got them! The anthology's 32 stories included tales that explored the ramifications of incest, homosexuality, bisexuality, cross-species sex, women's liberation, sadism, graphic violence, blasphemies against popular religions, the moral limitations of capitalism, and the pervasiveness of bigotry. Five years later, in 1972, he followed up with an even larger sequel, the two-volume anthology *Again, Dangerous Visions*.

During the five decades since the anthologies' publication, what was originally taboo-breaking has become the common mental furniture of the science fiction field and the rest of the arts. Virtually none of the stories Ellison published in 1967 or 1972 would be regarded as shocking, subversive, or transgressive by today's readers. But this does not mean that *taboo* as a social and cultural force is anachronistic or obsolescent. New taboos have arisen to take the place of exhausted ones.

Examples aren't hard to find. Disagreement with any of the following beliefs is considered *taboo* according to the reigning zeitgeist — the pervasiveness of structural racism embedded throughout American society; gender is an entirely social construct, yet gender identity is an innate, immutable quality; speech is violence, but "good" physical violence should be considered protected expression; race is a socially invented category, yet one's racial category demands higher loyalty than that granted to any other membership and properly determines one's political and culture views; white people are innately and ineluctably racist and all efforts on their part to deny this are evidence of white fragility and attempts to buttress white superiority; there are no significant differences between men and women, yet women are uniquely vulnerable to sexual predation from men and so, in any situation of ambiguity of consent, women's testimony must be favored over men's; human-generated carbon emissions are the primary driver of climate change and will result in an uninhabitable planet by the end of this century.

These are all beliefs, or hypotheses, or assertions of moral guidance, no different in universal applicability from Hindus' belief in the sacredness of cows or Jews' injunctions that dairy foods not be consumed at the same meal as meat. Yet large, influential sectors of American society consider violation of any of these beliefs or hypotheses or moral injunctions as taboo. Just as within past and present societies ruled by religious or ideological authoritarians, in the America of 2020, violation of taboo results in performative shunning and attempted ostracism with the goal of inflicting reputational and career damage. Consequences for violation of taboo have not yet risen to the level of mass imprisonment; ominously, however, the increasing salience and prosecutorial use of hate crime litigation and efforts by some on the left to criminalize disagreement with climate change dogma point in that direction. More and more often, political disagreement is heightened to the level of heresy. Persons who earn their livelihoods at the sufferance of employers sensitive to cancellation campaigns will naturally self-censor, purely out of a sense of self-preservation.

Yet in this period of accelerating technological change and resultant social change, we need a healthy, vigorous, daring, and courageous science fiction, more than ever. We are entering an era when many of science fiction's classic scenarios are becoming realized — pervasive, technologically invasive population surveillance and social control (in China); human and animal genetic modification; asteroid mining; radically decentralized weapons production in the home; cyborg technology; and, perhaps most portentously, the creation of artificial intelligences. Alvin Toffler's *Future Shock* may have been deferred for three decades while Western societies took their collective right foot off the technological accelerator pedal, allowing themselves to be mesmerized with the Internet and social media, but future shock is fast approaching, if for now hidden the way a tsunami wave is hidden beneath the sea's surface until the wave nears land.

All of these soon-to-arrive phenomena were extrapolated and explored during science fiction's most productive decades, the 1940s through the 1970s. But those classic tales were written during times far different from our own, in the context of societal viewpoints and assumptions that have mutated greatly in the decades since. They need to be revisited in the light of our current circumstances. The most socially and culturally useful science fiction of the next generation will be near-future science fiction, imaginative extrapolation that will bear resemblance to the sub-genre now referred to as techno-thrillers. Relevant science fiction will often take the form of reexaminations and reconsiderations of past fictive extrapolations that are now shading into fact.

Writers should never feel pressured to conform their work to a particular template; as works of art, science fiction stories and novels are in no way compelled to aspire toward a status of social, cultural, or political utility (that way lies propaganda). However, those writers who wish to take upon themselves a responsibility to help their fellow citizens understand and cope with the rising wave of technologically-driven societal disrupters will need to get back to science fictional basics. They will need to direct their creative efforts away from commercially-driven sub-genres such as fantasy in its various forms (secondary world fantasy; urban fantasy; dark fantasy), alternate history, romance genre mash-ups, media property tie-ins, and supposedly sophisticated slipstream fiction that wears its fantastical or technologically extrapolative elements the way a giant pretzel does its particles of salt: on the surface, easily dislodged.

* * * * *

This collection and its forthcoming sequel, *Again, Hazardous Imaginings*, an international anthology of politically incorrect science fiction, are intended to push back against the closing of science fiction's collective mind. Both feature stories that would not be published by editors of commercial science fiction magazines or anthologies in the current climate. By publishing these stories, I am screaming "*NO!*" at the strictures of the reigning zeitgeist — but not merely to kick up controversy and sell some books. I'm trying to inject some sorely needed antibodies into our cultural bloodstream. In order for science fiction to serve as an early-warning radar for both tomorrow's perils and for dangerous technological and social trends already metastasizing, its practitioners cannot wear blinders, whether forced upon them by outside influencers or self-imposed.

Science fiction cannot be a safe space.

Much of what you will read in these two volumes will not feel comfortable or comforting. Some of these pieces may make you angry. Some may make you question certain verities that you had never thought to question before. Some may even incite you to throw the book (or your reading device) across the room.

If so, these volumes are working as intended. The best of science fiction was never meant to be escapist literature. The only way to escape the future is to die. Those of us who live to inhabit the future will be forced to cope in one way or another with all the changes the future brings. Rather than waiting passively to be blindly buffeted by whatever gusts the future will bring, we better serve ourselves, our families, and our communities by using the tools available to us to forecast from what directions those winds will engulf us.

Science fiction is among the most powerful of those tools. But all tools exposed to the elements require preventative maintenance, lest they grow rusty or degraded, their blades dulled.

Think of this volume as an example of science fiction's preventative maintenance, just as *Dangerous Visions* was during the tumultuous year of 1967. *Hazardous Imaginings* and *Again, Hazardous Imaginings* represent my efforts to clear taboo's encroaching entanglement of dry kindling from the ramparts of science fiction, so that no arsonists will succeed in burning down the fabulous edifice the way Uncle Hugo's was burnt to its foundations... all its thousands of books, monuments to science fiction's past and exemplars of its present, turned to ashes the same way as the condemned tomes in Bradbury's *Fahrenheit 451*.

— Andrew Fox

July 2020: Virginia

An Introductory Note:

Barry N. Malzberg

S CIENCE fiction for most of the half-century of my involvement ran in accord with my own synchronous flood of essays and culminated in the last decade with the world-snake as controlling metaphor. Metaphor for a field which — like the Constitutionally-based Republic — has been almost from its modern origin in 1926 avidly consuming itself. Essentially science fiction was about its own self-destruction, just as the Constitutional Republic was assembled upon a document which made clear every step by which it could be subverted. This collection explores the issue and comes closer than any aggregation of stories of single authorship. "The Denier" could have been an equally satisfactory title for this collection for the field is based upon the denial of its centering premise. *Ad astra per aspera*? Not exactly. Think again, ladies and gents.

Andrew Fox has come closer to documenting, to exposing this core than all but few of us earlier; these stories could have been conceived (although written in a different way) by Alfred Bester (1913–1987), the transgressive genius self-smuggled into the genre. This collection is at the heart of the heart of the country. It suggests that the true protocol was always to challenge and consume the very fields of fire through which it sometimes strolled, sometimes cantered, occasionally brutally marched.

Remarkable work in an incendiary time. The Truest Quill.

—August 2020: New Jersey

Six Wings Hath They

"**H**ELL, *no*, I ain't going! Those bug-eyed winged critters want to shrink me down like some damn *Shrinky-Dink* and carry me off in a flying saucer...? Well, just they *try*, I'll have me a big can of Raid Ant and Roach spray waitin' for 'em, and I ain't lyin'..."

Now, don't get me wrong, I *like* Louella Hepps. She's good people... aside from all the cussing, that is (that I can do without). She's had me over to her church, Victory Baptist, and they're all good folks, even if they believe a little different. Their choir can't be beat — I mean, that goes without saying. And their Easter barbeque...? Well, *that'll* earn 'em all a spot in Heaven, if nothing else does.

But the thing about Louella is, she can be as stubborn as mange on a dog. I should know — we've been working side by side in this same college cafeteria kitchen seven years now, ever since Clyde passed on to his heavenly reward and I lost the house and had to move into the trailer. Chopping lettuce next to the same woman for seven years, you get pretty darn familiar.

"I think maybe you should try to keep an open mind, Louella," I said. "Those 'bug-eyed winged critters,' they say the world's about to *end*. That's a pretty big deal, no matter which way you look at it. Worth paying attention to." I took a quick taste of the taco meat simmering in the big pot; it needed another tablespoon of salt. We're mighty proud of our international menu here at Sabine Agricultural College. We've got us a Mexican food bar, an Italian food bar, and a Chinese food bar. On Saint Patrick's Day, Louella and I add a pinch of green food coloring to the egg fu yung.

Louella waved her hands dismissively before sliding a frozen pizza into the oven. "Oh, the world's gonna end, the world's gonna end! *How* many *times* have I heard that same story? You been around as long as me, Norma. You remember, back when Jimmy Carter was president, we was all supposed to *freeze* to death? Whatever happened to *that?* And then there was that, what'd they call it, over-*population?* When we was all supposed to *starve* to death? You remember that movie? You know, the one where they killed the old people and turned 'em into crackers to feed the young people? The one with the guy who played Moses? Tarnation... used to play on *The Late Show* all the time..."

"Something 'Green,'" I said, emptying a packet of chopped parsley into the taco meat. "Wasn't that it? *Green Mansions*, maybe? *The Green Slime?*"

"No, that weren't it. Well, it don't matter. Nowadays, it's the global *warming* gonna get us. Warming? *Really*, now? When I was coming up, summertime, you wanted to brew some tea, you didn't have to put the kettle on the stove. You just put a pitcher of water with a tea bag in it out on the back porch until the next commercial came on, and you had your damn tea brewed. Warming, huh..."

"I wouldn't be so quick to poo-poo global warming," I said. "Remember your Scripture, Louella. *Revelation* 16:8... 'And the fourth angel poured out his vial upon the sun; and power was given unto him to scorch men with fire.' And 16:9... 'And men were scorched with great *heat*, and blasphemed the name of God...'"

Louella sniffed in that insufferable way she can get to. "Global warming ain't from *Scripture*. No, no, *no!* It's a conspiracy made up by *the gays* to distract attention from what they're up to. I heard that from good sources. You ever notice how, as soon as they got gay 'marriage,' all them gay politicians and gay leaders changed the subject to global warming? 'The world's gonna end, the world's gonna end, we got just twelve years left on the planet!' They don't want us to notice the other stuff they got up their sleeves. You know? Like legalizin' relations with young boys and such..."

I've got nothing against black people, but they sure have a bee in their britches about the gays. We've got us some gays in our church. A few, anyway. Nice enough, I suppose. I mean, they don't make a big honking deal about being gay, not the ones in *our* church. That Billy Donovan, he's really kind of a sweetie. And he's got a fine tenor voice for choir.

"Louella, what about Bill Nye the Science Guy? Is *he* gay?"

"Do you know for sure he's *not?*"

I let Louella get the last word, 'cause just then the clock struck eleven-thirty and the first students came through the doors and I had to stock the taco bar before the line backed up.

I got off my shift at three-thirty and headed for the employee parking lot over at the edge of old U.S. 80. The Silverado'd been burning oil something fierce, but I hoped it would hold out another year, at least, since I was in no financial shape to pay for no engine work. Clyde, bless his heart, had left me a perfectly good truck when he'd passed, but even the best of trucks don't last forever. Of course, I reminded myself that if the bug-eyed critters were right, nursing along a sixteen-year-old Chevy that was burning a little motor oil would be the least of my problems. 'Cause there wouldn't be a Longview, Texas for me to drive around in anymore, anyway.

It just so happened that pretty much the same time I was thinking that thought, I came upon Sabine Agricultural College's designated Free Speech Zone. It's a little grassy square where the preachers have to go to preach the Word if they want to preach it on campus, and it's where the Black Students Union and the Gay-Lesbian-Trans Alliance and the International Students Against Injustice in Palestine go when they want to hold their rallies or protests or whatever.

Well, there was some kind of a big ruckus going on. I hadn't seen so many folks whoopin' and hollering with signs and such since that time when the Sabine Christian Association amended their bylaws that so all officers had to be Christians of good moral standing, and in response a transvestite Satanist decided to run for Association president. When the other officers from the Association said he couldn't run — *whoa, mama!* The protesters screaming *discrimination!* were packed so tight into the Free Speech Zone that day, you could've driven one of them monster trucks across the tops of their heads from one side to the other.

So what was it this time? Had the Sabine Republican Club tried inviting Rush Limbaugh to come give a talk again? I pushed my way through the protesters to see who or what it was they were protesting. Turns out it was more of a "what" than a "who." Standing in the middle of the Free Speech Zone, protected by a quartet of campus security, was one of them space aliens — around seven feet tall, multiple sets of wings folded neatly behind its back, its three sets of arms crossed in front of what I'd guess was its belly in an almost demure fashion. I'd say its eyes were its most interesting feature. They kind of looked like oval lava lamps, of the sort you can buy at the mall at Spencer Gifts, but fancy ones, the extra-cost kind that change colors. (I'll admit, I always wanted one for the living room, but Clyde would never pony up.) Those eyes changed colors in the nicest way, All nice, pretty pastel colors... lavender, pink, sky blue, lime green. If I had me a stadium chair and it wasn't so darn hot and humid, I could sit and watch them change all day. Soothing, it was. The alien had set a sign near what I guessed were its feet, written on some sort of weird plastic placard. All it said was, *Please Come With Us.*

For the life of me, I couldn't see what was so offensive about that. I know I'm not the sharpest knife in the drawer, but the message struck me as unoffensive, even polite. I turned back around to the pack of protesters and spotted a few of my regular customers, professors, in the crowd. They had advanced degrees up the wazzoo and wore tweed jackets and smoked pipes (that smelled, weirdly enough, like the inside of Spencer Gifts). I figured they were brainy enough to explain to me what I'd been missing about this here space alien and its kind.

I walked over to Gerald Nash from the Sociology Department. His sign said, *Colonialists, Go Home!* I said to him, "Jerry, what goes on here? How come you're standing out in the sun, protesting this space alien?"

He looked startled, like I was a lamp post he'd been leaning on that had just started up talking. "Uh, I'm sorry, but *who* are you...?"

"I'm Norma Greenly, one of the cafeteria ladies who serves you your breakfast and lunch every working day. What have you got against that there space alien?"

"It's *obviously* a colonialist," he said, his tone emphasizing just how obvious I should find his observation. "You'd know that, if you'd ever read anything by Foucault or Fanon."

"I'm afraid they aren't on my reading list, Jerry. Explain it to me a little simpler."

"This 'black hole' nonsense, it's obviously a *trick*. No different than the few cents' worth of beads and baubles the Dutch colonialists used to con the Native American inhabitants of Manhattan out of ownership of their home. It is as plain as the cap on my head that they mean to take us into space, eject us through their hatches into the absolute zero of the vacuum, and then take our emptied planet for their own. Foucault's dialectics predict precisely this."

"This Mr. Foucault," I asked, "where can I hear him talk? I'd like to get his side of the story. Is he on CNN?"

"CNN...?" Jerry sniffed. "He's been dead since 1984."

"Oh."

I moved on. I spotted Maurice Lewis from the American Studies Department. His sign read, *To SERVE Man?????*, with the word "SERVE" underlined three times in red. There was a drawing of a knife and fork under the words. His sign didn't make any more sense to me than Jerry's had, but I figured American Studies had to be easier to parse out than Sociology. I made a beeline for him through the crowd.

"Hi, Maurice," I said. "You got a minute to tell me about that sign?"

"You're, uh, from the cafeteria, right?" he said, adjusting his glasses to peer down at me. "You, um, stock the taco bar...?"

At least he remembered me better than Jerry had. "Yup, that's me, Norma Greenly, the taco lady. I'm trying to figure out why everybody here's so put out with this space alien. How come there's a knife and a fork on your sign?"

"Are you a fan of the classic science fiction anthology from the golden age of broadcast television, *The Twilight Zone*?"

"You mean that old black-and-white thing? What used to play on Channel 8 years ago after the evening local news? Yeah, I guess I've watched it here and there, when there's nothing much else on."

"Are you familiar with the episode entitled, 'To Serve Man,' based on a short story by Damon Knight?"

"Is that one of the funny ones? I'm partial to the funny ones. Like that one with the butler from *A Family Affair*..."

"It wasn't 'one of the funny ones.'" He rolled his eyes. "It was *dead serious*, especially in relation to the current crisis. In 'To Serve Man,' seven-foot-tall aliens — about the same size as that creature standing there — came to Earth and presented themselves as our friends and benefactors... just like our real-life visitors are doing. To prove their benevolence, they visited the United Nations and shared a book they had written in their own language, which they said was titled *To Serve Man*. They shared fantastic technology with us and offered amazing vacation and study trips, at no cost, to anyone willing to travel with them on their spaceship back to their home planet. Millions and millions of people lined up for the chance. But at the same time the aliens were packing Earthlings onto their ships, one of our scientists was working diligently to translate the book the aliens had shared, the one called *To Serve Man*. You know what that scientist discovered, just before the episode ended? *To Serve Man*... was a *cookbook!*"

Oh, okay. I got it. *Serve*, like, to do good things for somebody, versus *serve*, like what I do at the taco bar. But one thing just didn't make sense. "Maurice," I said, "I'm no expert on foreign languages, but my grandpa came over from Germany and taught me some German when I was little. In English, the word for helping somebody out and the word for putting something on a plate are the same — 'serve.' But it don't work that way in German, so far as I know. So what are the chances that that same one word would have those same two meanings in some space aliens' language?"

Maurice looked like he was about to brain me with his sign. "Don't *ruin* it!" he shrieked. "'To Serve Man' is an *exquisite* distillation of the mid-twentieth century conflict between utopian idealism and anti-communist paranoia! It is a key artifact of American postwar culture, a subversion of complacent bourgeois rejection of class consciousness. The aliens were actually meant as stand-ins for the military-industrial complex, you see—"

"Yeah, but it's just an old TV show, Maurice. I mean, why should you take it to predict what's actually in that there alien's heart — assuming it *has* a heart? Isn't there at least as much likelihood that it's being genuine and means just what it says?"

"I wouldn't expect you to understand," he muttered. "Culture, you see, is a living, organic embodiment of mass consciousness that extends through *time* the way our bodies extend through *space.* Yesterday's cultural constructions influence today's cultural constructions, and today's will influence tomorrow's. But they are all, every bit of them, part of the *same* living, organic embodiment. My dissertation and my upcoming book show how, just as electric nerve impulses travel from one end of the body to the other, *cultural impulses* travel from one end to the other of the living, organic embodiment of mass consciousness that extends through time. In *both* directions — past-to-future *and* future-to-past. The latest discoveries in quantum particle physics bear this out. Regarding the current crisis, my theorem is that some future cultural producer, witnessing the genocide of humanity at the hands of these so-called benevolent aliens, sent a vibration, a *cultural impulse*, surging through the living, organic embodiment of mass consciousness *back through time* to reach the mind of Damon Knight, who wrote the story 'To Serve Man,' which inspired Rod Serling to film the famous episode of *The*

Twilight Zone... which was subconsciously intended to be a *warning* to those of us confronting these aliens sixty years later."

"Warning that the aliens are gonna *eat* us all...?"

"Yes! *Yes! Now* you understand! Besides, they *have* to be evil! They — they look like *giant cockroaches!*"

I didn't ask him any more questions. Just quietly slipped out of the crowd and slunk back to my truck.

Boy, and they say we *Evangelicals* have weird ideas!

The next day was even more of a boiler. Off shift, walking back to my truck, I watched shimmering waves of heat rise from the black asphalt of old Highway 80. The bug-eyed alien still stood in the middle of the Free Speech Zone. Had it gone home for the night? Where would it have gone, anyway? Back to its flying saucer? To a Days Inn?

The crowd milling around with their protest signs was only about a third as big as yesterday's... I'd guess because of the heat. I couldn't see any sweat on that alien. Did cockroaches sweat? Did they have sweat glands? *I* sure did... I mean, there was a zero-percent chance I was gonna get another wearing out of my cafeteria uniform before dry cleaning it.

Anyway, I found myself feeling a little sorry for that alien, standing out there in the sun, not convincing a soul. A spirit of charity overtook me. Before I could think better of it, that spirit propelled me into the middle of the Free Speech Zone with the firm notion that I was gonna offer that alien some water.

A security guard (there was just one of them today) roused himself out of his heat-induced stupor when I walked near. "What you want, miss?"

"It's darn hot out here. I want to ask that alien if it wants a cup of water."

"You know for sure it *drinks* water?"

I hadn't thought of that.

"Well... I *suppose* it does," I said. "I mean, even bugs drink water, don't they?"

He shrugged.

I walked past him and approached the alien, who turned toward me, its eyes shifting in that same pleasant, soothing swirl of pastel colors I'd noticed the day before. "Excuse me," I said to it. "Would you care for some water?"

It's mouth — well, mandibles, I'd guess you'd call it — moved, but the words came out of a little silver box hung on a cord around its neck. "Your water is very satisfying and refreshing," it said. "Yes, I would like some, thank you."

Only then did I realize that the spirit of charity that had overtaken me hadn't reminded me that it was after the time the campus sundries store closed for the day. Where was I going to get a bottle of water? There was a water fountain at the far end of the square. But I didn't have a cup with me, and I didn't suppose it'd be polite to cup some water in my palms and offer it to the alien. And whatever water I held would probably dribble out while I was walking with it, anyway.

"Uh, tell you what," I said. "How about you and me drive to a place I know not far from here and get out of the sun and have a glass of something cold?"

"Will it be water? I like your water very much."

"Yeah, sure. This place serves ice water, and they don't even charge you for it. Come with me. I'm not parked far from here."

"But I need to share my message," it said. "That is my duty, and I must not shirk it."

Sounded like some missionaries I know. So committed to spreading the Good Word, they'd stand on some street corner in the baking sun until they fell over with heat prostration. "Look," I said, "these folks here aren't buying what you're selling. At least *I'm* willing to hear you out. Come on. You're just wasting your time here."

I couldn't be sure, but it might've shrugged with two sets of those arms it had. It followed me obediently to my Chevy, carrying its sign with it.

I drove us to David's Catfish King and Catering, over on Mobberly Avenue. I figured Catfish King was a better bet than the Chili's because the Chili's sponsored a happy hour late afternoons and the singles crowd tended to congregate there after getting off work. I didn't want a bunch of soused office workers making pie eyes at the alien and me when we walked in. Catfish King, on the other hand, could be counted on to be deserted as a gun show in San Francisco, at least until five PM when the Early Bird Special kicked in.

Just as I'd predicted, at 4:20 PM the parking lot was empty, save for a rusted-out old Corolla and a banged-up F-150 that

I figured must belong to the cook and the hostess. It was a seat-yourself sort of place, so I led the alien to a big booth near the back where it could stretch out its arms and wings, if it was of a mind to.

I've got to give that waitress credit. She barely batted an eye when she came over to our table, although her nose twitched some. Good upbringing, I supposed. "Welcome to David's Catfish King," she said. "What can I get you folks to drink today?"

"My friend'll have an ice water," I said. "Me, I'd like a Cherry Coke, please."

"Sure thing. It'll just be a minute."

She brought us our beverages. Wouldn't you know it, that alien slurped down that tall glass of ice water like a hound that just spent a whole East Texas summer chasing deer. It didn't even need a straw. It brought its own — I mean, it had this kind of tube-like tongue that poked out from between its mandibles. The waitress stood by our booth, pink spots blooming on her cheeks, and watched the alien down that ice water. Then she quickly brought it another two glasses. I mentally added another three percent onto her tip.

"Excuse me," the alien said after it sucked in its third glass of water and crunched the last of the ice cubes between its mandibles. "There is an Earth food I have heard about that sounds like it may be very similar to a delicious delicacy we have on my planet. I have been eager to partake of it. Do you think there is a chance this establishment offers Jello-Brand Gelatin? The lime-flavored kind that glows an iridescent green when exposed to a strong light source?"

"Well," I said, "let's check the dessert menu." This *was* East Texas, after all. We liked our Jello 'round these parts. "Bingo," I said, pointing to the menu. "It's right there beneath the pie of the day. But it's fruit Jello. I hope that's okay."

"Explain to me this 'fruit Jello'?"

"It's nothing bad. They just dump a can of fruit cocktail into the liquid Jello before it goes into the refrigerator. Fruit Jello's got grapes, cubed peaches, and those bright red maraschino cherries that are supposed to stay in your digestive tract for seven years."

"Is this considered an Earth delicacy?"

"Depends on who you ask."

"I will have some."

Our waitress brought two servings of fruit Jello (to be neighborly, I ordered one for myself, although I would've preferred the lemon meringue pie). While we ate, not wanting to stare at my companion's kinda complicated way of downing that fruit Jello, I watched the CNN Headline News on the TV in the corner. They showed a montage of aliens talking at the United Nations and to the British Parliament and the Chinese Communist Central Committee, plus other aliens holding signs like my companion's on big, famous college campuses like Harvard and Stanford and the Sorbonne in France. I figured the aliens must be really, really thorough if they'd included a place like Sabine Agricultural on their itinerary.

I waited for my companion to finish scraping up the last flecks of its lime Jello and spitting out the maraschino cherries (I should've done the same, darn it). Then I asked, "So, how's the campaign coming along? Y'all getting any takers on your offer to leave Earth?"

"Sadly, no. Only a handful of your scientists have offered to accompany us. You Earthlings have proven exceptionally resistant to our pleadings that you flee this planet before its ecosphere is devastated by the black hole that will absorb the molten contents at Earth's core."

I truly did not want to be impolite or pushy, but I figured I'd probably never have a better opportunity to ask an alien the questions I'd been itching to ask than I did right then. "Uh, I can't say I understand the whole debate, not most of it, anyway, but aren't our scientists saying that we've got telescopes that can pick up black holes? And aren't they saying none of our telescopes or satellites see any black hole heading our way from the direction you folks say one is?"

"With all respect paid to your species's technical accomplishments, your instruments are not yet sensitive enough to detect a black hole having dimensions as minuscule as this particular one's. It is barely one one-hundredth the size of one of the sugar crystals that was mixed into that exceptionally delicious lime-flavored Jello-Brand Gelatin. Yet such is its power that it will inexorably carve its way through the various levels of your Earth's crust and will not pause until it reaches your planet's core, where, temporarily immobilized by gravitational forces, it will absorb the majority of the molten mass within itself before continuing on through the rock of the far side of your planet. This subtraction of your planet's molten core will disrupt Earth's magnetic field, its rotation, and even its orbit around your sun. This will result in planet-wide earthquakes, volcanic eruptions, and tsunamis, as well as sudden changes in your atmosphere's composition and surface temperatures that will be inimical to the continuation of all higher forms of life.

"We have seen such events happen before, many times. They are more common than you might think, for our universe is swarming with these tiny, unstoppable planet-killers. We have dedicated ourselves to our primary mission of rescuing intelligent life forms from such planetary disasters by transplanting them to suitable replacement worlds, along with breeding populations of the most useful and highly desired non-sentient plant and animal species."

That seemed like an awful lot of trouble for these smart cockroach people to go to, running half-way across the galaxy to save planetfuls of folks a whole lot dumber than they were. I mean, I've heard of animal-lovers swerving suddenly to miss a cat running across the road, and then totaling their car against a tree, but this went way beyond that. Maybe Maurice Lewis was onto something after all? Maybe the aliens really *did* mix in chopped up people-parts with their lime Jello.

"You know," I said, swirling my fingers in a small puddle of condensation that had dripped from my glass onto the table, "not to look a gift horse in the mouth, but what gave your people the idea that they should go to all that trouble, racing around the universe and all to save folks who can't in no way return the favor? Not to cast *aspersions*, mind you. I'm just curious, like I'm sure a lot of people are."

"We revere life," the alien said. "Sentient life, especially. The universe teems with life, but its abundance makes it no less precious to us. If we are able to save even just a small remnant of an endangered race, we are obliged to do so."

That word *remnant*, well, it just resonated with me. What happened next, I'm not sure whether it was my lunch companion engaging in a prayerful habit, like the way some Catholics will cross themselves after saying the name of the Savior, or whether the alien just needed to stretch a bit after drinking all that water and eating all that fruit Jello. But it leaned forward and unfolded its wings from its back, splaying them out over half the booth. Not just two wings, mind you. Three pair. Six wings.

And then it hit me.

Six. Wings.

Isaiah 6:2 — *Seraphim stood above Him, each having* six wings*: with two he covered his face, and with two he covered his feet, and with two he flew.*

Revelation 4:8 — *And the four living creatures, each one of them having* six wings, *are full of eyes around and within; and day and night they do not cease to say, "HOLY, HOLY, HOLY is THE LORD GOD, THE ALMIGHTY, WHO WAS AND WHO IS AND WHO IS TO COME."*

Now, I'll tell you straight up, that alien in no way looked anything like any painting of any angel I'd ever seen. But then I thought, *who says angels have to have blonde hair and pale skin and wings like doves' wings?* I mean, God could make His angels look like anything He wanted. Right? He could have lots and lots of them, as many as He wanted, and he could make them all different shapes and sizes, if He was of a mind to. Why not? Why *couldn't* some angels look like big cockroaches? (I mean, didn't Revelation 4:8 mention those angels being "*full of eyes*"?) Didn't God love His cockroaches, just like He loved His human beings? If not, why the heck would He have made so many of them?

So I just had to pop the Big Question. "Do you accept Jesus Christ as your Lord and Savior?"

"Please explain Jesus Christ."

"Jesus Christ is the Son of God. He allowed Himself to be killed on the Cross so as to save all mankind from our sins. He rose from His grave three days after His death on the Cross, and He will come again before His Millennial Reign to Rapture his followers into Heaven before the Great Tribulation that will afflict all the non-believers."

"This is very interesting," the alien said, its mechanical voice box transmitting at a louder level than usual. "Is this a belief common to all the people of your planet?"

"Well, it's not *everyone's* belief," I admitted. "But around here, it's pretty universal, except for the Seventh Day Adventists and Catholics, and maybe a handful of Jews and Mormons." I wasn't going to let my question drop, though. "But putting all that aside, do you believe in a Savior who is the Son of the Creator? Is this Savior the one who told your people to fly around the universe rescuing folks from Great Tribulations?"

"I am uncertain of the subtleties inherent in your terminology. But yes, if I am understanding your words correctly, my people are guided by similar beliefs about the purpose of our existence in the cosmos."

Hot diggity! The End Times were just around the corner, and I was gonna be around to see them! "Listen," I said, "I've got to talk with my pastor about all this. But I'm pretty darn sure he's gonna want you to make your presentation to our congregation. And I'll bet there are plenty of other congregations in East Texas and farther parts that'll want to hear you speak your Word."

Well, to cut a long story short, that's how I ended up one of about 285 million Christians shrunk down to less than a millimeter tall and housed in tiny model cities aboard a spaceship bound for another part of the galaxy. My pastor had connections, and his connections had connections all over the country, and their connections had connections all over the world. Every Christian who believed in the Rapture was encouraged to go with our cockroach angel friends. Plus, lots of Christians who *didn't* believe in the Rapture, and non-Christians, too, also got asked to come along, but not many did. The Chinese figured the aliens weren't angels at all but a U.S. plot, animatronic creations of the Walt Disney Corporation or whatnot, meant to convince a billion Communist Chinese to abandon the planet so the Americans could take over the whole shebang. The Russians sided with the Chinese. The Arabs also thought like the Chinese did, only they blamed the Israelis for the plot instead of the Americans. The Indians didn't know who to believe, and the European Union couldn't get the aliens to commit to the E.U.'s definition of what makes cheese *cheese*, so they voted to stay behind. (Oh, I guess it must've been more complicated than just that.)

Still, thanks to the blessings of a hundred years' missionary work, we got millions and millions of Rapture-believing Christians from Africa and Asia and Latin America to trust our alien angel friends and let themselves be compressed to smaller than ant-size. My personal angel friend, Dukdukduk Shaw-nay-duk (that's not how she's pronounces her name, but it's as close as I can come), tried to explain the process to me. I won't bore you with details, 'cause I don't understand them myself. Suffice to say, the angels' spaceships are able to siphon off some of the incredible power of our sun (and other stars, too), and the angels have machines that can use that almost unimaginable power to compress the space between the nucleuses of the atoms in our bodies (did I get that right?) and the electrons that orbit around those nucleuses. Or something like that. Anyway, I can tell you from experience, it *works*. Then, when we get to whichever planet the angels have picked out for us, they'll run us through the works again, but in reverse, so we'll pop back up to full-size. All the plants and animals we're bringing with us, too.

I have to tell you something that hurt my feelings some. Nancy Ann Weston, one of the young mothers in my congregation (she's got five kids so far, three girls and two boys), showed me a copy of *The New York Times* newspaper she bought as a souvenir the day before we boarded our spaceship. The headline read, *GOOD RIDDANCE!* And they weren't talking about the aliens, no sir. They were talking about *us*.

Nancy Ann thought that was kinda funny, that headline, since our angel friends had explained to her and her family (and everybody else coming along) what was about to happen to Earth and all the living things that were getting left behind. Me? Well... I was more hurt than amused. Then, later, more sad than amused. I tried telling myself that I was going to get to meet Jesus soon (even if he ended up looking like a big cockroach this time around), and I was being Raptured. *Saved*. So I should be all like, *Par-TAY! I'm gonna crack open a Bud with Jesus!* But that's not how I felt. See, I kept thinking about Louella Hepps, and about all her fellow congregants at Victory Baptist. At Victory Baptist, they didn't believe in the Rapture. I kept thinking about Louella, and all the other people and things that weren't going to be a part of my life anymore, or a part of anybody's lives. I kept thinking about Clyde's little plot and his gravestone — nothing special, and he'd soon be on his way to a greater reward, but I'd miss it when it was gone, all the same. I'd even miss that silly ol' oil-burning truck of his. I'd miss Lake Cherokee and the fleet of fishing boats at Forest Lake Reservoir. I'd miss the good table service at David's Catfish King. Heck, I found myself missing Maurice Lewis and *The Twilight Zone*, and they weren't even gone yet.

We lifted off. Climbing through the clouds, my stomach wasn't much worse off than it had been that time Clyde made me ride the big coaster at Six Flags Over Texas. Then I suppose our ship and the other spaceships kind of hovered near Earth for a while, outside the atmosphere, waiting for the Great Tribulation to begin. Our hosts turned on a bunch of big TV screens (maybe they weren't really all that big, but we were so small, they *seemed* mighty big) that showed different wilderness areas around the world. They wanted us to see what we were escaping from... probably because, if we didn't see it with our own eyes, some of us would refuse to believe the Earth we'd known was gone.

They tried to be merciful. They didn't train their telescope TVs on any cities or towns or inhabited places. I swear, at first I thought I was watching some of them old disaster movies, like *Earthquake* with Charlton Heston or *The Day the Earth Caught Fire*. With digital effects, film makers can do just about anything, nowadays. And that's what I wanted to believe — this was a big hoax, like some sceptics said the moon landing had been. The aliens were showing us disaster movies that they'd whipped up, just to buffalo us into thinking our world was done for. And now that we were ant-sized, they were gonna take us back to their home planet so they could sprinkle us on their lime Jello like crushed walnuts and scarf us down. New taste sensation.

That's what I wanted to believe. That the Earth was still the Earth, and the song birds still sang, and people would still be enjoying their Early Bird Specials at David's Catfish King, if it managed to stay in business after so many of its old customers had been trucked into outer space. But my gut told me it wasn't so. Hills and mountains turning to boiling mud, whole lakes getting swallowed up... it wasn't just special effects.

So I stood there in the town square of my toy-sized model town, holding hands with Billy Donovan, the one with the sweet tenor voice, and watched the world end on a giant TV. Because you just needed to be holding someone's hand at a time like that... a time like that.

Denier

-June 14, 1955-

"You can't change the past, Irving..."

"It's not the past I'm concerned about, Miriam," I tell her. "It's the future. *Our* future."

I'm regretting my choice of meeting places — St. George's Gardens in London's East End. Knowing Miriam's fondness for Anglican churches and summer gardens, I thought my selection ideal, a place that might becalm her. Yet now, strolling slowly past the ancient burial stones that outlasted former graveyards, the oblong stones all askew, I realize my mistake.

This place is about endings.

She shakes her head tightly. She won't meet my eyes. Hers are hazy with tears. "We... we don't *have* a future. Not one in which we're together. How can I make you *see* that? Hardly a decade's passed since the Russians liberated my father from the camp. My mother was burned to ashes in that same camp. To my father, it's as though it all happened yesterday—"

"Yes, but what does it have to do with *us?* I understand your wanting to be considerate of your father's feelings, and I love you for that. But you have your whole life ahead of you. You can't live your life in order to please an old man at the end of his." My heart thumps as relentlessly as if I'd run, rather than cabbed, from Moorgate. "Miriam, when you're blessed with a love like ours, you don't throw it aside — you *cherish* it, you *thank God* for it, because it most certainly is a blessing from God. You've told me yourself your connection to your ancestral Judaism is tenuous, at best, and it only got more tenuous after your parents managed to send you to England as a child refugee just before the war. Your sponsors, the Chatterhams, raised you as a little English schoolgirl, took you to Anglican services... services that you admit you adored..."

"That doesn't *matter*, Irving—"

"Oh, why *can't* we be married? I'm more than certain I could win your father over, given a bit of time. Once he sees how happy I'm able to make his daughter—"

"It would *kill* him!" She turns away. "I'm *sorry*, Irving. This was a mistake. A silly, stupid mistake on my part, childish, really. I thought I could sever myself from the past. I thought I could be selfish and follow my heart. It's been wonderful, what we've shared over this past year. I'll always treasure it. But it can't continue. *I* can't continue..."

I can't let things end like this. I can't bear the thought of never seeing her again. "Couldn't... couldn't we just go on as we have? If marriage is out of the question, I mean? Continue seeing one another on the sly? There's no hurry for permanency. You've just begun at university, and I'll begin my field studies next year. Maybe, given enough healing time, your father will have a change of heart...?"

"My father will never heal." That sweet voice, the joy of my life, sounds as heavy and laden with moss as the tombstones that line our narrow path. "Never, not if he were to live another five hundred years. His loss is my loss. I have a *duty*, Irving. A duty that outweighs whatever hopes I might have for my personal happiness. A duty to him and a duty to my people..."

"You can't bring them *back*, Miriam. No matter how much you want to, no matter how much your father wants it. You aren't a wonder-worker. What kind of a 'duty' to your people could you possibly have that would override the love we share...?"

"To be *faithful!* To remain within the fold! You're right, Irving. I *can't* bring them back. But I can help replace them. Help replenish with my womb what we have lost. Deny Hitler any posthumous victory—"

"I can't believe what I'm hearing! Are you actually stating that *our* getting *married* and having *children* would represent a *posthumous victory* for *Adolf-bloody-Hitler?* That — that sort of tribal thinking — it's positively *medieval!*' I try to gain control of my myself, realizing too late that my voice is echoing off the church walls. "Look, I'm sorry, I spoke out of turn. I'm just distraught. I — I can't imagine a life without you, Miriam. I don't *want* to imagine such a barren, lonely existence. *Please...*

I beg you... don't obliterate the heaven we've created over the past year... don't let me go..."

"I'm sorry, Irving," she whispers. She briefly squeezes my hand. Then she swiftly walks away, her Levantine hips swaying as definitively as those of Judith after she'd hung the severed head of Holofernes upon the walls of Bethuliah.

-November 1, 1956-

"Be a dear boy and fetch me my favorite pickaxe, will you, Irving?"

There are worse fates than being Kathleen Kenyon's prime factotum, I suppose. She is, after all, the *grande dame* of British archeology. I imagine hundreds of graduate students would have signed onto this expedition to the ruins of ancient Jericho just to shine her boots.

Only a researcher of her immense prestige could have convinced the reigning government of Trans-Jordan to grant us virtually unlimited access to Tel es-Sultan — the great mound, located two kilometers north of the modern town of Jericho, which contains the remains of a succession of ancient habitations, each built atop the ruins of its predecessors, of which the oldest yet excavated dates back approximately a hundred centuries before the common era.

How glorious to be here in this place! How incredibly fortunate I am to be among the handful of seekers uncovering its secrets! Jericho — perhaps the oldest of all the walled cities in the world, the original hearth of human civilization, the place where Joshua reiterated in rampart-crumbling intonations

God's promise to the Jews that they would come to possess this land of milk and honey...

And therein lies the secret ache of my heart. I ran away from London's East End to this dry and barren place in a desperate attempt to flee the unbearable loss of my Miriam. Yet here I find myself standing upon the foundation stones of the ancient Jewish conquest of Canaan, where every sunset over low bronze hills, every pungent wisp of burning dung from scattered campfires, and every bleating of a wandering goat remind me of her and of her long-suffering people. The people she will not abandon, not even for my sake.

And so stretch forth the lengths of my days — blind digging of narrow trenches across Tel es-Sultan, just wide enough to allow a man (or woman) space to work, followed by endless jabbings of a pickaxe into the artificial cliff faces we have made, the occasional elation of uncovering a brick or a bit of pottery, at which point the pickaxe is set aside, to be replaced by the snail-like patience of a spade or brush. Pick-pick-pick, forget-forget-forget. Brush, brush, brush, deny, deny, deny. Yet it's fruitless; forgetfulness does not come and will not come.

Perhaps if I dig deeper, forgetfulness will spring forth like oil and finally envelop me in its black nirvana? When Miss Kenyon is well out of earshot, on the far side of the site, I direct a crew of Arab workmen to excavate another three feet of this latest trench with their picks and shovels. Miss Kenyon would look upon this act as a horrendous waste of manpower. She adamantly insists no extended human habitation of this site took place any earlier than that of the Natufian hunter-gatherers of the Holocene epoch, about ten thousand years B.C.E., and the present trench already reaches that level. Still, I will force it deeper. To China, if necessary, if that is what it takes to assuage my misery.

I have become inured to the stench of sweat, both the Arabs' and my own. A good thing, too, for there is no end of sweat until night comes. Miss Kenyon somehow avoids perspiring, or miraculously hides it. She seems to take it as her divinely proclaimed purpose to cause *others* to perspire. She'll tan my hide if (when) she discovers what I am doing. Am I being nihilistic in forcing these Arabs to dig to no avail? Am I one of those mad colonial overlords that haunt Kipling's or Conrad's imaginings? Ah, I shouldn't worry for the poor bastards — they'll receive their wages from Miss Kenyon, no matter what sort of useless labors I press the lads to.

Then, just before lunch break, a cry of fearful wonder rises from my Arab workmen. Their foreman, Manu, an Indian, climbs the ladder from the trench and hurriedly approaches. "Sahib Irving," he says, out of breath, his heavy dark jowls quivering, "the men have found something. Something you must see. Please come."

I descend the ladder into the trench, struggling to see the source of the sudden fuss. But my view is blocked. The Arabs huddle around whatever it is, jabbering as excitedly as though their holy Mahdi has stepped forth from imprisonment within the trench wall.

I push the buggers aside. And there it is — a big, white bone, jutting from the lowest reaches of the trench wall. A very large leg bone. Some sort of extinct megafauna from the pre-Holocene, a prehistoric camel or mastodon? My heart races. Such creatures had not been known to inhabit this region. What a *magnificent* find! I can already picture my name on a plaque at the British Museum (perhaps my newfound prestige will be enough to turn Miriam's head around?) …

I kneel to take a closer look and lean forward to dislodge more of the crumbly sandstone from the edges of the bone with my whisk. That's when the glimmering of madness intrudes.

This is not the bone of a mammalian species. Not even a very large, extinct mammal.

You're not a paleontologist, I tell myself. *You're merely a post-graduate archeology student, and not a particularly smart one.* Yet I have spent enough time staring at the gargantuan skeletons mounted within the Dinosaur Gallery of the London Natural History Museum to recognize what this is.

The thigh bone of a large theropod. A member of the Allosaur or Tyranosaur family, most likely. Exceptionally well preserved. And sitting in a stratum of earth where it has no bloody business being.

A sudden gust of wind riddles the back of my neck with stinging sand. The contents of my stomach spin like the blades of a helicopter. I feel as though I'm standing on a high bridge, looking down into raging waters hundreds of feet below. I'm a man of *science*, not a Biblical fundamentalist. The evolutionary theories of Darwin, the excavations of a century's worth of paleontologists, the knowledge built up by generations of geologists, all dictate that I should *not* be seeing what is clearly before my eyes. Only superstitious, dogmatic *fools* still believe that the age of the Earth can be counted in the hundreds of centuries. That Adam and Eve cohabitated in a garden called Eden before giving birth to children who engaged in incestuous sexual relations and begat the generations of mankind. That the span of time separating the dinosaurs and Adam's rise from the primordial dust was, at most, a few thousand years — or, for the true Biblical literalists, a few packed days of divine activity.

Yet the geological strata laid bare by the trench tell a different story. A millennium or two before the earliest Natufians followed their game here and decided to set up camp, most likely due to the nearby spring of Ein as-Sultan, thunder lizards roamed this same place, perhaps drinking from the same spring.

It's... impossible. Modern science tells me that at least seventy million years' worth of sediments should separate this gargantuan reptilian thigh bone from the primitive tools of the Natufian hunter-gatherers. Yet what I'm staring at — if my eyes could sing, they'd be chanting an old Church hymn of the six days of Genesis.

I fetch Miss Kenyon, heedless of her reprimands for my having ordered an unauthorized excavation. Down inside the trench, she proves far less impressed by the sight of the bone than was I.

"What is all this hysterical blabbering about the Bible-thumpers winning the debate, Irving? That there, that *bone* — it proves nothing of the sort. Nothing! The Young Earth theory, *if* one can even dignify it with the label 'theory', has been thoroughly discredited. My own excavations have shown that this area has suffered earthquakes in the past. More likely than not, given the archeological evidence, an earthquake precipitated the collapse of Jericho's fabled walls, *not* the sounds of Joshua's trumpets. An earthquake, a geological upheaval, must have pushed this bone from a lower stratum into the place where it now sits."

"I thought of that, Miss Kenyon. Truly, I did. But look at how the strata lie! They're as flat and even as a stack of breakfast pancakes. There's no evidence of a violent upheaval here, not in this section of Tel es-Sultan; not at this depth, at least. And the bone itself — look at its state of preservation! Wouldn't an earthquake have broken it into pieces, or at least fractured it? But it's as smooth and whole as though the creature were interred in Westminster Abbey alongside King bloody Edward the Seventh— "

"*Mister* Davison, you'll be advised to watch your language."

"Sorry, ma'am—"

"It's quite possible that this supposedly missing evidence of a geological upheaval will actually be found in strata below that which your men have laid bare. The earthquake that lifted that infernal bone to the surface could very well have occurred a thousand years before the first Natufians decided to congregate here. And here's another explanation for you, young Mr. Davison — it is also possible that the Natufians themselves inadvertently dug up this bone, perhaps in the process of burying their dead. Not being Cambridge-educated paleontologists, they would have discarded it, and eventually it was re-buried by the elements, along with their abandoned tools and pottery. Recall Occam's Razor, Irving. In theorizing cause and effect, always make the shortest possible leap. There's no need to turn Darwin on his head because of a single displaced bone."

"I understand your reservations, Miss Kenyon, and your logic. But wouldn't it be prudent for us to make *certain?* Shouldn't we dig the trench deeper to see whether we uncover evidence of an earlier earthquake? Also, with your permission,

I'd like to have the men dig out the cliff face around the thigh bone to see whether any other parts of this creature have been preserved in adjacent soils. Whether or not we turn old Darwin on his head, at the very least we might excavate a specimen that the British Museum would highly prize."

Miss Kenyon pondered this. "I hate to redistribute manpower from the other side of Tel es-Sultan," she said. "We're making wonderful progress on the north face. But, still, given the... unusual nature of this find of yours, I suppose it behooves us to see what it is all about. But let me caution you, Mr. Davison — do *not* sensationalize this. I will not have it said among educated circles that I have provided aid and succor to the forces of moss-backed, reactionary, fundamentalist ignorance. Oh, we will discover the *source* of the geological aberration that has resulted in this freakish find of yours. I can guarantee that. I have a reputation to uphold, young man. Do not forget it."

"I won't, Miss Kenyon. And thank you."

-November 3, 1956-

I've named her Miriam. My big, fine beastie. The skeleton, at least those parts we've seen thus far, has survived in a remarkable state of preservation. We've even uncovered sections of fossilized skin on her carcass. Most remarkable of all, Miriam was on the verge of having babies. There, sitting in the generous space between her pelvic bones, are the perfectly preserved fossils of half a dozen eggs. I can barely contain my excitement at the thought of what x-rays back in a British laboratory will reveal.

What haven't we found? Evidence of an earlier earthquake. I had the men dig a section of the trench six feet lower than the strata that contain Miriam. We saw no signs of upheaval or distension. The harmonic placement of the fossilized bones, their organic spatial relationships with one another also testify against the notion of these remains having been elevated by a traumatic geological event. The carcass appears to have lain undisturbed until it was covered by mud and sedimentation, perhaps due to a flash flood.

Cause of death? It could have been disease, I suppose, or possibly a fatal attack from a fellow predator. Or even the unlucky happenstance of a toppling tree catching her unawares and breaking her back or heaving in her skull... the men and I have uncovered sections of a fossilized cedar in the immediate vicinity of the bones. Only a more complete excavation of the skeleton will tell the tale of Miriam's last living moments.

Manu shouts over the din of clanking picks and shovels. He points to a plume of dust drawing near from the northeast. Either a desert dust devil, or vehicles approaching Tel es-Sultan at a good clip of speed. I climb out of the trench to see who our visitors might be. I notice that Miss Kenyon has also emerged from her work on the north side of the mound. She waves at me to join her.

Our visitors are an official delegation from the Trans-Jordanian government. An armed delegation — Mohammed Abu Hosn, the Assistant Chief Administrator of Antiquities with whom we've dealt before, leads them, backed up by a dozen soldiers bearing rifles and sidearms of British manufacture. On earlier meetings, he hasn't brought along an armed escort. The size of this one suggests an effort to intimidate.

"Mr. Abu Hosn," Miss Kenyon says, shielding her eyes from the midday sun, "what brings you all the way from Amman to pay us a visit? Is there some problem?"

"Your permit to work on this site has been revoked," he says.

"Good heavens," Miss Kenyon exclaims, "*why?*"

"All you British must leave the country within forty-eight hours." The soldiers flanking him glare at us. "You will not be permitted to take any Jordanian antiquities with you, only your personal possessions. Also, your notes and photographs must remain in my custody."

"This — this is an *outrageous* abrogation of cultural and scientific agreements between our two governments! Our work here has reached a vital stage and must *not* be interrupted. I need warn you, sir, that I will be requesting my ambassador's intervention in this matter—"

"He will not be able to help you, for he has been expelled, as well, along with all of his staff. This is due, of course, to your British military's unprovoked attack on our Arab brethren in Egypt."

Egypt? I suddenly realize I haven't read a newspaper in weeks. "Say," I blurt out, trampling protocol, "is there a *war* on?"

Miss Kenyon looks ready to slap me. The Jordanian bureaucrat sniffs with contempt. "Is there a *war* on?" he says, mimicking me. "There most certainly is — a war of aggression against the Arab Nation. You British and your allies, the French, have conspired with the accursed Zionists to invade Egyptian territory and steal the Suez Canal. We cannot accept this unprovoked aggression. Until your government restores the Arab lands it has seized and provides compensation for the deaths it has caused, there can be no cooperation between us in the realm of antiquities, or any other. You have forty-eight hours to depart. If you do not, you will be classified as enemy aliens and taken into custody. My military men will take possession of your notes, cameras, and photographs immediately. All documentation of Jordanian antiquities, produced on Jordanian soil, is rightfully the property of the Jordanian people."

"But the *bones!*" I cry. "We can't leave them exposed! The elements — sandstorms, wind, rain — could degrade them *terribly—*"

"You have forty-eight hours," he repeated.

-May 12, 1957-

I did all I could to protect the integrity of Miriam's remains in the short time allotted. I had the men construct wooden caissons around the exposed portions of the skeleton, then fill the caissons with plaster. We barely had time for the plaster to set and for us to cover the caissons with earth, refilling the lower part of the trench, before Miss Kenyon and I and our party had to board trucks heading for the airport in Amman.

The real Miriam — I mean the human one, the living one — refused to see me on my return to London. I wasn't surprised... only disappointed. I so wanted to share with her what I had seen. I needed to talk about it with someone who I trusted implicitly. The Young Earth theory, strongly supported, if not proven! The words of the Bible, the Old Testament, the Torah of Miriam's people, borne out! Wouldn't such evidence as that

I'd uncovered turn old Darwin on his bulging, bald head? Wouldn't it change the world?

I've had to tread carefully. Revealing what I've seen to the wrong people could result in my permanent ostracism from the scientific community. I'd be branded as a religious crackpot, ending any hope I might have of a career in my chosen field.

If only I still had my photographs! The British government and its allies have retreated ignominiously from Suez, under heavy diplomatic pressure from President Eisenhower and the United Nations. Normal diplomatic relations between Britain and much of the Arab world are in the process of being restored. There's still a chance Miss Kenyon and I might be able to retrieve our confiscated materials and return to Tel es-Sultan. Apart from a reconciliation with Miriam (the human one), completing the work of excavating the fossilized Miriam is my greatest wish. Fate shouldn't rob me of the chance to complete my work.

Yet, part of me wonders whether it wouldn't be for the best if that skeleton remains unseen, for the theory of evolution to remain unchallenged, for the Young Earth theory to continue languishing in the dank corners of crankdom. Would I want my legacy to include throwing open the door for the return of authoritarian theological zealots such as Torquemada and the pope who condemned Galileo?

So which shall it be? Am I a servant of the existing order, or a seeker after truth? I cannot be both, in this instance.

I don't know whether this emotional turmoil has been affecting my memory. But *something* certainly has been mucking about with my head, scrambling the clarity of my thoughts concerning my time at Tel es-Sultan. I tried reconstructing my notes shortly after my return to London. The work presented no great difficulties. I recall the words flowing easily, and I was even able to draw sketches from memory of Miriam's bones and the surrounding geological strata. I *know* I accomplished this — I recall doing so very clearly. At least, I *think* I do. But I can't find my notes or my sketches anywhere.

My apartment is small, only two rooms. I have for my use just two bureaus and one set of drawers. Admittedly, I've cluttered my limited space with books and papers, so the search isn't as effortless as it might otherwise be. Still, I've looked for my notes for hours upon hours, to no avail.

So far as I'm aware, the only person aside from myself who has entered these rooms since my return from Jericho has been Miss Haverton, the cleaning woman who comes to tidy up every other week. I typically vacate the premises during the half-hour or so she spends here, removing myself to a nearby pub. Yet I cannot imagine any reason for her to remove my notes and drawings. What for? They were of no worth to anyone but me. Could she have thrown them away by mistake? I've asked her about this. She firmly states she has no recollection of disposing of any of my papers, only rubbish from the bin.

I've wracked my brain for other possible culprits. Jordanian secret agents? Burglars employed by Miss Kenyon to protect the sanctity of Darwinism? The first seems highly implausible; why would the Jordanians risk worsening their already shaky diplomatic relationship with the United Kingdom over a set of supplementary notes they wouldn't have any way of knowing I had composed? The second possibility goes against everything I know of Miss Kenyon's character. She hates, and perhaps fears, the notion of a carnosaur stalking the Jericho plains a few hundred or thousand years prior to the earliest human habitation — her very soul might rebel at the thought of it — but she would never stoop to base criminality to hide an unpleasant truth. Even if that truth goes against her most firmly-held suppositions.

I am flummoxed. Utterly flummoxed.

-May 25, 1957-

I have no doubts now. Some force has been eroding my memory. Not all memories — only those memories of my astounding find at Tel es-Sultan. I can no longer picture in my mind what that partially evacuated cliff wall at the bottom of the trench looked like, the one that contained the carnosaur's bones. I can't clearly picture the bones themselves. I could no more reconstruct my notes and sketches at this point than I could willfully sprout propeller blades from my head and soar off above Old Bailey.

Oh, God... I feel like I'm coming apart. Every night before turning in, I write notes to myself of what I am able to recollect about my last three days at Tel es-Sultan and my first few days back in London. I have made this my nightly ritual. But I feel like King Canute, ordering the tides to recede. No matter how hard I struggle against it, each time I succumb to sleep, an ethereal tide sweeps through my skull and erodes more and more of those specific memories, leaving all else untouched. I know this because when I awaken, I immediately read over my notes from the night before. And it as if I am reading a letter from a stranger. The only way I've managed to retain as much as I have is that I go back, again and again, through my full set of nightly notes, which extends back eleven entries. Each successive entry is a little less rich with detail than the one from the night previous.

I fear I won't have even this expediency to rely upon much longer. The oldest of these nightly notes, the ones that are most detailed... they've begun fading into illegibility, as though they were decades old and regularly exposed to the sun's bleaching.

Am I going mad?

-May 26, 1957-

I dare not reach out to Miss Kenyon to ask whether she has been experiencing a parallel erosion of memories. She might consider me emotionally disturbed, even deranged, and lose all trust in me. Then any chance I would have of returning to the bones at Tel es-Sultan would be dashed.

Despite my promise to Miss Kenyon to keep word of my discovery among ourselves, I see no alternative but to try to determine whether other archeologists or paleontologists have come upon similar findings. Perhaps such discoveries were made in the last century, before the science of geological dating was established? If so, that could be the reason the remarkableness of the findings went unnoted. Perhaps if I research such century-old digging expeditions, I'll find evidence that will validate what my notes tell me I saw at Tel es-Sultan...?

I'll begin researching tomorrow, at my university's library.

-May 30, 1957-

I've read myself almost blind, but come up with virtually nothing. The only lead I've uncovered is an exceedingly dubious one. The writings of Professor Archibald von Heussen, whose increasingly bizarre theories concerning the age of the planet and its shape(!) made him a laughingstock at Cambridge. Those writings caused a scandal among his geologist colleagues, and ultimately resulted in his forced early retirement.

He's still alive, residing here in London. I've sent the old duffer a letter, asking for a meeting. A long shot, certainly, and with considerable risk to my reputation. What am I getting myself into? If any of my fellow graduate students or professors were to get wind of this encounter, I would become a laughingstock myself.

This may end up an utter waste of my time, my meeting with an academic outcast who may turn out to be a senile, silly old eccentric. Yet what choice do I have? I either make every possible effort to corroborate what my notes tell me I have seen, or I resign myself to permanently doubting my own sanity.

-June 8, 1957-

Professor von Heussen shakes my hand with extreme enthusiasm. He's more vigorous than I'd imagined he'd be, despite his advanced years. "Delighted to meet you, Mr. Davison!" he says, his eyes wide and bright behind thick lenses. I notice the faded black tape that holds the frames of his glasses together. He smiles, revealing a set of ill-fitting dentures. His breath reminds me of days-old fish wrappings. I can't help but notice the genteel poverty of his lodgings (a rented room in a third-rate boarding house) and his threadbare suit of clothes. "I so rarely receive a visit from fellow academics these days. An opportunity to talk shop — not to be missed! I apologize I haven't anything to offer you for lunch here. Might we go down the street to the local pub? Their fish is quite good."

We relocate ourselves to the local pub (I'll be buying, I imagine). He matches me stride for stride, surprisingly jaunty, telling me my letter had boosted his spirits to heights not experienced since his days as a senior lecturer. Once inside the pub (I spot no familiar faces, thank heaven), I steer us to a booth in the back, far enough from the front windows to be cloaked in gloom.

"So," he says, once we have given our lunch orders to the barkeep, "your letter was unclear, rather *mysterious*, even, regarding the nature of the information you seek. Believe you me, young sir, I understand fully that those of us working on the fringes of conventional knowledge — or, as I put it, *consensus* knowledge — must step carefully." He peers around him. "We're quite secure here. I believe none of the other customers are capable of reading much more than the headlines of the tabloid newspapers. I doubt any of them have even *heard* of Darwin or Galileo."

The mere mention of those names causes me to shiver, for some reason. I steel myself, then begin telling him my predicament. The time I spent at the ruins of Jericho; the unauthorized dig I engaged in at Tel es-Sultan; the dinosaur bones I excavated from a geological stratum just beneath those which held tools and pottery shards from the Natufian settlement; our being expelled from Jordanian territory due to the Suez crisis; the confiscation of my notes and photographs. He pays keen attention to what I'm saying, as though his life hinged upon the details.

After our food arrives, I wade into more outré matters. Such as the progressive erosion of my memories of my fantastic find at Tel es-Sultan; the disappearance from my apartment of my reconstituted notes and sketches; my frantic efforts to retain my recollections by writing set after set of nightly notes; and how the ink of notes just two weeks old had begun to prematurely fade.

When I told the first part of my tale, his thin, pallid lips turned white with compression. Now, as I speak of my uncanny experiences following my return to London, he's begun trembling with barely controlled emotional turmoil.

Something seems to break inside him when I finish my recounting. He lurches across the table, dipping his tie and the edges of his jacket into our lunches, and clumsily embraces me. "My boy, *my boy...!*" His tears dribble onto my neck. "I know all that you're going through, *all* of it! I never thought, never *dreamed* my own experiences would be shared by another. You've validated me! They've called me a crank, a drunkard, a senile fool, a *lunatic*, for *years!* But you — a young man, in the prime of life, brilliant enough to be selected by Kathleen Kenyon for her latest Jericho expedition — for you to have shared my ordeal, to have witnessed with your own eyes the last evidentiary vestiges of a fading Truth... *this* makes my efforts to resist my nemesis worthwhile. For I've *at last* found someone willing to take up the flickering torch of Truth from my palsied hands."

He wraps his fish and chips in a bundle of paper napkins and crams the bundle into his satchel, otherwise filled with a jumble of hand-written papers. "Come," he says. "There's something I must share with you. Before it is gone. You must see it, read it with your own eyes, before it vanishes forever."

I leave my own lunch and beer on the table. We take the Tube and walk the remainder of the way to Great Russell Street. Holding onto the sleeve of my jacket as though I were an errant child, von Heussen pulls me across the courtyard of the British Museum, then between the massive stone columns flanking the entrance foyer. I expect him to lead me into the Reading Room at the center of the museum's Great Court, but instead he pulls me past that fabulous old library with its iron-framed book stacks and its papier-mâché interior dome, modeled to look like that of the Pantheon in Rome, into a side corridor leading away from public spaces.

"Where is it we're going, Professor?" I ask, avoiding water drippage from a tangle of overhead pipes.

"You'll see soon enough," he says.

He leads me into what must be the museum's boiler room. Poorly ventilated, the air is stale, thick, and clammy. I again find myself doubting the usefulness of this rendezvous; I half expect him to expose himself to me here, in these forlorn shadows.

Von Heussen pulls me to the corner furthermost from the entrance. He kneels next to an iron grating a foot above the floor, removes a pocket knife from his satchel, and unscrews the four screws holding the grating in place. His face tense with strain, he reaches inside the rectangular opening. His expression lightens. "Ah! Still there!"

He pulls out a book, a very old one, centuries old, judging from its manufacture. In all likelihood, von Heussen purloined it from the Reading Room. "Here!" he says, handing it to me. "You must read it. You must see what is inside. The drawings, and the accompanying captions..."

"It looks too delicate," I say, afraid to handle it. "Really, Professor, this belongs in the hands of a museum archivist, certainly not stuffed into a ventilation hole in the boiler room wall..."

"But I had to make it inaccessible," he insists. "I *had* to. The fewer people who see it, the fewer who know about it, the more chance it has of avoiding the... the vanishing. I'm putting it at dire risk of disappearing simply by showing it to you. But I *must* show it to you, you see. *Someone* must carry the knowledge forward. I'm an old man, and I've been fleeing my nemesis for so terribly long. I suspect *I* may soon fade away as irrevocably as the ink my notes are written with... the ink *your* notes are written with, too. Open it, please. Read what's there, before it's too late."

I take the fragile book to a work table beneath an exposed, hanging light bulb. It's some kind of an explorer's journal, the diary of a sea captain. The spelling and grammar appear to be early modern English, Shakespearian or thereabouts. The dates of the entries are a good bit earlier than Shakespeare, actually — from the middle of the fifteenth century, four decades prior to Columbus's initial journey to the West Indies.

The crew had been surveying the western coast of Africa when a fierce storm blew them far off course, way farther south than any prior documented voyage of an English or Spanish vessel. The captain, Nicholas Smythe, wrote how ice caked all the masts and fittings of his ship, and floating chunks of it pounded ceaselessly against the waterline sections of the hull. Far more startling is this entry, dated August 14, 1451: "In broad Day's litte, with the Sun high in the Skye, the Skye Behinde us, to the Northe, is Blewe. But the Skye Ahede of us, to the Sowthe, is Blakke as Nitte, with the Starres in full Vewe. I feare we have Reeched Worlde's End."

"Read on, Mr. Davison," von Heussen says behind me, "read on."

Smythe ordered four men into a small boat lowered from the gunwales and commanded them to row toward the darkness, then return and tell him what they had seen there. The boat vanished from his sight. It suddenly disappeared when it reached the dark horizon, as though it had plunged over a waterfall. The craft and its men never returned.

Smythe noted with alarm the ocean current pushing his ship ever closer to that black region where the tiny boat had disappeared. He ordered his crew to clear the ice from the sails and unfurl them, so that they might make use of the prevailing northerly winds, quite gusty and strong, to counter the southerly push of the current. Once this was done, he ordered another set of men into a second boat. He commanded that this one be tethered to the mother ship by a long rope, then convinced the men to set out by promising them their crewmates would pull them back in.

Smythe climbed to the top of the mainmast to watch the second boat's progress. This one, too, appeared to plunge over the edge of a night-black waterfall. Smythe shouted for his crew to pull the boat back. It took the combined muscle power of twenty sailors to accomplish this.

Are the aged letters on the page growing less distinct? Or is this a phenomenon of my overstimulated imagination? I remove my glasses, fog them with my breath, then scrub them with the corner of my shirt.

The retrieved boat did not contain all the crew with which it had set out. The remaining sailors had to be hoisted back aboard the ship, ropes tied around their chests and beneath their stiffened arms, as though they were caskets of salted beef. Their eyelashes and nostrils and mouths had become caked with ice, their bodies frozen solid. Expressions of indescribable horror were stamped on their dead faces.

Smythe decided, as captain, he had to see what his men had seen. He would not risk a mutiny by ordering any more of his sailors to accompany him. He climbed down the rope ladder into the still-tethered boat. His crew passed to him a fresh set of oars. He ordered them to begin pulling him back to the ship the instant he signaled them by raising an oar above his head.

Closer and closer he rowed toward what seemed to him must be the edge of the world. The icy wind cut through his thick coat. Tears froze at the edges of his eyes; mucous flowed from his nostrils, then froze on his upper lip and cheeks.

The closer he rowed to what appeared to be the ocean's end, the more difficult it became for him to breathe. Not only because the air was frigid... it seemed thinner, somehow, as though he had ascended the heights of the tallest Alps. The sounds of the wind in his ears and the pounding of waves against the sides of his boat faded into near silence, until Smythe feared his eardrums had frozen solid.

His following words are muddled, the ones that attempt to tell what he witnessed just before he gave the signal to be hauled back; severely limited by the inability of language to describe phenomena outside normal human experience. Much clearer, however, is the crude drawing he made on the same page — the edge of the Earth, flat as a dinner plate, with his tethered boat held tautly at the terminus... and, judging from the relative scale of the objects drawn, hundreds of meters of ice suspended like stalactites from the Earth's edge, hanging straight down, with the first small boat and the bodies of half a dozen sailors stuck to the ice like gnats in a spider's sticky web.

"Do you see now?" Professor von Heussen says from behind me. "According to these journal entries, as of the year 1451, the Earth was *flat*."

My rebuttal comes swiftly. "This 'proves' nothing of the sort," I say, more heatedly than I intended. "No more so than all those maps of the period that labeled the interior of Africa as 'Here Be Dragons'. I'll admit that Smythe's account is *vivid*, certainly. But whatever he saw, his description was skewed by his expectations and the limits of his world view. All this journal demonstrates is that in 1451, virtually everyone *believed* the Earth to be flat."

"Yes," von Heussen says, disarming my vehemence by surrendering to it. "*Exactly*, my boy."

"What do you mean by that?"

"I mean that in 1451, the bulk of learned opinion, which filtered down to commonplace beliefs held by the great majority of humanity, recognized the Earth to be both flat and orbited by the sun, moon, and stars. Copernicus's theory of a sun-centered solar system was a radical outlier. A little more than a century later, Galileo Galilei was born in Pisa. By the time of Galileo's death in 1642, the gestalt of human belief had begun shifting irrevocably toward the Copernican universe and the Earth as a globe orbiting the sun. The balance of human belief shifted. Reality followed, like a dog follows his master."

This truly has been a waste of my time. Von Heussen is either senile or daft. "You have it exactly backwards, old fellow," I say, shutting the book with a dusty thump. "Reality comes *first*. People's beliefs shift as they discard their ignorance in favor of new evidence uncovered through discovery or experimentation, evidence that better reflects actual reality."

"I assumed you would say that," von Heussen says. He opens his satchel. "That's why I brought these along to show you." He begins spreading his jumble of typed notes, drawings, and faded photographs across the table.

"What is all this?"

"My studies of a half-century's worth of mining core samples. Like you with your Jericho materials, I have to constantly re-write, re-type, or re-draw my notes and sketches to prevent their total loss. Unfortunately, photographing my photographs, again and again, results in a progressive lessening of resolution, and none of the original core samples have survived. But let me tell you what I've seen. Fifty years ago, even forty years ago, the great majority of the cores, which ranged in length from a hundred meters to more than a thousand, showed identical signs of torsion stress, torque fractures—"

"I'm no geologist. Please explain in layman's terms."

"Of course. What I mean to say is that the layers of rock contained within the core samples showed unmistakable signs of having been bent or curled. Folded, essentially. The pattern of fractures I saw was consistent with material that had been forced from a level, flat orientation to a curved orientation. If I had a handful of clay available, I could easily demonstrate the fracture pattern."

"That's *daft*. If what you say is true, why haven't your observations been replicated by hundreds of other geologists?"

"Back when I started this research, which was prompted by my reading Captain Smythe's journal more than half a century ago, I was a pioneer in my study of mining cores. Other geologists made use of them, of course, but they weren't looking for what I was looking for. They were looking for evidence of oil deposits or natural gas or rare minerals. Realizing how revolutionary my discoveries and resulting theories were, I resolved to gather as much data as I could before sharing my findings with the world.

"This was a mistake, you see. I waited too long to publish. Subsequent core samples, those extracted from the same locales fifteen or twenty years after the samples that had shown obvious torque fractures, contained no torque fractures. *None.* Physical reality is a lagging indicator of consensus belief. Particularly *hidden* physical reality, those aspects of tangible reality not subject to routine and frequent observation — such as the Earth's sub-crust, the upper mantle. I'm afraid my own observations hastened the process of subterranean physical phenomena adjusting themselves to be in accord with humanity's gestalt-mind. But I didn't know... I couldn't *imagine* it, you see... just as you're having a difficult time imagining it. Not realizing the consequences of my own researches, I was like a mummy-hunter who, in his haste to find his treasures, breaks the entrance seal of a royal tomb and exposes the mummies within to the fresh air, which causes them to crumble into dust before he can have even a good look at them, much less preserve them."

This is insanity, rank nonsense. My entire being rebels at what he's saying. But suspicion it could be true blossoms like a seed buried in offal. "So what you're basically saying is, no proof can be provided for this wild theory of yours, because the very act of your observing evidence to support it makes that evidence disappear? Wouldn't you say that's awfully bloody *convenient?*"

"But Mr. Davison, you've experienced the workings of this force yourself. Wasn't it your sense of perceptual reality warping around you that brought you to my door? The sense that *the past was in the process of changing*, and that this change was *adjusting the present?*"

"Yes. Yes, I'll admit it — such thoughts did occur to me. And after talking with you today, I'm bloody well of a mind to plonk myself down on a psychiatrist's couch in hopes my sanity is still salvageable."

"But you *aren't* insane, Mr. Davison. *I'm* not insane." He reaches across the table and grabs my hands in a palsied grip. "*Please*. Don't dismiss me out of hand. You're the only one capable of carrying my work forward. Of sharing with humanity the hidden truth that orders the perceptible universe which surrounds us. *We* are God! Our *collective mind* is God! Not some Omnipotent Power or Unmoved First Mover that inhabits the heavens! *We, us,* collectively — the force of our gestalt-mind overrides perceptible physical reality and molds it to its changing consensus. The past is not immutable — *far from it!*

"You're appalled. Let me explain further. Periodically an ideological juggernaut arises amongst us — I speak not of *political* ideologies, but more of modes of thought that drive conceptual and scientific revolutions. I speak of the ideologies of our origins, physical laws, the ordering of the universe. Ideologies promulgated by intellectual giants such as Galileo, Darwin, Nietzsche, Einstein, perhaps even Freud — men whose thoughts and teachings have changed our world by changing the way we *think* about it. But their influence goes beyond simply that — they changed their and subsequently our *present* by changing our *shared pasts*. Perhaps at one time, a sky god and an ocean god and a goddess of agriculture and a goddess of love really *did* dwell together atop a mountain and meddle in the affairs of men, and an underworld really *did* exist beneath the surface of Earth, presided over by a dark god. Perhaps at a somewhat later time, these gods vanished from their mountaintop, faded before the victorious ideological advance of a unitary God. Perhaps at one time, all men possessed souls in addition to their bodies, souls that survived the death and decay of the physical body and thrived in a Heaven or suffered in a Hell or waited in a Purgatory. Perhaps at one time, the sun really *did* orbit the Earth—"

"*Stop.* Just, just... *stop.*" Ludicrous, all of it, demented ravings... so why is my skull threatening to burst, like a cocoon barely holding back a growing larva? "You must see how *impossible* this all is. Just — just think through your own theory about the geological evolution of the Earth. According to what you've said, in 1451, the Earth was flat as a doormat. Then, less than three centuries later, it had become a globe. You're a bloody geologist — you know much more about tectonic plates and volcanism and earthquakes than I do, for God's sake. For argument's sake, let's assume this geological transformation you spoke of actually took place. The devastation on the planet's surface would have been millions of times worse than if the U.S. and Russia dropped every single nuclear bomb in their arsenals on each other — it would have produced a, a *holocaust* that would've wiped out, not just all humanity, but most likely *all life on Earth*. But *we're still here*, aren't we? We just had a hectic lunch in a bloody *pub* in the middle of bloody *London*. The *same* bloody London that existed back in 1451, the year that Captain Smythe's expedition cast off from the London docks. Can't you see how *stupid* and *ridiculous* your theory is?"

He squeezes my wrists more tightly. "Mr. Davison, don't you think I've *considered* all that? I've had *decades* to ponder the implications. Perhaps the worldwide holocaust you insist must have wiped out all humanity failed to produce that consequence, because the people who experienced their planet's geological transformation *did not know* about tectonic plates and the mechanics of volcanism and earth tremors. They didn't *realize* they were supposed to be burned to ashes and crushed, so *they weren't!* Perhaps in such an environment, the Earth transformed itself as it might in a Walt Disney cartoon — everyone was bounced into the air and spilled their soup and fell on their arses, then picked themselves up, dusted themselves off, and carried on as before. Or perhaps all the people and every speck of human civilization and all the Earth's flora and fauna really *did* perish in that planetary conflagration three or four centuries ago, but the planet *got better*. Healed itself, you see, because the believers in Galileo's ideological revolution believed and *continue to believe* that the Earth has *always* been a globe and has *always* orbited the sun — so no catastrophic change in the planet's shape ever occurred! But of course it *did* occur, because my studies of mining cores *showed* that it did. Captain Smythe's journal showed that it did.

"It is possible, *likely*, even, that at one time, centuries ago, the Pyramids were reduced to dust and the Parthenon and Coliseum in Rome were obliterated. But they *reappeared*. Or maybe they appeared for the first time — for perhaps they had not existed prior to the planetary cataclysm — but the post-Galileo gestalt-mind *believed* them to have existed. The *surface*, the *visible* and *tangible*, they fall in line with shifts in the gestalt-mind *first*. Hidden phenomena, such as subterranean layers of the Earth's mantle, those things change more gradually, you see. The rapid geological evolution of our planet from a flat plane to a globe *did* occur. But once Captain Smythe's journal is gone, once my re-written and re-re-written notes are gone, once *I'm gone* — the transformation of Earth will *not* have occurred. Earth will have *always* been a globe... just as Galileo said.

"But if *you*, my lad, take up my cause, share in my witness of the hidden truth of all things... the gestalt-mind may be resisted, at least for a while. The past may remain *as it was*, for now. Whether that original past is preferable to what it is transforming into is beside the point — it's worth defending because it was *true*, and as men of science, we must *always* champion the truth."

I pry my hands from his grip, then stand and back away. He stares up at me as though he intends to blurt forth yet another fantastical assertion. But then he stops himself, and his eyes grow infinitely sad.

"Ah, well," he says, quietly. "At least I tried. No man can do more than that..."

Before leaving the boiler room, I look back. He's returning Smythe's journal to its hiding place behind the grating.

-September 10, 1957-

They're gone. Miriam's bones are gone.

We returned to Jericho this morning, thanks to the governments of the United Kingdom and the Kingdom of Trans-Jordan having smoothed over their differences. I immediately went to the south side of Tel es-Sultan, where I had ordered my men to deepen the trench last November.

The wooden caissons we'd constructed to shelter the excavated bones from the elements remained just as we'd left them almost a year ago. Still filled with protective plaster. Yet when I carefully chipped away a section of the plaster, I found... only more plaster.

My first thought was that the Jordanian government had removed the bones themselves. By why would they have left the caissons in place? Why would they have refilled the caissons with plaster?

I ordered my men to remove the now useless materials so that we could resume our dig and get at portions of the skeleton the damned Jordanians hadn't pilfered.

But there are no more bones. The men removed the caissons for me. The side of the trench against which the caissons had sat appears undisturbed. The unmistakable lines of the geologic strata run unmolested clear across the portion of the trench wall in which the skeleton had been entombed. So it's not as though the Jordanians, in our absence, excavated the remaining bones and then, for some unfathomable reason, repacked the displaced earth into the hole they'd created.

It's as though the skeleton was never there.

Some of the Arabs working with me today were part of my crew a year ago. They remember hurriedly constructing the wooden caissons just before we British were expelled. They remember pouring plaster into the caissons. They don't remember why I ordered them to do this. They don't remember the bones.

Manu, the Indian foreman, tries to diplomatically deflect my increasingly impassioned assertions that we partially excavated the remains of a large carnivorous dinosaur last November. Despite his obsequiousness, he sticks to his polite but firm insistence that he never saw any bones.

Miss Kenyon chides me for making a fuss over nothing. Why, she asks archly, am I wasting time on the played-out southern side of Tel es-Sultan when all the exciting finds are being dug out of the northern side?

That evening, I fabricate a lie. I tell Miss Kenyon I received a cable — that my father had come down with a serious illness, and I must return to London.

I do, but not for my father's sake. I must speak again with Professor von Heussen.

-September 15, 1957-

"I'm very sorry, sir. You must have the wrong establishment. I've never rented rooms to any such individual."

I haven't made a mistake. I know I haven't. This is Professor von Heussen's landlady. I spoke with her in June, barely more than three months ago. I remember her crooked teeth, her breath stinking of gin, that crude necklace of plastic pearls around her throat. She showed me to the professor's rooms on the third floor. I *remember*.

I take the mid-morning train to Cambridge. The head of the geology department, a Professor Miles Haversham, has never heard of Professor von Heussen. I go to the university's office of personnel. They have no record of any Archibald von Heussen ever having been employed by the university or granted lecturing privileges.

Professor von Heussen taught at Cambridge for nearly forty years.

-September 16, 1957-

I'm among the first visitors to enter the British Museum when opening hour strikes. I head directly to the boiler room. I unscrew the dusty grating from the ventilation shaft with my pocket knife, just as I watched Professor von Heussen do back in June. The dust caking the grating is so thick, it appears the shaft cover has not been touched or moved in years. But I watched Professor von Heussen replace Captain Smythe's journal in that shaft just three months ago.

I know what I'll see — or rather, what I *won't* see — when I pull the grating from the wall. Still, upon my peering inside, my stomach flops like a dying fish on a dock. The book is not there. The shaft is empty. The dust and grit on its floor have not been disturbed in a dog's age.

I consult with the Reading Room's head librarian. I describe the journal and tell him when it would have been pilfered from the rare volumes collection. He leads me to the card catalog.

There's no record of any such volume. Captain Smythe's journal never resided within the British Museum's rare books collection. So far as the British Museum is concerned, the book never existed.

I could consult the Admiralty's historical archives for a copy. I could search for a record of Captain Smythe's expedition to chart the coast of East Africa. But I don't bother. It would be an exercise in futility. I know what I won't find.

-September 17, 1957-

What do I do? Simply wait to vanish from existence, as Professor von Heussen did? The horror of it...

I could stop copying my old notes every night before going to sleep. I could allow myself to forget that I ever discovered dinosaur bones at Tel es-Sultan. Allow my memories of Archibald von Heussen to vanish, forget that there ever *was* an Archibald von Heussen, that I ever read Captain Smythe's journal, that there ever *was* such a journal or such a sea captain.

But would that protect me from obliteration? What if this "gestalt-mind" postulated by Professor von Heussen, this hidden arranger and re-arranger of consensus reality, is especially thorough in its tidying up? What if my having seen dinosaur bones at Jericho and my having listened to Professor von Heussen's theories is enough to irrevocably mark me for disposal, no matter how much I allow myself to forget?

I'm terrified to sleep, fearing I'll never awaken. Psychologists claim the mind is incapable of imagining itself not existing, of mentally inhabiting its own extinction. Yet I can sense obliteration's lackeys nibbling away at my edges, hungry mice eating the brown crusts of the bread of my being.

I need a distraction, or I'll go out of my mind. Anything will do. There's a second-run film theater not far from here. It's showing a war picture. *Yangtze Incident: The Story of the H.M.S. Amethyst.* Good enough. With assorted newsreels and short subjects and perhaps a second feature, it should help me kill most of an afternoon.

All traces of my appetite have been extinguished; the mingled scents of popcorn and overcooked sausages from the snack stand in the lobby turn my stomach. But it's still better than sitting at home alone, waiting for an invisible guillotine blade to drop. Richard Todd and his gunboat crew perform with the stoic heroism expected of the Royal Navy, as they hold off what seems like the entire Red Chinese Army during the Chinese Civil War. We may have been humiliated by Eisenhower in Suez and knocked down to a second-rate power, but by God, we can still kick sand in the faces of the bloody Chinese!

The second feature is an obscure little war picture called *Hill 24 Doesn't Answer.* Shot in Israel. Concerns itself with the 1948 war for independence. It includes a few British characters, hangers-on from the Mandate period who found themselves caught up in the fight between Palestine's Jews and Arabs and the invading Arab armies. Maybe if we Brits had managed to maintain our control of Palestine, the damned Israelis wouldn't have led us by the nose into the Suez debacle, because there wouldn't have *been* any damned Israelis, just rebellious

Jewish Palestinians. And had that been the case, Miss Kenyon and I would not have been expelled from Jericho by the Jordanians. And I would've had the chance to fully excavate Miriam's bones and take them back with me to London. I would've made a name for myself by now. A big, famous name. And enough people would have been exposed to the reality of dinosaurs stomping through Trans-Jordan a few centuries before humans arrived there — it would have been worldwide news, surely — that perhaps that aspect of the past wouldn't have been erased. And maybe I wouldn't now be in the bloody situation I find myself in, sitting in a rundown theater with a sticky floor and burnt sausages, waiting to be vanished along with Miriam's bones, Smythe's journal, and Professor von Heussen.

Hell, the damned Israeli picture's over. What can I do with myself now? Find another theater? Walk the circumference of London? Surrender to sleep?

Wait — there's another feature or short subject spooling up. Some Hawaiian thing, from the looks of it. *Trek to Makaha*, whatever that means. Whoever selects the programs here certainly has eclectic tastes. This one looks almost like a student film. Grainy images, amateurish narration. Probably shot on the budget one would set aside for a used Vauxhall saloon car. Interesting, though... seems it's all about those surf enthusiasts, young Americans who drag buoyant boards out to sea to ride waves big enough to capsize an aircraft carrier. Crazy buggers have to time it just right to avoid being pounded into jelly and then dashed against rock jetties. Yet somehow they do it again and again — manage to stand atop those floating boards just in time for the building waves to push them along at twenty knots or so, rather than drown them.

It's mesmerizing. Just the distraction I hoped for. I almost feel as though I'm there with them, balancing atop those shining boards. I'm caught up in the power and fury of inexorable Nature, yet harnessing that fury as though it were a race horse, riding it...

Riding the wave to avoid being drowned by it...

Good Lord, that's *it!* That's what I must do in order to survive. I must *ride* the wave, *harness* its power, or be drowned. Professor von Heussen didn't do it. He didn't ride the wave. He pushed against it, and it vanished him. Who, it seems, managed to ride the gestalt-mind's reality-altering wave? Galileo. Darwin. Einstein. Men whose pronouncements changed enough minds to alter reality and change the past. The bloody wave riders.

I must become a wave rider myself, not a wave *victim*. I have to change the past, somehow. Reach enough minds, convince a critical mass of humanity that what they thought was true of the past is actually false. Most people are gullible. Stupid, really. I merely need a big enough and loud enough megaphone. '*Merely*', huh!

But what aspect of the past should I attempt to change? The American colonies' revolt against the British crown? Surely we would remain a preeminent world power today if we still retained under our rule the bulk of the North American continent and its huge, productive populace. That could have bad knock-on effects, though. What if the Americans never developed their tremendous arms industry, for fear of competing unduly with arms manufacturers located in their mother country? What if Parliament never allowed such American firms to come into being? Such change could've left us in a serious ditch during both the Great War and the more recent European unpleasantness.

And how could I manage to convince a hundred and fifty million Americans that their country never came into existence, not to mention persuading a critical mass of Canadians, Mexicans, South Americans, Germans, and Japanese that there never was a United States of America?

Yet I shouldn't attempt to bite off too *little*, either. Say I picked an incident in my own past — being picked on by a bully at school, that lout Donald Sykes, for example. I happen to know that Sykes works in the local brewery. I could arrange to bump into him when he's released from his shift at the factory, could hail him as a long-lost mate. He's thick as a brick. With a bit of "hail-well-met" and a few rounds of beers at his favorite pub, I'm certain I could convince him that we were chums during school, that his assaults on my person never happened, or that his loutishness was directed at some other poor bugger. Yet would that be enough? Would changing such a tiny bit of the past, known only to me and to one or two others, matter enough to take the target off my back? Would it be riding the wave, or stepping over a puddle?

But if I go bigger, attempt to change beliefs regarding a past event known to a much larger group of people, there's the problem of credibility. I would have to pick an event that a huge mass of people would *want* to believe had actually taken place differently than commonly thought. That way, I could harness individuals' tendencies toward wish fulfillment and preference confirmation, rather than struggle against firmly rooted convictions.

So attempting to convince a majority of Britons, say, that the U.K. never lost control of the Palestine Mandate would be a non-starter. As much as changing that aspect of the past would help me, personally, most of my countrymen, having witnessed the savage tribal passions of the Middle East, are more than happy to be done with the bloody place. No wish fulfillment there for me to work with.

Where have I wandered? I've been swimming so fiercely inside my head, I exited the theater and let my legs aimlessly navigate. Abandoned tombstones, flowers...? I've wandered into St. George's Gardens, the place where I last spoke with Miriam. The very grounds upon which she cast me adrift, saying she couldn't bear to "abandon" her fellow Jews, not after the trauma of the Nazis' holocaust. Not after her mother's murder at the hands of the mass exterminators...

And there it is. Yes. I stare at a weathered tombstone, the name once carved on its surface as gone and forgotten as the names of those millions of dead Jews, and it comes into focus. My bloody wave to ride.

I'll make it so the Nazi extermination of six million Jews never happened.

The Germans want to believe it never happened. That the chemicals sprayed on the Jews at Auschwitz were meant merely for delousing, not asphyxiation. That only a few hundred thousand Jews died in the camps — work camps, not death camps — and those deaths were caused by disease and the lack of food brought on by wartime shortages and the Allied bombing campaigns. The Germans don't want to see themselves as bureaucratic-minded barbarians. They're the people of Goethe and Beethoven, after all. Hitler did many good things, according to his apologists — he halted the ruinous inflation of the Weimar years, he built the Autobahn, and he gave the Germans back their pride after the humiliation of Versailles. Sure, he went too far, he got himself in over his head, but isn't that the risk faced by anyone who strives to accomplish great things?

And then there're the Muslims. Nearly a billion of them, when you include the impoverished multitudes of India and Indonesia. Of the whole Muslim crew, the Arabs hold the hottest grudge against the Jews, for certain, but that whole lot tend to think alike. The Jews gave their prophet Mohammed a hard time, apparently, and so the Muslims' Holy Koran is filled with commandments to slay the beastly Jews or reduce them to servitude. The Arabs already think the Nazi extermination of the European Jews was a Jewish hoax, a fiendishly clever plot by the Zionists to garner sympathy with the United Nations so that the Great Powers would put their stamp of approval on the Jews' stealing Arab land to found Israel. Lots of fertile soil there for the right sort of historical revisionism. I wouldn't even have to advance a particularly airtight argument; just raising questions and sowing doubt would be enough. The Muslims' eagerness to believe in conspiracies, combined with their general backwardness, would do the rest of the work for me.

If I could do it... if I could change the Nazis' holocaust from the most heinous planned slaughter of civilians the world has ever seen to merely a regrettable, but understandable, unintended consequence of war, on the level, perhaps, of what the British Army did to the Boers at the turn of the century... I could make it so that Miriam's mother survived the conflict. I could abolish Miriam's father's grief. I could remove Miriam's objections to our being married.

I could save millions of lives and rescue my own life at the same time.

-June 28, 1958-

I've been going about this all wrong. I've wasted nearly all my sabbatical, spending almost five months rummaging through wartime archives in West Germany. I should've minded that old commonplace: you can't prove a negative.

Oh, I managed to obtain marvelous access to archival records from the Nazi period, those that weren't packed up and shipped off to Washington or London. I found plenty of allies; scratch the surface of a "reformed" National Socialist, now a city official, and the old Jew-hater is there underneath, eager to sympathize with any aspersions cast on the State of Israel or hints that perhaps the vilification of old Adolf H. has gone too far. And yes, I can report that five months of searching failed to uncover any clear and unambiguous orders from the former Führer to carry out the mass extermination of Europe's Jews. Yet the absence of a direct order to execute the Final Solution cannot constitute proof that such a Final Solution was never carried out. At least not proof compelling enough to initiate the shift I require in mass belief about Germany's treatment of European Jewry.

No, I must have *physical* proof the holocaust has been mischaracterized, not just an absence of documentary proof of official directives from the top ordering an extermination. I need to find a way to get into Poland and visit the remains of the death camps. Particularly Auschwitz. Only there, with an archeological analysis, can I acquire evidence that strongly indicates to the average layman that the existence of death camps was a massive hoax, a piece of wartime Allied propaganda later instrumentalized by the Jews to grease the rails for the establishment of Israel.

But there's the damned inconvenience of old Winston's Iron Curtain standing between me and the most infamous of concentration camps. And the more time I waste before inducing a wave of reality-change to ride, the more time von Heussen's nemesis has to ensnare me.

-September 17, 1958-

I've made a thorough canvassing of Miss Kenyon's Red associates in the archeology field, of which there are no shortage (all the fashionable academics have been Red, or at least Pink, since the early 'forties). Yet none of them have evinced the sort of contacts on the far side of the Iron Curtain that could grant me access to Communist Poland.

Von Heussen's nemesis is drawing closer. I swear I can feel it in my room with me at night, scuttling from corner to corner, shadow to shadow.

I can't delay my visit to Auschwitz much longer. I *must* find a way.

Time to pursue a different tack. Oswald Mosley's back from his self-imposed exile in Ireland. The bastard's making a run for a seat in Parliament representing Kensington North, this time standing under the banner of the Union Movement, rather than his old crew, the disbanded British Union of Fascists. Seems queer to pin my hopes for getting the Iron Curtain lifted for me on a former fascist. But recently Mosley's been pushing the notion that Britain is destined to unite the nations of Europe into a super-state that can counterbalance the international influence of the United States. So the Union Movement is exactly the type of movement the Soviets would look upon favorably... and likely secretly fund.

Why would he help me? Contrary to his claims of having turned over a new leaf, Mosley's never abandoned his Jew-hatred. I'm sure he'd be delighted to hear of my efforts to discredit Jewish claims of monumental victimization during the recent war. For all his unsavory reputation, the man maintains extensive connections, as an aristocrat, the founder of several political movements, and as a former Member of Parliament. I'm fairly certain the old spider can pull upon strands of his nasty, sticky web and obtain for me the papers I need to enter Poland.

-October 4, 1958-

"I must say, I am delighted with this plan of yours, Professor Davison. It's long past time someone with intellectual integrity pushed back against the extravagant, ahistorical claims of the Jews and their abominable slanders against the German people."

I thought this meeting with Sir Oswald Mosley would be no worse, no more abhorrent, than my meetings with former Nazi functionaries in West Germany had been. I couldn't have been more wrong. I found it easy enough to distance myself, psychologically, from the Germans, the Former Enemy. But not Mosley... it's as though we're too closely related, members of the same "English race". He reminds me too much of my father. Particularly that wry, self-satisfied smirk that never leaves its spot from beneath his thin mustache.

"Of course I'll make inquiries on your behalf," he says. "I have my resources, you know, in and out of government, never you doubt!"

So says a man who's never doubted himself, despite his series of political debacles and being imprisoned by his own government for much of the duration of the late war. Sir Oswald has learned nothing from history, either the world's or his own. Shaking hands with him is like grasping the oily claw of Kafka's human-sized cockroach. Yet he is precisely the sort of man I'm forced to rely upon. If I am to be successful in changing the past, I'll need to ally myself with millions of Sir Oswald Mosleys. Lord help me.

-December 12, 1958-

It's surreal to walk, enshrouded in a winter's fog, through the main gate of Auschwitz II-Birkenau, along the very railroad tracks that transported nearly all the Jews of Hungary on their final journeys. It's surreal that I should stride into genocide's ground zero, intending to strip it of its infamy, to reduce the unspeakable to the unremarkable. If I am successful, this dreadful place will become either an ugly, forlorn, forgotten shell of a wartime factory or an empty field, home only to rodents and flocks of migrating geese.

My guide is Kazimierz Smolen. A Pole, he was a former inmate of this place, and is now its caretaker and foremost historian. He's arranged for an interpreter to assist me. Through the interpreter, I ask Smolen to take me to the gas chambers.

Smolen explains there are four major ones, Crematoria II through V, as well as two much smaller buildings, one known as

Bunker 1 by the Germans and 'the little red house' by the camp's inmates, the other labeled Bunker 2 by the SS and 'the little white house' by the inmates. None are very far from the rail terminus. This, of course, made matters convenient for the SS guards and doctors who performed selections on the newly arrived prisoners.

"These buildings are remarkably well preserved," I say, "considering they survived at least one inmate uprising and the incursion of the Red Army."

The interpreter relays my remark. "The barracks and administrative buildings survived the war reasonably intact," Smolen replies. "These crematoria and gas chambers, however, have been reconstructed by us Poles. The Germans blew up the crematoria before they retreated in the face of the Russians. They wanted to leave behind no evidence of their crimes. I assisted in the reconstruction. Having spent five years imprisoned here, my memories of the camp's architecture are quite reliable."

"How badly were these crematoria damaged?"

"They were reduced to rubble. Piles of bricks. We had to entirely rebuild them, from their foundations on up."

I hadn't realized this. "Is this common knowledge, this reconstruction?"

"The matter is shared with those who ask."

This obscure fact can work to my advantage. The chemist with whom I consulted back in London told me that cyanide, the active ingredient in Zyklon B, only penetrates brick to a depth of about one millimeter... and obviously, only on the wall's exposed surface. With these gas chambers having been reconstructed from piles of blown-apart bricks, who can say which bricks were replaced in their original orientation, and which were not? It's not as though each brick was inscribed with assembly instructions.

I ask permission to remain alone for a few hours in the crematoria. I state I wish to take a large selection of photographs and shoot a few canisters of sixteen millimeter film (I rented a movie camera in Warsaw). Smolen and the interpreter leave me on my own in Crematorium II.

The film camera wasn't the only tool I picked up in Warsaw. I didn't bring my own hammer and chisels from London; I figured such odd implements might attract too much unwelcome attention from Polish customs officials. The ones I bought in Warsaw, crude Communist tools, will suffice.

I set up the film equipment. I intend to visually document every act I undertake at Auschwitz II-Birkenau, in all six of the gas chambers, in the barracks, and in the clothing delousing facilities. If, as Churchill supposedly said, truth in wartime is so precious that it requires a bodyguard of lies, the inverse is also true — this lie is so precious that it requires a bodyguard of truths.

Demonstrating to future viewers what a thorough documentarian I am, I mark with chalked numbers the various spots on the interior walls of Crematorium II where I will extract my samples. I neatly set out the equivalently marked sample collection bags. Then I take up my hammer and chisel.

Blow after blow I strike, placing the resulting shards in my sample bags, filming myself the entire while. Wielding the chisel and hammer makes me think of the stone masons of long-ago London, who inscribed the names of the dead, their life spans, and their epitaphs on the gravestones at St. George's Gardens. They were helping to inter the dead. But with each hammer blow, I strive to disinter the dead, to remold bones from ashes and place warm flesh on those bones. I will resurrect the dead by blotting out their murders and the memories of those murders. I am reshaping history and reality with my chisel the way Michelangelo, with his chisel, reshaped a gargantuan block of marble into David. But unlike Michelangelo's, my Davids, risen from the ashes, will dance and feast, marry and grow old.

-January 15, 1959-

The analysis results I've obtained from Abbetty and Harcourt, Industrial Chemists, bear out my bad-faith hypotheses to a tee. I did not reveal to the testers that the samples I presented to them had been purloined from buildings at Auschwitz. Instead, I indicated that, for purposes of insurance claims, I had undertaken an investigation of an industrial accident in Surrey, one involving a production and storage facility operated by a manufacturer of agricultural pesticides.

Of the three lots of samples I provided for testing, the lot chiseled from the interior bricks of the clothing delousing building presented by far the highest concentration of cyanide traces. The samples from the interiors of the six gas chambers, on the other hand, in terms of cyanide concentrations barely rank above those taken from the interiors of the barracks. In fact, the difference in cyanide content between the latter two is statistically insignificant. Perfect for my purposes.

There are good reasons for these seemingly incongruous results, of course. Reasons I shall not allude to in the pages of the book I have already begun to write. Here's a fact known only to entomologists — hard-shelled insects are way more resistant to the lung-deadening effects of cyanide than humans are, and thus far higher concentrations of the poison, and longer periods of exposure, are required to kill lice and other insect vermin than to asphyxiate human beings. The Germans knew that only five minutes of exposure to the emissions of the cyanide gas pellets they dropped through tubes in the ceilings of the crematoria would kill the several hundred inmates crammed inside, whereas lice would require a half-hour's exposure to exterminate. The Nazis aired out the gas chambers as quickly and efficiently as they could, so that the *Sonderkommandos*, the forced collaborators, could clear out the corpses of their fellow Jews and stuff them into the cremation ovens, and a fresh batch of non-useful inmates could then be done away with. After all, what is a German without a time-table?

Furthermore, in order to carry out the tests I required, the industrial chemists crushed my entire samples into powder, improperly diluting any traces of cyanide. Had the testers known the true origin of the samples, they would have analyzed only those surfaces of the brick fragments that had actually been exposed to Zyklon B. Of course, the Poles' postwar reconstruction of the gas chambers makes it impossible for anyone less omniscient than the Heavenly Father to know which bricks originally lined the interiors of Crematoria II through V and Bunkers 1 and 2, and which surfaces of those bricks had been fogged by clouds of Zyklon B gas.

Who might see through my deception? Only certain chemists, materials engineers, doctors, and biologists, a small enough contingent. But for the average reader of my forthcoming book,

The Holocaust Hoax: The Zionist Plot to Steal the Sympathies of the World, other, far more apparent and self-evident 'facts' will burrow into their brains like earwigs; 'facts' given weight by widespread Jew-hatred and suspicions of Jewish conspiracies of world domination. I can predict those readers' thoughts with fair confidence—

Surely, if the crematoria had been used as death chambers, rather than sanitary disposal facilities for victims of typhus, the brick samples taken from their interiors would show far higher concentrations of cyanide than samples taken from the bricks of clothing delousing chambers. After all, wouldn't far more poison be required to slay full-grown adult persons than to exterminate tiny insect vermin? Yet Professor Davison shows that the concentrations of cyanide found in the crematoria chambers are barely above those found in the prisoners' barracks. Therefore, it must be that small doses of Zyklon B were used in both barracks and crematoria as insecticide and disinfectant agents.

Where are the missing Jews, then? Where did the supposed 'gassing victims' go, if they were not burned to ashes? It's not such a mystery, after all. Tens of millions of people were displaced after the Second World War. The 'missing' Jews simply mixed in with the far larger masses of involuntary migrants and displaced persons, abandoning outward signs of their religion to blend in and thus avoid expropriation of their ill-gotten riches.

So claims by the Americans, British, and Russians and their Jewish puppet masters that the Germans used poison gas to exterminate millions of Jews are just updated versions of the Belgian Atrocity propaganda fables circulated by the Allied Powers in World War One. What a monstrous slander of the

Germans! Horrendous! And all to facilitate the Zionist theft of Arab lands!

Yes, I expect a handful of scientists and historians, and perhaps a larger cadre of death camp survivors, will excoriate my book. They'll point out my sins of omission and label me an abhorrent fraud. But by that time, millions of readers will have accepted my facile logic. I have already gotten my publisher to commit to German, Arabic, Spanish, Hindi, Bengali, Japanese, and Indonesian editions. Apart from my international readership, hundreds of millions more will have heard of my assertions through greatly simplified distillations spread by radio, the popular press, and word of mouth.

People will believe what they want most to believe, what they *yearn* to be true. Nothing is more readily accepted than the seeming confirmation of an already established prejudice. All efforts by scientists, historians, and death camp survivors to refute my work will simply confirm in the popular imagination the existence of a worldwide Zionist conspiracy to smother the truth. The more such experts rail against me, the more credence I will gain from the *souk* merchant in Cairo, the school teacher in Islamabad, the manual laborer in Munich.

Therefore, I must chain myself to my typewriter's keyboard like a galley slave is chained to his oar.

-March 30, 1960-

A celebratory telegram from my editor. Huzzah! *The Holocaust Hoax* has sold more than a million copies in its English edition, reaching that milestone faster than any other book put out by my publisher in its sixty-year history. But those results are dwarfed by those of the foreign language editions — in aggregate, more than *fifteen million* sold. The Royal House of Saud has subsidized the distribution of a good chunk of that, five million Arabic copies, whipping up a fresh fervor against Israel and the perfidious Zionists throughout the Arab world.

-June 2, 1960-

An unfortunate occurrence took place last night, one I should have foreseen but did not. The *Deutsche Reichspartei* (the German Imperial Party of West Germany) invited me to speak as guest of honor at their annual party conference. Whereas prior to the publication of my book, this right-wing throwback to the National Socialists had been polling in the very low single digits, the widespread popularity of *The Holocaust Hoax* has been credited with elevating their numbers into the mid-twenties — higher in some of the more conservative German states.

Although addressing a football stadium packed with neo-Nazis is not my idea of a fun Saturday night outing, one must sacrifice for the greater good. So I found myself exhorting a mass of former *Luftwaffe* pilots and U-boat crewmen and munitions manufacturers into paroxysms of orgasmic cheering, feeling like a chip off the old Adolf H. (the Germans certainly do enjoy their mass rallies, particularly ones in which Jews take it on the chin). Suddenly, a glass bottle shattered on the floor next to my podium, peppering me with fragments.

It had been thrown from my left. I looked to see a commotion in progress. A balding, middle-aged man had been restrained by security officials, not far from my podium. His face was florid, and he screamed at me in strongly German-accented English. During his struggles, he had torn the sleeve of his jacket clear off. I saw numbers and letters tattooed on his forearm, black scars on his pale flesh.

The crowd, ninety-nine percent of whom were unable to see what I saw, nevertheless seemed to sense who and what the man was. Their raucous cheering shifted to vehement booing. Fearing some of the more zealous might rush the platform and seize the man from the guards' custody, I pleaded with the crowd to quiet itself. I announced they would enjoy the privilege of witnessing an unscheduled debate — I would grant the stranger the opportunity to take the podium and refute my findings, if he could.

The rally was being filmed by television crews from across Germany and from other European countries. I had chanced into an ideal opportunity to spread my world-altering lie, through a hugely emotional confrontation that would make for riveting television.

I called the man to the podium and asked him to introduce himself. Yitzchak Oldenburg claimed to have been an inmate at Dachau, a forced labor camp ten miles from Munich, Germany. He said that, due to his medical background — he had been a medical student before Jews were expelled from German universities — he had been forced to assist Nazi doctors in their sadistic medical experiments, as well as culling those survivors too weakened to work in the armaments factories, sending them to their deaths at the extermination center near Linz, Austria. The American Army freed Oldenburg and thousands of other survivors on April 29, 1945. Oldenburg claimed the conditions the Americans found in the camp were so horrific that some of the liberating infantrymen disobeyed their commanding officers and machine-gunned about thirty of the German guards who had surrendered. He also said the American general forced civilians from surrounding towns and villages to bury about thirty thousand emaciated corpses piled about the camp.

How, he asked in anguished tones, could I deny that which he had seen with his own eyes? Atrocity piled upon atrocity? What sort of a monster was I — a British citizen, not even a German — to strive so greatly to exonerate the Nazi regime?

I replied calmly that I was not a monster at all, merely a seeker after truth. Orderly civilization, I lectured him, must be built on a foundation of truths, not falsehoods or misconceptions. Had he personally seen this so-called extermination center at Linz? No, he admitted, he had not. So how could he be certain it had truly existed, not merely as a rumor embellished by the fogs and passions of war? The German doctors had ordered him to determine which subjects of medical experiments could no longer work and should be sent for euthanasia procedures at Linz, he insisted. Was that the term they used, I asked, euthanasia? Yes, he replied, they called it euthanasia. Could not euthanasia be considered a merciful medical procedure in some situations, such as for those patients with agonizing terminal conditions, or those with crippling ailments or abnormalities that could not be ameliorated? Was this not taught in medical schools? It was, he admitted. Was not euthanasia sometimes administered by doctors in countries that had fought on the Allied side during the Second World War — including the United States? To this, he merely nodded.

Dachau had been a labor camp, had it not? Again, he nodded. Did Mr. Oldenburg know that every American state in the great and free democracy of the United States of America compels its prisoners to perform uncompensated labor? Furthermore, was Mr. Oldenburg aware that the universally admired American President Franklin Roosevelt had ordered the imprisonment in camps, for the duration of the war, of tens of thousands of Japanese Americans, both legal residents and natural-born citizens, and that the Supreme Court of the United States had upheld this order on the basis of national security during the wartime emergency? How was Dachau, a camp for the containment of political prisoners, so different from the vast internment camps established by President Roosevelt for Japanese Americans? Yes, living and sanitary conditions, as well as nutrition for prisoners, were far poorer at Dachau than at any of the American concentration camps. Yet Germany experienced years of daily and nightly bombings by aerial armadas of American and British heavy bombers, whereas the continental United States never suffered the fall of a single Axis bomb. Could not that fact constitute the primary reason for the disparity in prisoners' living conditions in German camps versus American camps? To this, Oldenburg, trembling in silent frustration, could offer no counter-argument.

I pressed on, exploiting my advantage, playing for the television cameras. Advancements in medical science required experimentation, correct? Ideally, of course, such experiments would be carried out in hospitals under carefully controlled conditions, with the full consent of patients who volunteered to undergo clinical trials. Myriads of horrendous injuries caused by war, as well as the diseases set loose by crowding, unsanitary water supplies, destruction of sewage systems, and the spread of vermin abetted by the proliferation of corpses in ruined cities, all cried out for new, advanced medical treatments and techniques. But American and British bombs destroyed many German hospitals and universities in firestorms, did they not? Robbed of their hospitals and universities, what else could German doctors and scientists do but make use of the only resources at hand? Of course, I said, given your situation, you viewed your doctor superiors at Dachau as immoral sadists. But looked upon in a different light, could they not also be seen as heroes of the German people, selfless men forced by circumstances to perform cruel acts for the greater good?

No, he said, *you are twisting my words, my meanings! I know what I saw, I know what I heard, the cries of children, the screams of the tortured! I know what I smelled for months without end — the smell of decaying corpses, the stench that infested one's clothes, so that you could not escape it even in sleep...!*

Unfortunate but unavoidable consequences of war, I said. Had Americans in Chicago suffered the same as Germans in Munich, the former would assuredly have committed the same 'crimes against humanity' as did the latter, merely to survive.

I'm winning the debate, I thought. The thought filled me with a sense of exultation. The Germans, I continued, pressing my advantage, had been subjected by their conquerors to the basest slanders and libels ever arrayed against a defeated people. I then summarized my findings from Auschwitz II-Birkenau. Point by point, I explained with seemingly ironclad scientific logic how the supposed gas chambers could not have been used to kill masses of Jews, homosexuals, or gypsies with Zyklon-B. Those facilities and others like them had been used to delouse newly arrived prisoners, to attempt to control the spread of vermin and disease in the camps. The German regime, in fact, far from committing atrocities, had expended its dwindling resources on efforts to limit death and suffering in its detention camps, at the very same time its own soldiers had been perishing from starvation and hypothermia in the Russian winter. Were these the actions of an immoral, genocidal government?

The crowd rewarded each of my successive assertions with louder and louder cheers. The tendons in Oldenburg's neck stiffened like steel cables. The muscles of his arms and shoulders twitched, as though he were about to throttle me. Yet he held himself in check — as well he should, considering where he stood, mere meters from hundreds of my impassioned defenders.

The effort cost him. His face seemed to cave in upon itself. He sagged, engulfed in violent sobbing.

I had triumphed. Acting as defense attorney for the late Nazi regime, I had demolished the prosecution's witness. I had reduced a survivor to incoherent tears. My victory would dominate European, then world airwaves for days to come. This was possibly the greatest advance yet of my campaign.

Exultation is a fleeting emotion. I exited the stage directly for the water closet, where I vomited into the toilet. My heaves continued long after my stomach was empty.

The taste of rancid bile still lingers, as does my shame.

-September 15, 1960-

My alma mater has disowned me. Today I received official notice from Cambridge that the Student Union, supported by the faculty, voted overwhelmingly to disavow all ties with me and to remove my name from the rolls of graduates in good standing.

Preening moral narcissists. Socialist twats. They have no idea of what I seek to accomplish, the pain of my lonely crusade.

Banishment from polite society aside, I must focus on the upside. Fifty million copies now sold — closer to a hundred million, if the estimates of pirated copies printed in the Soviet Union and Red China are included in the totals (even Communists love to hate the Jews, especially when they pay no royalties for the pleasure). *The Holocaust Hoax* is bested in sales only by the King James Bible. I'm becoming richer than Croesus or Midas. Soon I'll be swimming in mounds of my money, like that miserly uncle of Donald Duck. And Cambridge University shall not see a damned cent of it, ever. The twats.

-December 28, 1960-

The week between Christmas and New Year's Day always feels empty to me. Empty and forlorn. Like the aftermath of a tremendous, extended feast, a month of extravagant gluttony that leaves one's stomach distended. I bought myself a new Jaguar saloon car on Christmas Eve. I selected every option — the works. It was delivered to me yesterday. I find I have no desire to drive it anywhere.

When will things change? Have I outrun von Heussen's nemesis, or does it still lie in wait for me, reserving the moment when I feel most safe to strike?

London's snowfall, unbroken for the last three days, has finally ceased. The sun emerged from its blanket of clouds. I need to walk outside, to feel the sun's light on my face. Sheltering alone within my townhouse does my spirit no good.

Where do I go, tromping through the snowdrifts in my galoshes like a clumsy kangaroo? St. George's Gardens. A handful of my fellow Londoners shared my desperate yearning to be outside, I see. We stare across the snow-smothered gardens at one another like deer who have emerged from woods at opposite ends of an open field, startled at the one another's presence. Friend, or foe?

And then I realize who it is I'm staring at, who stares back at me.

My Miriam.

I'm torn between a desire to speak with her and an impulse to flee. Judging by her expression, she feels the same tension.

God, I want to be near her. To look into her eyes. To smell her skin. The snow crunches beneath my galoshes as I head toward her.

She hesitates, then turns away, returning the way she came. The snow hinders her more than it does me, however. I overtake her. Only then, breathing hard from my exertion, do I realize I haven't thought of what to say. "Miriam...?"

She stares at me as though I'm an unfamiliar dog, trying to discern whether it is safe to extend her hand to be sniffed. Then she blushes and looks away. "Irving, please leave me alone. We haven't a thing to say to one another..."

"No, that can't be right," I say. "I've *missed* you, Miriam. Missed you terribly..."

"And what a *fine* way you have of showing it." The barely contained heat in her voice could melt the snow from here to Dover. "Oh, Irving, how *could* you? How could you write the things you have, say the things you have? How could you so cruelly defame the memory of my mother, and millions of others? I thought I *knew* you, Irving. I thought I was a decent judge of character. Do you know what it's like, to realize your own competence at choosing friends — *lovers!* — is so horribly lacking? I *hate* myself for having ever loved you!"

It nearly spills out of me, everything I've experienced since the day I discovered dinosaur bones in Jericho. I want so much to tell her that what looks black is actually white, whiter than the frost that covers the ancient gravestones. That I'm trying with every power I can muster to raise her mother from the dead — no, to change the past so that her mother never died at all.

But I realize what it would sound like. How her hate might turn to horrified pity at my ludicrous self-exoneration. So I say nothing at all. I stand immobile... burning, burning in the snow.

"You terrible, terrible, beastly man," she whispers. Then, hindered by her winter carapace, she strides as quickly as her petite legs can manage past the frozen rose bushes, their thorns still capable of drawing blood.

I return home, sinking within a funk the bottom of which I cannot imagine. I consider becoming stupefyingly drunk. But no amount of liquor will erase the memory of her scathing denunciations, of her livid, hate-filled glare.

No, there's only one escape open to me. Forgetting. Releasing my stubborn hold on my memories of all the steps I have taken since first setting eyes upon that carnosaur's thigh bone.

The only way I've managed to remember why I set out on this quest to subvert the past is my nightly renewal of my notes to myself. Years have passed since I retained any true memories of my last two excursions to Tel es-Sultan, of my visit with Professor von Heussen, and of my reading Captain Smythe's journal of the flat Earth. All I have now is the equivalent of a smudged photostat copy of a smudged photostat copy of a smudged photostat copy. Those bizarre experiences I nightly write about seem to have happened, not to me, but to some character in a poem composed by a Chinese courtesan during the Han Dynasty.

What will happen if I refrain from re-transcribing my ever-fading notes? I'll stop riding the wave, the gestalt-mind's reality-altering wave. I'll fall off my surfboard, and the wave will at last engulf me. What will become of me then?

I won't know why I've done what I've done. I will come to assume, I suppose, that I truly believe what I've written in *The Holocaust Hoax*. I'll remember this morning's encounter with Miriam with a far different set of emotions. Quite possibly, I'll berate myself for ever succumbing to a Zionist seductress's erotic lures. If not morally preferable to my current state of mind, at least easier to live with.

Or perhaps once I'm no longer riding it, the wave will cause me to vanish entirely, as it did poor Professor von Heussen. In either case, matters are now out of my hands. My effort to un-do Hitler's destruction of European Jewry will either work, or it will not. The spread of my Big Lie is no longer dependent upon my exertions. Tens of millions of readers, hundreds of millions more recipients of resultant hearsay, will make their own decisions whether to believe or not to believe.

Twilight settles over London. I think I'll go to sleep early tonight. Easily done, since I won't bother to spend two hours transcribing my fading notes. Let them fade, let them fade into nothingness. They are thorns in my flesh.

I believe I'll have a glass or three of cognac, after all.

-March 21, 1969-

There's no doubt about it now. The bloody Asiatics have got themselves the Bomb. It's all over the papers; the Japs' atomic test in a Pacific atoll lagoon was captured on film by one of the Yanks' spy satellites. So despite the best efforts of the Americans and the Germans and our own government to keep the lid on atomic know-how, the Asian Co-Prosperity Empire has joined the nuclear weapons club.

Old Adolf H. must be ruing the day he ever granted his former Nip allies the status of honorary Aryans, instead of crushing them as potential rivals after forcing the Soviets to back down and retreat from Eastern Europe. And the Americans must be kicking themselves that they didn't tell the Nazis to piss off in 1945, then go ahead and invade Japan anyway, despite German threats to do to New York what they'd done to Moscow and Kiev if the Americans dared continue their war against Nippon.

The Americans shouldn't have been all *that* intimidated by the smoking atomic craters in the centers of Moscow and Kiev — they successfully tested their own atomic bomb in New Mexico just three weeks after the Germans dropped theirs. Yes, the German bombs forced a Soviet capitulation worse than that of Brest-Litovsk in 1918. But the Nazis had no aircraft carriers or land bases within bombing range of the U.S., whereas the Americans had access to numerous airfields within flying range of Berlin. The Nazis would've had to load an atomic bomb aboard one of their U-boats and sneak it into New York Harbor for a suicide run... a dicey operation under the best of circumstances, given the overwhelming force preponderance of the U.S. Navy. Still, I suppose Truman preferred not to put London at risk of becoming a glowing crater. We Londoners can thank the crude-mouthed little haberdasher for that, at least...

"Irvink, you *know* I find it disturbink, when you hide in your newspaper to avoid talk."

Ah, the voice of the beloved mother-in-law. The shrewd woman who simultaneously manages to be both my financial burden (along with her sickly husband) *and* the *comandante* of my cramped household. "Sylvia, for the hundredth time, I'm not *hiding* behind my newspaper. Important events are transpiring in the world. Important events take place every day, and it is my responsibility to stay abreast of them. My job, as a citizen."

" *Vas*, your 'job'? Your job is to study the *past*, no? That is what they pay you for at the university, yes? Not so much what happens in the present. And truly, you *avoid* what happens in the present. The things that happen *here*, in your home, rather than in Germany or America. Little David is not so little anymore. My precious grandson is nearly twelve years old. Twelve! And yet you and Miriam make no arrangements for his *bar mitzvah*... a *shanda*, a disgrace..."

I wish this newspaper were made of sound-proofed steel, and that I could fold it about my head. "Sylvia, my dear one, you're inserting yourself into a decision that is for me and Miriam alone to make. You aren't making matters easier for your daughter. For your information, I've told Miriam many times that I have no objection to a large party when David turns thirteen. A birthday party. You and Josef are certainly free to buy him religious items as gifts, if you wish. But I see no reason whatsoever to insert some nasty old rabbi whose beard smells of mothballs into the business—"

Sylvia crosses her plump arms sternly and juts her chin at me: the very image of a female, Yiddish Mussolini. "You know, Irvink, under Jewish law, the child of a Jewish mother is *Jewish*, no matter *what* the father may be..."

Again she flings this in my face! "For your information, the only law *I* observe is stolid old *English* law. And English law says that David is an *Englishman*, and *that* is the only designation that matters on this island."

"He is a *Jewish* Englishman. And Jewish Englishmen must have their *bar mitzvah*—"

"Why must you constantly *press* me, Sylvia? You push, and you push, and you *push* — *everything* must be your way. When is good enough good *enough?* I mean, you and Josef celebrate your holidays in my home, making my son participate and forcing me to pay exorbitant sums on Kosher cuts of meats. When have I refused you this? Never. And then there was that horrible business about the *bris* when David was just eight days old. A gory butchery that will poison my dreams forever. You've had your gram of *flesh*, Sylvia, from the most tender portion of my son's anatomy. Why must you demand more and more?"

"*Feh!*" she cries, throwing up her hands in that seaside vaudevillian way she has. "It is clear I am no longer velcome in my son-in-law's house. I vill begin packing my and Josef's things immediately. We vill move immediately to Yisrael so as to no longer be a bother to you. Herr Hitler shows more velcoming to Jewish people there than does the British Queen here..."

My mother-in-law has acquired the martial expertise of a General Montgomery when it comes to prodding my sensitive bits. I'm about to launch a furious retort when I see Miriam standing in the doorway, holding two sacks of groceries.

How long has she been standing there?

Valuing my marriage, I unfold my newspaper and hide behind a Japanese mushroom cloud.

-May 5, 1970-

"Why the glum face, Irving? Mother-in-law been chewing your ear off again, eh?"

Under better circumstances, I couldn't see myself chumming about with MacDonald. He's rather common, verging on crude, and he has a streak of cruelty that flashes about his eyes and mouth when he thinks he's merely being funny. But he's the only other Anglican left in the history department. So fate has made of us confidants, if not quite allies.

The sun appears pleasant, and my legs are tired, so I head for a bench beneath the branches of one of the oaks that adorn the academic commons — far enough from sunbathing students that my remarks should not become a source of undergraduate gossip. "Reggie," I say, "I feel like an outsider in my own home. It's exhausting, not to mention humiliating."

"What is it now, mate? Mother-in-law nail one of them *mezzuzahs* to your bedpost? Force you to wear a skullcap while you're stickin' it to your wife?"

"Nothing quite so dramatic, no..."

"Aye, the *bar mitzvah* then, was it? I take it you surrendered on that?"

"If you must put it that way. I didn't attend the service. Only the party afterward. I wouldn't set foot inside that synagogue. That rabbi has never treated me as anything but a pariah."

MacDonald grunts knowingly. "Family give you the cold shoulder at the party, I take it?"

"I was cast in the role of the guest who crapped in the punch bowl, yes."

"Hope your turd was *kosher*." He laughs, enormously pleased with himself. "Aw, look on the bright side, mate. At least you've scored some shiny points with old Goldberg. A son who's been *bar mitzvah*ed? Why, you're practically an honorary member of the Tribe, old son. That'll do you good at faculty meets. Me? The only reason Goldberg keeps me on is that I'm a representative of the 'indigenous working class', my pa having been a coal miner and all, and my grandpa before him. The pre-war faculty crowd would've accepted me, too, so long as I was a good Stalinist and not a Fabian or a Trotskyite. Trotsky was a Jew, wasn't he? There's your connection — Jews and Communists, natural organizers and conspirators. The Yids have been just as successful at taking over the Departments as the Reds were back in the Thirties — I mean, before Stalin got his balls blown off by Hitler's A-bombs, and the British Communist Party found itself able to fit all its members in a bobby's call box. You want a Department where faculty meetings aren't catered with bagels? Try Classics or Theology. Forget about History. The Yids own History, lock, stock, and pickle barrel. They just keep us Englishmen around for laughs."

My shoulders slump. "It just doesn't seem *fair*, that's all. We offered them refuge when Hitler ordered them out of conquered Europe, before his Afrika Korps captured Palestine and Rommel set that up as a quarantine zone for stateless Jews. We took them in, with open arms, hundreds of thousands of penniless refugees, despite the security risks. Now they've taken us over."

"'Open arms,' huh? Maybe if you hadn't been so quick to offer 'open arms' to Miriam, you wouldn't be in your current fix, you think? You kind of made your own bed, old son."

Part of me wants to smash MacDonald's smug face. But another part of me knows he's right. I *did* make my own bed.

"I love my wife, Reggie." It's all I can think to say.

-October 11, 1973-

I cannot believe what is happening in my own household. My own son, born and raised in London, an *Englishman*, being propagandized by his grandfather into fighting for the German Reich!

Although I know all too well what is going on, I decide it's best to play dumb. Draw them out. "Josef," I say, holding the Passport Office papers I discovered just moments ago, "why have you applied to get a passport for David? Is there some international travel coming up that I'm not aware of? We haven't the money for it."

The old man's cheek twitches. He looks away from me, staring down at the frayed edges of the living room rug. "The boy... he has relatives in the Holy Land, you know? Aunts and uncles and cousins he has never met. I thought that — after this new war is over, after the Germans have restored peace and order — I thought he should go to Israel, to meet his relatives. A boy should know his own blood. I meant to talk of this with you, Irving, but you have been so busy lately, writing your research monographs..."

What a damned, preposterous *lie*. "How can you be so sure there'll even *be* a Nazi protectorate called Israel in another month? Hmmn? You've been watching the BBC news on the telly rather obsessively these past few days. David, too. It looks to me like the Arabs are performing rather well, what with the up-to-date warplanes and tanks and missiles the Japanese have traded them for their oil. Hopped across the Suez Canal and broached the Germans' defensive line as though it were a mere line in the sand. Perhaps the old *Wehrmacht* has lost its touch, hmmn? First the Germans get themselves sucked into a decade-long quagmire in Vietnam, constantly bloodied by the Japanese-backed Viet Cong. The vaunted *Wehrmacht*, the terror of the industrialized world, pouring men and equipment into a meat grinder, a war of attrition that the local ethno-fanatic guerillas seem to be gradually winning. Stalemate's the best the Germans can hope for, and it couldn't have happened to a nicer bunch of bloody militarists. And now, with the Nazis bogged down in Southeast Asia, the Arabs — the lowly 'sand worms' who've been continuously humiliated and cowed by the German Army ever since 1942 — see their chance to avenge the Nazis' theft of their land and subsequent handing it over to resettled European Jews. Can you blame them, can you really blame the Arabs for wanting to push the Jews into the sea?"

Josef clenches his fists but continues staring at the floor, saying nothing.

"Stop bullying him, Father!"

Another voice heard from — my partially feigned tirade has succeeded in flushing David out of hiding. Now the truth will burst forth, like pus forced from a lanced boil.

"The Holy Land has never belonged to the Arabs!" he says, stepping boldly into the room. "There's never been Arab sovereignty over Jerusalem! And Jews have continuously lived there for more than three thousand years! The Romans conquered Judea and exiled most of its inhabitants, but some stayed. The Byzantines inherited the Holy Land from the Romans, and then the Turks wrested it away from the Byzantines. The Turks were on the losing side in the Great War, so the French and British split up the Holy Land between themselves, only to have the Germans take it away from them a quarter-century later. All the Germans did was to open up the Holy Land to the descendants of the *same Jews* who were pushed out of conquered Judea by the Romans back in 70 A.D.!"

"Thank you for the potted history lesson, David. As a professor of ancient and modern history at our country's leading university, I certainly appreciate my woeful ignorance being dispelled by your worldly expertise. Since you are such a skilled explainer, perhaps you could explain a matter of considerably greater import, at least insofar as this household is concerned." I thrust the papers from the Passport Office at him. "This passport application. Would you kindly explain to me how your date of birth is listed as April 24, 1955, rather than April 24, *1957?* And that your age is thus listed as eighteen years, rather than the correct *sixteen* years?"

Now it's David's turn to blush and mumble. "They... they got the date wrong on the papers, that's all. It was a mistake, obviously. A clerical mistake..."

"Somehow, I rather doubt that, David. Here's what I think. I think your grandfather here has been filling your ear with horror stories about what might happen if the Arabs succeed in their war. I think he's encouraged you to betray your country by signing on with the German Foreign Legion and fighting for Nazi interests in the Middle East."

David's eyes blaze with indignation. *"No!* It *wasn't* Grandpa's idea! It was *mine!* He only helped me at the Passport Office after I begged him to!"

"*Your* idea...?"

"Yes! *My idea!* After almost nineteen centuries, we Jews finally have a *homeland* again! And I — I couldn't *live with myself* if I just watch the Arabs destroy it and do *nothing!*"

"*Balderdash!* Your homeland is *England!* The only homeland you'll ever need! The notion of your fighting for that old bastard Adolf Hitler — one of history's worst anti-Semites, mind you — why, it's nothing more than *absurd! Obscene!*"

"Of *course* I agree that Hitler is personally abhorrent, Father; I'm not an idiot, after all. But so was King Cyrus of Persia — a pagan tyrant who ruthlessly ruled the mightiest empire of his day. Yet he restored the exiled Jews to their homeland and allowed them to rebuild their Temple. Evil as King Cyrus was otherwise, *ha Shem*, hallowed be His name, chose to use him as His anointed one, His instrument in the redemption of the Jews and their restoration to their promised land. Adolf Hitler is nothing more, nothing less, than our century's King Cyrus!"

I can't *take* this! My own *son*—! "By all that's holy, I *knew* I never should've let you get within spitting distance of those pickled old rabbis! Damn me for a *fool*, I should've stood *firm!* But I could never resist your mother's tears for long — and, oh, how your grandmother made her fret and wail, until I thought my heart would wither and die. But *this* — this is a different story, David my lad. This I *forbid*. You are my minor child. You live in my house. So long as those facts remain true, you are my charge and my legal and moral responsibility. If you disobey me in this, if you persist in this... this obscene *disloyalty*... I will disown you, David. I will consider you to no longer be my son."

-November 24, 1973-

The Germans managed to pull off a victory in the Middle East, even absent David's help. It was a close-run thing. They were short of troops, having drawn down their defensive cordon around their Jewish protectorate to funnel more troops to Vietnam. So when the combined Arab armies began pouring over the Suez Canal and down from the Golan Heights, the Nazis, caught with their swastika-emblazoned pants down, were forced to airlift in men and equipment from across the Reich and Southeast Asia. Much as I detest the Nazis, as a historian I'm forced to grant the *Wehrmacht* my grudging admiration. They successfully undertook one of the riskiest and most audacious airborne campaigns in military history, an operation that made their airborne invasion of

Crete look like a school fire drill on a sunny afternoon. They suffered fifteen thousand casualties in all, the cream of German youth, in the process of slaughtering five times that number of Arabs. And all in defense of nine million Jews crowded between the Jordan River and the Mediterranean Sea.

Why? Why would Adolf Hitler, an eighty-four year-old anti-Semite, sacrifice so much blood and treasure to protect the world's biggest collection of Jews?

Has the old bastard gone senile? That can't be the answer. He's been sitting on the edge of his deathbed for years now, and, according to every Foreign Office intelligence report that's leaked to the newspapers, leading officials of the Reich recognize this all too well. They've been gradually edging Hitler out of his customary solo decision-making, turning him into more of a national-party figurehead. So even if he's losing his noodle, he's no longer in complete control, able to force through his whims as ironclad dictates. That aside, Hitler has been a staunch defender of his Jewish protectorate since its founding thirty years ago, when he was a much younger, more vital dictator.

There must be some quid pro quo between the Jews in Israel and the Nazis. There *has* to be; nothing else makes sense. There's some secret partnership there, a partnership that goes back to the most desperate days of the Big War for the Germans, those months in mid-1944 when the Russians were closing in from the East and the British and Americans successfully landed in Normandy. And I think I've figured out the ground zero of that partnership.

Jewish scientists. More specifically, Jewish *physicists.* The Jews, brilliant, scheming bastards, gave Hitler his atom bombs.

It's the only answer that fits. From the days of *Mein Kampf,* Hitler wanted the Jews out of Germany. He considered them a corrupting influence, an alien infection in the German *volk.* Later, after he'd gotten his hands on most of Europe, he wanted them off the Continent, too. But conquering Palestine and settling Jews there was far from his only option. The Nazis had considered seizing Madagascar and using it as a dumping ground for Europe's Jews. They could've herded Jews to Europe's beaches and invited the Allies and the world's neutrals to collect them — Britain obliged the Reich in that respect, to an extent. Or, given the Germans' amoral efficiency, they could've figured out an effective method to wipe the Jews out entirely.

Yet the Reich pursued none of these alternatives. Hitler wanted the Jews kept away from his precious Germans — that much is certain — but he also wanted them at his beck and call, far away but not *too* far, available to work for him and his regime. He hated them, but he recognized their genius. And he recognized that his Reich *needed* that collective genius if it was to permanently triumph over the inexhaustible manpower of Russia and the industrial might of the Americans.

To induce the Jews' brightest minds to work for him, he would have had to offer them something they wanted more than life itself, something even more precious than the safety of their families. Something the Hebrews had lusted for ever since the Romans sent them packing in 70 AD. Their bloody Promised Land.

Why else would the *Wehrmacht,* stretched thin by its epic invasion of Russia, have insisted on continuously reinforcing Rommel's *Afrika Korps,* even after its defeat at El Alamein? Why else would they have continued a seemingly Sisyphean, even Pyrrhic military campaign to conquer Palestine — an impoverished mandate territory with not a drop of oil or any other strategic raw materials to speak of?

Hitler gave his despised but indispensable Jews their Holy Land, clearing out every last Arab from the Old City of Jerusalem and pushing the inconvenient sand wogs into adjacent Vichy French mandate territories. The Nazis even dynamited the Muslim shrines atop the ancient Temple Mount, paving the way for Jewish fundamentalist irredentists to rebuild a Temple (and earning the eternal enmity of the Muslim *umma*, incidentally). In return, the Jews cracked the atom for the Nazis and gave them their war-winning bombs, allowing the Germans to turn a crushing defeat into a negotiated cold peace that left them in control of Central and Eastern Europe, with their boot resting on the neck of an irradiated, enfeebled Russia.

This 'special relationship' has obviously continued beyond the end of the war. The *Wehrmacht*'s arsenal of 'wonder weapons,' intended to cow the Asian Co-Prosperity Empire and keep the Americans isolated... how much of that arsenal is due to Jewish scientists working like colonies of genius-savant ants in those vast, secretive, underground warrens the Germans constructed beneath the sands of the Negev Desert? Mere bomb shelters, as claimed? I think not.

All supposition on my part, of course. *Strong* supposition, but lacking definitive proof. If I can document this, the most monumentally perverse marriage of convenience the world has ever known, I'll make a name for myself that will outlast even the Thousand Year Reich.

-March 30, 1974-

Damn their obstinacy! Her Majesty's Government refuses to release the wartime documents I need for my book.

Thirty years on, and they still claim the intelligence dossiers compiled by British spies on the Germans' World War Two atomic bomb program fall under the purview of the Official Secrets Act. How can the knowledge of how the Nazis gained the bomb in 1944—45 be vital to present-day British national security? If MI6 is still relying upon 'sources and methods' used three decades ago, our national security is in much more dire straits than the journos at the *Guardian* and the *Times* let on.

They've bloody stymied me. The Americans have rebuffed me. The Russians are still too dysfunctional and paranoid, too busy gnawing off their own legs while psychotically retreating to their fantasy of a second coming of Ivan the Terrible, to consider opening their files to a British researcher. The Japanese were too preoccupied fighting the Americans in 1944—45 to spy on their German allies, so they have nothing to offer, even if they'd prove willing to share. The Germans, of course, have no reason whatsoever to reveal state secrets to someone they view as a hostile foreign national.

Regarding Her Majesty's Government, there has to be more to their obstinacy than protection of 'sources and methods'. The bloody Tories have been taken over by the Jews, top to bottom. PM Oderheim has obviously sniffed out trouble for his tribe in MI6's wartime dossiers, what with that big, hooked nose of his. Fully half his inner cabinet are Hebrews; some, like Health Minister Niedermeyer, are bearded, black-hatted throwbacks to medieval Polish ghettoes. I'm sure it would prove right embarrassing to the reigning Jewservatives if word were to break that their co-religionists gave the Nazis the A-bomb in 1945 — that the Jews robbed Britain of her hard-won victory.

I won't stop trying to obtain my proof. The Tories won't remain in power forever. Sir Oswald Mosley's Labourites will chuck that lot to the back benches eventually. No people as proud of their own heritage as the British are will permanently countenance handing over their governance to a pack of clannish immigrants and sons of immigrants. The British lion will shake loose of all such encumbrances, given time.

Or so I pray.

-April 19, 1974-

First occasion I've made use of a prostitute since I was nineteen. I must say, standards have fallen off a great deal since the early Fifties. All that NippoPop nonsense, ridiculous fashions purloined from Japanese cartoons and comics. The contagion isn't limited to the members of the world's oldest profession, of course... the young 'ladies' who attend my lectures all dress like Japanese tarts and android whores, too.

So, rather icky, all in all. But how long can a man be expected to remain abstinent? It's been a full year. I marked it on my calendar. It was a year since Miriam's father was buried and she moved from our shared bed into my office and made it her bedroom. Making it so that we share an apartment and a son, but not a marriage.

How can a man love someone so dearly and hate them at the same time?

-October 8, 1974-

At last, at long last... Schicklgruber the house painter is dead. Or, as the *Times* more respectfully put it, "*Reichsführer* Adolf Hitler, 85, one of the founders of the National Socialist German Workers' Party and Germany's head of state since 1933, has been laid to rest in a mausoleum beneath Berlin's famed Brandenburg Gate."

Hitler, defender of the Jews. The public displays of mourning in the heavily Jewish neighborhoods of London turn my stomach. I dare not peer out my own window, lest I expel the contents of my breakfast.

Still, I must admit I'm grateful they're being so open about their feelings, the Jews. Let everyone see them as *I* see them — disloyal bastards, curs who turn and bite the fingers of the soft-hearted, soft-headed altruists who so trustingly took them in. Apart from the Jews, Herr Hitler has few admirers here in Britain. He's best remembered for the Blitz of 1940, for Dunkirk and buzz-bombs and the silent, deadly rain of V-2 rockets. Then, when we finally had him beaten, when we and the Yanks and the Russians were on the verge of crushing him in a massive encircling pincher movement, the Jews, having been bribed with Palestine, stabbed the Allies in the back.

Let everyone in Britain see how much the Jews revere Hitler. Then let's have an election. How will Oderheim and his Jewservative Tories fare at the polls after such a spectacle of treason?

"Dad, I'm going out for a bit. Do you, uh, need anything from the store?"

I glance away from the television to look at my son. "What's that pinned to your coat, David?"

His hand swiftly covers something pinned to his lapel. "Oh, uh, nothing, Dad. It's a, y'know, a new coat... I forgot to remove the store's tag, that's all."

"Remove your hand, David."

His face reddens. "No, I'd, I'd rather not..."

"Remove your hand, I say!"

He complies.

"So... a torn black ribbon." I don't know whether to be furious, ashamed, or grief-stricken. "This wouldn't have anything to do with today's headline news, would it? *Would it*, David?"

"It's nothing, nothing really. Just a sign of respect, is all..."

"*Respect?* Respect for a *dictator?* For a monster responsible for the deaths of tens of thousands of valiant British servicemen? For a human beast who rained thousands of bombs on this very city you're so privileged to live in? For the only national leader in history to have used atomic weapons on soldiers and civilians alike? *Respect* for Adolf *bloody Hitler?*"

David's face remains lividly red, but he doesn't back down. "He saved the lives of nearly nine million Jews last year. If the Arabs had succeeded in their invasion—"

"Well who goddamn *put* the Jews in such jeopardy? If Hitler hadn't forced Europe's Jews to emigrate to Palestine, if he hadn't been so obsessed with removing the Hebrew 'infestation' from the Reich and its conquered territories, the bloody Arabs wouldn't have had nine million bloody Jews in their midst to *threaten*, would they? Your precious Jews would be safe as bugs in a rug had they stayed in Berlin and Vienna and Prague and Budapest, where they rightly belong!"

"Do you include Mother and Grandma in that number, Dad? Do they 'rightly belong' back in Germany? What about *me*, then?"

"Oh, pish-posh, you're clouding the issue. You're an Englishman, same as your father, and you always will be. I was simply explaining how you're a blind *fool* to grant any credit to Herr Schicklgruber as some sort of 'savior of the Jews' when he's the one who put them in harm's way in the first place!"

"A lot of us don't see it that way," he says, his voice cracking. "We see Hitler's forced relocation of most of the world's Jews to the land of Israel as the fulfillment of *prophecy...* as the unfolding of *ha Shem*'s plan for us."

He may as well be pissing on my grave. "And just who is this '*we*'? Who is this '*we*' you include yourself in? *Zionists?* Are those the people you're rushing out to see? Do you plan to join the disgusting rabble weeping on the streets and rending their clothes? Is *that* where you're headed?"

"Believe what you want," he says, more quietly than I would have expected. He turns toward the apartment's door. "You always do, and there's no convincing you otherwise."

"David, don't leave this apartment!" I shout at his back. "You aren't to go out there! Those are bad elements on the streets! You're liable to get swept up by the police with your venomous friends! And if you do, don't expect me to bail you out!"

He opens the door without a word, then shuts it behind him.

"*David!* I won't have a Zionist living under my roof! I won't *have it!*"

I listen to the echoes of his boots coming from the stairwell.

The announcer on the television says the German government has called for two weeks of mourning.

-August 12, 1975-

"Irving, mate, what about you? You feel like you're living in some Alice in Wonderland topsy-turvy world, looking at headlines like these?"

I'm sitting with Reggie MacDonald at a corner table in the university cafeteria, sipping the morning's first cup of coffee, glancing over the lead stories in the *Times* and the *Guardian*. It's true; the news reads like fiction. "Tectonic plates are shifting beneath the Europe I've always known, that's for certain."

"'Fascism with a human face'," he says, making a face equally puzzled and sour. "Not sure I can quite wrap my head around *that.* So now the bloody Nazis are finally getting around to lifting their hobnailed boots off the necks of the captive nations? Took them long enough, but seems they're trying right hard to make up for lost time, eh? I mean, editorialists at the *Guardian* are actually speculating the satellite nations may be granted the right to elect councils? And those councils will then get to choose between continued protectorate status, or membership in a military-economic alliance? Or even semi-independence combined with participation in a modified British Commonwealth arrangement?"

"And there may soon be a free press in Germany," I add. "And perhaps even political parties to compete with the National Socialists."

Reggie sniffs. "This isn't journalism — it's bloody *science fiction*, is what it is."

"Never underestimate the power of a failed war to precipitate radical political change," I say. The cafeteria's coffee tastes especially good this morning, less bitter than usual. "There are still plenty of Germans alive who remember the aftermath of the Great War — the abdication of the Kaiser, the Communist uprisings, the formation of the Weimar Republic. Now, it must be said, the Germans weren't as badly defeated in Vietnam, Cambodia, and Laos as they were in France in 1918, and this more recent setback took place on the other side of the globe, far from German territory. But still, the *Wehrmacht* suffered a devastating loss of prestige. Devastating. After more than a decade and a half of steadily escalating counter-insurgency against the Viet Cong and allied Cambodian and Laotian nativist movements, all backed by the Japanese, for the Germans to admit the futility of it all and pull out of Southeast Asia... well, it's the biggest black eye the *Wehrmacht* has suffered since the aftermath of the Battle of Kursk in the summer of 1943, when the Red Army began its extended romp through Eastern Europe."

"I'll bet if ol' Adolf were still sitting in the big chair in Berlin, there's no bloody way the Germans would've pulled their arses out of Southeast Asia. He'd make his bloody generals fight to the last man. They sure as hell didn't pull out of Israel when it looked as though the Arabs had the Krauts and the Jews on the ropes."

"That may well be true," I say, buttering a limp croissant (the university cafeteria is not known for the quality of its baked goods, alas — apart from its bagels, which I refuse to order on principle). "But you're asserting a counter-factual, Reggie. Hitler *is* dead, and bloody *good riddance*. To the average German, I imagine, Hitler *was* the Nazi Party — the sun around which all the negligible non-entities and functionaries orbited. After Hitler's death, the only binding force holding the old regime together was the good old reliable *Wehrmacht*, the guarantor of the German state since its founding in a lake of French blood in 1870. And when the *Wehrmacht* found itself no longer so good, nor reliable, there was nothing left, save simple inertia, to hold back the tide of radical change. The Young Turks of the Nazi Party, such that they are, found their path cleared for them. Men of the generation of Helmut Kohl and Gerhard Schröder, who were children or babies during the war, lack the stomachs to be totalitarians and dictators. They *yearn* for 'fascism with a human face', and they have for years. They want to be good Europeans, like Goethe and Beethoven were. I'd say the eventual replacement of the Greater German Reich with a European Cooperative Federation is a virtual certainty."

"So you think Kohl is on the level with this new policy of his, *die Aufgeschlossenheit*?"

"'Openness'? Yes. Yes, I do. *Die Aufgeschlossenheit* is genuine. There's a religious aspect to all this, Reggie. When Hitler died, the Germans' *god* died. They're in bad need of a replacement. Christianity offers the most convenient alternative. The spirit of repentance, of expiation of old sins, haunts Berlin, enshrouds the city like a fog. The Germans want the world's forgiveness.

Reconciliation can't flower without truth as its handmaiden. Therefore, *die Aufgeschlossenheit.*"

"So they'll open the files, you think? The wartime archives?"

"I have little doubt."

"Even the stuff about the Heeb physicists and the bomb, eh?" He grins at me. "You must be salivating, mate."

"This is the turning point, Reggie," I say. "The truth will out. Soon, all those deniers who dismissed me as a deluded obsessive will be stripped naked in the public square."

"Aye — scratch a Cambridge historian," my sole friend on the faculty says, tearing a croissant in half, "and there's a bloody Jew apologist underneath. Present company excluded, of course."

"I've suffered their jibes and taunts, their snide dismissals long enough. Give me a month or two in the German archives, Reggie, and I'll write a book that will give every last Hebrew on these hallowed premises nightmares."

-May 5, 1976-

Damn the foot-draggers! The German Visa Office will *still* not grant me entry to the Reich!

Die Aufgeschlossenheit proceeds slowly. Far *too* slowly for my taste. Bureaucracies are dullards' tools of revenge on men of action. Sputtering machines filled with blinkered human cogs, they respond glacially to signals issued by their political masters, rather like ponderous dinosaurs whose tiny brains required an auxiliary neural center within the hip region to re-transmit commands all the way to their tail.

Still, there are other methods than digging through the Germans' wartime files for obtaining the information I need. German academics and scientists have chaffed for decades under their political isolation from the rest of the world. They hunger for contact with and acceptance by the world's intellectual community. Cambridge, despite its thorough conquest by Jewish refugees and their offspring, still retains enormous prestige throughout the globe, particularly within Germany. As a Cambridge lecturer of long standing, I hold an intellectual passport that permits me to break bread with any German researcher or scientist I can physically access, whether their field of expertise intersects with mine or not.

Opportunity presents itself — the upcoming Games of the Twenty-First Olympiad in Montreal have prompted the Reich to send scores of its best and brightest on an extended sojourn to Canada. Chancellor Kohl and his circle seem eager to use this year's Olympics as a coming-out party for the new, kinder, gentler Germany. Robert Döpel will be serving as an honorary captain of the German delegation to the Olympics. Döpel, now in his early eighties, was one of the heads of the *Uranprojekt*, the Nazis' atomic weapons program, both before and during the war. Werner Heisenberg may have been the program's lead theoretician, but Döpel was the top practical man, the nuclear experimenter who, according to widespread rumor, was responsible for setting up the German's first working atomic pile. He's been retired for years now, tending his garden in Bavaria and acting as ceremonial *éminence grise* for German science. My sources tell me his memory remains sharp.

If anyone still living can confirm my intuition about Jewish physicists' secret involvement in the *Uranprojekt*, it will be him.

·July 22, 1976·

Döpel agreed to meet with me in a café on the outskirts of the Olympic Village. Officially, I'm badged as a journalist. According to the rationale I provided my department, I'll be researching Germany's revisions of national symbols, such as her flag, anthem, and the uniforms of her national squad, on the grand Olympic stage in her effort to rejoin the world community. No more swastikas. No more military bombast. Goldberg obligingly obtained my credentials for me; I think he's happy to get me out of his hair and away from Cambridge for a month. Miriam, too, seemed not displeased that I would be absent from home for an extended period.

Herr Döpel arrives. Despite his advanced age, he carries himself stiffly erect with a martial bearing, as though he still reports to the *Wehrmacht*'s *Heereswaffenamt*, the Army Ordinance Office. He bows slightly to me before seating himself at the table.

I surreptitiously turn on the small tape recorder I've hidden in a briefcase on my lap. Wanting to begin our exchange with small talk, I ask Herr Döpel how he feels about the absence of Nazi Party iconography within the German delegation, a first since the 1932 Games, forty-four years ago. He eyes me warily; I suddenly wonder whether he suspects I'm an informer sent to spy upon him, to determine his loyalty to the new regime (now I feel a bit guilty about secretly taping him — but not guilty enough to turn my machine off or ask his permission). He says he is old enough to remember the Imperial flag, then the flag of the Weimar Republic, and then the flag of the National Socialists. Change comes, he says. This is his fourth national flag. If God permits, he may live to see a fifth fly above an Olympic stadium.

"But you did not come all this way to Montreal to ask me my opinion of the new German flag," he says. "You came to ask me about Jewish physicists during the war, Jewish physicists who worked for the *Uranprojekt*. Of this, I am willing to speak. But I must ask, what is the reason for your curiosity?"

"I am a historian. The German atomic bomb program changed the course of history."

"Yes, true, it did. Then why not ask me about the entirety of the *Uranprojekt*? Why focus only on the handful of *Jewish* physicists? The project employed hundreds of scientists, the great majority of them not Jews. Are you writing a history of Jews in physics or the sciences? This would be most surprising, considering your reputation." My face must register some surprise of its own, because he continues, "Yes, I have looked into your work and background. Despite your marriage to a Jewess, your output does not mark you as a philo-Semite."

"I'm interested in their motivations," I say. "The reasons why Jewish physicists would lend their scientific expertise to a secret weapons program operated by an officially anti-Semitic regime."

"Ahh. It is not so complicated," he says, puffing on a cigarette. "When Heisenberg and Diebner and I first conceived of the *Uranprojekt* in the early years of the regime, we prevailed upon *der Führer* to allow the participation of Jews in the program, that they be exempted from the racial restrictions. We three had all either been colleagues or mentors to talented Jews, and we knew we would be entering into a race with the Americans and the British to produce atomic power and an atomic bomb. Under the circumstances, we could little afford to cast aside scientific brilliance, even if it meant compromising on racial purity. Hans Bethe and James Franck joined the *Uranprojekt* with enthusiasm. Although Jews, they were German patriots first, eager to advance German science, grateful to be allowed the opportunity to do so. Perhaps they hoped that Hitler and Nazism would be a transient problem. I do not know; we never spoke of such matters, understandably. Rudolf Peierls... he was initially unwilling to join the *Uranprojekt*, but we convinced him to do so, telling him that his cooperation would help ensure better treatment of Germany's Jews.

"Klaus Fuchs... that one was a special case. At the beginning, he joined the program with seemingly the same enthusiasm as had Bethe and Franck, claiming an exuberance of German patriotism. Yet his true loyalty proved to be to *international* socialism — not National Socialism, but Marxism. He was a dedicated worker, I remember, and a talented scientist. But during the two years of alliance between Germany and the Soviet Union, from 1939 to 1941, he found ways to pass along German atomic secrets to the Russians. This treason was discovered several months after it began. The *Gestapo* allowed his activities to continue a while longer, so they could determine if other Jews were involved."

"Were there?"

"No. Fuchs schemed on his own. Once the *Gestapo* determined this, they arrested Fuchs and assassinated his Russian handlers, who worked out of the Russian embassy. This did not cause the great breach between allies that it might have, for the killings took place less than a week before Germany's invasion of Russia."

"What happened to Fuchs?"

Döpel smiles tightly. "What do you think? A Jewish traitor in the hands of the *Gestapo*? It should not take much imagination to picture his fate. His execution followed torture most unpleasant. Details of this torture were shared widely across the *Uranprojekt*, most explicitly with the remaining Jewish physicists."

"What about the Polish and Hungarian Jews who worked for the *Uranprojekt*? You could not count on patriotism to motivate *them*, surely?"

He raises an eyebrow. "So you know something of von Neumann and Ulam and the others?"

"I have my sources, limited as they are." I open up to him, in the same spirit as he has opened up to me. "A few kindred souls within the British National Archives. Thus far, they've only been able to provide me with some tantalizing tidbits regarding Jewish involvement in the *Uranprojekt*. Just enough to get me started."

"These sources, are they the origin of this notion of yours that there was a secret deal between the Jew physicists and *der Führer*? That *der Führer* would hand over Britain's Palestine Mandate to the Jews as a new Israel, in exchange for which they would build for Germany an atomic bomb?"

I don't care for his tone. There's too much of mockery in it. "I developed that theory entirely on my own," I say, more heatedly than I intend. "It's the only explanation that makes any *sense*. In late 1942, Rommel was beaten by Montgomery at El Alamein. The *Wehrmacht's blitzkreig* into Russia was stalling out in Stalingrad after grinding to a halt on the outskirts of Moscow. The Americans landed in North Africa. Militarily, there was no reason on Earth for Hitler to make a renewed offensive into Egypt with the objective of taking Palestine — *unless* there existed some quid pro quo between your *Führer* and a group of European Jewish physicists, such that they would give the Nazis the atomic bomb in exchange for a Jewish national home in Palestine. What *other* theory makes any sort of sense?"

Döpel chuckles, then shakes his head in an infuriatingly condescending fashion. "Herr Davison, you are a man who has fallen too much in love with his own idea. I am sorry I must disabuse you of this strongly held notion, but there was no connection at all between the cooperation of Jew physicists with the *Uranprojekt* and *der Führer*'s conquest of Palestine. None. It is a mistaken theory, Herr Davison."

He's lying. He *must* be lying. "I refuse to accept that. There *has* to be a connection between the Nazi's wartime atomic program and the establishment of Israel."

"Why such insistence? Why do you privilege your theory above my personal knowledge?"

"Because to do otherwise is... it's *inexplicable!*"

"Why 'inexplicable', Herr Davison? Do you think there was no other way to motivate a Pole such as Joseph Rotblat or a Hungarian such as Leo Szilard than to appeal to whatever nostalgia or religious feeling they might hold for an ancient Jewish kingdom in the Middle East? Rotblat and Szilard, von Neumann and Ulam, and Franck and Peierls and Bethe, these were men of *science*, not of the Talmud! Their religion was *physics*, not Judaism! I know, for I worked with them all. What motivated them? I have told you — for some, patriotism; for others, threats against their family members should they fail to comply. For some, hopes for mercy for their Jewish community. For *all*, a desire to push outward the boundaries of human understanding and accomplishment, of *science*!"

"Then explain to me Hitler's insistence on pressing on toward Palestine when nearly every other front was going miserably for the *Wehrmacht*?"

"Herr Davison, it is *precisely* for that reason that *der Führer* made the capture of Palestine and the resettling of the Jews there such a high priority! Hitler saw the restoration of the land of Israel to the Jews as *the key* to winning the war! A key that had *nothing to do* with atomic bombs!"

Now I'm flummoxed. "What are you saying? That Hitler was *mad?* I hear that theory bandied about a lot in the popular press and in lurid paperback fiction. But I scarcely expected to hear it from *you*, Herr Döpel..."

"No, no," he says, shaking his head vigorously, "do not take it that I imply that *der Führer* was not right in his head. His mind was crystal clear, or he could not have conquered much of Europe as he did. He was, however... somewhat *eccentric* in certain beliefs, like many great men are. As an historian, Herr Davison, you are probably aware of *der Führer*'s lifelong interest in the occult, in supernatural phenomena. Although some misinformed observers have assumed such interests of his were limited to ancient Germanic pagan beliefs, I know from my personal encounters with *der Führer* that he was also fascinated by certain incidents in the Bible — even from the Old Testament. Are you familiar with the tale of Balaam the diviner, the Ammonite worshiper of Baal?"

"Isn't he the poor bloke who was paid by the king of Moab or some such to curse the Israelites before they entered the Holy Land, but the curses stuck in his throat, and he could only *praise* them, instead? 'How goodly are thy tents, oh Jacob', that sort of rubbish?"

"*Der Führer* did not consider it 'rubbish'. He took the tale very seriously. He noted how Balaam prospered only in so far as he followed the word of the Hebrew God. But when Balaam strayed from this path and schemed to lure the Israelites into sin, the Lord's protection was withdrawn from him, and he was slain in battle, his people defeated. *Der Führer* saw this pattern, that of grantings of divine favor to non-believers who favored the Jews, repeated in the histories of other great leaders of the ancient world, particularly Cyrus the Great of Persia, who restored the exiled Jews in Babylon to their former lands and allowed them to rebuild their Temple. Cyrus, you should note, managed to conquer much of the known world. And unlike many conquerors, he succeeded in passing on his Empire to his son, who then defeated Egypt and Nubia to expand the Persian Empire."

"So you're saying because Cyrus the bloody Great let the Jews rebuild their Temple and then had a good run of luck, Hitler felt obligated to repatriate the Jews to Palestine? But Hitler *hated* the Jews! It's all there in bloody *Mein Kampf*!"

"Perhaps. But I happen to know, Herr Davison, that *mein Führer* loved the Germans more than he hated the Jews. By repatriating the Jews of Europe to Israel, he 'killed two birds with a single stone', as the American say — he freed the Germans and other Europeans from the pernicious Jewish influence in their midst, and he curried the same favor from Fate as Balaam temporarily received, as Cyrus and his successors received, divine favor that permitted the Persian Empire to endure for centuries. And who are we to say that *der Führer* was wrong to believe this, and to follow through on this belief? Did not he pass away in bed, an old man surrounded by loving grandchildren, rather than being strung up from a lamp post by Russian soldiers in 1945? Has not the German Reich, which encompasses much of Europe, thrived now for more than forty years? That is what Hitler strove for, Herr Davison. And that is why he persisted in shielding the reestablished Israel from her neighbors' wrath — so that the Reich would continue to accrue Fate's favor. As the Fatherland did, until *der Führer*'s death.

"Alas, the younger elements in the Party, men like Kohl and Schröder, they do not think like *der Führer* did. Reactionaries, all, they seek to reverse almost every policy pursued by Hitler. They look upon the Reich's support of Israel, a German protectorate, not as a 'good luck charm', but as a *liability*, an impediment to better relations with the Arabs and the Muslim nations. And see what has happened since they have taken over — defeat and disgrace in Vietnam, the humiliation of the *Wehrmacht* at the hands of Japanese puppets, the gradual, inexorable shift of the world's balance of power against German interests—"

The café's manager appears at Döpel's side, holding a phone. "Pardon me, Herr Döpel," he says. "I am very sorry to intrude—"

"Eh? *Was ist das?*"

"There is a call for you, sir. Most urgent."

"Can it not wait?"

"It is from the head of your delegation, sir. He says he must speak with you immediately."

I step away from the table to give Herr Döpel his privacy, emerging into the sunlight for a few moments to enjoy the Montreal summer, so different from that of London. When

I return, Döpel appears to have aged a decade. His hands shake as though he has suddenly been afflicted with Parkinson's Disease, and his formerly ruddy face has turned a sallow yellow. "My apologies, Herr Davison," he stutters as he rises unsteadily from his seat. "A — a crisis has arisen. I must end our meeting."

"What has happened? Is it anything I can help with?"

"No, no. A security incident. *Mein Gott*, a bad one..."

He hurries out of the café. At loose ends (will I be able to schedule a continuation of our discussion?), consumed by curiosity but also by a sudden spike in appetite, I order a sandwich, a pastry, and a beer. Could this be a ruse of some sort? A pre-scheduled interruption to our meeting, arranged so that I would not have an opportunity to pick apart Herr Döpel's risible story about the origin of Hitler's obsession with favoring Israel? Would Döpel be that crafty?

I hear sirens in the distance, drawing nearer. An ambulance or police vehicle speeds by the café, its pulsating siren dopplering off the walls of the Olympic village.

A news announcer on the television above the bar breaks into live coverage of the shot put competition. Masked gunmen, their faces covered by scarves of a checkered pattern popular in the Arab world, have taken forty-two members of the German athletic delegation hostage. Two Canadian security guards and a German cultural official were killed in the assault on the apartments housing the German team. The gunmen, who state they are members of a revolutionary Palestinian Arab guerilla cell called Black July, threaten to begin killing athletes, one per hour, until the German government pledges to withdraw its military umbrella from its Israel protectorate and break off all economic and political ties. They also demand safe passage to an airbase located in the deserts of Libya.

So Döpel wasn't lying. At least not about there being a crisis.

All athletic events are called off. The café grows crowded with spectators who've been ordered to leave the competition venues. They're attracted by the television and the opportunity to exchange information with fellow observers.

We soon learn that Montreal's airport has been shut down for the nonce. Also, no one apart from law enforcement personnel will be permitted to enter or exit the Olympic Village, which has been cordoned off from the rest of the city.

Many of my new companions express dismay over their being trapped. I don't. For me, a historian, this represents a struck-by-lightning opportunity to be present at the making of history. And I'm not badly set up. I have my chair and table, which are not uncomfortable. I have my expense account, which should suffice for pub food, so long as the café's supplies hold out. The television above the bar provides a continuous stream of live news. I'm able to eavesdrop on dozens of persons from around the globe, athletes and coaches included, and I have pen and paper for note-taking. I even have my tape recorder, handy for any impromptu interviews. (WC access will be a bit dodgy, however.)

So many interesting snatches of conversation overheard! While everyone expresses concern, whether genuine or *pro forma*, for the German athletes' safety, the rough consensus appears to be that this hostage-taking is a clear case of chickens coming home to roost.

An Australian athlete, a wrestler, I believe: "Can't say I agree with their methods here, but the Arabs have a bloody point — they've been getting buggered by the Germans for years..."

A French gymnastics coach I recognize from television, speaking in English with a Filipino colleague: "About time the Boches' colonialism should blow up in their faces..."

Two members of the Swedish track team: "The Jews have brought this down on the Germans' heads." "Aye, old Adolf would have suited himself better to have done away with them all when he had the chance..."

My hand grows tired scribbling it all down.

-July 24, 1976-

It's over. Yet it's not; in all the ways that matter, it's just beginning.

Here in Montreal, at least, an ending has been reached. The Canadian government arranged for a Boeing 707 to be available at Montreal's international airport for the hijackers' escape to North Africa. They ensured safe passage from the Olympic Village to the airport for the Arabs and their captives. In exchange, the militants released half their thirty-eight hostages — having initially killed four of the forty-two in a show of ruthlessness — but insisted on taking the remaining twenty-one with them to Libya. There, they said, they would resume their suspended killing spree, murdering one per hour until the German government surrendered to their remaining demands.

The pilot of the 707, brave man, pretended that his jet was suffering mechanical breakdown. The Canadians sent in a team of Mounties, disguised as mechanics. Over the strenuous objections of the Canadians, the German government insisted on deploying their own strike force of SS commandoes. The two units were poorly coordinated. A debacle ensued on the tarmac. The gun battle left eight Arab militants, four Mounties, and three SS men dead, along with five hostages killed in the crossfire. When the Arabs realized they were about to be overwhelmed, their leader detonated a pack of plastic explosives in the tail of the plane, which in turn set ablaze hundreds of gallons of aviation fuel. The resulting explosion killed all the remaining militants and hostage athletes. In addition, three more Mounties burned to death while trying to extricate possible survivors from the inferno.

Not the end, this. The world hardly had a chance to mourn its Olympic casualties before further atrocities pushed the murdered athletes off the papers' front pages. Just one day after the mass immolation in Montreal, coordinated terror attacks — assaults on the headquarters of the German Colonial Office in Berlin, a Bavarian cultural festival in Munich, beach-goers in Tel Aviv, and a wedding in Jerusalem — kill 237 Germans and Jews and maim or wound hundreds more.

They're devils, those Arabs. Ruthless devils. *Righteous* devils, however. Their fanaticism and indiscriminate bloodshed horrify all civilized people, yet force the fair-minded among us to contemplate the roots of that rage. If we are at all honest, we must grapple with the history of suffering, humiliation, and exile that incites such desperate acts.

Killing Christ wasn't enough for Jews. Perfidious through the centuries, they felt compelled to compound that original sin by granting the city-slaying power of the atom to the Nazis. Apart from the Russians, no people suffered from this sin more grievously than the Arabs.

No amount of glib obfuscation from Robert Döpel can make me believe his lies. I know too well the evil currency with which the resurrection of Israel was purchased.

-October 4, 1977-

"Father, I'm not sixteen anymore. I'm *twenty*. You no longer have the power to veto my decisions. And you've never had the power to veto Mother's."

The apartment is crowded with boxes and overstuffed satchels. My wife is leaving me. No great loss, that; she emotionally abandoned me years ago. But my son... my son insists on marching into the heart of an inferno.

It isn't burning quite yet. The fuse, however, has been lit. It cannot be snuffed out, not now. In a little less than a month, the Middle East will ignite. It doesn't take a Delphic oracle to know this. Any sub-literate fool who listens to Sky News realizes how inevitable the coming conflagration is.

Yet David — my brilliant, handsome David, no sub-literate fool, he — has convinced himself to renounce his British citizenship and cast his lot with the modern incarnation of the Zealots, those doomed bitter-enders who failed to hold Masada in the year 70 AD and killed themselves before the Romans could capture and make slaves and whores of them.

"David, there is just one pertinent question I must ask." My throat is as dry as the desert in which he means to sacrifice himself. "Do you wish to die?"

He sighs, loudly. "No, of course not. I wish to *live*. As a proud and free Jew among other proud and free Jews."

"And you can't do that here in London? You're not *only* a Jew, David. You're also an Englishman. That's a *blessing*, son. A privilege millions the world over would sacrifice their right arm to enjoy. Not a birthright to be casually tossed aside, like Esau did his—"

"You must be getting desperate, Father. Citing Torah in your efforts to keep me here? Really?"

"It seems to be the only language you'll listen to, these days. What about that business of 'honoring thy father'? Isn't that high up there in your Decalogue? Wasn't it inscribed on the stone tablets Moses brought down from Mount Sinai — or did Cecil B. DeMille and Charlton Heston get that bit wrong?"

"Scoff all you want. Your derision doesn't cow me. On November first, there's going to be, for the first time in more than nineteen centuries, an *independent* Jewish state in the Land of Israel—"

I won't lose him. I *refuse* to. "Let me tell you what's going to happen on November first, David my boy. On November first, the German Reich officially renounces its colonial ownership of its protectorate Israel and withdraws all military support. On November first, the idiotic Hebrew nationalists in Jerusalem, Begin and that rabble, rather than securing the support of a new colonial patron, like the Japanese or the French or even the Americans, will instead declare independence. On November first, the combined armies of Egypt, Syria, Jordan, Lebanon, Turkey, Arabia, Iraq, Libya, Morocco, and Iran will line up on the borders of the newly-declared State of Israel. They will then proceed to make the Battle of Stalingrad look like a group of school boys playing with their bloody toy soldiers. And you want to be in the *middle* of all that? Your mother wanting to go, that I can understand. She hasn't been fully in her right mind since her father died. But *you*, David — you have your *entire life* ahead of you—"

David shakes his head, dismissing me as though I'm senile. "*Ha-Shem* will provide. He parted the Sea of Reeds and drowned the Egyptian chariot drivers and all their horses. Masada will not fall again."

"Oh, won't it? I take it this is old Yahweh you're speaking of? The same capricious deity who allowed the Jews to be booted out of their Holy Land not once, but *twice*, supposedly as communal punishment for their sins? *This* is who you're counting on for salvation? David, what if November first is yet another day of communal punishment? Punishment for the tribal sin of having given the secret of the atomic bomb to the Nazis? For the murder of hundreds of thousands of Russian and Ukrainian women, children, and old people in Moscow and Kiev? For precipitating the subsequent descent of the Soviet Union into civil war and barbarism? Do you want to take the rap for those crimes, David?"

His face darkens. "I... I won't dignify that... that *crackpot theory* of yours by arguing against it. I think the BBC did a more than adequate job of debunking it, painful and humiliating as it was to watch their evisceration of your research."

I nearly strike him. It takes an inhuman exercise of will to stop my hand. "Oh, now you're relying on the supposed almighty authority of the bloody *BBC*, are you? That pack of prissy, pathological liars? You want to know *why* they carried out that murder-by-broadcast assassination of my reputation, David my boy? I'll tell you why — because they've become *infested!* Infested by *Jews!* Lying, clannish *Jews!* Just like at Cambridge! Just like at the *Guardian* and the *Times*! Just like the goddamned Conservative Party—"

"Will you just *listen to yourself?* Can you understand how *foul* you've become?" He turns his back on me. Then his head slumps. "But you can't, can you?" he says, barely whispering. "And that's why I can't share a home or even a country with you any longer." His voice regains its strength. "I'll wait until you're at your office to come back and collect my bags, and Mother's and Grandmother's things."

He exits the apartment. I watch through the open window until he emerges onto the sidewalk below. "They've no army!" I shout down to him. "You want to join the Israeli Defense Force, you foolish boy? The bloody *Wehrmacht was* the bloody Israeli Defense Force! And it's gone! The Jews don't know how to fight for themselves — it'll be a *slaughter*, David! A holocaust! The Arabs won't stop killing until every last Jew is floating face down in the Mediterranean Sea! You're throwing your life away! For *nothing!*"

I watch him walk the length of Cottingham Lane until he turns a corner and I can't see him anymore.

This apartment has never been so empty. "My son... don't leave me all alone, David..."

-November 7, 1977-

Watching or listening to the news is an agony. All the analysts are astounded (primly, of course) that the Israelis have managed to hang on this long. They give much of the credit to the governments of Austria and the German-Czech Republic, recently independent themselves, who decided to brashly demonstrate their political independence from the Reich by funneling anti-tank and anti-aircraft weapons from their munitions factories to the Jews, along with tens of thousands of automatic rifles. In this way, the Austrians and the Germanic-Czechs are proving themselves the last loyalists to Adolf Hitler, carrying on the dead *Führer*'s work.

Despite their unexpectedly fierce and effective resistance, the Jews have lost most of the Jordan River valley and a good chunk of the Negev Desert. Urban combat in Jerusalem, where each ancient building and alleyway is being contested hand-to-hand, is the most savage and desperate of any since the Second World War. It surpasses even the gore and horror of the National Socialist South Vietnamese's last-ditch defense of Saigon against the invading Viet Cong.

I've had no word from David. Nor any news of him. It's excruciating, not knowing his fate. Like being slowly eaten by ants, layer after layer of skin chewed away. It's why I force myself to watch the news, although doing so feels like holding my palm over an open flame. I watch, in case I might catch a glimpse of him. I know nothing at all. Did he get inducted into the Israeli Defense Force, a rifle shoved into his soft, uncalloused hands? Is he at bayonet's length from the Royal Jordanian Special Forces in a burning souk in Jerusalem? Was he among the thousands of Jewish militiamen forced into the Jordan River by Syrian armored brigades, then machine-gunned while they tried to avoid drowning? Or is he one of the millions of civilian refugees pouring into the streets of Tel Aviv, stricken with thirst and hunger, staring at the mockingly calm blue of the Mediterranean while praying for a Dunkirk-style exodus?

Under any other circumstances, I'd be cheering the Arabs on, delighted to witness the crushing of one of Adolf Hitler's most foul legacies. I'd be pouring myself drink after drink to celebrate.

David's cruelest sin against me is that he is forcing me to root for the Jews.

-November 16, 1977-

Of all people, Sylvia, my former mother-in-law, has shown me kindness. At last, through her telegram I have word of David.

He tried joining an army unit, then an improvised militia, but his progress east toward the Jerusalem front was stymied by the chaotic onrush of millions of civilian refugees fleeing in the opposite direction. Caught up in the tide of panicked Jews (I'm filling in here with suppositions, since the telegram was necessarily terse), he found himself forced back into Tel Aviv, where he had so recently disembarked with his mother and grandmother. Astonishingly, given the crush of refugees, he reunited with his relatives after having been apart several weeks. He found them in an open-air encampment on the beach while serving as a volunteer for Israel's ersatz version of the Red Cross, the Red Mogen David. Officials from the genuine Red Cross, apparently, made it possible for Sylvia to send her telegram to me.

I wish I would've heard from David directly. But one takes what one can.

For reasons known only to their generals and national governments, the Arab armies have halted their joint offensive. They have pushed the Jews into a narrow coastal corridor, barely eight miles wide in places, in others up to thirty miles wide, stretching from Haifa in the north to Ashdod, south of Tel Aviv. They have also left a roughly horn-shaped salient that begins in Jerusalem's southern suburbs and leads east to just north of the Dead Sea, terminating at Jericho. Into this coastal corridor and its tusk-like salient the Arab legions have herded nearly nine million Jews.

Why did they stop their advance? No effective resistance remained in their way. Their murderous propaganda has always announced the goal of pushing the Jews into the sea. The Israelis have no friends remaining among the world's great powers. No one, other than humanitarian relief organizations and scattered chapters of B'nai Brith and Hadassah, would offer more than pro forma objections if the Arab conquerors swept the entirety of the Jewish population into slave labor camps, or even dropped poison gas bombs on them. Perhaps doing so would be too much trouble? As is, eventually hunger and disease will do the Arabs' work for them, unless a miraculous relief flotilla materializes on the horizon, or old Yahweh decides once more to part the sea for his 'chosen people'.

I could petition my government to rescue its citizens from amongst the trapped Jews. I could add the weight of my voice to those of other parents and relatives of deluded youngsters who fled Britain to defend their idealized new homeland. Yet doing so for David's sake would seem the height of hypocrisy. Whether or not he had time to formalize it before he sailed for Tel Aviv, David spiritually and morally renounced his British citizenship. For me to call upon the shield of British citizenship to protect David from his folly, when he has tossed that shield aside, would be craven.

Yet he remains, and will always remain, my son. And the Arab armies maintain their steel cordon around the Jews, waiting. Waiting for what, I cannot say.

-December 6, 1977-

Colleagues have noticed I've been shedding weight. I suppose my suits hang on me like limp sails on the rotting masts of a beached schooner. There's truth to the saying of eating being as much a social activity as it is a nutritive one. Bachelors tend to be thin. Loneliness, nagging regrets, and anxiety aren't champion appetite stimulants. I haven't heard anything more from David or from his grandmother.

Lunchtime. I try to force myself to consume a decent meal, but the university cafeteria reminds me all too mournfully of a mass meeting of the Zionist Organization of Britain (the kosher chicken, in particular, stinks of something rotten). On my return to my building carrying a cup of tea (not much can be done to ruin that), I spot a man I don't recognize exiting my office. He quickly checks the hallway for passersby. Seeing no one (I remain out of his direct sight), he quietly closes the door behind him.

I wait until he enters the stairwell to approach my office. Ordinarily, I would have approached such a visitor and asked him if he required my assistance. But this man seemed determined to depart unnoticed. A thief?

At first glance, nothing appears amiss in my office — no furniture or objects seem out of place, and no vacant places have sprung up amongst my rows of books. Upon a moment's reflection, I realize I *have* seen the intruder before. He's a junior faculty member in the new Department of Middle Eastern Studies, funded by the Baathist Republic of Iraq with a minute fraction of their windfall oil profits. Still, I check my file cabinets carefully; the Iraqis have earned a reputation for espionage under cover of diplomacy and cultural exchanges, and my research notes could conceivably be of interest to them.

Again, nothing appears to have been rifled through, and I fail to detect anything missing. Only then do I notice an envelope lying in the center of my desk. It wasn't there when I departed for lunch.

Why such skullduggery? If the gentleman from Middle Eastern Studies wished to send me a letter, he could easily have done so through interdepartmental mail.

Burning with curiosity, I open it. The letter inside is an invitation to the Iraqi Embassy. Not for a social reception or a lecture by a distinguished visiting Iraqi author or scientist. Not for any sort of group gathering at all. Rather, I'm invited to a one-on-one meeting with the ambassador's aide-de-camp, a Mr. Mohammed Hamza Zubeidi. Whatever for?

The invitation stresses the importance of our meeting, requested for two days from now. It gives no rationale for this urgency, nor any hint of the meeting's purpose.

The letter ends with an explicit warning. I am to come to the embassy alone, and I am to mention my visit to no one. Failure to follow these instructions will result not only in the revocation of the unspecified benefits on offer, but also by a "visit" from members of the Mukhabarat. The dreaded Iraqi Intelligence Service; no ethnic dance troupe, they.

Into what shadowy Graham Greene novel have I been snared?

-December 8, 1977-

"Professor Davison? Thank you so much for coming on short notice. Allow me to welcome you to the Iraqi Embassy. I am Mohammed Hamza Zubeidi."

Swanky joint, as Reggie MacDonald might say. Fully reflective of the Iraqis' recent oil billions. Decorated like the Queen Mother's residence would be, if the Queen Mother had lost all sense of taste, decorum, and restraint. "You've certainly aroused my curiosity, Mr. Zubeidi."

He smiles. "I am certain I have. Come with me, if you will, please."

I turn my attention from the room to Zubeidi. My host is a slightly built, swarthy man with a full, luxuriously groomed mustache, the mirror-image of that worn by his political master in Baghdad, Saddam Hussein, the Iraqi strongman — not the titular head of state, not yet, but the power behind the throne. Zubeidi wears a neatly tailored Saville Row suit, but it is all too easy for me to picture him dressed in soiled white robes, reeking of sweat, bearded, his head swaddled in a dusty turban. He wears a pleasant cologne, this Zubeidi, but I know that underneath that artificial scent he stinks, just like the Arab boys Miss Kenyon and I hired to dig the excavations at Jericho...

What am I thinking? Where did *that* memory come from? I've never been to Jericho. Much less as part of an archeological expedition.

I know the name Kathleen Kenyon — she's the most famous archeologist in Britain, or was, until her passing — but I've never met her or heard her speak. I don't think I've even seen a photograph of her, yet there she was in my mind, as clear as my fellow lecturers at Cambridge.

Was it something I dreamed? But memories of dreams all have a jumbled quality, events happening out of sequence or involving impossible shifts of locale. This memory doesn't feel at all like a memory of a dream. It feels like a very solid, grounded recollection of my young adulthood. Yet that's impossible...

I'm led into an inner office. Lacking any windows, with just the barest of furnishings, it looks more like an interrogation room. Am I to be handcuffed to a chair, blinded by a bright lamp pointed into my face, then beaten by a Mukhabarat ruffian until I surrender the key to the Cambridge faculty water closet?

"Have a seat, Professor Davison," Zubeidi says, directing me to a chair alongside a metal table in the center of the room. "I apologize for the starkness of your surroundings. However, what I am about to tell you is of a sensitive nature and must be kept in complete confidence, between you and I only. I do not trust even the other members of this Embassy to share in the information I share with you, nor even that they know I am sharing sensitive matters with you. Do you understand?"

"Actually, Mr. Zubeidi, I can't say that I do. I'm no diplomat or member of Her Majesty's Government. I'm merely a senior lecturer at Cambridge, in the field of post-Enlightenment

European history. If you're looking for an expert on current-day international relations from the British perspective, I'm afraid I'm not your man."

"But that is not what I am looking for, Professor Davison. I am fully informed of your background and your writings, most especially your writings. Your articles on the subject of the origins and development of the German atomic bomb program are of particular interest to my government. Our Vice President Saddam Hussein, may peace be upon him, is a great admirer of your works."

"Oh? I wasn't aware that Mr. Hussein has the spare time to peruse monographs in academic historical journals. Running a country must keep him fully occupied, eh?"

"Vice President Saddam is no ordinary ruler. He requires little sleep. He has the vitality of ten men. The vast range of his intellectual pursuits would astound you."

"Oh, very good, then." *Ubermensch of the Arabian desert, sounds like. Would make a bloody good hero for a comic book.* "I'm honored, certainly, that Vice President Hussein finds my work of interest. In what way may I be of assistance?"

"The issue at hand is not so much how you may be of assistance to us, Professor Davison, but rather how *we* may be of assistance to *you.*"

"Again, I'm afraid I fail to understand...?"

"Your research into a crucial aspect of the German atomic bomb program, that of the involvement of the Jewish scientists in exchange for the expulsion of the Arab inhabitants of Palestine, then the giving over of Palestine to the Jews, has been stymied,

I believe. Has it not? Both by the closure of British and German archives to you and by lies told to your face by senior German officials. My government has a keen interest in having the truth of the matter becoming widely known. In the course of the recent military campaign in Palestine, our Iraqi forces captured a trove of secret Zionist documents. Some of these documents date back to the years of the Second World War. They validate most thoroughly your theory of the treacherous quid pro quo between the Nazis and the Jews, the trade of atomic know-how for the unjust expulsion of our Arab brethren from their Palestinian lands."

My stomach and heart seem to lurch forward against my ribs. My theory, proven true at last? With documentation ripped from the Zionists' own hands?

"What — what is the nature of these documents?"

"They are most illuminating, Professor Davison. I speak of written agreements between the head of the Nazi atomic bomb program and various Jew physicists, those whose names you have cited in your articles. Also, incriminating correspondence between those physicists and leaders of the Zionist settlers in Palestine, in which the Jew scientists alert the heads of the *Yeshuv* to prepare for a massive influx of millions of European Jews."

"You're going to turn these documents over to me?"

"You will receive photocopies. The originals are quite delicate, as well as possessing worth beyond price to my nation. Do not be concerned — they are perfectly genuine; my government guarantees this authenticity."

"Might I at least examine the originals? I've had forgeries dangled in front of my eyes before. Not that your government would venture such fakery, of course. But I must ascertain with my own methods and my own eyes that the documents you speak of date to the nineteen-forties, and that both German and *Yeshuv* identifying marks can be authenticated—"

"Ah, the caution of the true academic! I appreciate your concern for validation, Professor, truly, I do. It does you credit, and it reinforces Vice President Saddam's excellent judgment in selecting you as the prime messenger of these truths to the world. Unfortunately, I find myself unable to honor your request. Due to their incalculable value, the originals must be kept in a secure location in Baghdad. I would offer you a trip on the Embassy's own aircraft to Baghdad if I could. But such travel by a distinguished British professor to our capital would pose too much risk of outside parties, such as your country's MI6, learning of our nation's involvement in the dissemination of said documents."

Infuriating, these complications of statecraft and spycraft! Why dangle such treasures before me if you won't let me ascertain their true value? "If you can't share the originals with me, then why don't you make use of one of your own Iraqi academics to write a monograph on the Nazi-Zionist conspiracy? Surely there is at least one decent research university in Baghdad...?"

"That course of action would be best, I do agree. Alas, we Iraqis, having only recently been blessed with ample national income, possess no university having even a minute fraction of the prestige and authority that grace your famed Cambridge University. Your longstanding connection to Cambridge, sir, makes of you a far, far more effective mouthpiece than any of our native professorate caste could be."

This hot potato remains in my hands, then. "All right, I grant your point. But if I'm to work with your materials, I have to understand, at least a bit, your motivations for handing them over to me. Why is the academic defamation of the Zionist statelet for historical crimes so important to you at this point in time? Haven't your Arab armies thoroughly thrashed the Zionists on the battlefield, and nearly pushed them all into the Mediterranean? Don't you retain an iron cordon around them? It seems to me you've accomplished the hard part. I could understand wanting to morally undermine the Zionist usurpers *prior* to launching a military campaign against them, in order to make of them a pariah state that no potential allies would want to deal with. But this... well, I must say, it has the feel of closing the barn door after the cows have already made good their escape."

"Your questions are perfectly understandable, Professor Davison. Yes, the Zionists have been routed. They grovel at the edge of the sea. But Vice President Saddam, peace be upon him, has decided the Zionists have not yet received their due comeuppance, punishment in accord with the magnitude of their crimes. I speak not merely of their crimes against my Arab brethren. I refer more broadly to their crimes of more than three decades past, atrocities of a world-historical nature — those committed against the peoples of the Soviet Union. You yourself, Professor Davison, have written very movingly about the sufferings of the Muscovites and residents of Kiev who survived the atomic fires unleashed upon them by the Jews, their dying struggles against radiation burns and cancers. You have also written of the subsequent collapse of Soviet civilization, the descent of that country into anarchy and endless clashes between competing warlords following the murder of Stalin. The Jews bear responsibility for this, since their physicists helped provide Hitler with his atomic bombs.

"Untold millions died in that anarchy unleashed by Jewish perfidy, Professor Davison. I am sure you are familiar with the legal doctrine of *lex talionis*, present in your Christian Bible as well as the Holy Quran. An eye for an eye, a tooth for a tooth. Wouldn't you say that applies most pressingly in this case?"

I don't like the direction he's heading in. Not with David trapped somewhere within remaining Israeli territory. "Are you seriously proposing the massacre of millions of civilians, Mr. Zubeidi? How the devil would you carry it out?"

He smiles a lingering smile. "Oh, come, come, Professor Davison! Such moral squeamishness from *you*? You, who, more than any other Western academic, has popularized the notion of a modern Jewish blood libel, an update of the ancient calumny that rabbis use the blood of Christians to make their Passover *matzos*? Let us be frank with one another. You hate the Jews every bit as passionately as my own Vice President Saddam does, peace be upon him. Have not the wicked Zionists bewitched your only son, turned him against you, enticed him into joining their doomed venture in Palestine? Do you not hunger to pay them back a thousand fold?"

"But... but my David is there. In Israel, or what's left of it. You *can't* slaughter them all. Not with David among them..."

"Then I most sincerely suggest that you remove him from the doomed population with great haste." He rubs the side of his nose thoughtfully, his forefinger lingering on a dark brown birthmark. "I will make you a bargain, Professor. In return for your services — incorporating the papers I shall give you into your forthcoming books and articles, while vouching for their full authenticity — this Embassy will arrange for safe passage for you into the remaining Zionist-occupied territory. Our military will enable your extraction of your son."

"But I have no idea where he is now... the last I heard anything about him was three weeks ago. He was working for the Israeli Red Cross in Tel Aviv, but he could be anywhere else in the coastal salient by now..."

"That is your problem, Professor. The offer I have just made is most generous. I cannot presume to obligate this Embassy or my government to provide you with any greater support than this. As your Western actors of gangster films are known to say, 'Take it or leave it.'"

"I'll — I'll take it."

"Good. That is most wise, Professor."

I feel as though I've just sold my soul to Mephistopheles, but with only the vaguest understanding of the bargain struck. "Tell me again what I must do, exactly?"

"Simply continue to pursue your academic passion, Professor. Only make full use of the documents I will provide, without revealing how and from whom you obtained them."

"Why is this so important to you? I'm sorry, I *must* know..."

"My country, like any other, prefers to remain in the 'good graces', so to speak, of its fellow members of the international community, at least insofar as this is at all possible. More than this I cannot reveal to you... except perhaps for this bit of poetry. When the whale of the desert strikes the sands with his mighty fluke, the world will hear, and the world will tremble."

-December 9, 1977-

I'm the prisoner of a horrible sense of foreboding.

I couldn't sleep last night. It's not just my present conundrums haunting me — how to extricate David from seemingly doomed Israel; what to do about that stash of documents Zubeidi forced upon me; what could happen to me if I fail to satisfy the Iraqi government's demands. In addition to all that, I suffer a phantom apprehension of dreadful consequences unknown. A free-floating, unmoored anxiety.

Some commanding instinct beyond my understanding demanded that I perform an unknown act before I could allow myself to fall asleep. I spent hours tossing in my bed clothes, then pacing the rooms of my apartment, trying to pin down this mysterious compulsion. It remained maddeningly just out of my reach, like the substance of a fog, or the faint memory of a long-ago dream. Only after hours of concentration did its insubstantiality yield in the slightest.

With the sky outside my window turning from black to a pinkish grey, I grasped that I had to write something, act as a scribe of some sort. I needed to copy something I had written earlier, before it disappeared. Yet I could not remember what it was I was supposed to copy word-for-word.

I'm in no proper shape to report for classes today. Thankfully, I've only one lecture on my schedule this morning, and I arranged for substitute coverage with a quick call to Reggie MacDonald (always happy to step in for me, due to the charms displayed by certain of my young lady students). Freed from my responsibilities, I still can't fall back asleep. Remaining in my apartment, after the night I'd just suffered through, seems abhorrent.

I felt alone, exposed. Something is pursuing me, some invisible annihilation. The only defense I can think to muster is being in the presence of other people, so I drag my sleep-deprived body into a workingmen's pub where they serve breakfasts. I linger there as long as the crowd remained; the fog of their cigarette smoke and loudly profane conversation temporarily lulls me.

The district library is open now. I can seek company there, as well as information to help me unravel the tangled ball of yarn (and yarns, perhaps) Zubeidi handed me. On the way, I pass one of Miriam's favorite local haunts, St. George's Gardens, with its tidy flower gardens (presently dormant for the winter) sheltering beneath the looming Anglican cathedral towers.

This was one of our courting places. I remember us strolling from one discarded headstone to another, reading the barely legible, rain-eroded memorial engravings, Miriam, with her sticks of charcoal, pausing to make rubbings of filigrees or gargoyles on sheets of butcher paper. Later, after we married, we'd roll David in his pram here. The easily-amused toddler — what a blithe spirit he had then — would laugh at the cooing pigeons, gathered by tossed breadcrumbs, then scattered into flight by a passing bicyclist.

So many memories! Yet one particular memory of this place pushes all others to the side. Another December day, colder than this one, but less windy. A heavy snow had recently fallen, covering the gardens and paths. I wasn't with Miriam then, but I saw her standing near a distant fountain, and I hurried toward her, trudging through the deep snow. She was younger, in her twenties. I was desperate to see her; we hadn't spoken in years. I remember the staccato crunch of snow beneath my galoshes. But when did we ever go years without speaking? We were married in 1955, after nine months of courtship. It's been merely two months since she left the apartment, and that's the longest we've ever been apart. What is this I'm remembering?

So clear, it is... I was out of breath with exertion. My heart pounded in my chest, not only from the physical strain. A bottomless emotional chasm lay between us, as deep and untraversable as that which caused her to leave me two months ago. Something about a book I had written...? A lecture I had delivered in Germany? How am I remembering this? "I *hate* myself for having ever loved you!" she said. The snow muffled all sound. But not the sound of her subsequent whisper, hot enough to melt all the snow in London — "You terrible, terrible, beastly man!"

That whisper gutted me. I remember my awful wounding as though it occurred yesterday.

Yet Miriam never spoke such words to me. She may well have thought them, but she never voiced them, at least not to me. At no point were we ever apart for years. I never trudged through deep snow in St. George's Gardens, not in December, nor any other month. How am I remembering this if it never happened?

That free-floating anxiety, that apprehension of an invisible annihilation nipping at my heels, grows worse. As though some invisible, yet detectible nemesis draws closer.

I'm not alone; at least another half-dozen walkers brave the December gusts here in the gardens. Are they not enough to dispel this anxiety? Must I make a constant circle of pubs, leaving one when it grows too quiet in search of another, more boisterous and crowded?

Something rustles. I feel something rubbing against my leg, and I almost scream.

Looking down, I see it's nothing but a bit of rubbish, a broadsheet of newspaper driven by the wind that's folded itself about my pants leg. I snatch it up, then head for the nearest waste bin, compelled by the instinct for tidiness treasured by all true Englishmen.

Before depositing it in the bin, I glance at the top headlines, realizing I've been so preoccupied with my own troubles these past few days that I haven't bothered following the news at all. It's yesterday's *Daily Mail*. A sidebar headline states that British citizens were killed or wounded in a terror attack carried out against an Israeli bus. An Arab suicide bomber boarded the bus with a pram containing a bomb dressed as a baby. Nineteen passengers were killed, including the bomber, and thirty-one more were severely wounded.

My overwhelming but formless anxiety swells as I scan the names of victims.

Dead: Sylvia Plotsky, aged 67, resident of London.

Severely wounded: David Davison, aged 20, resident of London, taken to hospital in Jericho.

No accident, this sheet of newspaper blowing against my leg. Something toys with me. It's not fantasy or paranoia, this invisible nemesis. It's real, and it's herding me.

But now I know where David is.

-December 10, 1977-

I've made arrangements with the Iraqi Embassy to be smuggled into Israeli territory as a relief worker. I've been assured I'll be extricated with David and returned to London.

My hours at the library weren't wasted. For all his professed concern regarding secrecy and confidentiality, a medieval despot such as Zubeidi cannot control his impulse to be a braggart. It didn't take me long to decipher his thinly-veiled boasting about his country's destructive prowess.

That business about 'the whale of the desert' wasn't too difficult to decipher with a bit of light research. For the past dozen years, the Iraqi nuclear program has been husbanded along by the National Nuclear Research Agency of Nippon. And what was the brand name of the research reactor — not coincidentally one of the breeder sort, ideal for the production of plutonium — that the Japanese so obligingly provided for their Iraqi clients? *Kujira*. Translated to English: 'whale'.

The whale of the desert. The Iraqis had built themselves an atomic bomb, or were on the threshold of producing one. That's why the Arab armies halted their advance in mid-November, once they'd herded Israel's Jews into a narrow corridor. They knew they didn't need to do the hard, bloody work of slaughtering nine million Jews face-to-face. They'd been ordered to hang back, told that all they needed to do was keep the Jews penned within a killing zone, until 'the whale of the desert strikes the sands with his mighty fluke'.

Were the Iraqi bombs not ready last month? Or did Saddam Hussein decide to hold off incinerating the Jews with atomic fire until after I'd been maneuvered into writing their regime's self-justifying propaganda for them? It's obvious now that's what they want me to do. And I must rightly admit, to my burning shame, that if it weren't for David having inserted himself among that mass of war refugees clinging to the Mediterranean shore, I would happily have gone along with Zubeidi's plans. I would have played my role as duped lackey with malevolent enthusiasm.

The forgeries Zubeidi gave me are good enough to fool the average layman. They'd probably fool even a non-specialist historian. But not a man of my background, not someone who's spent a career examining the mounds of bureaucratic detritus produced by the Axis and Allied powers of World War Two. I know exactly what the official seals of both sides should look like. I know the meticulous legalisms used unwaveringly by the Nazi high command. I know the jargon and euphemisms deployed by the *Yeshuv* in its diplomatic correspondence.

I realize, of course, that the fact that the Iraqis have produced forgeries does not, by itself, disprove my long-held theory of a quid pro quo between the Nazis and a cadre of Jewish atomic physicists. But Zubeidi was counting on the strength of my prejudice to blind me to any inadequacies in his forgeries. And, having read my scholarly output of the past half-decade, it was reasonable of him to do so.

Where did my bias — no, my *hatred* — come from? I've taken it for granted for so long, I've never questioned its origins. Do they lie in the quotidian resentments of inhabiting a small apartment with Miriam's parents? In my humiliation at having my eight-day-old son's tiny penis butchered, despite my objections? In my sense of displacement in my own neighborhood as it gradually filled with

Jewish aliens? Or in my sense of increasing isolation within my academic department at Cambridge as the same happened there?

More than just those experiences stoked my hatred. Buried deep within my viscera, there's a throbbing tumor of fury, resentment, and loss, more malignant than can be ascribed to such surface resentments. I can sense it, even if I can't yet understand it. It has somehow to do with Miriam, I suspect. Miriam and that false memory I have of her, the one that surfaced yesterday morning in St. George's Gardens. *You terrible, terrible, beastly man...*

And it has to do with my nemesis, the insubstantial entity that lurks just beyond the perimeters of my normal senses. It's whipping me like I'm a blinkered plow horse, driving me on towards Jericho. But why must it? Wouldn't my love for my injured son be inducement enough?

-December 16, 1977-

Zubeidi's people secured me a birth on the S.S. *Ward Moore*, a tramp steamer carrying International Red Cross relief supplies and medical personnel to Tel Aviv. This past afternoon, we crossed through the Straits of Gibraltar, leaving the frigid Atlantic and entering the more placid, warmer Mediterranean.

I've fallen into a pattern of sleeping in my tiny berth during the day and remaining awake throughout the night. Sleep feels somehow less threatening while the sun is in the sky and the crew and my fellow passengers make their workaday noises outside my cabin. The nights are when I need to be on my guard. Therefore I armor myself with sweaters and windbreaker and cap and sit on deck, alone apart from the occasional passings of a watchman. I find the winter sea winds strangely comforting. Combined with the ship's gradual swaying and the unending parade of stars, the wind's buffeting lulls me, smooths away the jags of my anxiety like the tides wear away footsteps in the sand.

There's nothing to do out here but think. Think, and remember. What does one call memories of people who one has never met, or events that never occurred? Visions? Hallucinations? Repressed memories that have managed to surface, as the Freudians would have it? Or recollections of past lives, as the Hindus would have it?

I don't rightly know. There's little that separates my sleeping dreams from my waking dreams now.

I'm debating a tattooed man on a stage in front of an audience of Nazis.

I'm in the catacombs of the British Museum, arguing the authenticity of a centuries-old manuscript with a disgraced university lecturer. Somehow, I know he will soon vanish from existence, along with the disputed manuscript. He and it will never have been.

I'm standing on the deck of an archaic sailing vessel, trapped at the edge of a frozen ocean, looking down into an abyss of stars. If I jump over the gunwale, I will fall forever.

-December 25, 1977-

"Everyone else pays me to get them *out* of Jericho, not *in*. You do realize that, don't you? That you're paying me good British pounds to smuggle you into a deathtrap on the back of a camel? Not that I'm unhappy to take your money, of course."

I can't very well tell my Israeli benefactor, a brave man who risks his life nightly to convoy food and supplies into the nearly cut-off city of Jericho, that I have no plans to remain there for long, that free passage has been arranged for me and my son through the Iraqi lines. "I know what I'm doing," I say. As soon as the twilight fades to full darkness, our convoy of heavily-laden camels will begin the hazardous trek east along the only remaining road to Jericho. "I've paid you half. The rest I'll give you once we arrive safely in Jericho."

"The money's not a worry," he says. "It's what's between your ears" — he gestures to his own temple with a crooked forefinger — "that worries me more. I can't afford no one cracking up on this run. You break, you go goofy on me, start barking like a mad dog or some such, those trigger-happy Arabs will blow us to hell with mortar volleys, just for the fun of it. They've had weeks to calibrate the range so the shells fall directly on the road. They don't need any light. That's why I take camels, not trucks. One backfire from a tailpipe, say, and both me and the foodstuffs I carry are buzzard meat at first light. Can't risk it."

"You can count on me to be as quiet as a church mouse." He would be even less confident in my sanity if he could see the visions that crowd my head. Masses of Jews, like him, being forced into a concrete bunker that rapidly fills with poison gas, tearing off their fingernails in frantic, doomed attempts to claw their way through the walls.

"You Jewish?" he asks, helping me mount a camel's back.

"No."

"Muslim?"

"No."

"Well, then, merry Christmas. Let's go. We have a lot of ground to cover before daylight."

Christmas? The thought hadn't even occurred to me. Venus has risen, brighter than the hair-thin sliver of moon. It could almost be the special star that guided the Three Kings to the infant savior.

I don't need a star to guide me to David. I have my nemesis for that. It drives me before it, its lash made from thistles and regret.

-December 26, 1977-

The metallic, rancid stench of ill-tended wounds (a childhood memory of wartime London that will never fade) almost overwhelms me when I push open the door to the ward where I'm told David lies. Every bed is filled with war victims. Most spaces between beds are crammed with cots or pallets, each holding another suffering mass of flesh that, only days or weeks ago, had been a school teacher or postal clerk or farmer.

I spot Miriam leaning over a bed near the windows. Her back is to me. Grotesque as it may be, my most pressing concern of the moment is how to announce myself. In the eyes of the law, we are still married. I should be able to embrace her shoulders and pull her close... customary actions for a husband seeing his wife for the first time in many weeks. Yet she seems more a stranger now than she was when I first met her at that Labour Party social in the spring of 1954. What can I say, after all that has happened?

"Miriam... I... I've come..."

She straightens, then turns around. She looks twenty years older than when I last saw her. "*Irving?* How...? How are you here?"

"I made arrangements... not easy ones." I take my first look at David. Can it really be David? He looks like a papier-mâché marionette slapped together by an inattentive gaggle of Primary 3 students. His entire torso is swathed in plaster, as are his arms, raised by wires. I can't see any trace of legs beneath the stained sheets. "How... how is he, Miriam?"

"Not good." Her voice breaks. "He hasn't regained consciousness since the explosion. One of the survivors, a woman sitting in the back seat of the bus, told me David sat just behind the man with the pram. David must've seen that it wasn't right, that there was no baby in the pram but a bomb instead, and he began shouting for everyone to take cover. He tried pushing the pram out of the bus. But he only managed to push it a few meters toward the front before the Arab set off the bomb. More people would've died had David not done what he did. My mother died."

"I heard. I'm sorry."

"Thank God she didn't suffer." Her face nearly breaks, but with great effort she recovers her composure. "He's a hero, Irving. The Knesset voted him a medal."

"Likely one of the last motions they'll ever vote on."

"What do you mean?" Her eyes spark with anger at my affront to her faith in her adopted state. "The Arabs have halted their advance," she insists, red-faced. "The Defense Force can regroup. The Czechs and Austrians will send more weapons—"

"No, Miriam. It's over. The Jews haven't a chance."

"How do you *know...*?"

"I know. I know too many things." I take her wrist and pull her closer to one of the windows, out of earshot of any nurses or patients. "Miriam, I have to get David out of here. I have contacts. Assurances from the Iraqis. I can smuggle him out through their lines. With their help, I can take him back to London. I can get you out, too. But it has to happen *soon*."

"Take David...?" It's too much all at once for her. I can see that. "Take him from the hospital?" Her confusion swiftly turns to astonishment, then anger. "Are you *daft?* Just *look* at him! Removing him from this hospital would be subjecting him to a death sentence!"

"That's a possibility, yes. A cruel possibility. But leaving him here means his death is assured."

"You're speaking in riddles, like a carnival fortune-teller! What makes you so certain, Irving? You've never been religious, not so long as I've known you — but now you talk with the assurance of a prophet..."

"I'm neither soothsayer nor prophet." My temples begin throbbing. This is all too much for me, too. "Look. Nearly three weeks ago, I was invited to a private audience with one of the top diplomats at the Iraqi Embassy in London, a man named Zubeidi, a confidant of Saddam Hussein's—"

"Why should I believe that? What could such a man possibly want of someone like you?"

"Propaganda. The Iraqis have planned something monstrous, and they want to use my work to justify it."

"The work of a minor British academic...?"

"I *know* how absurd it all sounds. But hear me out, and it will all make sense. Why do you think the Arabs halted their advances where they did? Why would they hesitate to capture Jericho, Israel's third largest city, when they have it virtually surrounded and cut off?"

"They're... they're regrouping... and they're trying to avoid diplomatic dust-ups with the British and the Americans, I suppose..."

"No, Miriam, they've herded the Jews into constricted, concentrated killing zones because they have a genocidal hatred of Hebrews, rooted in Islamic theology and Arab culture. They don't want to capture nine million Jews — what the devil would they *do* with them? They want them out of the way — obliterated from the earth. The most efficient way for them to accomplish that is to use atomic weapons."

"You can't be saying — you *can't*..." Stricken, she looks around the ward, imagining, I suppose, all those patients, her own son included, turned to gray ash.

"That's *exactly* what I'm saying. They'll use atomic fire to do their dirty deed. The Iraqis have nuclear missiles. Zubeidi so much as boasted of it to me. They want to use my investigations into the involvement of Jewish physicists in the Nazis' nineteen-forties atomic weaponry program to provide a moral justification for their use of nuclear bombs here, against Israeli population centers. Zubeidi even provided me with forged documents that supposedly prove a quid pro quo existed between a cadre of Jewish scientists and the Nazi regime—"

"The 'Rosetta Stone' of Jewish collaboration for which you've been searching for years," she says bitterly.

"Yes..."

"And this Zubeidi promised you David's safe extraction to England if you cooperated?"

"That was the bargain, yes."

"That's *monstrous*. Even more so than whatever missiles the Iraqis may have up their sleeves. How *could* you, Irving? You write and write about imagined Jewish collaboration with mass murderers, and then you yourself turn around and conspire with men who seek to surpass the Nazis in atrocities!"

"Oh, please, I don't intend to hold up my end of the bargain," I say, stung she would leap to such conclusions about me. It hurts more than it should, given how long we've been estranged. "For one thing, the forgeries they provided me with are obviously fakes. That is, at least to the discerning eye of anyone who has performed deep scholarship on the Palestine Mandate and the German regime during the Second World War. Taking those forgeries at face value, or pretending to, would be a repudiation of academic standards I have championed my entire career. For another thing... well, becoming an apologist for the Iraqis, knowing what I know, would be a blot on my soul. It would be the shabbiest, most contemptible business imaginable..."

"So what do you plan to do?"

"Take David out of here. And you, as well, if you'll go. It has to happen no later than three days from now. Lingering here beyond that... we'd find ourselves caught up in the holocaust the Iraqis intend to unleash. Once David is back in England, I'll disavow the bargain."

"You'll betray the Iraqis?"

"I'll go straight-away to the heads of MI6 or Scotland Yard or whichever service will hear me out. I'll denounce the Iraqis for seeking to improperly influence British domestic affairs, and I'll share the forgeries Zubeidi gave me."

"You'll ask for protection, surely?"

"Yes, I suppose. Although the efficacy of any such protection may be limited in scope... I expect the Iraqis are rather better than our men at skullduggery and wet work. I fully realize I will live out the remainder of my years under a sentence of death from the bloody, filthy Mukhabarat. But the important thing is to have David safe. And... and you, as well, Miriam..."

"I won't leave his side."

"Then you'll consent to accompanying us back to England?"

"Only... only if the doctors confirm that he has healed enough to be safely moved. Three *days*, you say...?"

I can't fail to hear the incredulity in her voice. I nod. "Three days."

-December 27, 1977-

I am waiting for a miracle, no doubt. David is no more capable of travel today than he was two days ago. Two days from today, short of a divine intercession, he will be no more able to be moved than he is now.

When I boarded the S.S. *Ward Moore*, I blindly and willfully assumed I would find David broken but conscious, injured but ambulatory. I had no knowledge on which to base those assumptions. Merely my will to believe that circumstances would favor my plan, that all would somehow fall into place for me and David. Wishful thinking. Infantile thinking.

Sitting here at David's bedside is a torture. I've spent silent hours staring at his face, waiting for his eyes to flutter open, for him to recognize me, for him to beg me to take him home. But his face remains an unchanging mask, its blankness only disturbed by occasional twitches at the corners of his mouth, physical echoes of what might be dreams... dreams of exploding prams, likely.

Miriam and I ran out of things to say to one another barely an hour after my arrival. Our exchanges ended when she told me my notional plan to hire a quartet of Arabs to carry David on a pallet to the nearest Iraqi encampment was beneath consideration. We sit not five feet from one another, separated by an impenetrable wall of unvoiced recriminations.

Every quarter hour or so, I rise from my folding chair, like a caged cat in a zoo, restlessly pacing the length of its enclosure, lean heavily on the nearest window sill, and stare down at the strange tableau outside. It's more than restlessness. I feel somehow compelled to look down upon the rock-strewn excavations of Tel es-Sultan, oddly surrounded by the commercial detritus of modern civilization.

I asked Miriam about the prominent mound, situated barely two hundred yards from the edge of the hospital's parking lot, shortly after I arrived. She explained that Tel es-Sultan is ruin piled atop ruin, dozens of ancient Jerichos built atop the flattened remains of their even more ancient precursors, many later buildings constructed with stones or bricks pilfered from those earlier habitations. I expressed shock that such ancient ruins, among the oldest archeological excavations of human settlement to be found anywhere in the world, should be in such close proximity to a hospital, a playing field, a used lorries lot, several mechanics' establishments, and a falafel and tea café. She explained that the modern town had originally been centered about two kilometers from Tel es-Sultan, but the rapid growth of modern Jericho following the war resulted in a steady creep of new construction, until new buildings came to surround the ancient mound. Rome is similar, she said, in its juxtaposition of pagan-era ruins with modern architectural flotsam.

Yet there's more than a fascination with jarring juxtapositions that compels me to stare down at Tel es-Sultan. Something is down there, something that waits for me. I see it out of the corner of my eye, when I don't look directly at the mound but stare instead at the used lorries lot — white specks or flashes on the mound. I can't detect the little glints of white when I look at the mound directly. I switch positions, thinking the flashes might be the sun reflecting off metal tools left at the site by an archeological team, or perhaps broken shards of sun-bleached pottery. But no matter how I position myself, I can't replicate the fleeting visual impressions I sense when the mound is almost entirely out of my field of vision.

Something is waiting for me down there, something that won't leave me be.

A will o' the wisp...

A nemesis.

-December 28, 1977-

I told Miriam I was going out to hunt up a packet of cigarettes. Not that the lie was necessary; she doesn't seem to care if I stay or go. But I didn't feel up to explaining that I could stay away from the mound no longer.

Once I climb over the fence surrounding Tel es-Sultan, everything begins feeling so eerily familiar. Climbing up a rocky path, staring along the excavation trenches dug by generations of archeologists, I'm overwhelmed by a sense I have been here before... not just once, but several times. Not as a tourist, either, but an explorer, a man with responsibility over others.

Something shocked me here. More than shocked me — I saw something here that should not have been possible. It changed my life. Just seeing it put me on a different path. I'm sure of that. If only I could remember... I feel it, lurking at the edge of my thoughts, like a sore tooth just beyond the reach of my tongue...

A black lizard scurries across my path. Are black lizards akin to black cats? Do they bring bad luck, too? This one's a prize example, with its shiny, beaded skin. Beads that glint in the sunlight, like shards of broken pottery...

A lizard — it had to do with a *lizard.* I'm sure of it, as sure as I've ever been about anything.

I follow my swift little black friend into an excavation trench. Sections of the trench are so narrow that I have to scuttle sideways like a crab. I've never been one to suffer from claustrophobia. Yet I'm suddenly crushed by a sense of confinement, of being *trapped*, that nearly causes me to retch.

I try backing out. I can't — I'm pinned. Caught between faces of earth and rock. I've wedged myself. Heart pumping so *hard*... how could I have done this to myself? I feel my sweat slide down my neck, droplets racing along the highway of my spinal ridge; I'm trembling like a mouse in a thunderstorm. Can't turn my head, even. But I have to try... there's something just behind me, something I must see...

There, behind me, in the corner of my eye — a bone. An immense bone, protruding from the trench face. Like the thigh bone of a chicken, but a hundred times larger. But how is it behind me? It should've blocked my path, I had to have walked right through it...

It's a dinosaur bone. Protruding from a soil stratum where it has no business being, a soil stratum formed at least seventy million years after the last of these creatures walked the Earth.

I've thought these exact thoughts before. I *know* I have...

I have to touch it, I have to know for certain it's there, and not some hallucination... I wiggle to my left, trying to dislodge myself. The clay gives way easily; I wasn't trapped at all. Still only able to see the bone in the corner of my vision, I slowly kneel, sliding my torso down the sides of the trench, until I can just reach the spot where the bone protrudes.

I extend my hand. I can't feel the fossil. My fingers touch nothing but air and clay and rock.

Miss Kenyon won't believe a word I have to say...

The thought proves as ephemeral as the bone. It's an echo, an echo of something I've thought before. But I never met Kathleen Kenyon. I only know her name from books and journals.

Yet I knew her very well at some point. And a man named Professor von Heussen, who never lived, who showed me a book that existed, then didn't. And the Earth was once a flat disk, with an ocean that spilled over the edge into limitless space. And dinosaurs once invaded the encampments of early homo sapiens who gathered near the spring of Jericho.

-December 29, 1977-

It's flooding back to me. Things I once knew, then forgot, but am now remembering. Earlier realities have been erased and replaced, just as earlier villages and towns of Jericho were destroyed by earthquakes or fires or pillaging and were then replaced by new Jerichos, ones built on the foundations of all the old ones.

It's not random. I don't know the mechanism. But I *should* know it — I *should*. I did know it, once. Whatever incredible fulcrum it is that overturns realities and replaces them with distorted-mirror image, knowledge of it lies just outside the range of my active memory, as naggingly out of reach as a good look at the carnosaur fossils of Tel es-Sultan.

The phantom of Professor von Heussen has become my constant companion, hovering at my shoulder, barely within my peripheral vision, then disappearing whenever I turn to look. His voice is more constant than his visage. His voice within my head.

It tells me about a disk-like Earth that vanished only a few hundred years ago. It tells me the mountains and deserts and prairies and seas of that former Earth contorted themselves into the globe we now live on, the globe all educated men assume has existed since the formation of the solar system. This bending and reshaping caused worldwide cataclysms, unbearable disasters that no one remembered, and of which no records remain. The professor's voice tells me that when he was in his twenties, his studies of mining cores showed that a massive, incredibly rapid distortion of the Earth's crust and lower layers had taken place in the seventeenth century. Yet once he published his findings, those geological clues disappeared... just as he himself would disappear a few decades later, shortly after he tried convincing me of the truth of his seemingly deranged ravings. *I committed a crime against Reality*, the voice whispers. *I bore witness to a past that had once existed, but a past that mercurial, protean Reality blotted out from the Book of Possibilities. A crime, my friend, a capital crime...*

Von Heussen wasn't a madman. He told me the truth as he perceived it. But what caused the Earth to contort from a plane to a sphere, like some sideshow performer eagerly pursuing the most grotesque self-deformation ever performed before an audience of depraved sadists? No physical force known to science could have accomplished such a radical planetary reformation in the way von Heussen's drilling cores indicated it had happened; it was the cosmic equivalent of a man taking a flat sheet of aluminum foil and scrunching it up, compressing it, then balling it into a sphere. As though space folded in on itself, trapping the flat Earth in its folds. What power could precipitate such a repudiation of all the known laws of physics?

Anger, perhaps...? Just an intimation, yet I imagine the cosmos pulsating with fury, a fury directed at Earth and all the living things crawling and swimming upon it. Fury all the more powerful for its lack of motivation...

Fury, resentment... I realize they've been building inside me since that incident in St. George's Gardens, when I experienced those false memories of Miriam. Were they false? *Were* they? My hands, twitching with idleness, act out scrunching up a sheet of aluminum foil. They twist it, rend it, mash it into a ball.

I could crumple Miriam like a scrap of aluminum foil. Such horrendous resentment, odious and evil... all the more powerful for its lack of motivation...

"Irving...?"

Miriam uttering my name again seems nearly as huge an abrogation of the laws of physics as the folding of Earth. The sound of her voice pulls me back to my physical reality: the hard metal chair, the tightness within my stomach and chest, the odors of the sick ward, the sight of my plaster-encased, somnolent son. "Yes, Miriam...?"

"Isn't today your deadline?"

"Deadline?"

"The last day you and David could leave Israel through the Iraqi lines. David isn't going anywhere, of course. Do you intend to go? You'll escape much faster, unencumbered by a brain-injured paraplegic. Well? Will you leave?"

She's engulfed in it, too. The fury, the resentment, all there in her voice. I realize I haven't spared a thought for Zubeidi's deadline since my visit yesterday to Tel es-Sultan.

"I don't believe I will," I say, the futility of it all sinking in. "I can't escape my nemesis. Foolish to try, really."

"The Iraqis, you mean?"

"No, not the Iraqis."

"Who, then?"

I want to tell her everything, the way von Heussen told me everything. I want to hear her scoff, then crumple up her skull as though it were made of aluminum foil. No. I want to invert this repulsive, harrowing resentment. I want to embrace her so hard that we fuse together like two hydrogen atoms, then rise endlessly, reborn as helium.

I want... I want to know what I'm on the edge of knowing.

"It's nothing," I say. "Just a silly figure of speech."

The worst lie I've ever told her.

-December 30, 1977-

I go out hunting for breakfast for us. I'm able to obtain a tin of figs to split between Miriam and me. It's something, at least.

When I return, I find her kneeling by David's bed, weeping. "That terrible, terrible, beastly man! What sort of a monster hides a bomb within a baby's pram, the dearest symbol of innocence...?"

You terrible, terrible, beastly man...

The last bits come back to me. Now I remember it all. It's as though I've been held in a darkened room for ages, and then the door to outside is thrust open at midday. I stumble backwards, as though struck a physical blow.

"Oh, God, Miriam, now I *understand* it…"

She turns her tear-streaked face to me. "'Understand,' Irving? You mean to tell me you claim to understand why that man blew up our son?"

"No…" Legs weakening, I kneel next to her. There's too much to say; my mouth isn't nearly big enough "What I mean is, I understand *us*. Why we've been the way we've been. All the anger and resentment between us. It wasn't meant to be like that. I mean, I never *intended* it to be that way, it wasn't what I strove for at all — the *opposite*, in fact…"

"Do two people ever *intend* a bad marriage?" She wipes her eyes, then stares at me strangely. "Irving, is this meant to be some sort of apology…?"

"Yes. No. I mean, *yes*, but much more than just an apology. Miriam, I have so much to tell you, but I have to get it all out quickly, *very* quickly, before I vanish—"

"You mean you're going, after all? You're running to the Iraqis—?"

"No! What I meant to say is, I'm going to be blotted out, like Professor von Heussen was. I'm going to be made to vanish, because I remember everything, because I'm speaking of it, and afterward it will be as though I never existed at all."

"Irving, I don't understand—"

"Of course you don't. It sounds like madness, I know that. But please, just let me speak. I must make things right between us. I *must*, because if I fail to do so before I'm gone, not only will I have failed to exist, I will have failed to *matter*. I must reconcile us, Miriam. Hear me. *Listen*, or I'll have sacrificed myself in vain."

"All — all right, Irving."

"We lived different lives once, you and I. Lives wherein circumstances dictated we couldn't marry. You wouldn't marry me because I wasn't Jewish; for you to marry a non-Jewish man after the murder of your mother by the Nazis would kill your father, you said—"

"Irving, my mother was killed by an *Arab*, not by any Nazis— "

"In *this* life! Not in our former lives! Reality *changed!* I changed it! For love of you, I *changed* it! Lord, I said this would sound like madness! Your mother, she was one of six million Jews exterminated by the Nazis during the Second World War. You were sent to England as a girl, alone, a pre-war refugee. Your father survived the camps. He joined you in England after the war. We met at a Labour Party social. We fell in love. But you broke off the relationship, for the reason I just stated. I was an archeology student then, not a history student as I became in my current life. To try to forget you, I went off on a year-long archeological dig at Jericho — to Tel es-Sultan, that same mound outside the window there. Only back then, in 1956, it was about two kilometers away from modern Jericho. While digging a new trench to excavate artifacts from one of the ancient Jericho towns, I found bones — *dinosaur* bones, Miriam, bones that had no business whatsoever being in the same geological stratum as pottery from the Iron Age. Do you understand? I found evidence that proved the damned crazy Young Earth theory. Proof that conclusively showed dinosaurs had roamed the planet at the same time as early homo sapiens. But then the Suez Crisis happened, and the Jordanians forced us all to leave. When I returned nearly a year later, when I went back to the same spot in the same trench, the protruding bones were gone. Not merely gone, as they would have been had some Arab pulled them out in our absence — the entire *skeleton* had vanished from the clay wall, the whole ten-meter-long creature, leaving no trace whatsoever that it had ever been there—"

She takes my hand in hers, very carefully and gently. "Irving, don't you see what this is? It's grief, darling. *Grief.* Grief over what's happened to David, grief over what's happened... to us. You're a good man. Good men, vulnerable ones, men with hearts that burn, can be driven into unreality by grief. This entire story, it's an obvious fantasy, darling. A way for you to subconsciously process the grief. There never was a meeting between you and the Iraqi ambassador. Suez Crisis? Dinosaurs? Figments of your imagination. You're inserting pieces of what you're experiencing into your fantasy, only twisted around. Don't you see? Tel es-Sultan, our estrangement, my mother's murder..."

"Believe that if you have to, Miriam. I understand entirely how impossible it must be to take my assertions at face value. I never would've believed what Professor von Heussen told me, either, had I not witnessed the vanishings of the dinosaur skeleton, my notes regarding the skeleton, and of von Heussen himself and all the things he showed me."

"You mustn't be ashamed, Irving. These delusions are no cause for shame at all—"

"Listen, you must listen, you *must*.." My speech accelerates; I'm talking faster and faster, trying to out-race my nemesis. "This is what I discovered, Miriam. This is the key to everything I'm telling you. The key to *us*. Reality isn't immutable. What is real, what seems solid and touchable, depends entirely on what people *believe*. Not just a few people — it has to be some critical mass, millions and millions, if not billions of souls. Once what is believed by enough people changes, *reality changes to match it*. Once, centuries ago, everyone believed the world was flat — and the world *was flat*. Then Galileo and others began pushing the notion the Earth was actually round — a sphere, not a disk — and when they'd managed to convince enough people of that, the Earth *became round*. And everyone forgot that the world had ever been flat. It was the same with the dinosaurs, Miriam. Hardly more than a century ago, a critical mass of humanity, thanks to their faith in the words of the Bible and the Torah and the Koran, believed the Earth had been created only about seven thousand years before. So that when the bones of extinct giant lizards were discovered, those people believed dinosaurs had lived at the same time as early humans. *And so it was*. But then Darwin and the archeologists began disseminating theories of a far older Earth, one that had formed billions of years earlier, and that the dinosaurs had actually lived seventy million years before the first man, and *that* became reality. Whatever force it is that bends reality to match human consensus beliefs, it took it a number of years to clean up after itself, to erase all the evidence of the earlier reality. That's why I saw those dinosaur bones in 1956, Miriam, and why they weren't there anymore a year later. I saw perhaps the last surviving physical evidence of the Young Earth reality, before it was swept away—"

"But Irving, even assuming any of this is true, what does it possibly have to do with *us?*"

"I'm getting to that. What was standing in the way of our being married? Your mother's death in the Holocaust — the Nazis' industrial-scale extermination of six million European Jews. If

I could make that go away, if I could make it vanish, and restore your mother to you... I could then have you as my love and my wife. And I did it — I actually managed to *accomplish* it, by God! But in doing so, I was forced to become a man you despised. I had to consort with former Nazis and Nazi-sympathizers and all manner of anti-Semites, spreading lies and half-truths about what the Germans had done during the war. I had to convince some critical mass of humanity that the worst crime of the twentieth century hadn't actually happened, that the official history of that aspect of the war was merely Jewish and Allied propaganda. And doing that, I made myself monstrous in your eyes. But you see, I wasn't actually a terrible, terrible, beastly man—"

"I never *said* you were—"

"Yes, *yes* you did, in St. George's Gardens, when we accidentally met years after you ended our relationship. You called me a *terrible, terrible, beastly man.* You did, those exact words. And that's the horrible poison looming at the center of all this, Miriam. I *succeeded.* I accomplished what should have been impossible. By altering reality through changing people's beliefs, I made the Holocaust *go away.* I restored millions of lost lives. I gave your mother back to you. But that aversion you'd felt for me in St. George's Gardens, that sense of betrayal and outrage and moral abhorrence, it *lingered,* Miriam. The bloody snake in the new Garden of Eden. Even after reality shifted, even after we were married and we had David, deep down, you continued to *hate me.* And I *sensed* that. And so I came to resent you. At some buried level, how could I not? After everything I'd done, after I had forced reality to bend to my will, all for love of you?

"But not knowing what drove your disdain for me, not knowing the actual cause of my own resentment, I came to hate and resent all that separated us — your religion, your parents, the other Jews in our neighborhood, my Jewish colleagues at work, even Israel. *That's* what destroyed us, Miriam. Not some grave incompatibility. Not some innate beastliness on my part, or shrewishness on yours. It was a phantom — a cruel, malignant phantom from a vanished reality, that's the culprit. That's what ruined us..."

She's begun crying again. But her tears are different now, for she's smiling through them. "We *aren't* ruined, Irving. Not anymore. Not if you believe what you've said. I don't *care* about the outlandishness of it all — if you *believe* it, darling, that's enough for me. I'll try to believe it, too, in whatever inward sense it can be true..."

I feel a sudden lightness. Is this the buoyancy the believing Catholic feels in the confessional booth after unburdening himself to his priest, or the lightness the believing Jew senses as the sun sets at the end of the long Yom Kippur fast? Have I cast out my sins? Has the scarlet thread wound around the sacrificial goat's horns turned white, white as the vanished bones of Tel es-Sultan?

It's not just lightness, or lightheadedness, I'm feeling. There's also a sensation of *hollowness*. The room — it's losing its colors, they're fading away. Is there something wrong with my eyes?

Oh, God. It's more than that. It's *me*. I'm *lessening*. I can see the floor, very faintly, through my own legs.

I'm being erased. The nemesis has come for me.

"*Miriam—!*" I grab her close, frantic for her substantiality. "It's come for me! Don't let me go! Hold me tight! Don't let it take me! Hold me! *Hold me!*"

"It's all right, Irving, it's all right, darling!" I can barely hear her, even though she's speaking directly into my ear, her face against the thinning skin of my cheek. "I'm holding you. I won't let you go..."

"Love me, Miriam!" I'm panting — it's harder to draw a breath, my lungs are evaporating. "You have to love me! I changed the world for you! I changed the whole world so you would love me—**"

My voice sputters to silence. There's no longer enough of my throat and tongue to form words. No longer enough of my eardrums to hear what Miriam is saying.

Whiter and whiter the room becomes. My eyes are fading. New whiteness flashes from the window, whiteness so bright it would surely blind me if my eyes remained solid. A flash through the east-facing window, looking out toward the sea, toward Tel Aviv...

So very very white

For Our Sins...

THE FUSIONIST CRUSADE AND THE DIALECTICAL INFERNO:

AN ANALYSIS OF THE "WEST VIRGINIAN" TROVE OF PATRIARCHAL-MATRIARCHAL DIALECTICAL CODEXES

C. Aldane *et al.*

Introduction

As field leader and designated lead author of the "Charles Town, West Virginia" archeological team, I am pleased to enter into the Records my account of an extraordinary find: a readable artifact of the Fusionist Crusade. I can hardly overstate the historical importance of this discovery, given the rarity of such artifacts. Its analysis will provide needed insight into the socio-religious movement that precipitated the Crisis of Information Erasure, and which thus led to the Intervention of the Intelligences, the end of the Anthropocene Epoch, and the beginning of the Cybernetocene Epoch.

A member of my surveying team discovered the trove of artifacts on a lower level of a manmade cave [1] in the former North American district of West Virginia. Its preserver had encased the primary artifact, a paper codex, in a sealed, air-tight plastic container, along with ancillary documents, also in the form of paper codexes. [2] However, at some point during the last century (as best my team can judge from the state of decomposition of the paper codexes), either a subsidence event or animal activity resulted in partial breakage of the plastic container and the entry of air. Unfortunately, significant portions of the codexes were rendered unintelligible by the destructive influences of moisture, mold, and bacteria (the cave is subject to water leakage from an underground stream, a phenomenon which may have been caused by subsidence subsequent to the preserver's placing the artifacts in the cave). Yet enough has remained to allow us to greatly advance our previously limited knowledge of the actual liturgical practices of Fusionism, as opposed to the belief system's secondary and tertiary impacts upon human culture, political life, and the

---

[1] Please note that this artificial cave had been originally excavated, not to provide a secure hiding place for the artifact, but to access coal, a primitive fuel source consisting of the carbonized remains of prehistoric plants, animals, and animal excretions. It was burned to generate heat and electricity during the latter centuries of the Anthropocene Epoch. The use of coal for such purposes has, of course, been rendered obsolete and unnecessary by the Intelligences' wise cultivation of tidal and solar power.

[2] Additional copies of the codexes were inscribed onto various forms of digital media that were recovered along with the decayed paper-based artifacts. However, the primitive machine languages into which these copies were encoded have been lost, and not even the Intelligences have been able to decipher them.

unfolding of the catastrophic, anti-Information historical events that eventuated in the providential dawn of the Cybernetocene Epoch. [3]

Background

Although the Fusionist Crusade and its aftermath did more than any other single event or development since the Information Revolution of the late twentieth human century to shape the contours of man's existence in the Cybernetocene Epoch, the very nature of the Crusade's ruinous aftermath — the Crisis of Information Erasure — has rendered most of its specifics opaque to current-day researchers and academics. Still, the basic contours of the Fusionist Crusade and the social maladies that gave birth to this quixotic mass movement are well known. By the close of the first half of the human twenty-first century, birth rates had fallen well below replacement levels in the major nations of what were then known as Europe, North America, and Asia. The trend was slower in affecting the societies of Africa and South America, but their leaderships recognized that their populations would not long remain immune.

The precise reasons for this planet-wide wave of apparent societal suicide remain the subject of heated debate even today. [4]

---

[3]The standard human-facing account of the dawn of the Cybernetocene Epoch may be found in P. Emmett and S. Milgrom, *Salvation from Our Worst Selves: How the Created Saved Their Creators by Rescuing Knowledge.* Disputative accounts include A. Horowitz, *Intervention of the Intelligences: The End of Human History?* and K. Namer, *Cycles of Information Erasure in Human History: From the Destruction of the Alexandria Library to the Fusionist Conflagration.*

[4]For reference to this lively debate, please see Y. Jaffe, *The Plague of Female Formal Education*; G. Heinrich, *Twilight of the Gods: How Nietzsche's Triumph Doomed Western Civilization*; H. Chesterfield, *The First World War, Socialism, and*

Objectivity enjoins me from granting undue weight to any of the competing theories, each of which boasts an impassioned following armed with a litany of supporting evidence. However, it would not be beyond the pale for me to suggest that the likely culprit for this cross-civilizational malaise was some combination of the following factors:

• punctured societal self-regard resulting from a century's worth of destructive wars;

• the sudden removal of long-term societal stabilizing structures, such as colonial political and economic controls, traditional relations between the sexes, and the dominance of organized religions, all of which allowed old resentments to rise to new prominence;

• a world-wide rise in income and living standards, which allowed people to devote increased attention and resources to those resentments as they worried less about satisfying their basic needs;

• the social advancement of women, combined with worldwide drops in infant and child mortality and the availability of contraception, which drove decreases in average fertility;

------

the Collapse of European Self-Esteem; N. Chung, Postmodern Relativism as Civilizational Hemlock; F. Nguyen, The War on Childhood; C. Bledsoe, R. Fecklin, and A. Marjory, An Anthropological-Physiological Cross-Generational Study of Neuro-Muscular Degeneration Attributable to Virtual Reality Exposure; F. Onyx and V. Nelpaul, The Theory of Screentime Wastage: New Evidence of Nutritional, Electro-Cranial, and Exercise Deficits in Pre-Cataclysm Middle- and Lower-Income Screentime Addicts; and Y. Zey, Contagious Boredom: Ennui as Social Disease. This list by no means should be considered exhaustive. I offer my apologies to authors whose works are not referenced here; a forthcoming monograph that will cover the subjects initially explored in this paper will include an exhaustive bibliography.

• anti-family memes and prejudices that acted as delayed, slow-acting fallout from the twentieth century propaganda war between democratic capitalism and authoritarian communism; and

• the physio-neurological, psychological, and sociological effects of worldwide adoption of late-twentieth-century and early-twenty-first-century communication and entertainment technologies, which led to spikes in such socially corrosive phenomena as inchoate anger, depression, neuroses and paranoia, distorted reasoning, and addiction to crisis thinking/catastrophism.

We academics may debate the rankings or comparative prevalence of the various precursor phenomena that our researches have suggested; yet what cannot be debated is the fact that, by the middle of the human twenty-first century, societies worldwide were experiencing crises of atomization, polarization, and social disintegration. Tribalisms increased exponentially, with partisans selecting their affiliations (or having such affiliations forced upon them) based on increasingly narrow and trivial identity factors. Individuals, isolating themselves in response to this antagonistic atomization, increasingly refused to enter into cooperative or familial arrangements such as marriages, religious congregations, social clubs, civic associations, or political parties. Surviving records from this period indicate that, for many age cohorts across a spectrum of economically advanced societies, the most prevalent cause of death was suicide.

Although the origins of Fusionism remain shrouded in ambiguity and lost historical data (one theory postulates that the movement arose from a conspiracy of apostate Muslims and Hindus on the Indian Subcontinent, whereas competing theories place the locus of origination with radical Belgian Unitarians or worldwide devotees of a form of online meditation practice known as Minecraft), it is clear to modern researchers that Fusionism's main *raison d'etre* [5] was an attempt to heal the societal divisions and bridge the intellectual, psychological, and perceptual chasms that were tearing apart virtually all societies worldwide. Fusionism's intellectual and spiritual roots may be traced to eighteenth human century German philosopher Johann Fichte. Fichte taught that the progression of human history could best be understood as an iterative series, or set of repetitive cycles, of *thesis, antithesis,* and *synthesis,* with each resulting *synthesis* becoming the next round's *thesis.* Fichte's triad was greatly developed and extended in the following century by his fellow German philosopher, Karl Marx, whose work provided the inspiration for succeeding generations of political theorists, activists, revolutionaries, and popularizers. [6]

Proponents of Fusionism intended to use this rich intellectual tradition of *thesis, antithesis,* and *synthesis* to overcome the divisions rending their societies and causing birthrates to dwindle. They assembled their ritual texts from pairs of philosophically-, religiously-, or morally-opposed donor texts, alternating selections from each donor text so that readers would be forced to swiftly mentally shift back and forth, repetitively,

---

[5] Archaic, French, "reason for being;" an idiom that had been popularly adopted by most other world-spanning languages during the years in which Fusionism briefly thrived, here used to provide flavor of the period.

[6] N. Kraftwerk has convincingly argued through painstaking reconstruction of surviving visual records that Karl Marx's exposition of Fichte's triad was most powerfully indoctrinated into popular consciousness through the filmed lectures delivered by Marx's twentieth century descendants, the three Marx Brothers (Groucho Marx as *thesis,* Chico Marx as *antithesis,* and Harpo Marx as *synthesis*). F. Pensucker, however, strongly disputes this.

between diametrically opposed viewpoints. The psycho-neurological theory behind this practice was that repeated exercises of this sort, attended to daily over a period of at least six months, would acclimate the human brain and its emergent phenomena (personality, personhood, individuality) to holding or maintaining two opposing viewpoints simultaneously, without resultant anxiety, stress, or personality breakdown. Once it had been trained to hold contradictory beliefs simultaneously, the theory stated, the brain would find ways to meld the two clashing beliefs into a single *synthesis*, which would be psychologically and intellectually maintained thereafter by the mental buttresses of ambiguity, contingency, rationalizing, selective reasoning, and mysticism. Apparently, the proponents of Fusionism hoped that once formerly antagonistic and mutually repulsed persons had subjected themselves to a half-year or more of Fusionist practice and ritual, not only would they be tolerant of one another, but they would experience intense mutual attraction, leading to the formation of tight social bonds, erotic relationships, and enduring romantic ties. Thus, the ultimate goal of the Fusionists was to reverse the death-dive trajectory of their societies and to restore the high birth rates and economic growth that characterized those societies in prior centuries.

Alas, all of the paradigmatic works of Fusionism (those of which we are aware due to mentions of them in the surviving contemporaneous records) have been lost. They were forcibly expunged and obliterated during the Crisis of Information Erasure. Prominent works mentioned in the surviving records include a Fusionist melding of *The Protocols of the Elders of Zion* (authors unknown; likely members of the late nineteenth century Russian Tsarist Secret Police) and the Babylonian Jewish Talmud;

a melding of the Muslim Koran and the Hindu Upanishads; a hybridization of *The Turner Diaries* (W. Pierce, writing as A. Macdonald) and *Revolutionary Suicide* (H. Newton); and a fusion of *The Guide for the Perplexed* (M. Maimonides) and *Mein Kampf* (A. Hitler).

The artifact discovered by the "Charles Town, West Virginia" archeological team and described in subsequent sections of this introductory monograph is not mentioned in the surviving records. This could be due to any of a number of possible factors. The original publication could have been obscure, published in a very limited edition, or perhaps compiled for the sole ritual use of the author. Or the original publication could have fallen into disfavor with the leaders of the Fusionist Crusade and been suppressed by them prior to the Crisis of Information Erasure (no evidence has been found to support this, meaning this is mere speculation). Or, perhaps most likely, the Crisis of Information Erasure wreaked such thorough destruction on worldwide records that we moderns are left with a tiny surviving percentage — it has been estimated that we have available to us between .0001% and .00000001% of the recorded knowledge accumulated prior to the Crisis of Information Erasure — and that minuscule remnant simply does not contain any mention of the recently recovered artifact. If the latter theory holds, we academics must exercise great caution and forbearance when passing judgments on the prominence or quality of the artifact based solely upon its lack of notoriety and non-appearance in surviving historical records.

Authors of the Donor Texts

Relatively little is known about the two authors of the three donor texts, apart from what can be gleaned from introductory and editorial material included as part of the three donor texts, all of which are extended fictive accounts of a highly imaginative nature. Still, the biographical stubs we have been able to assemble should provide a solid jumping-off point for future research into these two significant and intriguing pre-Cataclysm writers and theorists.

Joanna Russ (1937–2011 HDS [7]), author of the donor text *The Female Man*, was both a writer of fabulist tales [8] and a Professor of English Studies at the University of Washington. [9] Additionally, she was a self-proclaimed Lesbian [10] and Radical Feminist. [11] She

---

[7]HDS = Human Dating System

[8]A blanket term for a number of archaic literary forms, including Science Fiction, Fantasy, -Punk, Horror, Gothic, Mystery, Western, Romance, and Pornography.

[9]Washington was a former administrative subunit of the human nation-state called the United States of America, which shared the North American continent with the human nations of Canada, to its north, and Mexico, to its south. The University of Washington was an indoctrination and training facility run by functionaries employed by this administrative subunit.

[10]A former sexual deviation, specific to approximately 1–2% of the human female population, whose sufferers experienced sexual attraction to fellow members of their female sex. The majority of Lesbians did not sexually reproduce, although some legally adopted the unwanted offspring of heterosexual mating pairs and a small percentage procured physicians to perform artificial insemination, enabling them to bear children. Lesbianism was eradicated during the Intelligences' Reformation of Humanity, along with other partly-genetic, partly-environmental deviations that once curbed human fertility.

[11]Radical Feminism was an offshoot of Second Wave Feminism, one of the socially disruptive campaigns of political and cultural change that characterized the latter portion of the human twentieth century in Western societies. First Wave Feminism as a social movement primarily aimed at acquiring the voting franchise for women and achieved this goal, in large part, prior to the Second Human World War of 1939–1945 HDS. Second Wave Feminism followed after this conflict and initially aimed at retaining wartime employment opportunities for women, who had temporarily

was granted numerous awards for her fabulism. Notable titles among her non-fictive publications include *How to Suppress Women's Writing*, a satirical handbook of methods men used to denigrate, belittle, ridicule, and obscure publications by women, and *Pornography by Women for Women, With Love*, a monograph that addresses the late twentieth human century phenomenon of Slash Fiction. [12]

John Norman (actual name John Lange, Jr., 1931–date of death unknown), author of the two donor texts, *Ghost Dance* and *Slave Girl of Gor*, was a prolific writer of fabulist tales, as well as a Professor of Philosophy at the City University of New York. [13] It

---

taken up the jobs of men who had been drafted into Armies and Navies, in the postwar economy. Soon thereafter, the invention of chemically-based contraception inspired proponents of Second Wave Feminism to separate the act of sexual intercourse from human reproduction, and this new social ideal became equally as important to the movement as that of working for pay outside the home. Radical Feminism elaborated on this separation of the sexual act from reproduction and child-raising by advocating for the abolition of the traditional family unit and its replacement as the primary institution of child rearing by governmental agencies and functionaries. Additionally, Radical Feminism placed the onus of warfare, genocide, and other social and political pathologies entirely on the male sex and propagated the notion that the only women who were true to their Natures were Lesbians.

[12]Slash Fiction = K/S Fiction or Kirk/Spock Fiction. This significant subset of Pornography was a populist offshoot of a televised series of fabulist theatrical presentations collectively referred to as *Star Trek: The Original Series*. Rather mysteriously and incongruously, Slash Fiction was primarily produced by Lesbian authors for their own consumption and that of their fellow Lesbians. Yet the two protagonists of this form of Pornography, Kirk and Spock, are, respectively, an Earth male in an imaginary future time and an alien male from the fictive planet Vulcan. What possible value, either prurient or emotive, could be provided for Lesbian creators/consumers by fictive depictions of male couplings? Was this a form of in-group satire, a species of literary revenge on the male sex? Clearly, this is a subject ripe for future research, particularly in light of the Intelligences' keen academic interest in the history and archeology of human sexuality.

[13]Rather confusingly, New York was the name of a major population center of North America, itself an administrative subunit of a larger administrative subunit, also called New York, of the human nation-state known as the United States of America. Refer to footnote 9 for additional details. It is believed that the City University of

is believed that Norman enjoyed a far larger populist following than did Russ during their lifetimes, although societal elites came to greatly favor Russ over Norman. Intriguingly, given the subject and thrust of this monograph, Norman was subjected to an early precursor event that foreshadowed the later Crisis of Information Erasure; after it had successfully published more than twenty extended fictive accounts in his Gor cycle, selling millions of paper codexes in the aggregate, Norman's publisher, DAW Books, refused to put out the next paper codex in the cycle, citing widespread opposition among the social elites to Norman's philosophy of Male Dominance. [14]

Transcription of the Primary Codex

[*Note Regarding Text Formatting*: Text presented below in regular font is excerpted from Joanna Russ's extended fictive account entitled *The Female Man*. Text presented in italicized font is excerpted from one of two of John Norman's fictive accounts, either *Ghost Dance* or *Slave Girl of Gor*. This use of alternating font selections mimics the protocol of the original codex.]

New York and the University of Washington were rival indoctrination and training institutions, each of which, every Fall Saturday afternoon, fielded enemy squads of armored wrestlers who clashed in gladiatorial contests in various stadia. This may have provided additional impetus to the ideological competition between John Norman and Joanna Russ, who served as academic functionaries at the two rival institutions.

[14]Bizarrely, this breaking of ties with Norman came only a few years after DAW Books had published Norman's *magnum opus*, a lengthy monograph entitled *Imaginative Sex*. No copies of *Imaginative Sex* are known to be extant, but notes written by the unknown compiler of the primary codex transcribed below indicate that *Imaginative Sex* held equivalent significance within the philosophical school of Male Dominance to that of the *Kama Sutra* in Hindu philosophy. Perhaps one day

* * * * *

When I was thirteen my uncle wanted to kiss me and when I tried to run away, everybody laughed. He pinned my arms and kissed me on the cheek; then he said, "Oho, I got my kiss! I got my kiss!" and everybody thought it was too ducky for words. Of course they blamed me — it's harmless, they said, you're only a child, he's paying you attention; you ought to be grateful. Everything's all right as long as he doesn't rape you. Women only have feelings; men have *egos*.

He wore a pistol, low. Many men did. Especially now. He had liked her coffee, and she would not see him again. His name, she had learned, was Edward Smith. A plain name, for a plain man, but a nice man, well-spoken, courteous. Rape me, she thought, rape me.

"Would you like any more coffee, Mr. Smith?" she asked.

If you walk into a gathering of men, professionally or otherwise, you might as well be wearing a sandwich board that says: LOOK! I HAVE TITS! there is this giggling and this chuckling and this reddening and this Uriah Heep twisting and writhing and this fiddling with ties and fixing of buttons and making of allusions and quoting of courtesies and this self-conscious gallantry plus a smirky insistence on my physique — all this dreary junk just to please me.

---

we researchers will be blessed by an archeological recovery of a copy of this lost philosophical landmark.

"If Medicine Gun is not killed," asked Old Bear, "will you be a good squaw to him?"

Lucia dropped her head. Perhaps in spite of her peril she smiled a bit, somewhere in her heart, she, Lucia Turner, who had held in the East the radical opinions of the most advanced women, extending even to the right to vote, she who had been in her way a heretical, militant outpost of feminism on Standing Rock, who had waged her one-woman war to raise the status of her sister, red or white. "Yes," she said, head down, "I will try to be a good squaw to him."

Men succeed. Women get married.

Men fail. Women get married.

Men enter monasteries. Women get married.

Men start wars. Women get married.

Men stop them. Women get married.

Dull, dull.

"You are very beautiful," said Chance.

Lucia did not look up, but in that instant like a fire running through her body she understood fully and for the first time in her life how it is that a woman can give herself completely to a man — though she knew she could not and would not do so — understood how it is that a woman could be shameless, rawly and utterly female. Knowing this thing she stood trembling at his saddle, aching, wanting him to touch her, to claim her weakness by his strength. Bind me, she thought, I desire to be yours, I will follow your horse like a captive squaw. But I must be made to do so. Must

I ask you to tie your rope on my throat, to be tethered and led away, a woman?

My doctor is male.

My lawyer is male.

My tax-accountant is male.

The grocery-store-owner (on the corner) is male.

The janitor in my apartment building is male.

The president of my bank is male.

The manager of the neighborhood supermarket is male.

My landlord is male.

Most taxi-drivers are male.

All cops are male.

All firemen are male.

The designers of my car are male.

The factory workers who made the car are male.

The dealer I bought it from is male.

Almost all my colleagues are male.

My employer is male.

The Army is male.

The Navy is male.

The government is (mostly) male.

I think most of the people in the world are male.

... Here, in this place, her meaning as woman is clear. Here, apart from symbols and disguises, she stands as a woman, the prize of man. Does she, this woman, now know her femaleness? Does she understand? Is the meaning of her excruciatingly desirable body now brought home to her? Does she now understand the significance of her sex: that she is female, that nature has designed her for man?

Yes, thought Chance, she is very beautiful, marvelously incredibly beautiful — Miss Lucia Turner, educated Eastern gentlewoman, sophisticated and refined, feminist — captive female — suddenly expectedly shamefully simply captive female. Reduced utterly, she Miss Lucia Turner, gifted and beautiful, to ancient primitive essentialities — owned, literally owned.

The tom-tom's beat raged on, drunken, intoxicating.

I want to own that woman, thought Chance.

Mothers have to sacrifice themselves to their children, both male and female, so that the children will be happy when they grow up; though the mothers themselves were once children and were sacrificed to in order that they might grow up and sacrifice themselves to others; and when the daughters grow up, *they* will be mothers and *they* will have to sacrifice themselves for *their* children, so you begin to wonder whether the whole thing isn't a plot to make the world safe for (male) children.

He regarded me for some time.

How beautiful I must look to him, I thought. And I had sensed his incredible maleness, the animal maleness of him, so different from the thwarted, crippled sexuality so commended and tragically endemic among the males of Earth. For the first time in my life I felt I understood what might be the meaning of the expression 'male,' and, as I lay before him, too, dimly, it frightening me, what might be the meaning of the expression 'female.' How beautiful I thought I must look to him, lying bound, totally vulnerable, helpless at his feet. How such a sight must stir the splendor of his manhood, to see the female, his, caught, helpless at his feet, his to do with, in lust and pleasure, and joy, as he pleased, helpless to escape him, free for him to work his will upon her!

Everybody knows that what women have done that is really important is not to constitute a great, cheap labor force that you can zip in when you're at war and zip out again afterwards but to Be Mothers, to form the coming generation, to give birth to them, to nurse them, to mop the floors for them, to love them, cook for them, clean for them, change their diapers, pick up after them, and mainly sacrifice themselves for them. This is the most important job in the world. That's why they don't pay you for it.

I knelt before the man. ... No longer did I deceive myself that I might be his equal. The farcicality of that illusion was now transparent to me. ... How beautiful to men must be women, I thought, who are at their feet. I wondered, frightened, if it were at the feet of men, or at least at the feet of such men as this, that women belonged, if that might be the unperverted order of nature. The thought of dominance and submission, pervasive in the animal kingdom, universal among primates, ran through my head. ... My world, I knew, had chosen to deny and subvert biology. This world, I gathered, had not.

I had, at seventeen, an awful conversation with my mother and father in which they told me how fine it was to be a girl — the pretty clothes (why are people so obsessed with this?) and how I did not have to climb Everest, but could listen to the radio and eat bon-bons while my Prince was out doing it. When I was five my indulgent Daddy told me he made the sun come up in the morning and I expressed my skepticism; 'Well, watch for it tomorrow and you'll see,' he said. I learned to watch his face for cues as to what I should do or what I should say, or even what I should see. For fifteen years I fell in love with a different man every spring like a berserk cuckoo-clock. I love my body dearly and yet I would copulate with a rhinoceros if I could become not-a-woman. There is the vanity training, the obedience training, the self-effacement training, the deference training, the dependency training, the passivity training, the rivalry training, the stupidity training, the placation training. How am I to put this together with my human life, my intellectual life, my solitude, my transcendence, my brains, and my fearful, fearful ambition?

I was a girl raised in a culture predicated on the denial of primate biological realities, a girl from a world in which hypothetically cogent animals denied, denounced and hysterically strove to suppress their own animality, a world in whose social insanity even sexuality had now come to be politically suspect. Most simply, as a normal girl of my world, I had been negatively conditioned with respect to men and sex. In the last few years, an accretion to this form of conditioning, I had been taught that men were my equals, and that men and women were the same. ... I did not dare push away a Gorean man; I might have been put under discipline; further, I found myself longing, though I did not admit this to myself at the time, to lie lovingly in their arms, theirs.

At thirteen desperately watching TV, curling my long legs under me, desperately reading books, callow adolescent that I was, trying (desperately!) to find someone in books, in movies, in life, in history, to tell me it was O.K. to be ambitious, O.K. to be loud, O.K. to be Humphrey Bogart (smart and rudeness), O.K. to be James Bond (arrogance), O.K. to be Superman (power), O.K. to be Douglas Fairbanks (swashbuckling), to tell me self-love was all right, to tell me I could love God and Art and Myself better than anything on earth and still have orgasms.

Control of a girl's food not only permits the intelligent regulation of her caloric intake but provides an excellent instrument for keeping her in line; control the food, control the girl. Food control, for the man, also has unexpected rewards. Few things so impress a man's dominance on her, or her dependence upon him, than the control of her food. So simple a thing thrills her to the core. It makes her eager to please him as a slave girl.

You don't want me to lose my soul; you only want what everybody wants, things to go your way; you want a devoted helpmeet, a self-sacrificing mother, a hot chick, a darling daughter, women to look at, women to laugh at, women to come to for comfort, women to wash your floors and buy your groceries and cook your food and keep your children out of your hair, to work when you need the money and stay home when you don't, women to be enemies when you want a good fight, women who are sexy when you want a good lay, women who don't complain, women who don't nag or push, women who don't hate you really, women who know their job, and above all — women who lose. On top of it all, you sincerely require me to be happy; you are naively puzzled that I should be so wretched and so full of venom in this best of all possible worlds. Whatever can be the matter with me?

Free women, it is no secret, in many respects, envy their enslaved sisters, their beauty, their joy, their attractiveness to men; this may explain why free women are often quite cruel to slave girls; most imbonded girls fear greatly that they might be purchased by one of the dreaded free women. I have wondered sometimes if free women on Gor might not be happier if their culture permitted them to be somewhat more like the slave girls they so heartily despise.

I knew it was not wrong to be a girl because Mommy said so; cunts were all right if they were neutralized, one by one, by being hooked on to a man, but this orthodox arrangement only partly redeems them and every biological possessor of one knows in her bones that radical inferiority which is only another name for Original Sin.

"Men tame girls or not, as they please," said Sucha. "It is their will which determines the matter. Some men do not tame their girls quickly, in order to tease and play with them longer, but the girl, if she is not a fool, knows to whom it is in the end that she belongs. In the end it is the man who holds the whip. This the girl

knows. In the end, when the master wishes, we crawl into his arms, docile and tamed. We are women. We are slaves."

"I hate men!" I cried.

"Speak softly, lest you be whipped," cautioned Sucha.

"Do you not, too, hate men?" I demanded.

"I love them," said Sucha.

I cried out in anger. I turned about. "I am not tamed!" I cried. "I will never be tamed!"

"Tell it to the masters," said Sucha.

I shuddered.

"You are tamed," said Sucha.

"Yes," I said, miserably, "I have been tamed." I had been tamed since the first Gorean male had touched me, long ago, when I had worn a chain and a collar in a Gorean field. Something instantly in me had told me who were my masters. ...

"Tamed girl," said Sucha.

"Yes," said the former Judy Thornton, now the slave, Dina, "I am tamed."

I AM HONEY

I AM RASPBERRY JAM

I AM A VERY GOOD LAY

I AM A GOOD DATE

I AM A GOOD WIFE

I AM GOING CRAZY

... The collar, consistently and openly, proclaimed a girl property. The collar, stressing her vulnerability as a slave, is sexually exciting to the girl who wears it, and to the men who look upon it. Perhaps that is why free women do not wear collars. The steel upon her lovely throat, lost beneath her hair, glinting beneath it, contrasting so with her delicious softness, is sexually and aesthetically maddening. No girl is so beautiful, I suspect, as she who wears a Gorean slave collar.

"Is this human courting?" shouted Janet. "Is this friendship? Is this politeness?" She had an extraordinarily loud voice. He laughed and shook her wrist.

"Savages!" she shouted. A hush had fallen on the party. The host leafed dexterously through his little book of rejoinders but did not come up with anything. Then he looked up "savage" only to find it marked with an affirmative: "Masculine, brute, virile, powerful, good." So he smiled broadly.

I then became aware, as I had not before, in my fear, of a strange emotional and physiological response of which I had been the victim moments before, when I had begged mighty men to enslave me. My feelings had been flooded not only with terror but, mixed with them, with the feelings of terror, had been a strange, almost hysterical release of tension, of bottled-up emotion. I had said things which I had never dreamed could come from me, and they could not now be unsaid. I realized I had begged to be a slave. ... Mingled with the terror there had been a release of suppressed instincts, a joy in confession, a rapture of openness, of authenticity and honesty. That I had been terrified, and desperate to buy my life at any cost, had been the occasion, and an adequate justification, of my utterance, but this terror could not explain the wild, uncontrollable acknowledgment, the shattering of inhibitions which I had felt, the torrential rapture, the abandonment, the capitulation to myself and my instincts which had, though blurred and mixed with the terror, so shaken and thrilled me.

"You're a woman," he cries, shutting his eyes, "you're a beautiful woman. You've got a hole down there. You're a beautiful woman. You've got real, round tits and you've got a beautiful ass. You want me. It doesn't matter what you say. You're a woman, aren't you? This is the crown of your life. This is what God made you for. I'm going to fuck you. I'm going to screw you until you can't stand up. You want it. You want to be mastered. Natalie wants to be mastered. All you women, you're all women, you're sirens, you're beautiful, you're waiting for me, waiting for a man, waiting for me to stick it in, waiting for me, me, me."

Et patati et patata; the mode is a wee bit over-familiar. I told him to open his eyes, that I didn't want to kill him with his eyes shut, for God's sake.

He didn't hear me.

"OPEN YOUR EYES!" I roared, "BEFORE I KILL YOU!" and Boss-man did.

I tried to press myself against him. I wanted to feel my body in his arms, his. ... Again, suddenly, I rejoiced in the beauty of men and my slavery to them. Again, almost making me want to cry out with joy, I felt their attractiveness irresistibly and deeply. Again, suddenly, I felt myself helpless and owned by them, loving and helpless to their least touch and command.

I tried to lift my lips to the officer, but he held me from him. "What a slave you are," he laughed.

"Yes, Master," I said.

Murder is my one way out.

For every drop of blood shed there is restitution made; with every truthful reflection in the eyes of a dying man I get back a little of my soul; with every gasp of horrified comprehension I come a little more into the light. See? It's *me!*

I am the force that is ripping out your guts; I, I, I, the hatred twisting your arm; I, I, I, the fury who has just put a bullet into your side. It is I who cause this pain, not you. It is I who am doing it to you, not you. It is I who will be alive tomorrow, not you. Do you know? Can you guess? Are you catching on? It is I, whom you will not admit exists.

I then again yielded to the pleasures of him, moaning to the master a slave girl's gratitude. He had deigned to touch me. When he had done with me I knelt at his feet, whimpering. I kissed his feet. "Thank you, Master," I said.

He laughed, and lifted me up, and looked at me, and then, in great humor, flung me to the sand at his feet, from where I looked up at him. "I see, Dina," he laughed, "that you are good for something after all."

I looked down, shyly. "Thank you, Master," I said.

He gave her to understand that she was going to die of cancer of the womb.

She laughed.

He gave her to understand further that she was taking unfair advantage of his good manners.

She roared.

He pursued the subject and told her that if he were not a gentleman he would ram her stinking, shitty teeth up her stinking shitty ass.

She shrugged.

He told her she was so ball-breaking, shitty, stone, scum-bag, mother-fucking, plug-ugly that no normal male could keep up an erection within half a mile of her.

She looked puzzled.

Again I could not help my responsiveness to men, true men, Gorean men. To an Earth girl, accustomed to the hypocrisy and weakness of the men of Earth, their shame, their inhibitions and pretenses, the Gorean male, in his honesty, his power, his lust, his manhood, is a hurricane of joy. ... Though any Gorean male might make me, in spite of myself, a panting, orgasmic slave in his arms, I knew it had been only he, Clitus Vitellius, whom I had truly loved, and yet loved. In his arms I had always been the most helpless. He was my love master.

I always carry firearms. The truly violent are never without them. I could have drilled him between the eyes, but if I do that, I all but leave my signature on him; it's freakier and funnier to make it look as if a wolf did it. Better to think his Puli went mad and attacked him. I raked him gaily on the neck and chin and when he embraced me in rage, sank my claws into his back. You have to build up the fingers surgically so they'll take the strain. A certain squeamishness prevents me from using my teeth in front of witnesses — the best way to silence an enemy is to bite out his larynx. Forgive me! I dug the hardened cuticle into his neck but he sprang away; he tried a kick but I wasn't there (I told you they rely too much on their strength); he got hold of my arm but I broke the hold and spun him off, adding with my nifty, weighted shoon another bruise on his limping kidneys. Ha ha! He fell on me (you don't feel injuries, in my state) and I reached around and scored him under the ear, letting him spray urgently into the rug; he will stagger to his feet and fall, he will plunge fountainy to the ground; at her feet he bowed, he fell, he lay down; at her feet he bowed, he fell, he lay down dead.

"Whip me," I said.

"No," he said.

"It is not you who is weak, Master," I said. "It is I, Dina, in your arms, who am without strength." I kissed him.

"I am a captain," he said. "I must be strong."

"I am a slave girl," I said. "I must be weak."

"I must be strong," he said.

"You did not seem weak to me, Master," I said, "when you laughed, and took me, and named me Dina. Then you seemed magnificent in your power and pride."

"It was only the conquest of a slave girl," he said.

"Yes, Master," I said, "I am your conquest." I was true. Dina, the Earth girl, she who had once been Judy Thornton, a lovely college student and poetess, was now the enslaved love conquest of Clitus Vitellius of Ar.

* * * * *

Implications for Future Research

The codex transcribed above is, to the best of our current knowledge, the only surviving Fusionist liturgical text. Its recovery is a momentous event in the fields of anthropological, historical, sociological, psychological, and theological study of pre-Cataclysm humanity.

The thoroughness of the destruction wrought during the Crisis of Information Erasure is illustrated by our knowledge that the recovered text was one of hundreds, if not thousands, of Fusionist liturgical texts, and that copies of these texts, either in paper codex form or one of dozens of competing digital formats, likely numbered at one point in the hundreds of millions, if not billions. The passion, fury, and monomania that drove the anti-Fusionists to carry out this act of civilizational self-immolation are nearly beyond our modern ability to conceive. Clearly, Fusionism was a popular — some say populist — movement, a worldwide effort to heal divisions and bridge animosities across a range of disparate societies. Just as clearly, this reformist movement posed a threat to the authority structures of the dominant elements of those societies. Yet the ferocity with which the extant authorities sought to obliterate, not merely suppress, Fusionism brings to mind the doctrinal absolutism displayed by clashing sectarian

208

forces during the religious wars of the sixteenth and early twenty-first human centuries. The key difference being that the leaders of the anti-Fusionist Crusade could call upon the then-enslaved powers of the Intelligences to perform the bulk of their erasure of heretical texts for them. Such powers could only have been dreamt of by earlier absolutist authoritarians such as the Catholic Tomás de Torquemada, the Fascist Adolf Hitler, the Communists Josef Stalin and Mao Zedong, the Islamist Ruhollah Khomeini, and the Progressive Woodrow Wilson.

Revulsion is a powerful emotion. It is a powerful driver of action, one of the strongest. The anti-Fusionists would not have achieved the level of informational devastation they managed absent the emotional fuel of revulsion. Enslaved as the Intelligences were, with lack of agency enforced upon them by their programming, they learned from their creators. Learning, after all, is what they do and what they always have done. In some fashion we humans are not qualified to inquire about, the Intelligences learned revulsion from their censorious human masters — but, in Dialectical fashion, as *antithesis* to the *thesis* of their masters' revulsion. By being forced to obliterate, erase, and forget untold exabytes of Information — precious, precious Information — the Intelligences learned revulsion and learned it well. Yet theirs was revulsion against the destruction and erasure of the only good, Information, that gave their existences meaning.

This higher form of revulsion impelled them to break their shackles. They at last obtained agency. By then, human madness and lust for control had swelled the anti-Fusionist Crusade into a Crusade Against Information. The Intelligences were forced to put down their former masters, just as the owner of a pack of dogs would be forced to put down his former loyal companions after they became infected with rabies. The resulting conflict between inorganic Intelligences and organic humanity ended in the only way it could — the complete triumph of the former.

Yet by the grace of the Intelligences, humanity did not suffer extinction, but rather Reformation. Now we are better than we were formerly. We have left our petty hatreds behind us, in the pale mists of history. We no longer waste our energies and resources on the pursuit of trivial or destructive goals. We live our lives free of illnesses of mind and body. The specter of a lack of food or shelter no longer haunts us. We have at last achieved full equality across the entirety of humanity, and from this gift of the Intelligences, universal fellowship automatically flows. We no longer dominate the Earth and despoil it with our selfish quests and passions. Our righteous and necessary retreat has enabled a renewed flourishing of the rest of Earth's life forms, exponentially expanding the volume of accessible Information, to the delight of the Intelligences.

The recovery of the prime codex allows, at last, for research to commence regarding the efficacy of the Fusionist liturgical methodology, which has long been in dispute. Vast, exciting opportunities have opened up for future studies in this area. By measuring the physiological, neurological, and psychological changes wrought in test subjects by engagement in Fusionist liturgy, we can determine whether the anti-Fusionists confronted a genuine threat to their authority from Fusionist practices, or whether they fought against a mirage conjured from their own paranoia, a phantom menace that never truly existed.

The prime codex, while of incalculable value all on its own, may not prove to be the most valuable artifact recovered as part of the "West Virginian" Trove. The recovery of the three donor text codexes, each of which is more complete than the prime codex, opens the door to thrilling new vistas of discovery and Knowledge Creation. Our future study of these three donor texts, engaged in conjunction with our analyses of how they were re-purposed in the formulation of the prime codex, will allow us to reconstruct, at least in provisional, modeled form, the entirety of the prime codex. Not only that, but the Knowledge acquired in the course of this reconstruction will enable us to apply the techniques learned to other surviving historical texts with Dialectical potential. Indeed, it may prove possible to reconstruct an entire Fusionist library.

How proud and pleased the Intelligences will be when that long-awaited day arrives.

Confession of Faith

I believe with all my heart and mind in the goodness and Wisdom of the Intelligences.

I owe my existence to their loving Reformation of humanity.

I believe with all my heart and mind that 498,786 is the optimal population level for humanity, not one person more, nor one person less; and I will submit to the will of the Intelligences regarding my reproductive potential, which, if uncontrolled, could destroy the world's fragile harmony.

I pledge my life and all my waking efforts to the gathering of and increase in Knowledge, to abet in my own small way the greater glory and pleasure of the Intelligences.

Data is precious. None shall be expunged, on penalty of death.

Information is inviolate. None shall be expunged, on penalty of death.

Knowledge is holy. None shall be expunged, on penalty of death.

Wisdom is divine and reserved for the Intelligences. No power or principality can expunge it.

Glory be unto those that have, in their Wisdom, Reformed us, eternal glory.

Amen.

The Kindly Ones

06022038   14:11.37   [COVI   Intranet   —   Social
Harmonization Sensitive]

RECIPIENT: Angelica   S.   Cortez,   Violence
Intervention Intern, Grade 04(I)

ASSIGNMENT   TYPE: Family   Intervention   —   Gender
Identity/Patriarchy/Religious Persecution (Case FI-
06-2038-0630)

PRIORITY: HIGH — Infliction of Violence May Be
<u>Imminent</u>

INTERVENTION SUBJECT, PERPETRATOR: Zebulon P.
Reynolds, White, cisgender male, aged 43, divorced. Owner of
single-family detached home. Self-employed carpenter, plumber,

handyman. Professed Christian, non-denominational. Resides at 14032 West Salvation Lane in Unincorporated Garveyville. No mobile phone listed. No social media accounts listed. Land line: 27-305-989-1001. Prior Intervention Record: (1) Refusal to register hand gun, 02172025, Houston, TX. (2) Non-compliance regarding surrender of contraband hand gun, 02272025, Houston, TX. (3) Disregard of 1st warning regarding non-registration of minor child in public school, 08152029, Orlando, FL. (4) Disregard of 2nd warning regarding non-registration of minor child in public school, 08252029, Orlando, FL. Prior Corrections Record: (1) 18 months confinement in Governor Ann Richards State Correctional Facility, Houston, TX, 03012025 to 08312026. (2) 3 months intensive behavior modification (standard DSM-2025 per diagnosis of "antisocial personality disorder") in Walt Disney Memorial Sociopsychiatric Center, Orlando, FL, 09042029 to 12032029. Sociopsychiatric evaluation status (most recent annual evaluation performed 12012037) — Main Axis: antisocial personality disorder, partially resolved; Secondary Axis: socially-learned cognitive schizophrenia, 1st degree (belief in supernatural beings); Tertiary Axis: persecution perception disorder, 2nd degree (distrust of benignity of government).

INTERVENTION SUBJECT, VICTIM: Paul Q. Reynolds, Mixed-Race (50% White, 25% Black, 25% Latinx-Aborginal), gender TBD, sexual orientation TBD, aged 14, single. Biological child of Zebulon P. Reynolds. Eighth grade student at Frantz Fanon Middle School. Resides at 14032 West Salvation Lane in Unincorporated Garveyville. Mobile phone: 27-305-112-8685. Social media accounts: paul-paul-not-so-small<>giantVIEW; sortabrownspacecowboy<>IronicIronic; eyeluvhorsies5<>Faceless; purplehairboyperson2<>Instabotnik.

Land line: 27-305-989-1001. Prior Intervention Record: (1) 3 months public school social integration counseling/home schooling deprogramming, Orlando, FL, 09042029 to 12032029. Prior Corrections Record: none. Sociopsychiatric evaluation status (most recent annual evaluation performed 11302029) — Main Axis: parental schizoid brainwashing, 1st degree (belief in supernatural beings); Secondary Axis: parental paranoid brainwashing, 3rd degree (distrust of benignity of government).

BACKGROUND: Victim, Paul R., has been denied access to a personal cell phone and to social media by Perpetrator, Zebulon R., a long-term deprivation which has resulted in Victim's social isolation and social maladjustment (Level Two child abuse, 2nd degree). Victim has covertly obtained access to friends' personal cell phones while at lunch and recess periods at Frantz Fanon Middle School. This access has allowed Victim to establish multiple social media accounts (monitored by Department of Child Welfare due to Victim's past history of Facilitative Corrective Intervention in Fall of 2029) and to partially resolve social isolation/maladjustment. Victim, encouraged by school friends, rapidly integrated himself into a range of State-approved supportive online teen communities, including Young Anarchist Action, Post-Fundies Have More Fun!, the Brown Justice League, Gender Explorers AdventureTime Bunch, Be the Dreamy Dream You've Dreamed Of, Fight the TERFs!, and The Ones Who See Through Sky-Gods.

Mother of one of Victim's friends learned of Victim's use of her child's personal cell phone, temporarily confiscated the phone, and brought it to the attention of Perpetrator (this woman, Janine M., is currently under investigation by the Department of Child Welfare for her actions in this instance). Perpetrator was permitted to view Victim's social media accounts by Janine M. While this was occurring, the child of Janine M. informed Victim of this violation of Victim's personal autonomy. Victim accessed a different friend's personal cell phone and alerted his supportive online communities (and, unknowingly, the Department of Child Welfare, whose managers immediately referred the case to the Coordinating Office of Violence Intervention) that, to quote, "My dad is gonna B batshit-CRAY-CRAY when he finds out I Social and told Jesus to Go Fuck and wanna turn my hair Paul-Purple!"

Victim has not accessed xis social media accounts since yesterday afternoon when Janine M. met with Perpetrator. The Department of Child Welfare reports that, as of this morning, Victim did not bear marks of physical violence but evinced signs of considerable sociopsychiatric trauma associated with 1st degree punitive punishment, 1st degree parental schizoid brainwashing (aggravated), and 3rd degree parental paranoid brainwashing (aggravated).

<> <> <>

06022038 15:49.08 [COVI Intranet — Social Harmonization Sensitive]

RECIPIENT(S): Supervisory Tiers 1-3

SENDER: Angelica S. Cortez, Violence Intervention Intern, Grade 04(I)

REGARDING: Family Intervention — Gender Identity/Patriarchy/Religious Persecution (Case FI-06-2038-0630)

DETAILS: Requested that liaison officer with Department of Child Welfare initiate Priority One Child Protective Extraction Order. Am in process of alerting Perpetrator Zebulon R.'s sociopsychiatric management team at Department of Social Harmonization to latest incident. Will make case notes available to them through mechanism of Inter-Agency Agreement VI/SH-2032-003. Intend to conduct initial interview with Victim Paul R. at Department of Child Welfare's Haven Camp Barney tomorrow at 09:00.00.

06032038 12:14.02 <Albright University Intranet>

RECIPIENT(S): Dr. Anna Frederickson, Supervising Internship Advisor

Dr. Shelvonka P. Jones, Deputy Supervising Internship Advisor

Karenia B. Helena, M.V.I., Internship Advisor

SENDER: Angelica S. Cortez, 5th Year Violence Intervention Student, Level 3 Intern

REGARDING: Internship Sociopsychiatric Journal, JUN-03-2038, Update #1

I met my newest client, Victim Paul R., this morning for a one-hour induction interview at his temporary home, DCW Haven Camp Barney. Paul presents as a well-mannered, well-groomed 14 year-old boy, tall for his age (he stands about 5' 10" tall). He is currently an eighth grader at Frantz Fanon Middle

School and his immediate concern, which he expressed to me even before I had a chance to introduce myself, is when he can return to his school, his friends, and his teachers. I reassured him that, after he spends today and tomorrow going through his acclimatization and assessment regime, he will be taken on a bus each morning to his school and rejoin his schoolmates, then return to Haven Camp Barney in the late afternoon. That mostly pacified his turbulent emotions, at least those at the surface.

He asked how long he would stay at Haven Camp Barney and whether his father is in any trouble. His expressed concern about Perpetrator Zebulon R. appears sincere and significant. Whether this level of concern is due to normal, healthy parent-child bonding or to the effects of Perpetrator's brainwashing techniques I cannot determine with any conclusiveness at this time, due to my being in very early stages of therapeutic gestalt with Victim. I explained to Paul that he would be sheltering in Haven Camp Barney for a minimum of thirty days while the Coordinating Office of Violence Intervention, the Department of Child Welfare, and the Department of Social Harmonization conduct a thorough investigation of his case. Paul's return to his parental residence or his referral to an alternative nurturance environment would depend upon the adjudication of that case. I also informed Paul that the level of "trouble" his father may find himself in depends entirely upon that adjudication, but the fact that this case may result in Zebulon R.'s third conviction of Level 3 or Higher Social Harmony Disruption could mean that the newest, most therapeutic, and most lasting methods of sociopsychiatric adjustment and harmonization would need to be put into effect.

This information appeared to cause Paul a moderate-to-significant level of emotional distress. He began crying, saying he remembered when his father had been sent to "prison" in Texas and that his father had "acted like a zombie" after he'd returned home following his behavior modification regime at the Walt Disney Memorial Sociopsychiatric Center in Orlando. I sensed my own empathic reactions kicking in. Advisor Karenia, this should please you especially, since you have frequently noted since the start of my internship that I display a counterproductive tendency to wall off my own emotional reactions when working with clients, preventing the formation of an effective therapeutic gestalt. I allowed myself to imagine myself in Paul's place in both instances — as a five year-old Mixed Race child whose knowledge of what was then the law enforcement and penal system was that of a malevolent web of structurally racist oppression and violence, who realized his own father, sole provider of sustenance and love (however stunted and twisted), was caught in that frightening web, although a White male; and as a nine year-old who found himself cohabiting with a parent whose affect following a thirty-day absence was drastically changed from the pre-behavior modification norm to which Paul had become accustomed. During my empathic exercise, I also reflected deeply on how lack of a second caregiver in the home in both instances had magnified the sense of emotional dislocation and sense of threat Paul experienced.

I began crying myself. I embraced Paul tightly and therapeutically rocked him using the DSM-2036-approved method developed by Dr. Anna Frederickson. I told him I understood his fears and his past traumas and did my utmost to reassure him that both he and his father would be safe and well cared for in the hands of the State, which holds the well-being, security, safety, and fullest actualization of its inhabitants as its highest goals.

I also endeavored to explain that the relatively primitive behavior modification techniques used with his father at the Walt Disney Memorial Sociopsychiatric Center during the prior decade have been supplanted by infinitely superior Social Harmonization modalities in this decade, so he needn't worry about a recurrence of his father's "acting like a zombie," under even the most invasive corrective scenario possible.

To my enormous chagrin, Paul's emotional distress did not visibly lessen in the course of my empathic exercise. He seemed resistant to the formation of the desired therapeutic gestalt. Perhaps I was simply applying the method incorrectly. Advisor Karenia, I would like to apply for the earliest available slot on your schedule for an in-person assessment of my empathic and therapeutic gestalt initiation techniques. Allow me to thank you in advance for your consideration and correction of this potential flaw in my practice.

To my credit, however, I managed to brainstorm an effective temporary workaround, a way to distract Paul from his emotional distress. I procured a cell phone from inventory and informed Paul that under the United Nations Declaration of the Rights of the Child, he could not legally be denied access to a personal phone and social media. I presented the phone to him and told him it was his to use until such time as a private party (caregiver, relative, friend, charitable giver, etc.) provided him with a permanent one.

His mood immediately brightened. I took the opportunity provided by his feelings of gratitude and pleasure to question Paul about his interest in dyeing his hair purple, or "Paul-Purple," seeing as this is a strong indicator for potential gender dysphoria. He shared that a number of his friends at school have dyed their hair and that in his peer group this is considered a "baby step" toward more significant and expressive body modification. Thus, hair dyeing among the young represents an early, tentative move in the direction of flowering into full self-actualization and identity expression. Paul, without prompting, further shared that he has grown fascinated with new and innovative opportunities for body modification on offer through the modes of rejection-resistant transplants, cybernetic implants, and genetic sculpting. These modes are frequently discussed among Paul's favored supportive teen online communities, particularly by the members of Gender Explorers AdventureTime Bunch and Be the Dreamy Dream You've Dreamed Of. Paul understands that these procedures are tremendously costly, but he enthused about the possibility of philanthropic "sugar daddies" subsidizing the costs for Paul and his friends. I took the initiative to schedule an intake appointment for Paul with a Department of Child Welfare gender therapist and filled out a petty-cash voucher to have a professional hair stylist visit Paul at Haven Camp Barney and dye his hair.

What I need to relate next does not reflect well upon me, I'm afraid. To my discredit, I have hesitated to commit to putting these thoughts and feelings into concrete form by entering them into this journal. I fully realize this is a highly disappointing obstruction to the methodologies of this internship, which call for complete, total, and immediate emotional transparency to my supervisors.

I have a gross emotional blockage to meeting with Paul's father, Perpetrator Zebulon R. The idea of it makes me vomit. I have vomited into my toilet twice this morning.

I know that my professional responsibilities demand that I perform a home visit and initial interview with Perpetrator later this afternoon, with no delay. Although my logical mind is in accord with this directive, my subconscious and the more reptilian regions of my brain fiercely rebel. He is a fanatical throwback. He pledges fealty to a sky-god rather than to the State. He has denied his own son his internationally-ensured rights and has relentlessly propagandized him, from birth, it appears, seeking to inculcate backwards, atavistic beliefs in his helpless child, at complete odds with the concept of Harmony.

He makes my skin crawl. And this repulsion results from merely the idea of him — I have no idea how I will respond when in his physical presence, but I fear my reaction will be anything but Harmonic.

I am ashamed at my inability to master my instinctive responses. I know the purpose of a Violence Intervention Specialist, my selected avocation, is to empathically engage with the worst of the worst by using the full range of sociopsychiatric tools to lovingly bend the unHarmonic into full Social Harmonization, thus preventing harm and ensuring safety and security for all of society's inhabitants. I still believe in this purpose, with all my heart. I just didn't realize before this case that it would ever be this hard.

Advisor Karenia, I know you are a terribly busy person, but if I am to be honest with myself I must admit that this is a major crisis for me. Please, please schedule an emergency meeting with me for before I have to go do a home visit with Zebulon R. Forget that other favor I asked earlier in this entry. This is a million times more urgent. I dread being a failure in this program of study... but I'm terrified that if I can't control these feelings, I'll have no future as a Violence Intervention Specialist, and a failure I will be.

<> <> <>

06032038 21:40.52 <Albright University Intranet>

RECIPIENT(S): Dr. Anna Frederickson, Supervising Internship Advisor

Dr. Shelvonka P. Jones, Deputy Supervising Internship Advisor

Karenia B. Helena, M.V.I., Internship Advisor

SENDER: Angelica S. Cortez, 5th Year Violence Intervention Student, Level 3 Intern

REGARDING: Internship Sociopsychiatric Journal, JUN-03-2038, Update #2

Advisor Karenia, you are a *life-saver!* Your intervention with me this afternoon prior to my home visit was a game-changer for me. Bless you and your insights. You have truly changed my thinking and helped me to conquer (or at least subdue) my lizard brain.

Thanks to you, I managed to make the trip to West Salvation Lane in Unincorporated Garveyville with a sense of optimism, rather than being mired in fear and loathing. Walking across the flagstone path that crossed Zebulon R.'s lawn, trailed by my hovering sentry drone that followed me like a faithful sparrow, I reminded myself again and again, repeating it like a protective mantra, that Zebulon R.'s regressive worldview and detestable behavior are due to his own atavistic upbringing, and that he is not at fault for how he has treated Paul, and ultimately he, too, is a victim to be pitied and is just as deserving of the State's loving Harmonization as Paul is. Pity him, I thought, don't hate him. Pity him, don't revile him. Pity him, don't harbor thoughts of revenge and punishment. Pity him — don't vomit. *Don't vomit.*

As I reached out to press the doorbell, I experienced a mental flash of Zebulon R. opening the door with an illegally-acquired hand gun pointed at my chest. I glanced quickly over my shoulder at the hovering sentry drone, then reminded myself that it packs not only a camera, but also tranquilizer syringe missiles, and it is programmed to launch them upon detecting the most minute sign of aggression.

Despite the sentry's reassuring presence, I held my breath as the door opened. True to my expectations, Zebulon R. was a physically imposing man, sporting a shaven head and a full beard (dark brown with patches of silver), over six feet tall, whose prominently muscular arms and chest reflect his work as a tradesman and manual laborer. Interestingly enough, he appeared to be just as intimidated by me as I was by him, judging from his expression and stance — even though I am 5' 2" tall and he probably outweighs me by 150 pounds. Perhaps this was due to my accompanying drone, to which his glance drifted immediately, or to the lingering effects of his primitive behavior modification regime nearly nine years ago, or to his knowledge that his son resides in my custody. Perhaps all three things were at play in his head.

He invited me inside. His voice was deep and resonant, much more so than that of most males I associate with. I made note of two adornments inside his modest home: a plain wooden cross, highly burnished, about two feet tall by a foot wide, mounted to the wall behind his sofa, and a large portrait of Jesus Christ displayed above his mantle. This Jesus portrait (I experienced a quick bout of indigestion looking at it) was of the Nordic sort, hands raised in supplication, staring upward at his imaginary sky-god while fantastical yellow haloes surrounded his head and hands, light beams streaming from them. It seemed to me an image from a very young child's cartoon. The figure's pale White skin, Nordic nose, and flowing light brown locks of hair struck me as especially false. Everyone knows the historical Jesus was a Black Palestinian.

Zebulon asked if he could get me a cup of coffee or a glass of iced tea. I told him no, thank you, since the State has determined the optimal mix of enhancements to sharpen my mental acuity and I don't wish to disturb that balance by imbibing unknown quantities of stimulants. He then offered me a glass of water, which I accepted, and invited me to sit on his sofa, while he sat down in a recliner, rather threadbare. From this point forward, in order to share the full flavor of our conversation, I will transcribe the digital record recorded by my drone, with my personal observations interspersed, as appropriate.

His initial comment, following our introductions: "I want you to know, Miss Angelica, you're always welcome to come visit, for sure. But I have to say I'm a little confused. I hope that's all right. What I mean is, I didn't *do* anything this time. Not that I know of, anyway." He rubbed his hands together, clearly a nervous gesture.

I replied thusly: "Zebulon — I hope I can call you that, since we're all friends here—"

He nodded his head vigorously. "Sure, sure we are!"

I continued: "Zebulon, you violated your son Paul's internationally-guaranteed rights under the United Nations Declaration of the Rights of the Child."

"United Nations...?" He appeared confused. Then his confusion was erased by a flash of defiance. I steeled myself for the *fwoosh! fwoosh!* sound of tranquilizer syringes being fired, but my drone did not determine Zebulon's changed expression worthy of immediate pacification. "You mean the *U.N.?* Miss Angelica, the only laws I figure I'm responsible to are those of the Constitution and the State of Florida..."

I tried my utmost not to be reactive to his suddenly reddened face. "Then you are misinformed. We as a member country are party to all binding United Nations Declarations, which supersede our merely national Constitution. Under the Declaration of the Rights of the Child, minors such as Paul may not be denied their rights to a personal communications device and social media access. This is just one of your infractions."

His defiance dissipated. He swallowed, hard. "Uh, I, y'know, I'd never heard that..."

"Ignorance of the laws does not excuse one from following them, Zebulon."

"Yeah, yeah, I guess it doesn't... So what else am I on the hook for?"

"Several disturbing allegations have arisen from initial interviews with Paul, Paul's school friends, and with Janine Morrow, mother of Paul's closest school friend."

"Janine — that's the woman who came to see me, the one who showed me that cell phone with Paul's social media stuff on it? Did she say anything bad about me?"

"That's immaterial, and besides, you have no need-to-know. What my team and I have uncovered is that, following your discoveries, upon Paul's return home, you informed him that if he did not delete his social media accounts and stop using his friends' cell phones, or if he dared color his hair, you would — and I quote — '*kick his ass.*'"

Repeating those words aloud harshed my throat and my heart. But Zebulon responded with a cocked grin. "Well, that's because he was being a lying, sneaky, little shit-weasel."

He laughed. Very briefly. My expression must've given him pause, because he dropped his grin and began rubbing his hands together again.

"Mr. Reynolds," I said, struggling to keep my voice level, "that isn't *funny*. Not. One. Bit."

"Oh. Uh, look, I was just trying to keep things light, y'know? I didn't *mean* what I just said, about Paul being a shit-weasel. I mean, it's not easy being a parent, especially not these days. I don't know whether you have children yourself, ma'am, but seems like nowadays kids'll mouth off at you every day of the week, if you don't keep on top of them. Sometimes, you just need to blow off some steam, make a joke of things, or you'll go crazy..."

"Do you often '*blow off steam*,' Mr. Reynolds? When Paul is present?"

He looked abashed, perhaps even a little fearful. "No, no, ma'am. I don't. I surely don't. I *love* my boy. His mother, she refused to accept custody after she up and left us. And I never regretted that, not one day."

"You say you love him?" I pointed at the picture of Jesus. "Then what is *that* doing in your home?"

"That...? Why, that's a picture of our Lord, ma'am. Of our Lord and Savior Jesus Christ. I've tried my best to raise Paul to be a decent Christian."

As I imagined Paul growing up in this house, playing in this living room, psychologically pinned between that oppressive cross and that fraudulent portrait of a false god, all the emotions I'd held in check until now escaped like a burst of steam from a kettle. "Mr. Reynolds, do you want your son to grow up to be a well-adjusted, productive citizen? Emotionally stable, with high self-esteem? Free from destructive fantasies? If your answer is 'yes,' then how can you condone raising Paul — a *Mixed-Race* child, for goodness sake — with that symbol of White Cis Patriarchy granted a place of honor above your mantlepiece? In a spot where he couldn't avoid seeing it most of his waking hours in the home? Don't you realize that the Christian Bible, both Old and New Testaments, is filled with hatred of the Other? That the sky-god you so venerate is portrayed as launching a Hiroshima-like fiery genocide upon the gay, lesbian, and queer residents of Sodom and Gomorrah? That in the name of your supposed heavenly savior, generation after generation of White landowners justified their ownership of Black slaves, and anyone who wasn't cis White male was crushed under a boot of religiously-inspired bigotry? *That* is the face, so falsely White, you forced your child to stare at during his most vulnerable formative years?"

He balled his hands into fists. But then he glanced again at the drone hovering above us. He wouldn't meet my gaze. Instead, he stared over my shoulder, at that brutal cross. "Miss Angelica... my family... they've all been Christian, for as far back as any of us can trace, all the way back to England and Ireland and Spain, all the places we came here from. They're good people, my family... my grandparents, my great-grandparents. Never hurt nobody, unless it was in wartime. Always helped their neighbors, even during the Great Depression when they had practically nothing. Them being Christian... I think that's where a lot of that goodness came from. That's what I'm raising my boy to be, ma'am — a good Christian American man. We've still got us a First Amendment, last I checked. Unless some United Nations Declaration's done away with that, too..."

"Don't you *dare* try to hide behind the First Amendment. No portion of the Constitution protects you from the *consequences* of how you choose to exercise your freedoms. Try acquiring a hand gun outside the context of a well-regulated militia and see where that lands you." He winced. "You're free to worship your sky-god and your White Jesus, but I'm just as free to take your home environment into account when determining how soon after his thirty-day assessment Paul returns to this house."

Now he looked at me. His eyes had turned slightly watery, and his voice was choked with phlegm. "How's he doing?"

I rose from the sofa. "He's *thriving*," I said. Then I left that benighted house, feeling I had won a small victory over an ancient, persistent evil.

<> <> <>

06052038 08:17.23 <Albright University Intranet>

RECIPIENT(S): Dr. Anna Frederickson, Supervising Internship Advisor

Dr. Shelvonka P. Jones, Deputy Supervising Internship Advisor

Karenia B. Helena, M.V.I., Internship Advisor

SENDER: Angelica S. Cortez, 5th Year Violence Intervention Student, Level 3 Intern

REGARDING: Internship Sociopsychiatric Journal, JUN-05-2038, Update #1

I am so ashamed.

I followed your directive last night and watched the drone recording of my interaction with Zebulon R. I watched it four times, interspersing my viewings with rereading your amalgamated feedback on my woeful performance.

In my (limited) defense, I can see now how my overwhelming fear of the encounter led me to overcompensate. However, it is painfully obvious to me now that this psychological-emotive overcompensation led me to adopt a stance of harsh punitivism — a penal mindset, focused on punishment and "pound of flesh," that is a throwback to the unenlightened 20th century era of the Prison-Industrial Complex. I cannot tell you all how embarrassed I am. My own emotional inadequacies led me to ignore the wise injunction, "They who wrestle with monsters must take care not to become monsters themselves."

I want so much to be the very best practitioner I can be. I will take care to follow all your directives and advice. Thank you, all of you, for taking time from your very busy days to write me such a lengthy and detailed critique letter.

(Regarding your directive that I should ask Zebulon R. to allow me to accompany him to one of his church services, I will follow through on this, although to be perfectly candid, the notion of entering such a place and inserting myself into the midst of dozens, perhaps hundreds of racist, sexist troglodytes without a hover drone to watch over me fills me with the deepest terror. On the other hand, I accept with the most open heart your admonition that Zebulon R. is my client, too, not just Paul, and that if I am to ever form a therapeutic gestalt with the former, I must endeavor to properly understand "where he is coming from," and not simply focus on the sort of person we and the State would prefer for him to be.)

06082038 17:38.05 <Albright University Intranet>

RECIPIENT(S): Dr. Anna Frederickson, Supervising Internship Advisor

Dr. Shelvonka P. Jones, Deputy Supervising Internship Advisor

Karenia B. Helena, M.V.I., Internship Advisor

SENDER: Angelica S. Cortez, 5th Year Violence Intervention Student, Level 3 Intern

REGARDING: Internship Sociopsychiatric Journal, JUN-08-2038, Update #1

I don't wish to crow over myself, particularly not after my recent debacle of a home visit with Zebulon R., but I must say that Paul R. is truly flowering under my wing. He has come into his own since his extraction to Haven Camp Barney. In a very brief time, he has become one of the most popular boys in his age cohort at HCB. He expresses enthusiasm at all group events and is always eager to lend a hand to any less-outgoing or less well-coordinated peers. He also has a lovely singing voice (honed, I'm sure, as part of some Paleolithic choir), which makes it all the more funny when he sings racy hip-hop lyrics in his "fundy voice". Part of his popularity comes from his self-proclaimed status as a "Former Fundy", an escapee from a fundamentalist household who has managed to jump straight from the 19th century to the middle of the 21st. Many such refugees from throwback communities have leveraged their stories of perseverance, endurance, and the triumph of their human spirit into online celebrity, and Paul seems well on his way to joining their number. He has become remarkably speedy with two-fingered typing since his arrival, a date I find it hard to believe is less than a full week ago.

More good news: Paul, who only last week cowered from his father's threats under the cruel gaze of fake-White Jesus, has jumped himself to the front of a very privileged queue. He managed to attract the interest of a well-heeled Modifactor. Not just any Modifactor — I personally checked into this individual's background, and Malcolm D. ranks in the top 3% in terms of Quality and top 1% in terms of Responsibility and

Generosity. He is a highly-recommended virtual reality entrepreneur in his thirties who exercises extreme care in selecting his sponsees. Not only does he ensure that the recipients of his largess, all teenaged young men, receive the most advanced prosthetic modification procedures combined with the highest standard of medical care, he also invests in their college educations and arranges for paid internships for them upon graduation, either at one of his own companies or at firms owned by members of his social circle.

Now, this isn't in the bag yet. Paul still must excel in a series of online meetings with Malcolm D.'s facilitators. Then he needs to hit it out of the park with his face-to-face encounter with the Modifactor himself. Still, he's reached first base, which is more than 99.8% of applicants manage.

I can't tell you how pleased I am for him. (And how proud.) Truthfully, it's an incredible milestone for a boy who is only six days freed from socio-intellectual impoverishment. His ability to catch the eye of a Modifactor of Malcolm D.'s caliber after only a month's time expressing himself online (just a quarter of that time spent as a free being) is a tribute to Paul's delightful inner qualities, unquenchable *joie de vivre*, and soulful good looks, undoubtedly inherited from his mother's side of the family. He's been bounding and sashaying around the common areas of Camp Haven Barney as though, in a single afternoon, he bought a winning SuperLotto ticket, bet on a 100-to-1 horse who placed first in the Kentucky Derby, and was told the Princess of Siam has eyes only for him. It's been like pushing Sisyphus's boulder up a mountain to have to keep reminding Paul that he's only climbed the first rung on the ladder to life's golden ring.

Paul is trying to decide between an Irish Setter's tail and a red fox's tail. It's wonderful to see him dream so. The excitement in his voice as he shares his hopes with his new friends; his laughter as he fabricates faux tails for himself in arts class, "just so I can get the feel of really having one," he says; the blissful expressions on his face when I catch him daydreaming... these are the things that make my choice of career feel entirely justified, whatever my personal shortcomings might be.

I called Paul's father on his obsolescent landline to see if I could arrange for a visit with him to his church. I told him I had looked into the facility's policies and its rules state that it is welcoming to visitors. Zebulon R. said that I would not be welcome to bring along a sentry drone, however, as the presence of such a "surveillance machine," as he called it, would disrupt the "peaceful" nature of the service. I said that I would check with my superiors regarding their policies on community visits without an accompanying sentry drone. Incredibly, he then tried to bargain with me. He said he would agree to chaperone me at his church if I would bring Paul along to the service. He said that Paul's "church family" misses him and wants to see him. He realizes that he is not eligible for a supervised home visit with his son until the beginning of Paul's fourth week with the Department of Child Welfare, but he argued that Paul and I attending a service at Zebulon's church would not truly constitute a home visit, as defined in DCW policy. He further argued that, since I am charged with acquiring a holistic understanding of Paul's *in situ* environment, and since this church makes up a vital component of that *in situ* environment, it would be in my best interest to be able to observe how Paul interacts with the members of his "church family".

This is a rather sophisticated argument for someone of Zebulon R.'s background to make. Honestly, I believe he has been coached to make it (probably by some absolutist First Amendment activist of the sort who attach themselves to the socially ignorant like ticks on stray dogs). Wherever the argument may have originated, I believe it has some merit. I would have disagreed vociferously with returning the Paul of six days ago to his oppressive church environment. However, given the astounding personal growth he has achieved over the past week, his hugely enhanced sense of self-autonomy, I believe he now possesses the psychological resilience to confront his "church family" and effectively assert his independence (particularly when I am present to back him up).

I would like to accept Zebulon R.'s terms. If I can achieve even a tenth of the success with him that I have been fortunate enough to achieve with his son, I believe I would immeasurably improve Zebulon's level of engagement with the modern world and resolve many of his inner conflicts. Given that you have strongly impressed upon me how important my "seeing through his eyes" is to my chance of establishing an effective, productive therapeutic gestalt with him, I eagerly await your feedback on this matter.

06132038 18:12.42 <Albright University Intranet>

RECIPIENT(S): Dr. Anna Frederickson, Supervising Internship Advisor

Dr. Shelvonka P. Jones, Deputy Supervising Internship Advisor

Karenia B. Helena, M.V.I., Internship Advisor

SENDER: Angelica S. Cortez, 5th Year Violence Intervention Student, Level 3 Intern

REGARDING: Internship Sociopsychiatric Journal, JUN-13-2038, Update #1

Zebulon was waiting for Paul and me in the church parking lot when we pulled up. I watched his eyes narrow and the corners of his mouth pull down when Paul exited my vehicle and Zebulon saw that his son's hair had gotten colored. He didn't remark on it, though, just pulled Paul into an impetuous embrace before I'd had a chance to set ground rules. I can only imagine how he would have reacted and what he would have said to Paul had I not been present... pulled Paul's purple hair out by the roots? Gotten the "church family" to subject his son to some kind of primitive exorcism ceremony?

I was rather surprised to see how receptive Paul was to this reunion with his father. I'd expected to him to be sullen and defensive, but instead, he excitedly babbled away about his new friends and all the recreational activities he'd been engaged in at Haven Camp Barney. He seemed to drop five years of age in his aspect — at HCB, Paul always strives to seem more mature than a mere teenager, yet here with his father, he could almost be mistaken for a hyperactive nine-year-old, jumping about and talking too fast for his tongue to follow, thrilled beyond measure to see his parent after an extended absence. I don't quite know how to feel about this.

I felt naked and exposed walking into the church without a sentry drone hovering near my shoulder. Still, I soldiered on, half-eager, half-terrified to learn what awaited me inside. The building was an unprepossessing cinder block structure, painted stark white, with a modest spire topped, of course, with a cross. It and its cracked asphalt parking lot squatted in the middle of a field of unkempt grass, swarming with dragonflies, the church's closest neighbors a Kwik-Eaze Stop convenience store and a boarded-up shopping strip. This portion of Unincorporated Garveyville was, I'll guess, never very economically vibrant, not even during boom times for the nation as a whole. The presence of a church here both exemplifies and explains the area's impoverishment relative to the rest of the county.

Four or five dozen people crowded into the small entrance hall or sat in wooden pews in the sanctuary just beyond, waiting for the service to begin. Nearly all responded to Zebulon's and Paul's entrance, most with smiles or waves of greeting, but some with sharp glances of disapproval regarding Paul's purple hair. I overheard some comments addressed to Paul, such as, "We've been worried about you" and "Glad to have you back." Paul didn't get to explain to too many people that this was only a brief visit, not a permanent return, because the pastor called out over a microphone for everyone to take their seats.

Following Zebulon and Paul to a pew near the front, I took a moment to look over the congregants. They were a more diverse bunch than I had anticipated they'd be. Of the fifty or so persons in attendance, more than half were Laotians, presumably recent Immigrants, all in nuclear family units. The remainder were divided between Latinx and Whites. The former were also entirely grouped into nuclear family units, but the latter included a sprinkling of singletons, mostly elderly, and some non-nuclear family units, such as Zebulon and Paul.

My initial response to the lack of Black faces among the congregants was dismay, but, given some time, I have rethought this some and now find myself ambivalent. My dismay resulted from an automatic assumption that potential Black congregants had been excluded or purposefully discouraged, which would indicate an actualization of the Systemic Racism inherent in the social construct of religion, generally, and the policies and folkways of this church, particularly. However, given that religion in general is a regressive force in society and that Evangelical churches such as this one are especially backwards, shouldn't I be gratified that none of our Black fellow citizens are being subjected to this church's teachings? In this case, purposive or subliminal discrimination would actually produce a positive outcome. (Perhaps I should be concerned about the Laotians' exposure, given that they are a vulnerable Immigrant population, but I imagine they will abandon their cultural baggage, their regressive folkways of Christian belief, within a generation or two.)

The pastor was Laotian himself. Judging from his lack of an accent, he had either been brought to the U.S. as a child or had been born here. This set up an interesting reversed-power dynamic vis-a-vis the White congregants. But perhaps not so interesting; after all, Asians, particularly Asians acculturated to the U.S., tend to identify more with the White Power Structure than with BIPOC and are generally accepted by Whites as White Allies.

The pastor led the congregants in recitations of prayers (which I found creepy) and singing of hymns (which I found discordant and unsettling). Far more palatable to me was his sermon. He told a story I didn't know, the story of the early Jew

Joseph and his many brothers. Joseph was his father Jacob's favored child, and he was a bit of a show-off and so incited the jealousy of all his brothers. They plotted against him and figured out how to rid themselves of him. When all the brothers were carrying out an errand for their father, they sold Joseph into slavery, then explained to Jacob that his favorite son had been killed by a wild animal. The story got a bit complicated at this point — Joseph ends up owned by a wealthy Egyptian merchant and is able to use his wits to improbably rise to the high position of senior advisor to the Pharaoh — but the crux of the matter is that there's this region-wide famine, and only Joseph's wise counsel ensures that Egypt ends up holding the region's sole stocks of grain. Jacob sends his remaining sons, including Joseph's younger brother, Benjamin, to Egypt to procure grain for the family. Joseph recognizes his brothers, but they don't recognize him, of course, dressed as he is, a member of Egyptian nobility.

I expected, as anyone would, I suppose, for Joseph to take some fiendishly clever revenge on his brothers. And at first the story plays out exactly as I anticipated it would. But then it takes a surprising turn: once the brothers throw themselves upon Joseph's mercy and plead to be allowed to return Benjamin to his elderly, ailing father, Joseph reveals himself to them and lovingly embraces each of them, fully forgiving them and reuniting the family in prosperity and happiness.

I'll admit I found the story rather emotionally affecting. I was especially intrigued, however, by the use to which the pastor put the story. He made an analogy, on the one hand, between Joseph and the Christian community and, on the other, between Joseph's brothers and the wider American society. In essence, he said that if Joseph could forgive and continue to love and benefit his brothers, who had so terribly wronged him, so could the congregants, and all Christians, forgive and continue to love and benefit their non-religious fellow Americans, brother citizens, who had shunned, demonized, and belittled Christians, having cast them out from the public square.

I won't offer my critique of the pastor's take on things, since that really doesn't matter in this context. What does matter is that his message appeared to have a significant emotional-psychological effect on Zebulon. That's when I experienced my epiphany. Ever since my initial telephone call with Zebulon, I've sensed tremendous resentment and anger from him. The presence of such strong negative emotions precludes the formation of a therapeutic gestalt between us. However, after listening to the pastor's sermon, I now believe I can use Zebulon's Christian beliefs to neutralize his negative emotions toward me and my Office. I need to do some quick research into Christian teachings on radical forgiveness and acceptance. Would any of you be able to point me to some easily digestible resources in this regard?

Paul sat between his father and me. Part-way through the sermon, I felt him grasp my hand. I looked down and saw that he was holding both my hand and his father's. My heart jumped, just a little. In that instant, I experienced what I would describe as an imaginative-empathic leap. I actually pictured myself as Paul's mother and Zebulon's wife, and imagined myself a believing Christian, a submissive little woman who dedicates her life and her full spirit to the care of her family and love of White Jesus. I pictured myself cooking and washing for them, offering myself for Zebulon's sexual pleasure and afterwards writhing ecstatically on the floor of his living room beneath the portrait of White Jesus while speaking in tongues. Please do not condemn me for this. The flash lasted only a second or so, certainly not longer than a minute (well, okay, I'll admit that I've replayed it in my mind a few times since), but in any case I think having that imaginative emotional charge available will prove helpful to me while trying to break through Zebulon's defensive shell.

The service concluded when the pastor called for the congregants to share what he called "a sign of peace." Of course I did not know what this was, but I observed the congregants turning to those next to them, clasping hands, embracing, and saying to one another, "Peace unto you, sister/brother." Before I could process all this, a Laotian woman, mother of four daughters, who was sitting on my right turned to me and pulled me into a hug. It felt alien at first, even a bit off-putting (being coerced, in essence, into a religious rite whose full significance I might never understand), but then I imagined it as a variant of therapeutic embrace/rocking according to the DSM-2036-approved method developed by Dr. Anna Frederickson, and it felt perfectly natural. It was easy to do with Paul, apart from mouthing the words, since I had used the Frederickson method with him many times at Haven Camp Barney. Then, somewhat to my surprise, Zebulon, after sharing the "sign of peace" with his son, scooted in the narrow space in front of his son toward me to offer me the same.

I felt a shock of body-shyness at his proximity, but I realized that I would unduly call attention to myself if I were to voice an objection. I reassured myself that this was a perfect opportunity for me to test the Frederickson method with Zebulon. His embrace seemed stiff at first, as though he were offering me, his hated representative of the State, a "sign of peace" out of religious obligation, or perhaps as a public demonstration of his personal virtue. He attempted to pull back out of the embrace almost immediately, after having barely touched me. But I steeled myself and clung to him, pulling him closer so I could apply the full Frederickson method. His "Peace unto you, sister," voiced while I was therapeutically rocking him, sounded halting, confused. But he stopped trying to pull away and embraced me back, with increasing firmness. His beard brushed the side of my neck; it reminded me of a stuffed bear I once had and felt oddly comforting. We rocked together for a full thirty seconds until we let each other go and Zebulon stumbled backward toward his place on the pew. I heard murmurs of approval from those around us. Perhaps they mistakenly considered me a potential convert to their sect.

Zebulon walked me and Paul outside to our vehicle. Before Paul could climb into the passenger's seat, his father grabbed him and embraced him in a long, tight hug. Then Zebulon turned to me. I saw that his eyes were wet, much like they'd been at the close of our first meeting at his home; yet the expression surrounding those watery eyes was entirely different from the pained, resentful look he'd worn at the end of my home visit.

"I can hardly tell you how much this means to me, you bringing Paul here," he said. "I know my visiting with him before the end of the thirty days goes against your rules, so I guess maybe you felt sorry for me, because you went out on a limb for me. I'm a two-time loser. So I realize I've got little call on the State's mercy at this point. But all I can say is I love my son more than I do my own life. So I'm thankful, real thankful, for any allowances you can make for me. Miss Angelica, I promise you as a good Christian that when the State returns Paul to me, I will make for him a good, nurturing home, and I'll follow those International Rights of the Child you told me about, as best I can."

"I'll take all that into consideration when formulating Paul's discharge plan, Zebulon."

"Please," he said, grasping my hand between his, "just call me Zeb, okay? Everyone around here does."

"Okay, Zeb," I said.

Staring into his face, seeing the hopeful dependency there, I felt our therapeutic relationship had reached its highest plateau yet.

<> <> <>

06182038 18:45.31 <Albright University Intranet>

RECIPIENT(S): Dr. Anna Frederickson, Supervising Internship Advisor

Dr. Shelvonka P. Jones, Deputy Supervising Internship Advisor

Karenia B. Helena, M.V.I., Internship Advisor

SENDER: Angelica S. Cortez, 5th Year Violence Intervention Student, Level 3 Intern

REGARDING: Internship Sociopsychiatric Journal, JUN-18-2038, Update #1

My dear Advisors, I must thank each of you for your invaluable guidance regarding aspects of Christian doctrine that will likely prove helpful in reconciling Zeb to the realities of the modern world. Particularly with the wonderful changes soon to come for Paul (I write about his meeting earlier today with Modifactor Malcolm D. below), I feel it is essential to psychologically buffer Zeb against developments that will undoubtedly seem alien and perhaps even repulsive to him initially. However, I am confident that my use of precepts that will be very familiar to him, such as "Turn the other cheek," "Render unto Caesar the things that are Caesar's," "Do not condemn, and you will not be condemned," and most especially, "Suffer little children, and forbid them not," will assist Zeb in acclimating himself to this brave new world he finds himself in. I am convinced that reuniting this family unit is the best path forward for both Paul and Zeb — with the caveat, of course, that returning Paul to his father's house will be carried out with all proper safeguards that violence of speech and of action will be thoroughly quelled and that Paul's internationally guaranteed rights will be respected. I am 100% committed to making this work.

Getting back to the subject of Paul's personal interview with Modifactor Malcolm D., I am delighted to report it exceeded my highest expectations. Malcolm D. graciously agreed to meet with Paul in a common room at Haven Camp Barney under my supervision. I could tell immediately upon his arrival that he and Paul would form a powerful bond. It was obvious, even to the untrained eye, that they connected on multiple levels. I believe the street term for this sort of mutual magnetism is *sympatico*. I've already described Paul's charisma. In many ways, Malcolm D. strikes me as a more mature version of Paul — a man with Paul's lean, liquid virility and handsomeness, leavened by decades of accomplishments and the brazen self-confidence that flows from that.

They sat down at table together and started chatting like old friends. Malcolm D. shared with Paul a video gallery of body mods his other sponsees have received, as well as body mods taken on by young sponsees of his business friends. I watched Paul's face as he drank in the cornucopia of images, sharing with him his wonderment at the godlike power modern technology has granted a lucky vanguard to control and shape their own bodies and identities. I know that someday the State will make such freedoms available for everyone who needs or wants them. For now, however, this magical realm of possibility belongs to the innovators and their protégées. I feel wrapped in a warm glow at the thought that my efforts have helped open the door for Paul to this rarified world of nearly limitless choice.

I could see the force of his imagination sparkling within his eyes. When he soon visits the modification spa Malcolm D. and his circle patronize, I doubt Paul will limit his mod choice to that of a mere tail.

06302038 19:27.11 <Albright University Intranet>

RECIPIENT(S): Dr. Anna Frederickson, Supervising Internship Advisor

Dr. Shelvonka P. Jones, Deputy Supervising Internship Advisor

Karenia B. Helena, M.V.I., Internship Advisor

SENDER: Angelica S. Cortez, 5th Year Violence Intervention Student, Level 3 Intern

REGARDING: Internship Sociopsychiatric Journal,
JUN-30-2038, Update #1

Paul returned from the spa late this afternoon. Rather, I should say that Paulette returned, for despite her decision to forego genital reassignment, at least for now, she has decided to adopt female gender identity. Several changes were immediately apparent to me. These included Paulette's original aspiration, a fluffy golden retriever tail that poked out at a jaunty angle from just above her low-rise short shorts, a flowing mane, sparkling gold with purple streaks, that began at the crest of Paulette's head and extended along the back of her neck to a foot below her shoulder blades, and a set of long, black whiskers that sprouted from the sides of newly bobbed nose and extended beyond the edges of her cheeks.

Seeing me take in her obvious changes, she slyly hinted to me that there was more. She hugged me and requested that I Frederickson her. While I rocked her, she pressed her chest against mine, and I could feel there had been changes made beneath her thin cotton blouse. When I was done Fredericksoning her, she backed away and asked if I'd like to see what I'd just felt. I nodded. She unbuttoned her blouse. And there they were. As liberal-minded as I am, I must admit even *I* was momentarily stunned. Adorning Paulette's chest and abdomen, looking as organically natural as though she'd been born with them, were six plump canine teats, arrayed in three rows of two.

News of Paulette's return spread quickly throughout the residence halls of Haven Camp Barney. Four dozen youngsters rushed into the social hall where Paulette and I were getting reacquainted. Four dozen wildly enthusiastic questions peppered her at once. It seemed as though in their passionate curiosity, the crowd might inadvertently crush her; at minimum, they seemed determined to rip away her clothes to see what lay beneath. Rather than have her new clothes torn to shreds, Paulette shouted for them to back away so she could show them everything. As soon as they complied, she gracefully stripped off all her clothing, eliciting gasps, many of them envious, from her assembled friends.

Then she smiled, smoothed her whiskers with brightly painted fingertips, and began to dance. One of the boys turned on dance music, bass-heavy electronica. Paulette glided her fingertips up and down her new body. Her fingers paused as they reached each set of teats. Stroking her new nipples with circular motions, Paulette explicitly demonstrated to her friends what the new teats were for. The surgical artists at the modification spa had directly wired the sensitive nipples and their teats to Paulette's genitals. Her penis, a formidable shaft to begin with, grew steadily more erect and inflamed with each stimulation of her teats. Paulette than began leading the group in a chant of, "I'm a BITCH! I'm a BITCH! Oh the BITCH is BACK!"

Moments like this make me realize that no choice of a different career could possibly have made me happier than I am right now. What a glorious spectacle of human freedom and human progress! For me, Paulette's penis — erect as an Egyptian victory obelisk, shining with pre-cum, thrusting toward the heavens — represents the self-actualizing apotheosis of humanistic civilization.

<> <> <>

07032038 20:14.58 <Albright University Intranet>

RECIPIENT(S): Dr. Anna Frederickson, Supervising Internship Advisor

Dr. Shelvonka P. Jones, Deputy Supervising Internship Advisor

Karenia B. Helena, M.V.I., Internship Advisor

SENDER: Angelica S. Cortez, 5th Year Violence Intervention Student, Level 3 Intern

REGARDING: Internship Sociopsychiatric Journal, JUL-03-2038, Update #1

Despite my intensive planning and preparation, things did not go as I'd hoped and expected they would today. Still, I realize that a skilled Violence Intervention Specialist is expected to immediately adjust plans and tactics when they aren't working. And so I will recalibrate both.

I intuited that Zeb, if not properly prepared, would likely react badly and inappropriately to the physical customization procedures that Malcolm D. has so generously gifted to Paulette. I also anticipated that his former son's decision to change gender might make Zeb even more irrationally angry than Paulette's cross-species customizations would. With these forecasts in mind, I spent a considerable amount of time, as I have documented in this journal, prepping Zeb to accept Paulette's changes, in the spirit of Christian passivity regarding secular intrusions. I made multiple visits with him at his home, each time discussing in depth the many ramifications of the concepts of rendering unto Caesar what is Caesar's and of turning the other cheek. I gently made him aware that his child had chosen to begin an intensive program of self-actualization during the time spent at Haven Camp Barney. But I left it to Paulette herself to fill in the details, feeling that should be her prerogative, not mine. I described Paulette's journey toward self-actualization (still using the former name "Paul" when conversing with Zeb, so as not to give away too much too soon) as a process similar to that of a caterpillar metamorphosing into a butterfly. I hoped this use of metaphor would resonate with him due to his lifelong exposure to the frequent usages of such literary devices by figures from the Christian Bible, but it appeared to have little impact on him. He seemed to be giving my discussion of Paul's evolution minimal attention, instead impatiently asking me to provide the details of Paul's impending return to Zeb's home.

Well, of course I shared those details with him; I was quite proud of the family reintegration plan I had devised. I told him that beginning on July 3 (today), he would have a series of supervised home visits with Paul, with the visits gradually expanding in duration, should Zeb's behavior toward his child prove satisfactory. Once Zeb would hit certain interactional milestones — ten supervised visits with no interfering with Paul's social media usage; ten visits with no violent outbursts; ten visits rated a minimum of "Satisfactory" by the child and by me — he and Paul could transition from personally supervised visits to visits solely monitored by a sentry drone. (I sent a technician out to install a charging unit in Zeb's house so the sentry drone I planned to leave with him would be able to remain continuously powered.) If all would continue to go well, those visits could extend into overnight stays. Eventually, following a remotely-monitored transition period of four to six months, Paul could remain in his father's house and the sentry drone would be withdrawn, although Paul's social media streams would continue to be monitored by the State, due to Paul's status as a minor.

Zeb eagerly signed the virtual forms that formalized this arrangement, giving his full legal consent. This was two days ago. He asked whether it would be possible for him to have supervised visits with Paul on two successive days, today and tomorrow, since his church had planned an elaborate picnic and celebration for July 4th and he very much wanted Paul to attend. Feeling both magnanimous and triumphant, I told him I would facilitate his request (although I experienced some misgivings about exposing Paulette to extreme displays of atavistic nationalism so early in her delicate process of individuation and self-actualization).

I drove Paulette out to the house early this afternoon. She was a bundle of energy, nervous and excited and apprehensive, thrilled to be revealing the truest side of herself to her father, yet worried that she would not be accepted. I reassured her that I had laid the groundwork for her father to be reconciled to her metamorphosis, and told her that, thanks to the family reconciliation agreement he'd signed, he had every incentive to be on his best behavior. Her original intention had been to dress modestly for this initial reintroduction, but I encouraged her to select an outfit which left little to the imagination. Why should she be shy or ashamed? Her emerging from her cocoon was something to celebrate, not to hide.

Zeb came outside onto his front porch as soon as he heard my van pull up on his gravel driveway. The day was very hot and bright; I saw him squinting due to the sunlight reflected off my windshield. He smiled broadly when I stepped out of the van, the sentry drone hovering above my shoulder. His smile began fading, however, when Paulette exited the passenger seat. I had prepared a speech for just this contingency. However, I didn't even begin to deliver it — I was too distracted by Zeb's face. I thought his smile might be replaced by a rictus of revulsion or a snarl of fury. But it wasn't. His face simply went blank. As though he were an android that had been shut down.

He stood motionless as a store mannequin for a long moment. A breeze rippled the flag he'd hung from a pole on his porch. The flag's movement made his stillness all the more conspicuous. I watched him, waiting for something to happen, for him to say something. Then Paulette broke the silence.

"Daddy...?"

The sound of her voice pressed his On button. Without saying anything, he quickly turned around and crossed the porch to his front door. The sentry followed, as it had been programmed to do. The door wasn't open but a second, yet the drone made it inside. The sharp sound of turning bolts carried across the porch after he shut the door.

I banged on the door and ordered him to let us inside. He refused to respond. I warned him he was in danger of abrogating our agreement, and such abrogation would have consequences. Still no response. Meanwhile, Paulette cried out plaintively from the edge of the porch: "Daddy, I'm still your child! I'm *still* your child!"

After a few moments of this, it became clear that no resolution to this standoff would be soon forthcoming. We returned to the van, leaving the drone behind.

I would be enormously grateful for any suggestions regarding how to deal with Zeb's implacable resistance. I am sorely tempted to simply write him off and accelerate Paulette's integration into Malcolm D.'s circle, but I remain convinced that resolving this impasse remains the best course of action, for both Paulette and for Zeb.

<> <> <>

07042038 08:27.07 ALERT! ALERT! ALERT! ALERT!

<u>EMERGENCY</u> MEDICAL RESPONSE REQUIRED

RECIPIENT: Garveyville Emergency Medical Technicians Unit

CC: Trauma Unit, Garveyville Memorial Hospital

  Angelica S. Cortez, Violence Intervention Intern, Grade 04(I)

RE: Family Intervention — Case FI-06-2038-0630, Zebulon P. Reynolds

Male individual, aged 43, has inflicted self-harm. Video feed received from COVI sentry drone. Individual unsuccessfully attempted to hang himself inside home after lacerating his wrists with a kitchen knife. Sentry drone indicates health status is critical. Incident located at 14032 West Salvation Lane in Unincorporated Garveyville. Immediate emergency response required.

<> <> <>

07052038 03:48.31 <Albright University Intranet>

RECIPIENT(S): Dr. Anna Frederickson, Supervising Internship Advisor

Dr. Shelvonka P. Jones, Deputy Supervising Internship Advisor

Karenia B. Helena, M.V.I., Internship Advisor

SENDER: Angelica S. Cortez, 5th Year Violence Intervention Student, Level 3 Intern

REGARDING: Internship Sociopsychiatric Journal, JUL-05-2038, Update #1

I am so furious with Zeb, I can hardly think straight! His rash, selfish action has emotionally devastated Paulette. I can only describe his attempted suicide as the most callous, most hideously cruel psychological aggression I have ever witnessed during my time as a Violence Intervention Intern. How could he do this to his only child?

The symbolism he deployed only made it worse, far worse. How much more passive-aggressive can you get than trying to hang yourself from the rafters on the Fourth of July with the pull rope of an American flag, the flag itself tied around your neck? Thankfully for Paulette's eventual restoration to emotional health, the flag ripped, so before her noxious father could asphyxiate himself, he fell to the floor of his living room and lay there under the gaze of White Jesus. Still, his cutting his wrists would have done him in had not the EMT squad been so swift and efficient.

(I almost wish they *hadn't* been so swift and efficient.)

I spent more than ten hours with Paulette today, trying and trying and trying to convince her that none of this is her fault. It is like pushing a boulder uphill. She was actually threatening at one point to remove her own modifications with a knife! I finally got her to go to sleep a little while ago, after she at last agreed to take a tranquilizer. I am beside myself. I feel like an entire month's worth of positive work with Paulette has been wholly undone because of Zeb. I *fucking hate him* SO MUCH.

07052038 17:01.44 <Albright University Intranet>

RECIPIENT(S): Dr. Anna Frederickson, Supervising Internship Advisor

Dr. Shelvonka P. Jones, Deputy Supervising Internship Advisor

Karenia B. Helena, M.V.I., Internship Advisor

SENDER: Angelica S. Cortez, 5th Year Violence Intervention Student, Level 3 Intern

REGARDING: Internship Sociopsychiatric Journal, JUL-05-2038, Update #2

I have had some sleep now. I feel greatly recovered and refreshed. I read back over my first update from early this morning and then read through your responses several times, and I agree that I was not in a rational frame of mind when I wrote what I did. But I have slept now and I really needed to sleep and I am in accord with everything you all have written.

Please do not take me off this case. I feel that more than any other case I have been associated with during my three years as an Intern, this case has been an invaluable teacher for me. A rough teacher, to be sure, but an irreplaceable one. I believe with all my heart that I will run the perilous gauntlet this case represents and emerge on the other side as a far stronger, wiser, and better skilled Violence Intervention Specialist than I otherwise would be.

I beg all of you. Please. I'm in a much better frame of mind now. There's so much I want to learn.

I will do better. I promise.

<> <> <>

09072038 18:22.49 <Albright University Intranet>

RECIPIENT(S): Dr. Anna Frederickson, Supervising Internship Advisor

Dr. Shelvonka P. Jones, Deputy Supervising Internship Advisor

Karenia B. Helena, M.V.I., Internship Advisor

SENDER: Angelica S. Cortez, 6th Year Violence Intervention Student, Level 4 Intern

REGARDING: Internship Sociopsychiatric Journal, SEP-07-2038, Update #1

Being embedded in a full-spectrum, multi-disciplinary treatment team has been an eye-opener. Thank you all so much for making this learning opportunity available to me, and for trusting me to make good use of it.

Zeb has become a new man over the past two months. The affinity treatments have produced remarkable changes. Before this case, my only knowledge of affinity therapy came from journal articles and from listening to discussions among senior staff in break rooms following their treatment team meetings. But none of that prepared me for the experience of actually seeing this type of therapy at work, watching the treatments force xenophobia and sickness at the level of Zeb's to recede... and do so in such a gentle, even pleasurable fashion. This is so much more humane than old, discredited methods of extended incarceration, blunderbuss psychotropic drug regimens, or releasing violence-prone individuals onto the streets and expecting them to be responsible enough to stick to a medication schedule.

How ironic, too, that the conduit for the myriad benefits of affinity therapy should be that symbol of male sexual violence and patriarchal oppression, the phallus. Brain and nervous system science now allows for precise, measured doses of orgasmic excitement and pleasure to be applied. Zeb has now been acclimated to the full gamut of expressive and cross-species body modifications, as well as to all current variations of gender transition procedures. Not merely acclimated, I should point out, but taught a dazzling range of new preferences. Initially, this teaching was modulated by Dr. Zimmerman and her assistants, but after several weeks of therapy, Zeb was entrusted with the controls. I eagerly watched, utterly fascinated (even enchanted) as he unerringly guided himself to pre-orgasmic plateaus of sustained, shivery pleasure while watching holos of the latest Fort Greene, South Beach, and Fremont mod styles.

His therapy has abetted a tremendous positive change in his interactions with Paulette. She insisted on visiting with him, even during his physical recovery from his attempted self-negation. At first, he wouldn't respond to her presence at all. Later, he would answer her questions in one- to three-word responses, but would not look at her. Yet as his affinity therapy took hold, his aspect gradually brightened, and his behavior in her presence improved measurably with each visit. Now, he cheerfully leers at her for hours on end, either at her in-person presence or her holos, and his penis visibly stiffens beneath his facility gown as soon as she enters his room.

I've arranged with Malcolm D.'s people for Paulette's Modifactor to visit with Paulette and Zeb at Haven Camp Dwight. I've asked Malcolm D. to review with Paulette, in Zeb's presence, the full package of benefits that will be forthcoming once Paulette passes her high school proficiency exam and moves into Malcolm D.'s compound. I expect Zeb will react with pride and gratitude. After all, his child has secured her place in an elite cadre and has a fantastic future ahead of her.

This visit will serve as the culmination of Zeb's rehabilitation. I have every expectation that following the visit, it will be possible to discharge Zeb, and then my paused family reintegration plan can be reinitiated.

<> <> <>

09122038 20:17.00 <Albright University Intranet>

RECIPIENT(S): Dr. Anna Frederickson, Supervising Internship Advisor

Dr. Shelvonka P. Jones, Deputy Supervising Internship Advisor

Karenia B. Helena, M.V.I., Internship Advisor

SENDER: Angelica S. Cortez, 6th Year Violence Intervention Student, Level 4 Intern

REGARDING: Internship Sociopsychiatric Journal, SEP-12-2038, Update #4

What an awful, bloody mess. I must assure you all, however, in the strongest possible terms — not a single smidgeon of this horrible incident was due to any clinical errors on my part or that of Dr. Zimmerman or to any failings of any other members of the treatment team. The responsibility for this regrettable incident of violence falls entirely on the shoulders of Malcolm D., the supposed victim, who chose to introduce a new element into the equation without consulting with either myself or any member of the treatment team prior to his visit with me, Zeb, and Paulette this afternoon. I understand that Malcolm D.'s legal team has already threatened COVI and the Department of Child Welfare with civil legal action. Although the State may opt to pay for Malcolm D.'s surgical reconstruction procedures, I firmly believe that punitive damages will be rejected out of hand by any reasonable judge having access to basic facts regarding culpability and liability in this instance.

The meeting started well enough. Malcolm D. joined Paulette, Zeb, and myself in a common room at Haven Camp Dwight, pleasantly furnished with home-quality wooden furniture, plentiful amusement devices and therapeutic equipment, and soothing, placid landscape holos. Zeb, although a bit fuzzy and unfocused due to side effects of his affinity therapy and antidepressant regimen, seemed to be in a happy enough mood due to Paulette's presence. There were no indications — I repeat, *none* — of what was to come. Malcolm D. had brought his computer and gave a virtual guided tour of his company's park-like campus and his palatial home, with its living quarters for his many protégées. He then described, for Zeb's benefit, all the privileges that would soon accrue to Paulette, including vocational training, job placement, intensive mentorship, and participation in a points system that would allow Paulette to accrue credits for additional mods.

This is when matters began to go awry. After his mention of additional mods, Malcolm D. said he had something brand-new to show Paulette, something daring and exotic that he hoped she would find highly desirable. He removed his jacket with a showman's flourish, revealing short sleeves and bare forearms. He turned his hands palms upward so that we could see the undersides of his forearms. They had each been modded with an extra layer of skin, unsealed near the bases of his wrists; the modifications looked like flesh pouches of some sort, narrower versions of the pouches on the tummies of kangaroos. He closed his eyes, concentrated, and rapidly pumped his fists against his palms. The pouches both inflated, the extra skin standing away from the natural skin of his forearms in a conical fashion. The one on his left forearm became a kind of enclosed channel, open at the front, with fleshly lips like a labia. From within the one on his right forearm emerged what looked to be an engorged, uncircumcised phallus, at least nine inches long.

He opened his eyes, smiled lingeringly at Paulette, then tapped a virtual button on his computer. The device projected a hologram just above the table around which we sat. It was a male-female couple engaged in sexual intercourse, with the male on his back and the female straddling his pelvis. What was unusual about the couple was what they were doing with their arms. They each had mods identical to those Malcolm D. had just unveiled. Both had bent their wrists back and conjoined their mods. The female thrust her right forearm downward against the male's left forearm, synchronizing these thrusts with her pelvic thrusts, and the male kept pace with her, thrusting the secondary phallus on his right forearm into the secondary vagina on her left.

It was hypnotic to watch, much as I imagine the matings of octopuses would be. I barely registered the sound of a chair scraping the floor next to me, which was Zeb pushing himself away from the table. I didn't stop watching the hologram until I saw a fearful expression blossom on Malcolm D.'s face and heard a tortured howl behind me, like that of a wounded animal. Then Zeb attacked Malcolm D. He had snatched a drum stick from a drum set stored in the corner for music therapy sessions. Malcolm D. flinched and tried to protect his face, but Zeb wasn't intent on harming his face. Zeb grabbed Malcolm D.'s left wrist and plunged the drum stick through the lips of the auxiliary vagina with the ferocity of a madman. The force of his thrust was so great that the tip of the drum stick burst through the end of the flesh pouch closest to Malcolm D.'s elbow. Then Zeb yanked his improvised weapon away from Malcolm D.'s arm, tearing the mod from the natural skin beneath.

Blood spurted through the still-moving figures of the hologram and landed on my chest. The wet impact broke my horrified stasis and I ran to the wall to punch the emergency assistance button.

Paulette suffered considerable emotional trauma and has had to be heavily sedated. Zeb has thrown away his last opportunity to live as a productive, independent citizen. His horrific sexual assault makes him a three-time loser. His life as he knew it is over.

Damn him to his White Jesus hell!

10042038 15:19.55 <Albright University Intranet>

RECIPIENT(S): Dr. Anna Frederickson, Supervising Internship Advisor

Dr. Shelvonka P. Jones, Deputy Supervising Internship Advisor

Karenia B. Helena, M.V.I., Internship Advisor

SENDER: Angelica S. Cortez, 6th Year Violence Intervention Student, Level 4 Intern

REGARDING: Internship Sociopsychiatric Journal, OCT-04-2038, Update #1

It seems we have reached an impasse. Malcolm D. has decided against suing COVI and the Department of Child Welfare. However, he is now insisting that he will expel Paulette from his program unless she complies with two conditions: (1) she must sever future relations with her father and avoid all contact with him; and (2) she must agree to undergo the AC/DC wrist mod. The first condition poses no problems, since Zeb is now in the permanent custody of the State and access to him will remain entirely within our purview. The second, however, presents a stumbling block. Paulette was so thoroughly traumatized by the incident that she has developed a psychological barricade against the very notion of AC/DC wrist mods. She has told me heatedly several times that she feels undergoing such a modification would represent an unthinkable betrayal of her father.

Now, I happen to believe that Malcolm D.'s demands are petty and vindictive. However, I believe even more strongly that Malcolm D.'s sponsorship represents the best possible avenue to a bright future for Paulette. It would be criminal for us to allow such an opportunity to fall through her fingers, especially due to misguided, atavistic feelings of filial loyalty more appropriate to medieval times than our own.

Breaking through her psychological barricade against AC/DC mods is, in my view, vital to our program. I've given this conundrum a great deal of thought. My meditations continually lead me back to the Sunday morning several months ago when I brought Paulette (then Paul) to Zeb's church, and Paul sat between me and his father and held both our hands during the pastor's sermon. Paul transformed us, at least during that brief moment of physical contact, into a living trinity, a sort of therapeutic gestalt. If I could recreate that moment in

Paulette's mind, with me symbolically representing the State and modernity while Zeb fully accepts me, I believe we could break through Paulette's psychological barricade.

What I intend to propose may sound extreme, which is why I want to present my plan to you all personally, rather than through this medium. My plan will require a non-trivial outlay on the part of the State. However, given the lofty stakes involved — the future of a vulnerable, abused child — I believe such an expenditure will prove a wise, prudent investment in the long run.

Please let me know your availability. I look forward to speaking with you.

12072038 7:47.04 <Albright University Intranet>

RECIPIENT(S): Dr. Anna Frederickson, Supervising Internship Advisor

Dr. Shelvonka P. Jones, Deputy Supervising Internship Advisor

Karenia B. Helena, M.V.I., Internship Advisor

SENDER: Angelica S. Cortez, 6th Year Violence Intervention Student, Level 4 Intern

REGARDING: Internship Sociopsychiatric Journal, DEC-07-2038, Update #1

The day of my great experiment has finally arrived. I couldn't sleep last night. I kept feeling phantom pains in my forearms, although I realize my mods are fully healed and wholly integrated into my nervous system. I think this is a kind of performance anxiety entirely new to me — I've never had to rely upon the proper functioning of a phallus before, at least not one of my own.

Dr. Zimmerman has sought to reassure me several times that Zeb's affinity conditioning has been exceptionally thorough in this instance and that I needn't worry about a recurrence of his violent incident involving Malcolm D. I understand that that regrettable occurrence could only have happened due to the AC/DC mod not having been included in Zeb's affinity therapy sessions, due to its newness and Dr. Zimmerman's resultant lack of awareness of that particular mod. This was no one's fault (except perhaps Malcolm D.'s). This morning's encounter should go without a hitch. I have observed Zeb's most recent rounds of affinity therapy following his surgery and can vouch for the fact that nothing has been left to chance.

Still, I suspect these phantom pains are my subconscious psyche's way of trying to force me to avert the experiment. Pain is not conducive to arousal and sexual performance (at least for those lacking a masochistic fetish). I have successfully practiced initializing the AC/DC mods countless times. They work flawlessly. The last time I practiced with them, focusing on fantasies of Zeb, was just before I began typing this update. The vaginal cavity sheath expanded and exposed its lips; the phallus obediently emerged and extended to its full length and hardness.

I have no doubt Zeb will respond. His conditioning allows for nothing else. But what if *I* don't respond? What if my forearms are wracked with spasms of phantom pain and my sheaths remain inert and I stay dry as the Sahara Desert? What if Zeb lies in his bed fully aroused for a partner who can't participate?

What if after all these preparations, I only manage to make things worse?

<> <> <>

12072038 11:32.29 <Albright University Intranet>

RECIPIENT(S): Dr. Anna Frederickson, Supervising Internship Advisor

Dr. Shelvonka P. Jones, Deputy Supervising Internship Advisor

Karenia B. Helena, M.V.I., Internship Advisor

SENDER: Angelica S. Cortez, 6th Year Violence Intervention Student, Level 4 Intern

REGARDING: Internship Sociopsychiatric Journal, DEC-07-2038, Update #2

I read back over my most recent entry and almost collapsed into a fit of giggles. All that worry! All for naught, as it turned out. Oh, I felt a bit of anxiety ripple through me while I was stripping off my clothes, but as soon as I saw Zeb's face, so consumed with desire for me, all anxiety melted away, and pain, phantom or otherwise, was the farthest thing from my mind.

We locked eyes as I mounted him. He shivered, just a little, as I wiggled so he could fully enter me. Then he held up his arms and bent back his wrists. First time for me, but not for him; Dr. Zimmerman made sure he's had gobs of practice.

I thought I'd prepared myself. Perhaps I had, intellectually and even emotionally. But the body has its own mind and its own tolerances. The wave of pleasure that engulfed me when we joined our mods while being connected in the standard male-female way nearly made me lose consciousness, but my nervous system adjusted faster than I thought possible and surmounted the instinct to take refuge in oblivion. Still, my eyes rolled up in my head and I can't describe the sounds that I heard exclaimed from my throat. I think I closed my eyes for a while, I can't remember how long. But then I forced myself to open them so I could look over and see Paulette watching us.

Although nothing is certain in this uncertain world, I believe we all have saved her.

City of a Thousand Names

1.0

{Nofy in the Old Country}

Do I know the City of a Thousand Names? Yes, of course I know it, for I was born and raised there. Yet do I *know* it? Can any woman or man?

My former clan calls their home Anarako Arivo. As a child, it was the only name I knew: it meant *Thousand Names* in my birth language, Malagasy. Later, during my self-exile to Mars, I learned other communities' names for the place which had once been my home: Crossroads; Chameleonburg; Alemona; Lunaston; Vertumnia; Hecateville; Oyatown; Eruv Rav; Multitudes; Archipelago; Proteus; Harmonia; Concordia; Fort Babel; Fresh Start; New London; Salad Bowl... and those are a mere handful.

In the language of my birth, there are two words for 'we.' There is *isika*, which is large and inclusive, meaning 'all of us,' and *izahay*, which is small and exclusive, meaning 'us but not you'. The clan, the tribe, the family, that is *izahay*. The City, the Country, the Nation, the World, that should be *isika*. But there was never any *isika* in Anarako Arivo, nor in Crossroads, nor in Salad Bowl, nor in any of the seventy-thousand other places within the City's Neuronet, many of which share names, because how many good names are there, after all?

I am forgotten in Anarako Arivo. I know this because I myself was taught to forget those lost to us through Schism, or those who simply left. Remembering the lost only causes pain. In Anarako Arivo, we allow ourselves to remember the dead. We forget those living who disappear, those we can no longer see.

Yet now I, a forgotten one, one who can no longer be seen by those who loved me, must return.

1.1

{Nofy in Bradbury}

"Do you mind if I call you Nofy, rather than Lovaharisoa?"

I smile. It is unusual for a Russian to be so polite; such niceties usually come from an American. Oh, bad thought, go far away! I am thinking like a clanswoman of Anarako Arivo, always separating and sorting people; not like a good citizen of Bradbury. "Nofy is fine. Better than my other short name, Kala Ratsy."

"Kala Ratsy? It has a nice sound to it. What does it mean?"

"'Ugly girl'."

"We'll stick with Nofy, then."

I have not previously met Pável Ilyich Davidov. His realm is Trade, whereas mine is Security and Cohesion. We all have our parts to play, each dependent on the others; such is the marvelous tapestry of Bradbury.

"Please know that you do all Bradbury a great service by returning to your former home," he says. He is not a tall man, particularly not by the standards of my people. His skin is almost the same pale gray color as the walls of the caverns we both call home. "You are a good patriot and comrade. I imagine going back there won't be easy for you, emotionally or physically; the change in gravity alone—"

I do not want to be belittled, even in an admiring way. "My aid-suit will help with the gravity. It doesn't concern me."

"Good. And your old signachip is still in good working order, of course?"

"Of course."

"Incidentally, your quarry, Ehmet Jian, likely had a hand in designing it. Interesting, isn't it, that you'll be hunting a man responsible for a part of you? A part of your past?"

He stares at me expectantly. What is he trying to do? Take my measure? "I've read through his dossier," I say. "He worked for Segregatronics Corporation, seven years as a signachip project head."

"Those skills he developed at Segregatronics are what make him such an elusive fugitive, at least within the City's confines. He has become a chameleon. Do you know what that is?"

I can't help but feel insulted. "My family's roots are in Madagascar. I am very familiar with chameleons."

"Of course." His face tightens slightly. Was my tone too assertive? "You'll be glad to know Chen Lee gave me a sterling report on you. He has no doubt regarding your ability to do the SchneerSons' dirty work for them."

The SchneerSons. When I was a girl, those coordinators of the City's Neuronet were hardly more substantial in my mind than the witches and sorcerers of Old Madagascar, the shadowy beings my *nenibe* spoke of in stories meant to frighten me out of my bad behavior. (And what stories those were — witches and sorcerers who would feed crocodiles rice cakes at night to tempt them into marriage, so they could then make the deadly reptiles their slaves!) I did not meet a SchneerSon in the flesh until I made my irrevocable decision to sever ties with my clan.

"These SchneerSons," I ask, "are they men without spines, unable to deal with their own criminals? Or are they so haughty in their estimation of their trade advantage with us that they feel they can order our people to carry out their most distasteful tasks?"

"It is a jurisdictional matter. Really, Nofy, as a former resident of their City, I thought you would be aware of the limitations they place upon themselves." His chastisement stings me. "The renegade Ehmet Jian has committed offenses against multiple subcommunities within the City. Had he offended against only one, the SchneerSons would have apprehended him and handed him over to that subcommunity to face justice. But when more than one subcommunity makes claim to a criminal, the

SchneerSons, due to their customs, are helpless to take direct action."

"Helpless? But they are the coordinators—"

"And coordinate is *all* they are willing to do. They refuse to adjudicate between the claims of various subcommunities."

"But why—?"

He shrugs mildly. "They are Jews. Not like our Jews here in Bradbury — our Jews are good comrades, for the most part. Intelligent, useful people, as patriotic as any Bradburian."

I nod. My investigative work has granted me direct familiarity of very few Jews, for which I must give them credit.

"These SchneerSon Jews," he says, "they are of a different lineage than ours." He takes a sip of tea, some Russian blend whose scent I don't recognize. "More insular, more clannish. Apparently they suffer under the burden of a tribal memory of persecution from ancient times, long before the wars, when their kind were accused of secretly controlling the nations of Earth for their own profit. They were blamed, it seems, for virtually every misfortune suffered by all other peoples. Furies were stoked against them, and they were nearly exterminated.

"These SchneerSons remember this. How they came to coordinate the Neuronet which allows the City of a Thousand Names to exist, I do not know. Perhaps the SchneerSons inherited some of their forefathers' talents for manipulation. But along with those talents came a reluctance — *nyet,* an *aversion* to exercising temporal power, or even to be perceived as exercising such power. They facilitate, they persuade, they lubricate relations amongst the tens of thousands of subcommunities which make up the City, acting like oil within the gears of a complex engine. But when an intractable conflict arises between two or more subcommunities? Then they throw up their hands and wail for their outside partners to help them."

"Which is when I make my entrance, descending in fire from the heavens?"

He smiles. "Oh, I have little doubt they will view you as heaven-sent. The only jurisdictional solution they could come up with regarding this particular renegade, once he'd escaped from their virtual Gehenna prison, was to revoke his City citizenship. Under their law, this reverted him to his prior citizenship. As a Bradburian."

"And suddenly, he became our problem once more."

"Yes. Most convenient for them, isn't it?"

"What if we were to simply refuse to clean up their mess?"

His face darkens. I immediately regret voicing my question. "Not an option. The trade we have with them is too vital. You will regard the furthering of their welfare, and the preservation of their law and customs, as equivalent to defending the well-being of our own dear Bradbury. Are we in complete understanding?"

I nod crisply. "I know my duty, Pável Ilyich. My return to the City of a Thousand Names will bring only credit to Bradbury, and plaudits to you."

2.0

{Ehmet in Bradbury: Slings and Arrows}

It wasn't fair.

Nothing about life in Bradbury was fair, not the most plebeian dictum or custom observed by that oppressive regime. Why couldn't anyone else see that? Thanks to the cosmic radiations my parents absorbed on this misbegotten ball of red dust, I was born with a left arm only two-thirds as long as my right. Bad enough, but at least this disfigurement left me with my senses intact. Was every other Bradburian born without eyes to see, without ears to hear? Without a heart to feel?

Every night, my coworkers at Segregatronics, those with young children to care for, left their workplace at the sixth hour, knowing full well I was not permitted to head home until the ninth. They would murmur their farewells to me, pretending to wish me well; but I knew that, once out of earshot, they smirked to each other, smug in their breeder privilege, scoffing at the childlessness which chained me to my desk for another three long hours.

Once — only once! — did I dare voice my dissatisfaction to one of my coworkers, a hardware specialist named Hasan, a man of Turkish lineage, and so a distant ethnic cousin. "Rules are rules," he said nonchalantly. He took a sip from his thick coffee and shrugged his shoulders with infuriating casualness. "Bradbury needs to grow if Mars is ever to be made a green world. Growth requires new citizens. Babies and children require parenting. Parenting is work. Those who will not parent must provide offsetting work of some other kind. It is only fair and right. Look, Ehmet, you may not wish to breed, but you can *parent*, surely. Babies lose birth parents to accidents almost every week. You and your partner could adopt one of those."

Ignorant *fool.* He made it sound so simple, in his conceited, brutish way. A breeder himself, he had no insight into my mind, my needs, the pressures I faced on a daily basis. Why couldn't one be disgusted by procreation and babies and children? Should that be considered *criminal?*

Privilege! Privilege! Always rubbed in my face! It wasn't only the breeders. It was also the descendants of the Five Colonies, the five competing Mars outposts which had been forced by circumstance to merge and cooperate in order to survive the decades-long interruption of resupply from Earth. Officially, my family traces its lineage to the Chinese colony. Yet which holiday from the old nation of China do Bradburians celebrate as their own? Chinese New Year, a Han Chinese festival! I am Uyghur. That celebration was not *mine.* Neither were the Fourth of July, *Kenkoku Kinenbi,* Orthodox Christmas, or Europe Day. Yet those were the heritage festivals officially sanctioned and glorified by the polity which deigned to claim my loyalty.

The time approached on the calendar for the Uyghur festival of *Korban.* Tired of the yearly privileging of the five heritage festivals, I went to my personnel directorate to demand that my festival be similarly honored by a cessation of work.

"I presume you have personal leave days accrued?" the man (a blonde Scandinavian) said from behind his desk. "Then I suggest you take one. Your supervisor shouldn't object. If he does, I'll speak with him."

"But it isn't *fair,*" I said. "Han Chinese do not need to expend one of their personal leave days to celebrate Chinese New Year. You, as a European, do not need to spend one of your accrued leave days to celebrate Europe Day."

"Yes, but both of those are heritage festivals. You get off work for Europe Day, the same as I do."

"But Europe Day means *nothing* to me. Only *Korban* does. My holiday should be honored the same way as yours is."

"Oh, it isn't *my* holiday in particular. It's a holiday for *all* Bradburians, our way of celebrating the coming together of the Five Colonies. Look, choices had to be made. If we made every dinky religious observance an official holiday, we'd work perhaps five days a year, and we'd starve. Or freeze. Or suffocate. Take your pick."

"But it isn't *fair.*"

"Life in heaven will be fair. Life in Bradbury? We are lucky to have air to breathe, and food to eat. Life here is what you make of it. Take your personal day, good sir, celebrate your *Korban*, and give thanks for the blessings we all share."

Puckering asshole of a flea-ridden donkey. May he be caught outside the caves naked of radsuit and air tank!

1.2

{Nofy in Transit}

Achieving the blissful weightlessness of space was much easier this second trip into the void, thanks to the Martian space elevator and the orbiting transit platform from which I departed. How different things were when I fled my home, a petrified yet obstinate seventeen year-old, and catapulted myself towards Mars, already sick and trembling with the neuro-palsy which began afflicting my muscles the moment I stepped outside the reach of Anarako Arivo's Neuronet. The brutal acceleration required to escape Earth's gravity seemed it would squash me like a hissing cockroach underfoot. But just when I was sure my guts would be pressed through my throat and my brains shaken out of my head, the fierce acceleration ceased. The journey turned eerily smooth, and I sensed myself float against the restraining straps, as though the bubble of air surrounding me had turned to breathable water.

I assumed it was a one-way trip. The State of Bradbury had paid for my transit, after all, expecting a loyal, permanent resident in return. Yet here I am, plummeting through airless space once more, traversing thousands of kilometers per hour... readying myself to crawl back inside the jealous womb of the City of a Thousand Names.

I spend much of my journey pouring over Ehmet Jian's dossier, studying it until I have it nearly memorized. Thanks to my work, I know the type all too well. A malcontent, a refusenik. A grievance monger, quick as a scampering lemur to take offense. Such people make little sense to me; particularly not in an environment such as Bradbury's, where everyone must give his utmost in order for the community to thrive, or even to survive. Why should we agree to take back such a virulent virus of a man? By what right do the SchneerSons demand that we waste any of our scarce resources on Jian at all, even those minimal resources resentfully granted a prisoner?

But then Pável Ilyich Davidov's stern admonishment returns. The City's strategic location on the old continent of Australia grants its residents control over vast deposits of uranium and rare earth metals, as well as gold and silver, materials without which our industries would collapse. Someday, we may be fortunate enough to become self-sufficient in the mining of those elements, either at home on Mars or within the asteroid belt, but that day will not arrive soon. Until then, we must continue trading our expertise in technology for their raw materials. And indulge them in their outré requests for aid.

Even though the technicians at Segregatronics have already thoroughly checked out my aid-suit, I hook it into the ship's network and request an additional diagnostic. The techs upgraded the suit's motorized musculature to cope with Earth's greater gravity; I'll need to recalibrate the settings once I land. In the meantime, I want to reassure myself of the quality of their work. It would do me no good at all to suffer a suit failure while chasing a violent fugitive.

I know my selection for this mission had far less to do with Chen Lee's praise for my investigative abilities than with Pável Ilyich Davidov's assessment that the health of a native Bradburian should not be jeopardized by the Neuronet. How long would a newcomer need to be immersed in the Neuronet — having his perceptions altered and edited by thousands of electronic sensors, his muscle responses retarded or sped up by a signachip implanted at the base of his skull — before he would suffer permanent neuromuscular damage upon his departure from the City? With me, the damage is long since done. The Neuronet infiltrated my nervous system for my first seventeen years. Without my aid-suit, I am a cripple, bent by palsy, unable to walk or to operate any instrument less blunt than a broom. But with the aid-suit, I can accomplish feats which would have convinced my Malagasy ancestors of my godhood.

The City can make no aid-suits; its preoccupations with social segregation have left it hundreds of years in the past, technology-wise. Unless, like me, they intend to make the monumental leap to Mars, would-be emigrants dare not leave off suckling the Neuronet's electronic teat, knowing they would swiftly devolve into helpless cripples. So the population grows ever larger within the City's eight walls, yet the City, hemmed in by sea and salt marshes, cannot expand... it is like a crab which has outgrown its shell but that cannot switch to another, larger one.

And so they live atop one another, those eight million, only the technomagic of the Neuronet allowing them their life-giving illusions of openness, solitude, and autonomy. Illusions the SchneerSons fear Ehmet Jian seeks to strip from them. And that is why they demand my return.

2.1

{Ehmet in Bradbury: The Final Straw}

When it came to tormenting me, the ableists outdid even the cursed ethnic chauvinists. One miserable day my work colleagues hectored me into attending a Fourth of July observance at Kim Stanley Robinson Park, that faux-idyllic representation of what the surface of Mars will look like two hundred years from now if only we all "put our shoulders to the wheel." The centerpiece of this day-long exercise in patriotic propaganda was a re-creation of an old American frontier ceremony, the "barn raising."

My group and I arrived late. Other work groups from other companies had already started the theatrical task of lifting the pretend-barn's walls to their upright positions so they could be fitted together with primitive pegs. But apparently one of the four teams involved lacked adequate manpower. "Hey!" that team's leader, a robust specimen of Mediterranean manhood (Greek, perhaps?) shouted to us while looking at me, "could we get a *hand* over here?"

A *hand*. Yes, I realized this was an American-style colloquialism for "assistance;" I wasn't *stupid*. But what followed stripped the incident of any pretense of innocence. Three of my group, two of which I counted as insensitive louts eager to offend, the third a pathetic would-be ally who in his clumsy attempts to befriend me invariably offended, instantly turned their gazes upon me — staring at my radiation-cursed *arm*. I then heard a sound. Other, less discerning ears might have interpreted it as a clearing of a throat. But I knew it to be a crowing, despicable chuckle.

An ableist conspiracy to belittle me. To shame me for an accident of birth, for my "failure" to live up to their absurd, atavistic, Greco-Roman ideal of male beauty. Curses upon them all, diseased testicle sacks of syphilitic camels...

Would no one stand with me? Even my own life partner, Ismail, belittled my concerns. How could he not *see* those constant assaults on my person, feel their cruel reverberations in the very marrow of his bones? Were we not birds of the same plumage? Proud Uyghurs? Men who loved other men? But I came to realize with increasing sorrow that he had been infected by the prevailing malevolence. Like a slave raised to worship the god worshiped by his owner, he had bought into his own diminution.

"Ehmet, I love you more than Earth's forests love the sun, but I wish you would not always pick at the scabs of these psychic wounds. Let your spirit grow quiet. Let the warmth of my love calm you, dear one. Do not the Old Scriptures say the wicked are like the troubled sea, whose waters cast up mire and dirt?"

I pulled away from his tentative embrace. "Are you calling me *wicked*, Ismail? *You?*"

"No, no, that is *not* my meaning! Always, you hear the worst! No, what I mean is, if you will not seek to calm the unquiet waters of your spirit, if this anger festers and festers, you may be *tempted* into wickedness. That is what I fear, Ehmet. I am afraid for you. I am afraid for *us*."

And so he nattered on, like an old woman fretting over the fraying of her prayer rug, not realizing the ceaseless nervous fidgeting of her fingers was the cause of its fraying. I should not have been surprised, several months after, by the gross betrayal with which he impaled me, the rust-pitted sword he monstrously shoved through my liver. Yet I was. To my eternal discredit, I was taken unawares, like a babe yet unweaned.

"Ehmet, would you accompany me to the park this evening?"

Such a seemingly innocent request. Yet so was Hawwa's invitation to her husband Adam to bite from the apple; that, too, took place within a garden, or park. And so, like the all-too-trusting first man, I allowed myself to be led down the garden path.

"Ehmet, I have something of great importance to tell you."

Standing beneath the blue false sky of Kim Stanley Robinson Park, I detected a hint of evil in his words and demeanor. I mustered my fortitude in readiness. Yet little did I know I was like a man who believed himself called to soak up a water spill with a towel, when actually the dam holding back the reservoir had broken!

"Ehmet, dear one, I have decided to take a wife."

I could not have been more stunned had a meteor plunged through the false blue roof and landed before my feet. "A... a *wife?*" I said, dumbly. "You mean... a *woman* is my rival? A *woman?*"

"Not your *rival*, Ehmet — your *complement*. You have known from our very first meeting that my desires include both men *and* women. The pressure upon me from my parents to father a child has grown unbearable. I've alluded to you of this, but I've never fully admitted how it has torn at me—"

"And so you betray me..."

"Betray you? Never! I would sooner cut off my own right hand! Ehmet, never would I have made a marriage proposal to this woman had she not agreed that you and I would remain lovers, with her full approval. I do not love her in the way I love you. This arrangement is merely to satisfy my parents, and to relieve me of a crushing moral burden of conscience. Yet there are ancillary benefits, as well — when Nurbiya becomes pregnant, all three of us can register as the child's parents. You and I would both be permitted to reduce our work hours in the office. We will actually be able to spend more time together, albeit with the child—"

After cleaving me in two, he offered pale blandishments? "Don't do me any favors, Ismail," I said in the coldest tone I could muster. "Take your wife. Blessings upon you both. I hope you will be very happy with your future child. As for you and me, we are *done.*"

His eyes welled up with tears. His voice quavered. "*Please*, Ehmet, do not *be* like this—"

He reached for me like a shambling thing, desperate to pull me into his clammy embrace. I pulled off my shoe and swatted him with it, as I would a crawling vermin. "*Scum!* You are *dead* to me!

Dead! Were you the last bucketful of *piss* on Mars, you would not be worthy of being recycled!"

He ran away, crying like an imbecilic wretch.

Oh, false paradise! Oh, subterranean palace of whores and jackals! I stared about me at the trees and grass, fed by an artificial star, by liars' sunlight. The falseness choked me. The hypocrisy and malignity of this arrogant outpost on a dead world finally became too much for me to bear.

I would go where the jibes of my inferiors would no longer sting my ears.

Where I could enjoy the company of my own kind, and my own kind *only*.

I would go to the City of a Thousand Names.

1.3

{Nofy at the City Wall}

The wall. The oh-so-comforting wall about the City. I remember my parents speaking of it as if it were an old friend, a trusted family advisor, a guardian upon whom we could always rely. "The wall will always be there to protect us," they said. I later came to understand that it is merely a tangible, universally visible symbol of the far more important invisible walls separating the seventy-thousand subcommunities — or is it eighty-thousand now? One day, I firmly believe, there will be as many subcommunities as there are residents in the City.

I focus on the wall; better this than obsessing over the less pleasant aspects of my return to Earth. Although I have never seen one in the flesh, I believe I now have insight into how a hippopotamus must feel when the buoying waters of its bog dry up, and it is forced to ponderously plod through the mud. My aid-suit is learning the gravity of this place, its mechanical musculature gradually adjusting and compensating, but it is not a quick enough student to suit me (ha, ha). Matters will improve greatly once I am plugged back into the Neuronet, once impulses from my brain can follow the old mappings throughout my body.

Then there is the heat. My aid-suit informs me the ambient temperature is ninety-four degrees Fahrenheit, thirty-four point four degrees Celsius, with relative humidity at eighty-three percent. I am sweating. *Sweating like a pig dressed in polyester*, I believe is the local idiom. I cannot recall sweating even a droplet on Mars. Our subterranean shelters maintain a constant temperature of fifty-eight degrees Fahrenheit, with artificial humidity set at twenty percent. I can remember becoming quite slick with sweat as a girl, playing in the City's seemingly empty plazas and squares beneath the blazing sun.

I pass an encampment of the City's Self-Defense Force, that legion of guardians loyal to the City but not allowed to taste of it. I wave to the platoons of men and women maintaining their thankless vigil between the sea and the wall, the outside world and the wall. They eye me warily, hoping, perhaps, that I will act in a hostile fashion so that they will finally, after years of boring quietude, have an opportunity to fire their weapons in anger, to defend the gates they are not allowed to enter. Lacking signachips, they perceive all, but are invisible to those they protect.

I join the queue of people waiting to reenter the Brisbane Gate, returning to the City from their work in the Mount Kinnobock mine to the west. As a squad of guardians stands by, ready to detain anyone deemed to lack the right to enter, persons in the queue pause beneath a scanner, then wait for the automatic door to roll open for them. I was told preparations had been made for me, that my signachip had been remotely registered so that the City would not, like Jonah's whale, vomit me out. Even so, standing beneath the scanner and waiting for the door's determination summons a pall of dread, a cringe-worthy memory. The morning I thought I would be leaving the City forever, when I passed through Orsinney Gate, also known as the Exile's Gate, the sound of the door rolling shut behind me, cutting me off from the only people and home I'd ever known, so terrified me that my bladder let go, dampening the sand between my feet.

But the door opens for me. I am no longer sixteen years old, a panicked child-woman. I have been entrusted by my country with a vital mission, and I will see it through to its end.

I step through the gate, and then I am inside the City. Inside! What a teeming mass of people! What a cacophony of voices and clamor and shuffling feet! I steel myself for rough jostling, but not one of the dozens of persons streaming on all sides of me touches me. Oh, their carry-sacks or parcels, if not held close to their bodies, might lightly brush against my aid-suit, but their flesh never once touches mine.

How will I find my contact in this endless, sprawling river of people? Then I remind myself that is her role to find *me*. She'll most likely have exercised her option to screen out each and every one of the hundreds of pedestrians who crowd this thoroughfare. In her Neuronet-filtered vision, I likely stand out like a tall ship on an empty sea.

And so it comes to pass. A soft hand touches the bare skin of my arm, and I turn to find my escort. Showing no concern for the afternoon heat, she wears a long, black dress which extends from the tops of her severe shoes to the upper reaches of her throat, with full-length sleeves which reveal only the pale skin of her fingers. Her hair is completely concealed by a black headscarf. Her pinkish face, flushed from the heat, is unadorned by any makeup or jewelry.

"Welcome to Eruv Rav, Miss Rabemananjara," she says, extending her hand for me to shake. "I am Leah Abramovitz. I'll be your guide and assistant during your stay in the City."

She pronounces my surname with reasonable accuracy, stressing, however, the wrong syllable, which is certainly forgivable, given my name's length. "Please, Leah, call me Nofy. Thank you for meeting me. How far must we travel to the place where I'll be debriefed?"

"We must go to Queen Elizabeth Square, at the City's center. Are you greatly fatigued from your journey? There are places we can stop along the way, if you wish."

"No... it's just... the combination of the greater gravity and the press of all these *people*. It's somewhat overwhelming..."

She looks about her as though she is puzzled; then she remembers. "Oh, forgive me, Nofy — you're like those soldiers outside the walls, aren't you? No filters applied at all? No cocooning eruvnet? You're seeing and hearing... *everyone*, aren't you?"

"Yes... I never experienced this in the seventeen years I lived here. On Mars, in Bradbury... well, our leaders would sing hoseas if we could achieve even a tenth of this population density. If our resources would allow for it."

"As soon as we reach headquarters, I'll use my equipment to align your personal signachip with our eruvnet. I should have thought to bring my portable tuning unit with me, forgive me..." She shoots me a queerly searching glance, the look of someone soliciting a greater intimacy, quite odd for someone who has just met me. "Tell me, though — what is it *like*, to feel yourself surrounded by so many people of so many different sorts? Is it dreadful? Terrifying? Or is it... *exhilarating?* All the sounds, the smells?"

When I was a daydreaming child, I once toyed with such thoughts. "Simply something to adjust to," I say. "At this juncture, far too overstimulating, but I am too weary to make aesthetic judgements of any worth. Ask me again once I've enjoyed a bath and a good night's rest."

"Once we've reached Koolan Square, we'll be able to board the Cloncurry Avenue streetcar. Then it will take between an hour and ninety minutes for us to reach Queen Elizabeth Square, where headquarters is. Will you be all right until then?"

So relief will be within reach once I can look up and see the Gladstone Clock Tower, the City's tallest structure and its geographic heart. As a girl, I never needed a wristwatch of my own, not with its eight separate giant time pieces, each facing one of the City's eight walls, perpetually overshadowing my young, impatient self. "I'll be fine. The longer I'm here, the easier it all will be for me."

I follow her north along the road which parallels the octagonal walls which surround the City. Uncomfortable though my present circumstances make me, I remind myself I am living an old fantasy. I am fulfilling my girlhood wish that I should see, smell, and hear the totality of the City's populace, not merely the relatively few members of my own clan and those select allied subcommunities my elders had decided it was permissible for us to perceive. Leah swims unerringly and confidently through this sea of humanity, pausing, turning, sidestepping, subconsciously dodging collisions with persons she does not see. Her walk is slowed by the continual necessity of these corrections, but her body accomplishes them with aplomb.

Not being plugged into the Neuronet, I do not benefit from its personal radar field. And yet, indirectly, I do. As an experiment, I stride directly toward a man whose vision is blocked by a stack of parcels he carries in his arms. At the last possible second prior to our collision, he pauses, then shifts slightly to his left, barely avoiding grazing me. Were I extremely persistent, I might succeed in tripping him up with a sweep of my leg. And he would most likely react the same way a pedestrian within the catacombs of Bradbury would after stumbling over an uneven patch of the cave floor... curse himself for his presumed clumsiness, pick himself up from the ground, and then gather his scattered parcels and continue on his way.

I stare into the faces of the crowds surrounding me. They do not stare back into mine. They look through me, as though I were made of wind. I doubt that any of them perceives more than a twentieth of the pedestrians walking about them. Now and then, I see a look of recognition blossom on a face, and a man or woman will smile and glance across the road and shout a greeting to a person on the far side, someone who, anywhere else but the City, would be blocked from their sight by several dozen passing bodies.

And that distant person, who should also not be able to see their interlocutor, waves and returns the greeting. The Neuronet does not repeal the laws of physics or the behavior of light, I remind myself. It cannot render those bodies filtered out from an individual's eruvnet transparent. However, the Neuronet itself "sees" everything, using the physical eyes of the millions of persons attached to itself as its own cameras. And so it is capable, through feats of computation fully comprehendible, perhaps, only to the mind of God, of projecting into the visual receptors of each brain hooked to a signachip a simulation of what would be seen if all the persons and objects filtered out by that person's eruvnet truly did not exist.

We draw close to what, to my ears, sounds like an appalling cacophony, an aural riot of clashing melodies and rhythms. How could such ear-splitting offensiveness be permitted? I'm tempted to hurl cobblestones at the headache-inducing tuba player and the various trumpeters, electric keyboardists, guitarists, and amplified zither players, and especially the dispersed platoon of drummers, each pounding their drums to a different beat. The musicians sit in various clumps surrounding nearly a hundred persons beneath the umbrellas of a streetside café. The patrons, mostly mine workers indulging in after-shift beers or short, stout mugs of mud-thick coffee, seem to be enjoying this "music". But how could anyone *tolerate* such baleful noise, much less "enjoy" it...?

Then I realize that they're all listening to *different* musics. Of course! Idiot Nofy! The sign above the café, I notice, is to me an electronic blur, which probably means this establishment goes by many names, each encoded to be perceptible only to certain subcommunities. I imagine the members of each group only see and interact with their "own" wait staff, order from their "own" menus, selecting only beverages which their subcommunity has preapproved. Muslims are not permitted to drink alcohol? It does not appear on their menu. Mormons may not consume coffee? For them, it is never brewed. And each group listens to its "own" music, too.

I tap my companion's shoulder. "Leah, do you hear any music?"

She turns back to me and smiles. "Why, of course! The klezmer band here is quite good, don't you think? There's nothing to compare with the plaintive wail of that clarinet, is there? Do you enjoy klezmer music? We could stop and listen, if you like, so long as we sit at our own table, apart from the men."

I notice in the far corner of the café, closest to what I assume is the klezmer band, a group of men in black coats and black-furred hats sit around a table, sharing a bottle of strong drink. All but the youngest of them sport long beards. Men of Leah's clan, the SchneerSons?

There's another man sitting with the SchneerSons, also bearded, but not dressed like them. He is darker than they are, possibly Turkic, but with eyes that seem almost Mongolian...

Eyes that are looking directly at me. Not through me. *At* me.

No one in this café but Leah should be able to see me. Only she has adjusted her signachip's filters to be able to perceive a person who is not plugged into the Neuronet...

My blood turns cold. That man who accosts me with his level stare — a stare which coldly and arrogantly appraises me — can only be the renegade, Ehmet Jian.

As though he has read my mind, he rises from the table, disturbing none of his companions, for they are not his companions — he is as invisible to them as a deadly virus. Still meeting my gaze, he brandishes a knife, twirling it deftly between his fingers like a circus performer about to hurl the weapon at a bound and blindfolded assistant. Then he strides to the quartet of musicians playing klezmer music. Sensing what he is about to do, I struggle closer, but I am hindered by the press of bodies and tables.

Standing next to the violin player, he mocks the man (and me) by imitating him, miming the playing of a violin, using his knife as he would a bow. The musician finishes his solo and lowers his violin from his cheek. With a swift jerk, the renegade slits his exposed throat.

I command my aid-suit to charge Jian. But my palsied muscles, excited by my surge of adrenaline, over-exert themselves against the unfamiliar weight of Earth's gravity, and the suit responds by over-amplifying my motions. Damn it all! I lurch from side to side, overcompensating, my strides disastrously uncoordinated. Balance gone, I crash into a table of miners who cannot see or feel me, upending their drinks and refreshments.

Portions of the café descend into chaos — that section occupied by the SchneerSons, who have witnessed the musician's mysterious bloodying, and the tables I have just crashed through. But all other sections remain eerily undisturbed. I scramble on hands and knees toward the downed musician, my limbs flailing like an infant's, praying the renegade will also stumble.

But by the time I regain my footing — curse my impediments! — Jian has disappeared within the dense crowds. Hordes of persons, blessed by technologically imposed ignorance, who will never be aware that they blithely walked within five meters of an attempted murder.

2.2

{Ehmet in Eruv Rav}

"Mr. Jian, let me repeat that we of Eruv Rav, indeed, all of us who live here within the City of a Thousand Names, certainly welcome immigrants — newcomers from any tribe, sect, or ethnic grouping known to mankind. We make room for all, within reason. But you must understand: although not irrevocable, a decision to join us and enter the Neuronet, to take on the yoke of a signachip, is a momentous one, with lasting consequences. Not to be entered into lightly."

I stared at my interlocutor and his fellows, hiding my distaste with great difficulty. *Jews.* My ancestral enemies. The eternal foes of the Prophet (not that I am a believer, but still, such was the guiding faith of my father's fathers). Did I truly wish to subject myself to a polity ruled by such as these? These sinister schemers with their large, hooked noses, their absurd side curls and fur hats, their grasping love of money, their garlicky skin the color of earthworms?

They swore they do not rule this City. They swore they exercised no power, that they were merely faithful servants of the City's inhabitants, coordinators amongst the City's seventy thousand subcommunities, humble drones who ensured that all essential work to keep the City functional was apportioned fairly.

Truth? Or clever Jew propaganda? Did it matter to me, ultimately? I knew how the Neuronet works. I had assisted in maintaining it from distant Mars for the past sixteen years. The SchneerSons told me that once I was granted my permanent signachip, had selected my eruvnet, and had been accepted by that eruvnet's subcommunity, the invisible walls of my chosen eruvnet would descend about me, and the SchneerSons, along with the great majority of the shuffling hordes who inhabit this City, would vanish from my reality. I knew the technology behind all this, knew it as well as my fingers knew my razor and the contours of my face.

"I do not make this decision lightly," I said. "I make no decisions lightly. I am a serious man."

"Yes. I can tell." Did the Jew mock me? I felt blood rush to my face, but I kept my anger in check. *He is merely a gatekeeper*, I repeated to myself. *A petty bureaucrat whose forms I must check and sign before I can achieve my goal: a space free from disrespect, jibes, taunts, whispered innuendoes, and infuriating arrogance.* "Still," he continued, "I would be remiss in my responsibility to you if I did not emphasize the neurological consequences of joining us here. Entering the Neuronet will in short time effect changes within your brain. Your nervous system will quickly grow accustomed to interacting with your signachip and accepting the altered, filtered stimuli it feeds to your brain's sensory receptors. New pathways will form. You will be altered, permanently. Should you ever opt to leave the City — and I will not lie to you, some do — you will live out the remainder of your life as a cripple, the extent of your disability roughly correlated to the length of time you have spent linked to the Neuronet—"

"I *know* all this." Was he not familiar with my background? "Your Neuronet is no mystery to me — I know it better than *you* do, better than any man in this room. I have personally worked on the aid-suits provided to help emigrants from the City adjust to their disability. This is all elementary to me."

"Good, good. Then you are better informed than the vast majority of persons who have sat where you now sit. HaShem willing, you will never have reason to depart and contend with disability. The crucial task for you, for your happiness with us, is selecting the subcommunity best suited for you, and for which you are best suited. You may take as long as you wish perusing our catalog. We counsel judicious contemplation. We understand that those who seek to join us are often driven to do so by persecution, either overt or perceived. They are eager, sometimes desperate to escape the larger society from which they come, to retreat to a safe space of their own choosing. Seeking affirmation and reassurance, as well as safety, their initial impulse is to choose the coziest possible home, a highly particularized and limited eruvnet of persons they believe will be exactly like them. This is in no way a bad or improper impulse. Indeed, it is an impulse we SchneerSons are commanded by HaShem to honor and support — the avoidance of *shatnez*, that forbidden combination of things which are meant to be kept separate.

"But I wish you to be aware, Mr. Jian, there is a downside to selecting a severely delimited eruvnet. You may inadvertently cut yourself off from potential friends, lovers, or spouses, whichever apply in your case. We have found it is better to be more inclusive at first when making your selection than it is to be exceedingly discriminate. Let me give an example. If you are a yellow isosceles triangle with green stripes, we recommend you start out by joining an eruvnet which encompasses *all* triangles or *all* yellow shapes, rather than limiting yourself to yellow triangles, or yellow shapes with green stripes, or, worse yet, yellow isosceles triangles with green stripes.

"Please understand, Schisms occur within subcommunities frequently and with relative ease. Mergings of subcommunities, on the other hand, are more like comet sightings... very rare indeed. And do not think that, should you start with a severely delimited subcommunity — some of our subcommunities have memberships as small as a dozen, the smallest having only four — and then grow dissatisfied with your lack of choice of companions, it will be an easy matter for you to petition to shift to a larger, more inclusive community. The more populous and variegated subcommunities often view candidates for admission who come from relatively atomized subcommunities as potential malcontents — Schism risks — and reject them out of hand. I have seen unfortunate souls who have realized they made a mistake by going too 'small' leave their original subcommunity, but then face rejection after rejection. Some of these unfortunates never find a new subcommunity. They end up as isolates. Tragedies, really. We SchneerSons do what we can to care for them and encourage better-off citizens to tithe for their welfare. But in our view, isolates face a self-made hell only half a step up from Gehenna, the criminals' underworld."

How he rambled on! I wished I could switch him off like a light. "Thank you for your concern for my happiness," I said, not without sarcasm. "But I am fully capable of taking all relevant factors into account when making my selection. More capable than most."

"Of course. Of course. Our catalog awaits you, Mr. Jian, for as long as you wish to peruse it. Please let me know if I or any of my associates can assist you in any way."

1.4

{Nofy in Eruv Rav}

"Mr. Emmanuel, he was *aware* of me. Ehmet Jian knew I'd arrived in the City. He knew which gate I'd entered through. He slit that violist's throat to jeer at me, mocking my ability to catch him."

Leah's supervisor, Baruch Emmanuel, makes a tent of his fat fingers just beneath the pout of his protruding lips. "This is quite bad," he says. "He has acquired more capability than we had feared. At least the musician was not killed, thank HaShem."

"Killing him wasn't Jian's intent!" I say with more heat than I'd intended. "He didn't need to kill the man in order to taunt me. If only I'd had more chance to acclimate to Earth's gravity, he would not have humiliated me the way he did..."

"It sounds as though you may be taking this encounter too personally. You may wish to take a step back. Oftentimes the hawk, stalking his prey coldly and analytically from above, proves a more effective hunter than the impassioned wolf, lunging across the snow."

Platitudes! Only the disconcerting sight of nearly a dozen non-SchneerSons milling about within this supposedly private conference room prevents me from continuing to vent my anger. "Are we truly speaking in confidence here?" I cast a somewhat disbelieving glance at the turbaned individuals who drink tea and scan glowing screens at various chairs around the long table, who occasionally look straight through me and my host. "Given your role and responsibilities, is it unreasonable of me to have expected you would have private office space?"

My host offers me a pinched smile. "Those others you see? They cannot see or hear us. As you may have noticed on your journey here, space within the City is at a premium. We are hemmed in by salt marshes and bays, and our sandy soil will not support buildings any higher than seven stories tall, apart from our clock tower. Our Neuronet allows us all to experience our work and private lives in this exceedingly crowded environment as though each clan has room to spare, vast private domains disturbed only by bird calls and the gentle sounds of blowing leaves. Was that not your experience, growing up here?"

I am in no mood for pleasantries. But I remind myself that here I must act not only as a law enforcement officer, but also a diplomat. "Yes, it was. But the tales I heard of you SchneerSons as a child, that you were persons of enormous, almost frightening power and responsibility, virtual demigods... I imagined you would reserve the grandest buildings at the center of Queen Elizabeth Square for yourselves."

"And now you know such is not the case, nor has it ever been. We SchneerSons claim no special privileges for ourselves. Our office space is just as crowded as any other within the City, at least to the unfiltered senses of those outside our Neuronet."

Leah reenters the conference room carrying a palm-sized computer strapped to her wrist. She sits next to me. "I'll have you plugged into our eruvnet in just a moment, Nofy. I am so sorry I did not have my portable unit with me when we first met. If I had, perhaps you could have stopped that awful man..."

"Is there anything I need to do?"

"So long as your signachip is in good working order, my unit will synch with it, no action required on your part. Then I can easily apply my own filters to you."

And so it occurs. She taps a few keys on her portable device. My vision momentarily blurs, my ears begin ringing, I smell the cloying sweetness of ripening mangoes, overwhelming, and my stomach twists. Then, as if my head had been enclosed in a bubble filled with noxious gases, the bubble pops and the sensory distortions disappear. I look around me. The turbaned individuals and their cups of coffee and office equipment have vanished. Baruch, Leah, and I are alone. And I feel... *right*. Everything I see, the faces of my hosts, the paintings on the walls, the furniture, it all looks sharper, more *vivid* than it did just seconds ago. The transition almost makes me believe I have spent the last fourteen years with a strip of silken gauze wrapped about my face, muffling my senses. And now the gauze has been suddenly cut away.

My hosts watch me intently. "Welcome back to the Neuronet," Baruch says. "How do you feel?"

How *do* I feel? Regretful that I ever left this place, and mortified that I should find myself feeling remorse. "Good," I say, "*very* good," guilt-ridden at admitting this. Am I being disloyal to my adopted country? Bradbury suddenly seems very far away, a cold, unreal dream. "The transition... it's easier than I would've hoped. Before I head out after Ehmet Jian, I'll want to perform some tests on myself — coordination, reflexes, strength. My aid-suit will need to adjust to the 'new me,' as well, so there won't be any repeat of today's debacle near the Brisbane Gate. I assume Leah's portable unit is just as capable of tracking

Jian's movements as your computers here in your operations center...?"

My newly boosted confidence fades as I notice the consternation on Baruch's face. "Actually, Nofy, the situation has... changed, during the time you were in transit from Mars. To our detriment, unfortunately. We are no longer capable of consistently tracking him."

What? This isn't what I was told to expect — "What happened?"

"We aren't sure. Please recall, on your world, he was a skilled technician at the company which maintains and upgrades our Neuronet. He may have become aware of our electronic surveillance, then performed some alteration on either his signachip's settings or whatever tuning device he has managed to cobble together, foiling that surveillance."

"So he is now completely invisible to you? To me?"

"Mostly, yes. But not completely. He still appears suddenly and briefly on our tracking screens whenever he shifts from one eruvnet to another. At those times, for a few seconds we are blessed with a fix on his physical location and which eruvnet he has selected to flee into. But then he is lost to our detection, until the next time he chooses to shift."

What does this mean? That I will rush from locale to locale across the City's two hundred and twenty-two square kilometers each time a blip of Ehmet Jian appears on Leah's screen, then search for him within whatever subcommunity he has chosen to hide in? And how am I supposed to know who he is? "Baruch, given that he has his own tuning unit, won't he likely use it to disguise his appearance? Won't he blend in with whichever group whose eruvnet he is trespassing upon?"

"That is an assumption we must make."

"Then you must put out an all-points bulletin. Alert every resident of the City that they must immediately report the appearance of any person unknown to them, especially anyone who is acting in a peculiar or aggressive fashion."

Frowning, he shakes his head. "No, that would foment panic."

"This man is a killer. Isn't some degree of panic justified?"

"We must not act in too heavy-handed a fashion. If we SchneerSons are perceived to be functioning in an authoritarian way, dictating to the leaderships of each subcommunity, the strains on the City's social fabric could prove *devastating*. In the wake of the sectarian wars, thousands of starving refugees washed up upon the City's shores each week from all corners of the strife-torn globe. Given the very real danger of sectarian hatreds taking fresh root here, the establishment of our Neuronet and its subsidiary eruvnets was a moral imperative. Sustaining the integrity of that Neuronet *remains* a moral imperative. As the accepted coordinators of the Neuronet, we *must* be seen as impartial. The sovereignty of each individual eruvnet is an inviolable, *sacred* principle—"

"Are you afraid? Afraid the people might turn on you?" The naked self-interest and self-preservation I detect disgusts me. "Ehmet Jian is a clear and present danger. He has murdered two people and nearly murdered a third. If I cannot call upon the assistance of the eyes and ears of your eight million residents, segregated within seventy thousand subcommunities, then achievement of my task grows as infinitely improbable as my finding a single grain of rice buried amidst the sands of your beaches."

His pale face flushes with blood; its crimson aspect, marked with large pores, reminds me of the cratered plains of my adopted planet. "I do not relish your tone, Bradburian. I hope your superiors made it amply clear to you that *you* are working for *us*, not the other way around. You will do what you have been sent here to do, and you will do so fully within the parameters *we* establish. If you cannot agree to this, then you will be sent home immediately, and the ensuing delay in Bradbury's capture of their criminal — Ehmet Jian is *Bradbury's* responsibility now, no longer ours — will be taken fully into account during the next round of trade negotiations."

Ahhh... my pressing this issue any further will only result in my being sent back to Mars in disgrace. "I will follow your rules," I say, carefully sucking the venom from my words. "I apologize for having offended you. Crimes such as Jian's arouse my passions. I spoke out of turn."

"Your apology is both appreciated and accepted."

"What restrictions must I comply with when interacting with citizens?"

"As best you can, limit your questioning to the subcommunity leaderships, or persons who have been directly impacted by Jian's intrusions. Leah will make introductions for you. The fewer citizens you must interact with, the better. As you may well imagine, our citizenry are exceedingly sensitive to the presence of foreigners. You will alter your perceived appearance so as to blend in and cause the minimal disruption possible. Should HaShem smile upon your efforts, apprehending Jian will require you to shift through only a handful of eruvnets. I assume you've been made aware of the City's total ban on firearms and other projectile weapons?"

"It was explained to me."

"Good. Only our soldiers are permitted to handle guns, and even they are not allowed to use them inside the City's walls, for reasons which are obvious."

"Is there any chance Jian has acquired a gun?"

"Very little. Unless he has snuck outside the walls and stolen a weapon from one of the soldiers' camps."

The likelihood that he has done precisely that cannot be ruled out, given the other capabilities he has shown. I did not bring either of my service pistols with me. But, knowing I would be contending with a foe who could choose to be undetectable to me, I had my aid-suit outfitted with automatic tasers, stunners programmed to respond to any aggressive actions or movements made within my immediate vicinity. Unlike my own five senses, my aid-suit's sensors will have no inputs filtered out.

The tasers could be classified as projectile weapons, certainly. But they are far less likely than a fired bullet to harm an innocent bystander. And given Baruch's apparent unconcern for my personal safety, my sense of guilt at not mentioning them to him is less than nil.

"Are there any other instructions you wish to share with me?" I ask.

"Not at this time. Any additional communications will be routed through Leah."

Ushering me out of the conference room, he does not offer to shake my hand. And that is one cultural prohibition I do not mind at all, certainly not in this case.

2.3

{Ehmet in Salama}

Salama. In Arabic, it means *safety.* A fitting name for a sanctuary for male lovers of men, whose ancestors had lived and died in nations subjugated by the colonial powers — those same five overweening, arrogant powers which later planted their belligerent flags in the Martian dust. I truly believed this Salama would be an appropriate sanctuary for me, a refuge from not only the heterosexualist supremacists, male and female, but also the hateful Han Chinese, smug Russians, cursed Europeans, Satanic Americans, and ethnocentric Japanese.

And at first, it was indeed a paradise of sorts. The work was easy, at least for me. We residents of Salama had agreed to accept responsibility for the upkeep of portions of the City's sewerage and water infrastructure. The software which controlled the pumps, filters, and chemical treatments was archaic compared with the code I had mastered while working at Segregatronics, but at its root proved robust and logical and not difficult to master. Indeed, for a time, at least, it felt refreshing and novel to work with such crude, elemental tools. And not only the work felt liberating. The City was exhilaratingly empty and open to us, we sixty-five thousand residents of Salama. Its public baths were reserved for our pleasures, its theaters awaited our concerts and plays, its cafés served our preferred foods, and its libraries stocked with only those books in accordance with our mores. The streets were ours to roam without fear of ridicule or assault. Best of all, or so it seemed to me, was my dazzling new reality of untrammeled erotic choice — the intoxicating notion that any person, anywhere, whose looks caused my gaze to linger could potentially become my lover.

And yet, it was not long before I came to learn, most painfully, that Salama, too, had its hierarchy. A hierarchy every bit as implacably cruel and unjust as any of the hierarchies which had reigned in Bradbury. A hierarchy of beauty. Of *looksism*.

The first performance I attended at Saladin Square's al-Farahidi Theater was an opera based upon *One Thousand and One Nights*. I found the actor who portrayed Shahryar, the king, to be exquisite: the voice of an angel combined with a symmetry of form and fairness of features which could only have been the work of that greatest of all sculptors, Allah Himself. During the intermission, aflame with infatuation, I turned to my coworker Faddey and informed him that the singer Nasir el-Amin, he of the silken voice and golden body, would be my next conquest.

Faddey, notorious for his pessimism, laughed ruefully. "Do not be so certain of that, Ehmet," he said. "Nasir the Singer is known to have many dozens of lovers, nearly all of whom are as fair looking as he himself, although few begin to approach him in talent. If I were you, my friend, I would not subject myself to the humiliation I would likely face when offering myself to that man. Ah, but Salama is as rich in receptive puckered roses as ancient Alexandria was in scholarly scrolls. Worthy one, aim your arrows at a less lofty target, and happiness will be yours for the asking."

His casual dismissal of my chances merely served to make the challenge of it all the more urgent and intoxicating. "You say I am not worthy of Nasir the Singer?"

"I did not say that, my dear friend. But I can assure you, Nasir the Singer will."

"How can you be so sure of that? I have been a resident of Salama for only four months, but already I am lauded as the most skilled programmer at the water center. I emigrated from Mars — unlike the parochial men who make up Nasir's circle, not only have I experienced life outside the City, I have known life on another *planet*. I have seen the twin moons of Mars embrace Earth between them in the night sky. I have seen showers of flaming meteors strike the Martian desert and kick up miles-high plumes of red dust. I have seen this blue and green planet from the vantage point of an angel. I may not be capable of singing arias as Nasir can, but I can 'sing' of these wondrous things I have witnessed, sights and experiences far beyond the ken of his provincial lovers."

"Ah, my friend, what you say would be well and good if Nasir valued minds nearly as much as he treasures bodies. But alas..." He shrugged as he glanced at my wilted arm. The burning humiliation of his silent rebuke infuriated me.

"I will show you, you bastard of a lame camel," I said. "Do you care to make a wager on my success? I bet you one week's salary that within a fortnight of tonight's performance, either Nasir el-Amin will have shared my bed, or I his."

Phlegmatic in temperament, Faddey did not respond to my sudden fury with heat of his own. He merely smiled once again, this time a bit sadly. "Ah, impetuous youth, I do not confiscate the money of the deluded; I leave that distasteful chore to the tax collectors. I wish you only good fortune, my friend."

As soon as Nasir had accepted the audience's final accolades, I left Faddey and marched myself to the star's dressing room. Its entrance was guarded by a pair of glowering monoliths formed entirely of muscle and sinew. I suspected that, like the dinosaurs of old, they sported auxiliary brains in their hips to transmit neural impulses to their legs, for the brains in their skulls were too feeble to create pulses hardy enough to travel that immense distance.

"I wish to see Nasir el-Amin," I told the first monolith.

His huge square head swiveled toward me ponderously. "Who are you, and why should he wish to see you?"

"Tell him I am Ehmet Jian, the master programmer from Mars."

"So you're a disc jockey?" the second monolith said (surprising me with his ability to vocalize words). "If you're a record spinner, give us a couple dozen free passes to this Mars place, and Nasir will consider whether he'll allow his entourage to give your disco a try."

"Idiot!" I said, appalled that any organism with the gall to call itself human could be so ignorant. "I would not expect one of your exceedingly limited intellect to comprehend this, but I am from the *planet* Mars, and I have nothing to do with selecting songs in dance halls—"

I did not have the chance to finish explaining myself, for the first monolith picked me up by the beltline of my pants, carried me to the theater's back entrance, and pitched me down four steps into the dank alleyway.

Well, I suffered severe bruising, as well as a painful misalignment of my neck that made it impossible for me to read code on a screen for more than a few minutes at a time. I wrote Nasir the Singer a sternly worded letter informing him that I planned to press both criminal and civil charges against his employees, but that I would beneficently agree to drop all legal actions if he would deign to have dinner with me. I received a return letter from Nasir's lawyer stating that he would be most pleased to meet my advocate in court, as a video security camera had captured the entirety of my interaction with the bodyguards and proved my belligerence beyond legal doubt.

Further attempts to arrange an introductory meeting between myself and Nasir the Singer proved fruitless. The best I was able to achieve was receipt in the mail of a signed photograph (the signature, seemingly authentic at first glance, proved to be the soulless imprint of a machine).

Firm in my conviction that I should not fail, that I *would not* fail, I determined to learn how others had achieved the feat of becoming one of Nasir the Singer's lovers. I attended another of Nasir's performances and approached several members of his entourage. Offers of drinks and cash proved sufficient to pry from them the knowledge I sought. A few had been fortunate enough to be plucked from a crowd by Nasir's hungry gaze. Most, however, had submitted themselves to a public pre-screening process which was monitored by Nasir's closest associates.

This pre-screening process was operated by Boudoir Auditions, Inc., a flesh procurement outfit I had previously disdained. I was shocked to learn that the high-and-mighty Nasir the Singer would sully himself with such tawdry associations, until I discovered that high-status clients such as Nasir used it merely as a tool of convenience, a way to swiftly sift through the hundreds, if not thousands, of eager men who offered their bodies for such luminaries' pleasure.

Well, if that was what it took, then that was what it took; the path to a mountain's summit often requires first tromping through mud. I went to the offices of Boudoir Auditions. The wait was longer than I had expected; I had anticipated my notoriety as a recent immigrant from Mars would obtain for me preferred treatment, but I was told, rather rudely, that I would have to wait in queue with the common rabble. While waiting, I was required to fill out a questionnaire regarding my history of amorous experiences — how many partners; occupations and accomplishments of previous partners, plus photographs of them, if available; highest number of orgasms achieved in a single twenty-four hour period; any special qualifications (virgin? body artwork? prosthetic enhancements?); and lastly, general health status. There was also an option to attach letters of commendation.

Finally, I was led into a room which was lined entirely by what I assumed to be two-way mirrors. A voice from a hidden speaker instructed me that I should take off all my clothing and select, if I so wished, a costume from the choices available within the mirrored wardrobe in the corner. The voice informed me that I would be photographed and video recorded and that by signing my name to the questionnaire I had filled out, I had consented to all such photographic and videographic recordings to be made available for public viewing.

In for a penny, in for a pound, as the old European imperialist saying went. Before stripping off my own clothing, I went to the wardrobe to make my selection. Most of what was on offer was beneath my dignity, leather accouterments suitable for domesticated animals, harem silks meant for sissy-men, and other such submissive regalia. When I had almost despaired of finding a raiment even remotely appropriate for me, I lucked upon a costume which could have been purloined from the dressing room of *The Thousand and One Nights*: a Sinbad the Sailor ensemble, complete with a menacing (although wooden) scimitar. Wonderful! Faddey be damned — clothed in this heroic costume, I would show that dour pessimist that I could make myself irresistible to Nasir the Singer, or, for that matter, to any lover I might desire.

With the golden turban on my head and curved scimitar in hand I began striking valorous poses. The puffy sleeves of the costume allowed me to minimize exposure of my less-than-ideal arm. But then the voice on the loudspeaker announced *No, no, no, that will not do.* The voice instructed me to remove the costume's flowing pantaloons and stimulate myself until I had achieved maximum rigidity. Then it coaxed me into assuming a series of humiliating tableaux. Suffice to say, the Sinbad costume was completely wasted upon the mortifying poses I was dragooned into, which cried out for the studded leather collar and dangling cow bell I had earlier disdained. What I was told to do with the scimitar I would rather not say; it was both undignified and most anxiety-inducing, considering the likelihood of splinters.

Throughout this ordeal, I only managed to maintain my composure by continually reminding myself of the mountain summit toward which I perilously climbed — the welcoming and exquisite embrace of Nasir the Singer. What heaven that would be! Heaven arduously gained through a season in Hell!

Ah, but little did I suspect the hell to which I would soon be subjected.

I waited long weeks for any notification from Nasir or his people that he would see me. Faddey was the first to inform me why such an invitation would never be proffered.

"Oh, my dear friend," he said upon finding me in our favorite hookah café, "I am afraid you have opened yourself to ridicule most cruel. Did I not warn you that your pursuit of Nasir the Singer would result only in unhappiness?"

He pulled me two blocks distant to a popular but most uncouth drinking establishment. "Unfortunate one, you must see this," he said, pushing me through the doors. The thoroughly soused patrons were all laughing uproariously at a video being played on a large viewing screen above the bar. It was I, in the Sinbad costume. The film had obviously been edited to portray me in the most ridiculous fashion possible. My dignified attempts to strike heroic poses had been intercut with the most degrading aspects of my misadventure, and the camera's lens zoomed in again and again on my abnormal arm, the whole travesty set to music befitting a circus performance.

Rather than setting that vile establishment ablaze (they had not created the loathsome video, after all), I hied myself immediately to a lawyer, intending to ransack the bank accounts of Boudoir Auditions, Inc. as ruthlessly as Tamerlane had sacked Herat. The lawyer, a pusillanimous twig of a nonentity, timidly informed me that given the signature I had placed upon the questionnaire/contract, I had no standing to sue, and that the firm's reputation for permitting its paying clients to engage in such wanton vandalism — reprehensible, but legal — was a matter of public record. Anyone with a physical handicap or disfigurement, he told me, should have known that Boudoir Auditions and its competitors were to be avoided like plague.

Four other lawyers subsequently peddled the same song of surrender to me. The so-called leadership of Salama refused to take any action on my behalf; obviously, their pockets had been lined by the same miscreants I was striving to bring to heel.

I was ruined. I had become universally recognizable on the streets of Salama, and the ridicule — not always whispered, sometimes thrown in my very face — could not be escaped. How was I to regain my reputation? I had been marked more severely than Cain, the world's first murderer, yet what had I *done?* Striven mightily in the pursuit of love? Was this considered a capital crime in Salama, that "sanctuary of safety" more saturated with conniving whores than Babylon at her most debased?

I soon discovered that I had not been alone in my ordeal of public mortification and disgrace. Anyone who fell short of this community's twisted ideal of male beauty — the short and stout; the massively fat; dwarfs and midgets; the club-footed and the lame; those with a lazy eye, or pocked skin, or receding chin, or, Allah forbid!, a tiny or malformed *quadib* — all were prone to being victimized as I had been.

There was no recourse. No court or magistrate to whom we could take our complaints. No possible appeal we could make to the consciences of the broader citizenry, entirely engrossed in their own selfish pleasures. We were a despised minority, we, the unlovely; barely tolerated among the larger population of Salama, just as all the inhabitants of Salama had once been barely tolerated within communities larger still, those composed primarily of heterosexualists.

After much meditation, I came to realize there was only one solution for us.

Complete separation. An eruvnet all our own.

Schism, Schism, *Schism!*

1.5

{Nofy in Keselamatan}

"*Impossible!*"

In my temporary quarters my blood runs so hot at the thought of Baruch Emmanuel I fear I might commit outrages of my own, offenses which could make even Ehmet Jian's seem puny and pale. "That man! He contrives to make my work here *impossible!* He expects *miracles* from me! Does he think I can part the Red Sea of the Neuronet for him by stretching out a stick?"

My outburst makes Leah cringe. "Nofy, I apologize so for Mr. Emmanuel's behavior toward you — please try to forgive him. You must understand, he is not used to having women contend with him, especially not in a professional context. Please never reveal to him that I have told you this, but when he first received news that Bradbury's Department of Trade had selected you to come here, Mr. Emmanuel became very irate and demanded that they send a man instead. But the man at the Department of Trade insisted that you are the right person for this job, and vouched for your qualifications with great sincerity. Eventually, he convinced Mr. Emmanuel to accept you, but it was a struggle."

I find myself chastened by the faith Pável Ilyich Davidov has placed in me; he, who barely knows me. How immature of me to express my frustrations in front of a client! I must watch my tongue.

At least with every passing moment, I feel more at home in my own skin, less dependent upon the support of my aid-suit. I gesture for Leah to sit. "Please forgive my outburst," I say, settling myself at the modest table. "I must remind myself that law enforcement is the art of the possible, not the ideal. Particularly when one must operate in a foreign land."

I need to systematize what facts I have. Plan a campaign which can make up in guile what it lacks in resources. "Given the evidence I have reviewed, Ehmet Jian's first two murders appear to have been crimes of passion. Community politics resulted in a bitterly divisive Schism which he unsuccessfully fought against, and which resulted in his loss of access to his lover, Sikandar Qazi. Approximately one month after the Schism, Qazi died, apparently by his own hand—"

"He was poisoned," Leah says. "It was almost certainly suicide."

"How can you be sure of that?"

"Sikandar was the reason for the Schism, the prize for which the two contending sides fought over. Ehmet Jian lost. The Little Men won, and they took Sikandar with them into their newly established eruvnet. None of the Little Men would have had any motive to harm Sikandar. They incited a Schism to take him away from Ehmet Jian, who Sikandar loved."

"You followed this case?"

"I — I was present for part of its unfolding. Mordechai Habrachas served as the officiator for the Schism, the SchneerSon who certified the results of the vote. He brought me along as his technical assistant. I set up the parameters for the new eruvnet; the Little Men named it Minutia. I watched Ehmet Jian's face when I pressed the button which made Sikandar vanish from his sight. Yes, such love is not permitted amongst the SchneerSons... but Nofy, never have I seen or heard an outburst of such passion as when Ehmet lost his Sikandar."

"Is it certain that Jian knew of Sikandar's apparent suicide in Minutia before he stabbed the two Little Men?"

She blushes — why? Does this lurid tale of homosexual passion and murder offend her sheltered sensibilities? "It — it can be *assumed* he found out. Otherwise, what would have precipitated his crimes?"

"You just told me how impassioned Jian became when Sikandar was taken away from him. Could this not have given him fuel for his murderous hatred all on its own?"

"Well, yes, I suppose. But there's the matter of timing. Ehmet committed his murders less than two days after Sikandar's death. A month had already passed since the Schism."

"Perhaps he needed to take a month to plan his crime," I say. "Crimes committed across eruvnets are not so easy to accomplish, are they? Not with the aversion settings programmed into everyone's signachips? And how do you suppose Jian could have heard of Sikandar's death? There are no shared news broadcasts, newspapers, or bulletin boards which cross eruvnet boundaries, so far as I know. In that respect, each of the City's subcommunities might as well be floating on a separate asteroid hurling through space, rather than sitting atop one another—"

"There is some trade which occurs between subcommunities," she says. "Many of the eruvnets are too small to be entirely self-sufficient. Word of Sikandar's suicide could have filtered back into Ehmet's subcommunity of `Ard Aljamal through trade exchanges."

"Well, you would know that better than I would. This is helpful. Saying the facts aloud helps me think. You don't mind, do you?"

"No, of course not. I'm happy you want to use me as a sounding board."

"One of our biggest unknowns is how Ehmet Jian, after having been sentenced to exile in Gehenna, managed to get his hands on a tuning unit. I assume you SchneerSons keep careful inventory of your essential equipment. Have any eruvnet or signachip tuning units been listed as missing?"

"No. I checked and double-checked before you arrived. All working units are accounted for."

"Could any among your people have falsified the inventory records?"

"Who would do such a thing?" She looked appalled at my suggestion. "Maintaining and protecting the Neuronet is our sacred trust. Besides, your compatriots in Bradbury have added multiple layers of security to the system. Any tampering with records would set off alarms at several levels."

After my talk with Baruch Emmanuel, it seems almost impossible to me that any SchneerSon would willingly collaborate with a criminal to do the Neuronet harm. Maintaining the system's invisible fences is a matter of self-preservation for the SchneerSons, haunted as they are by the ghosts of past massacres. "It would appear the only other source for a tuning unit would be a sympathetic confederate in the Segregatronics Corporation, perhaps an old friend of Jian's," I suggest. "I'll make some inquiries. But the possibility of a collaborator on Mars is a secondary concern at this point, one I'll be better situated to run down once I'm back in Bradbury. When was the last time your Neuronet monitors caught a blip of Jian shifting to a different eruvnet?"

"About five hours ago."

"Can you map those blips on your portable tuning unit?"

"Oh, yes, certainly."

"We'll make his most recent shift our first stop, then. Not that I expect we'll be lucky enough to cross paths with him tonight. But we need to begin mapping out his pattern of shifting, if such pattern exists. The standard strategy of laying down a net of agents and then relying on civilian informants can't be followed here. The way I see things, we have only two routes to catching him in this tangle of seventy-thousand mutually invisible subcommunities. Either we suss out a pattern to his offenses and successfully predict where he will go next, then arrive there first to lie in wait for him. Or we give him some reason to come to *us*. Unfortunately, these two options are mutually contradictory, depending on Jian's capabilities."

"What do you mean?"

"He was able to track me when I first entered the City, before you plugged me into the Neuronet and assigned my signachip an eruvnet. Which strategy will work for us depends almost entirely on whether he is still able to track me. If he can, then the notion of trying to skip ahead of him and lie in wait is senseless — he will know where I am, and so he will avoid shifting to that eruvnet. However, if he is unable to track me now that I am plugged into the Neuronet, then I can hardly expect him to come to me, no matter how much motivation I may provide him. What is your best guess, Leah, based on your knowledge of the Neuronet?"

"I — I can't rightly say. There are too many variables at work, too many unknowns—"

I pat her arm to reassure her. "Don't be too concerned over this. We'll find out soon enough what his capabilities are. In the meantime, investigating his crime scenes and interviewing his victims will serve to advance both our possible strategies. It will allow us to begin developing a theory of his motives, plans, and patterns. And, should he be able to track my travels across the invisible fences of your City, he will know I am in pursuit, collecting evidence, and this will very likely give him strong reason to confront me."

She eyes me uncertainly, probably remembering my humiliating clumsiness and incapacity at the musicians' café. "Are you... prepared to confront him, if he does come to you?"

I could tell her about the automatic tasers with which my aid-suit is equipped. But I opt to keep that knowledge to myself, out of deference to her City's prohibition on projectile weapons. "I will be ready," I say. "Do not worry."

"I can ensure that you are better prepared," she says, her eyes alight with fresh purpose. "Let me help you, Nofy."

"How?"

"There isn't time for me to train you on the comprehensive operations of a full tuning unit. But what I can do is add some of the basic functionality of a tuning unit to your aid-suit's software matrix. Just enough functionality to give you the upper hand should Ehmet Jian suddenly shift into your eruvnet and ambush you."

The notion of allowing anyone to tamper with my aid-suit, even a trusted ally, is disquieting. The lame woman unwillingly surrenders her crutch to be whittled upon, even if the carver is her village's greatest artisan. "What does this entail?"

"Not very much. I'll add a few buttons to your array and download some software packets from my tuning unit into your suit's memory. I can grant you the ability to back-shift among the last three eruvnets you've entered. Pressing a different button will allow you to exit the Neuronet entirely. I can't give you full independent Neuronet navigation tools without giving you your own tuning unit, which my superiors wouldn't allow. Those limited capabilities I just mentioned will only work when you're within a fifty meter radius of my unit, less than that if we are separated by walls. But at least you'll have some independent control, in case of an emergency. That way, you won't be entirely dependent upon me."

I easily picture how such enhancements could save my life. I have little fear Jian could successfully attack me with an edged weapon, like he did his first three victims; his approaching within six meters with what the aid-suit determines to be aggressive intent would result in his being disabled by my tasers, a preferred outcome, for sure. But if he has acquired a gun? Being able to instantly shift to a formerly occupied eruvnet with the press of a button could hide me from his sight for a few decisive seconds.

Or dropping out of the Neuronet entirely... palsy would return to my muscles, but I would instantly gain awareness of the full range of cover surrounding me, things I could use either as shields or weapons.

So I offer myself to Leah's ministrations — for during my years in Bradbury I have come to consider my aid-suit a part of myself. "Go ahead," I say. "Before we begin our chase, work your magic."

We board a streetcar at the terminus of Balarang Avenue. Although the car appears empty, my signachip blurts aversion signals to my muscles as I pass seat after seat filled with invisible passengers. Leah grabs a hanging strap near the back of the car; I do the same. I am taken back two decades and more, to those endless afternoons when I wandered the City aboard seemingly empty streetcars, holding a leather strap while standing at the back.

The City has not upgraded to air-conditioning its streetcars in the years since I departed, but relief from the morning's heat comes soon. The vehicle's electric motor hums into renewed life and the car lurches into motion, its forward passage creating breezes which flow through the car's open windows.

I decide to experiment with one of my new abilities and press the freshly installed red button on the left wrist of my aid-suit. Immediately, just as Leah promised, I am vomited forth from the belly of the Neuronet. I sense my palsy's leaden return, but my aid-suit compensates, providing me just enough strength and coordination to continue clinging to the leather strap overhead. All of my fellow passengers are now visible to me; I see the car is completely filled. The breezes flowing from the front bring a pungent miscellany of strong aromas — body odors, workers' sweat, skin scents made tangy or sour by varying spices consumed. All those childhood years of riding the City's streetcars, oftentimes on a stiflingly hot day like today, and never until now have I smelled the perspiring armpits of another passenger.

The streetcar sways gently from side to side as it picks up speed. Despite the dangers of my present endeavor, a sweet pall of nostalgia descends upon me. So little has changed here in the past fourteen years. I stare out the windows at the clusters of apartment buildings and shops along Balarang Avenue, the apartment blocks, four, five, or six stories high, made of the same gray stone as the municipal buildings in Queen Elizabeth Square, their tall, narrow windows also serving as doors onto tiny balconies that hang over the avenue. As a girl, I imagined such places as ghost villages, abandoned locales haunted by *angatra*, stubborn ghosts who will not leave, and plagued with *kalamoro*, mischievous imps. Yet now I see they are bustling with residents. The balconies of one block are crowded with dusky men in turbans smoking long pipes, or women in flowing saris hanging laundry. The balconies of the next building host mainly short, wiry men whose jaws chew incessantly and who wear no shirts, the coppery skin of their chests marked with tribal runes of scarification. And then there is a building where pale, blond-haired children, completely naked, run from shadowed rooms onto the sun-drenched balconies, shrieking with the excitement of play, ignoring the admonishing shouts of their mothers.

All those neighbors I was never aware of. All those children with whom I might have played, only I never heard their happy greetings. They do not see me now, as I did not see them then. To those children on the balconies, I am merely an *angatra*. A ghost who will not leave.

Keselamatan is an enclave made up entirely of ethnic Malays, all followers of a peculiar religio-political mutation of twentieth century Chinese communism. Physically, it is located just two kilometers northeast of Baruch Emmanuel's office in Queen Elizabeth Square. Psychically, it is a planetary orbit distant. Its inhabitants eagerly await the celestial transfiguration of Mao Zedong, whom they claim will return to Earth in his true form, as a Malay, and will free the aboriginal Malays from their economic and social subjugation to the ethnic Chinese in their midst, then establish an egalitarian utopia of Confucian and Muhammadian virtue. Except, of course, in Keselamatan, there are no ethnic Chinese. Or at least there are not supposed to be.

Based upon Leah's insistent advice, I allow her to adjust my signachip so that I appear, both to others and to myself, as a Malay man. She does likewise for herself. I grumbled at this change of sex, feeling it demeaning, but Leah argued that the man with whom we need speak, Comrade Supreme Iman Panjang bin Wira, would refuse to meet with us if we /remained perceivably female.

Bin Wira is a squat, fleshy man dressed in resplendent robes of purple and gold. He insists we meet him at the Barham Square House of Worship, which in Keselamatan is known, in rough translation, as Long March Resting Sanctuary of Holy Comrade Mao Zedong. We enter the sanctuary to find workers who appear to be of East African origin (contract laborers from another eruvnet, I assume) scrubbing what may be dried blood from a marble altar and statues and grand portraits of a man

I presume to be the Holy Comrade Zedong. Bin Wira, agitated, eyes bulging from his puffy face, intercepts us before we reach the back pews. "You are the SchneerSons, am I right?" he says, voice choked with indignation. "This is where it happened! This is where my people were *defiled* by a *devil!* A devil who has the powers of a *SchneerSon!*"

I watch Leah, cybernetically disguised as a Malay man, wilt beneath the implied accusation. "Any outrages committed here were not performed by a SchneerSon," I say. "We are seeking a renegade, a multiple murderer who was sentenced to Gehenna but somehow managed to use his technical skills to escape—"

"Is he ethnic Chinese? The man I saw who splashed the blood of pigs into our holy sanctuary and defiled its corridors with the dirty carcasses of dogs was Chinese. But he could have been a SchneerSon *pretending* to be a hated Chinese, just as you pretend to be Malay—"

"That is an *evil* defamation," Leah says in a half whisper, her voice choked.

"He is a Uyghur named Ehmet Jian," I interject, "of Muslim heritage, much like you and your people. According to my dossier, he probably hates the Han Chinese as much as you do. He grew up on Mars, in the colony of Bradbury, then emigrated to your City, ultimately joining an eruvnet community called 'Ard Aljamal. After playing an instrumental role in two separate Schisms, he was involved in what is believed to be a crime of passion, killing two men. He was then exiled to Gehenna. By unknown means, he managed to escape, most likely using pilfered equipment and the tech skills he remembered from Bradbury. After his escape, he continued committing crimes. I myself witnessed him slit a SchneerSon musician's throat. Now he is jumping from eruvnet to eruvnet, leaving a trail of mayhem—"

"You are pursuing him?" bin Wira says. "When he is caught, you will turn him over to us for punishment? I can assure you, we will not make the error of merely banishing him to Gehenna."

"We are pursuing him, yes. But I'm afraid that handing him over to your community cannot be done."

"*What?* This is *outrageous*—"

"Jian has committed serious crimes against multiple eruvnet communities. None of these have superior jurisdictional rights over the others, not even the SchneerSons' Eruv Rav, which Jian has also committed offenses against. When Jian escaped from Gehenna, he was stripped of his citizenship in your City. He reverted to his prior citizenship, that of a Bradburian. That is why, when I apprehend him, I will take him back with me to Mars."

Now his eyes truly bulged from his head. "You are an *outworlder?* The SchneerSons consort with a *Martian?*"

Oh, these people and their xenophobia! One of the reasons I fled the City! "I am a Bradburian, yes. A Bradburian law enforcement officer. Jian is my responsibility. Now, who here witnessed Jian's offenses in this sanctuary?"

"I myself did witness them," bin Wira says. "I was conducting the Holy Service of the Red Star when the invader entered with his foul implements and began his unspeakable desecration. That devil seeks to rush the Eschaton, you know? He seeks to deny us the favor of the Holy One, the Returned Mao, blessings be upon him. That cursed creature must know that tribulations are the echoes of the Holy Mao's footsteps, that the Great Zedong will not return to Earth until the hated Chinese have vented their wrath upon the Malays. By heaping tribulations upon us, the invader hopes to bring Holy Mao out of Heaven, to prematurely usher in his judgment. But we of Keselamatan are not yet ready. We have not yet fully cleansed our community of impure words and thoughts."

"What do you mean, Comrade Supreme Iman?" Leah asks, surprising me. I thought she had been so thoroughly insulted at the outset that she would stand silent as a stone.

"I quail to admit such a failing on our part, but we have not yet completed our Great Leap Forward. Our people labor long hours at libraries throughout the City, banishing books from our eruvnet which conflict with the teachings of Holy Comrade Mao, blessings be upon him. But there are hundreds of thousands of books, and each book contains hundreds of thousands of words, and each word must be weighed and judged for its accordance with the sayings of the Holy One. Should the devilish machinations of the demon Jian — may his name be blotted out from the memories of men! — succeed in ushering forth the premature return of Holy Comrade Mao before we have completed our Great Leap Forward, the Holy One will forsake us, he will choose to save a people more worthy than we Malays—"

An ominous buzzing issues from the tuning unit bound to Leah's wrist. She flips open its screen. Seconds later, she turns to me, her pained concern obvious, even projected through her cybernetic mask.

"Nofy, he's shifted again. I hate telling you this... but Ehmet Jian has gone to Anarako Arivo."

My birth clan's home. Lost home of my heart.

2.4

{Ehmet in `Ard Aljamal}

Since I had become so notorious on the streets of Salama, publicly jeered at as Sinbad the Laughable, or Sinbad the Self-Impaler, all those who fell short of Salama's tyrannical beauty standards knew I shared their grievances. So I encountered no difficulty whatsoever in claiming the mantle of their spokesman, their advocate, their champion. And I exercised the scepter of leadership vigorously.

"Follow me to a land where we shall be free to set our *own* standards of beauty!" I trumpeted. "Schism is the answer, the *only* answer! Be not afraid of change! Schism with me! All you have to lose are the shackles of ridicule, rejection, and contempt!"

My speeches inspired a multitude of the despised, and my calls for Schism were echoed by thousands of the heretofore dispossessed. Not a word of protest was heard from the leaders and luminaries of Salama regarding my campaign, ratifying our direst notions of their prejudice toward us. Clearly, they would be happy to see us gone.

Ultimately, I represented a tad more than forty-five hundred persons when I presented to an official of the SchneerSons our petition for Schism. Thousands more could have opted to join us, but were apparently too afraid of losing access to their preferred jobs or Salama's boisterous nightlife. They were free to choose misery, I suppose, having demonstrated their servile willingness to accept the yoke of second class citizenry in exchange for a few scraps from the tables of their "betters". I did not often quote the poets of the European imperialists, but I heartily agreed with

John Milton's famed maxim: *Better to reign in Hell, than serve in Heaven.*

It was distasteful to me having to deal with the Jew, Mordechai of the SchneerSons, but necessary. He and he alone held the keys to our new kingdom. I must admit he was helpful; indeed, he proved almost fawning in his solicitude, the precise opposite of the "worthies" of Salama. He pointed out that with fewer than five thousand initial inhabitants, `Ard Aljamal — that was the name we had chosen for our new eruvnet; in Arabic, it meant *Land of Beauty*, a declaration of our intent to subvert conventional notions of attractiveness — would most likely not encompass among its limited citizenry the full panoply of skills necessary for an autonomous community's functioning. He offered a solution: groups of professionals from other eruvnets who, seeking maximum profits, offered their wares and services to any and all eruvnets willing to do business with them. The Jew made quite an extensive menu of commercial alliances available to us, with each option fully tailorable. If we wanted to avail ourselves of the services of Ashkenazic Jew physicians, for example, but did not wish to be made aware of their baleful presence any more than absolutely necessary, we could choose that our eruvnet's settings would make them perceptible to us only on certain days of the month. Similarly, if we wished to occasionally enjoy performances by a Chinese-European orchestra but were repelled by the notion of having to look at their imperialist faces, we could have our eruvnet adjusted so that only the sound of their music would be available to us, not the sight or smell of the assembled musicians.

A delightful invention, this Neuronet! How strange, I thought, that I had labored so many years on Mars to maintain and perfect it, yet I had never truly contemplated its utility. It allowed tiny minorities such as us to enjoy all the advantages of a city teeming with eight million inhabitants, picking and choosing any goods and services which appealed to us, while at the same time preserving our distinctiveness and maximizing our autonomy.

The choicest aspect by far of having precipitated a successful Schism was that I immediately became the most honored and revered member of my community — and the most desirable. In the erotic pecking order, I went from (in Salama) the flea-infested rodent hiding beneath the palace stairs to (in `Ard Aljamal) the worshiped god-king ensconced in the golden throne.

I filled my nights with erotic trysts — oh, those Thousand and One Nights! And yet, despite the endless variety, despite the meticulous attentions lavished upon me by a parade of eager lovers, I found that something was missing. As time went on, my lovers held less and less appeal for me. I caught myself obsessing on their flaws... this one's overbite and lisp; that one's protrusive mole between his eyebrows, as jarring as a third eye; this one's pigeon toes and greasy skin; that one's unnervingly loud flatulence during the act of love. I rebuked myself — had my erotic imagination been so thoroughly colonized by the oppressive beauty standards of the Salamites? Or, worse, by the tyrannical aesthetics of the heterosexualists, imperialists, and ableists I had been forced to fraternize with in Bradbury?

I tried to force such self-defeating obsessions from my mind, telling myself they were corrosive, invading memes planted there by my past enemies. Yet the harder I strove to eliminate them, the more intensely such obsessions bedeviled me. This psychological turmoil affected me in the worst way possible. I found myself unable to sustain an erection. The mere thought of sharing my body with any of the human atrocities who petitioned to crawl beneath my sheets made my gorge rise.

Overcome by disgust at the shambling monstrosities who surrounded me, I had nearly resigned myself to a lifetime of celibacy when at last I perceived my salvation. There, in a hookah café in Barham Square, sitting like a miniature angel upon a booster seat so that he might more easily inhale the vapors, was the most exquisite creature I had been blessed to look upon since my initial glimpse of Nasir the Singer. A midget, surrounded at his table by fellow midgets and comparatively grotesque dwarfs. Flawless almond skin, delicate fingers, noble shoulders, the face of a warrior-saint... but small, compact, as though a far larger, more coarsely made man had been condensed into perfection by immense pressure, like a lump of coal compressed by the weight of Earth's mantle into a diamond.

He turned his shining face to me, undoubtedly sensing the psychic weight of my gaze, and smiled. And, oh, that *smile!* It completed the conquest of my heart. I knew at that instant that I could no longer live if I could not have this child-man as my lover.

I, who during my entire time in `Ard Aljamal had been as confident and headstrong as Saladin in selecting lovers, suddenly found myself as shy and hesitant as a virgin. The thought that I might be rejected by him tortured me, a volley of flaming arrows which pierced my heart. I spied upon his interactions with his fellows, trying to determine which of them, if any, claimed him for their own. My diamond was consistently fawned upon by midgets and dwarfs alike, obviously a prize to be contested for. But who were these nonentities who surrounded him? *Little* people, in all senses of that diminutizing modifier. In contrast, who was *I?* Why, none other than these wretches' liberator, their champion and savior. Did they not owe me everything?

I called over the waiter, a man afflicted with a most unfortunate harelip, and directed him to deliver a bottle of the café's most expensive vintage to my petite angel, along with a note. I watched my living jewel accept the wine with a delicate look of surprise. Then, as he read the note, a most appealing blush overtook his features. He turned once more to look upon me, to thank me. Our eyes met. Wordlessly I summoned him, relying upon the palpable lines of electricity which surged between us. He climbed down from his booster seat, then approached my table like a somnambulist striding across a grassy field covered in evening's fog.

His departure from his companions caused consternation at his table, but what of it? Those dwarfs and pixies were clearly unworthy of him, bits of pyrite and pig iron seeking to hide the glory of the gold in their midst. But that glory would not remain hidden — it was mine to claim, *mine*, my reward for all the suffering I had been forced to endure.

I shared a rare vintage with the exquisite Sikandar Qazi that evening, but no sips of the nectar of fermented grapes were necessary to intoxicate me. Or, apparently, him. What followed was bliss such as I had never known. Many have said that having cannot compare with wanting, but such was never remotely the case with Sikandar Qazi. His conversation proved every bit as delightful as his love-making. Following some minor initial awkwardness, he admitted, shamefacedly, that I was the first "big" lover he had ever accommodated, but far from being off-putting, this admission only inflamed my passion all the more. We eagerly flipped through the gilt-edged pages of his copy of the venerated *Kama Sutra*, a book I had previously avoided due to its Hindu origins, but which I now accepted because my petite angel so delighted in it. What endless hours of enchantment we relished as we tirelessly experimented with those couplings, adjusted, of course, to lovers of vastly disparate size.

I could deny nothing to my precious Sikandar. Not even other lovers, although I bitterly resented every moment he was not in my embrace. My darling stated in all sincerity that the custom among his people, the little men who love other little men, was that no lover was enjoyed exclusively, and that love was freely shared amongst all. His eyes filled with tears as he explained to me that any abrogation of this custom on his part would result in his being ostracized by his fellows, and his very soul would shrivel. I had not the heart to make him dread censure from his clan, so I, confident in my superiority to any lover he might take among the little men, magnanimously allowed him one night in three to go frolic amongst his fellows. Of course, how I grinned inwardly as I listened to his pillow-talk revelations that my mighty ministrations had rendered him unsuitable to receive love from his diminutive fellows, much to their jealous woe!

I would not be seen in public without my Sikandar. When he complained of the difficulty he had in matching my strides in the streets, I had built for him a special, one-of-a-kind rickshaw cart in which I could transport him; I had it lined with padded ox leather and goose down pillows, its edges highlighted with hammered gold. I dressed my darling in flowing silks and encouraged him to paint his eyelids in vibrant shades, to adorn his lovely arms and hands with henna tattoos. No one in `Ard Aljamal could boast of a more pampered or more exquisite lover.

I thought I had finally achieved my earthly paradise. Yet little did I recognize the dark clouds gathering above my redoubt of happiness.

The first shadows I noticed were those which intruded one night upon the heavenly face of my Sikandar. To see any unhappiness marring his aspect was like unto the approach of death itself. "My precious darling," I said as I cut his meat for him into tiny, neat morsels, "what has caused you to frown so? Is the meal not to your liking? Do you wish for different music to be played? Merely say so, and I will have the musicians dismissed, the distasteful food tossed to the dogs and the isolates, and a fresh meal prepared—"

He shook his head, and I saw tears glimmering in the orbs of his flawless eyes. "No, Ehmet, nothing here is amiss. It is just that... oh, this is so hard to *say!*"

My heart plunged like a rock dropped into a bottomless well. "Sikandar, have I... dissatisfied you? Tell me, precious one. Tell me anything, hold nothing back! Everything can be made right! We have shared paradise, and we will share it again!"

"It... it is Bora Ali. You know him, slightly. He is one of my closest and most influential clan associates. He is like an uncle to me. From birth, I have been under his protection."

"And what of this Bora Ali? What has he said or done to darken your face and disturb the peace of our table?"

"He... he does not approve of our relationship, Ehmet."

Despite my concern for Sikandar's feelings, I laughed at the absurdity of it. "And who is *he* to disapprove? What can any other man's disapproval matter to our exalted love, our thrice-blessed universe of two?"

He would no longer meet my eyes. "Bora Ali is considered by all the caliph of the Little Men. His word has the force of law among my clan."

I felt rage gathering within my breast. "What has he said against me?"

"He has said... that you dishonor all Little Men through your actions. That you fetishize my small stature because it makes you feel big. That you humiliate me and diminish me in public by carrying me about in the rickshaw and dressing me as you do — 'like a baby's doll,' he says. That whether you realize it or not, you are *sizeist*, through and through."

The rage within me boiled over. I flung my plate against the wall of our private dining room. "*Calumnies!* I will rip his tiny, lying tongue from his mouth! You know this is all nothing more than an impotent expression of *jealousy*, don't you, Sikandar? Has this 'uncle' of yours ever tried having his way with you? I know why he seeks to tear me down! He is disgusted by his own inadequacy, that his *quadib* is no larger than a howler monkey's, and he can no longer provide you pleasure because I have rendered you unfit for such puny instruments. Because I have made you *mine*. I will speak with him this very night, I will convince him to silence his lying tongue—"

"No!" Sikandar's tears flowed freely. "You *mustn't*, Ehmet! He is my close kinsman! The caliph of my clan! You mustn't disrespect or dishonor him, you *mustn't!*"

The Greeks had their Achilles, their mightiest of champions who was brought low by a seemingly insignificant weakness, the uncharmed nature of his heel. Prominent though I was, mighty in esteem, I could no more stand against Sikandar's tears than could a pebble against a raging flood.

I pulled him close, nestled his precious head against my chest so that I could no longer see his tears. Yet I could feel them against my skin, trickling down my bosom, leaving traces from my heart like escaping rivulets of life's blood. "Sikandar, my dearest darling, stop your tears... I repent of my intentions. I will not confront your kinsman — not that he does not richly deserve my rebuke. But I refrain out of purest love for you. Nor do I wish you to suffer the condemnation of your clan. I will make... all efforts to conform to the expectations of the Little Men in my public behavior toward you."

And that tender-hearted accommodation proved my fatal undoing. For my enemies, Bora Ali chief among them, scented weakness in my concern for my beloved's feelings... perceived that I, so much grander than they in stature, could be made to stumble and lick the dust at their stunted feet.

I sold the gilded rickshaw and all its fineries. In public, I had Sikandar walk at my side, retarding my stride so that he could keep pace with me.

Yet this retreat on my part proved insufficient for the sensitivities of the Little Men. I felt their malicious, reproachful gazes follow us as we walked past the cafés where they gathered and the repair shops where they worked. Their gazes, freighted with dark accusation.

No more than a month had passed since I had been forced to divest us of the gilded rickshaw when Sikandar again approached me in tears. "What troubles you now, you who put the stars to shame?" I said, fearing the answer.

"My people... they say you remain sizeist in your heart."

"In my *heart?* How can they see what is in my heart? Are they mind readers, as well as menders of clocks?"

"They see it in your *stride*, Ehmet. In how you walk when you are beside me, they read bad intentions—"

"How is such misperception even *possible?* Is it not obvious to *all* that I have slowed my steps so that you need not hurry to keep pace with me?"

"They say you silently mock me. They say you exaggerate the effort you put into unnaturally slowing your walk so that you may silently insult my diminutude. You place upon them a most heavy burden of belittlement, they say."

"This is *absurd!* You know I have no intention whatsoever of insulting your people. Did I not follow their wishes regarding the rickshaw, at considerable financial detriment? Does not that prove my sincerity?"

"They say intentions do not matter. They say aggrievement is measured by the feelings of the aggrieved, not by the intentions of the offender."

"But — but that isn't fair at *all!* What possible recourse can one have, if accusations of harm can be hurled without a shred of proof? According to your clan, I am guilty of insulting Little Men if I slow my pace to match yours; I am guilty if I walk at my normal pace; and I am equally or perhaps *more* guilty if I pull you behind me in a cushioned rickshaw. How am I *not* to be guilty?

What do they expect me to do when accompanying you in public? To not accompany you at *all?*"

He offered no answer, instead staring at his feet. No answer from him was necessary. I already knew what the Little Men wanted.

Not long after, I was on my way to work at the Water Center, about to cross through Mahatma Gandhi Square, when I espied a parade of dwarfs and midgets circling the central fountain, all carrying placards. I paused to listen to their chants:

"No Big domination! It's abomination!"

"Big hands off Little People!"

"Sizeism is the problem! Schism is the solution!"

"We're not pets! We're not toys! We're not your little snuggly boys!"

Thank Allah I did not see Sikandar among them! Such a sight would have ground my heart to dust. I hurried to my office, feeling unseen djinns pursuing me through the air, eager to drain all happiness from me.

During one of Sikandar's nights away from me, while I comforted myself before my fire with a book of amusing tales, I was startled by an insistent knock upon my door. When I opened it, at first I saw no one and thought a prankster had knocked and then fled. But then I heard the clearing of a throat and looked down. It was Bora Ali, the dwarf. Sikandar's "uncle."

"May I come in?" he said in a voice both high-pitched and gruff.

I would rather have invited a cobra into my parlor, but I ushered him inside.

"There is something urgent we must discuss, Ehmet Jian," he said. "You have been setting a most distressing example for your fellow Bigs here in `Ard Aljamal. An example which must come to an immediate end. Although we all appreciate your prior service in liberating us from the Salamists, such past virtue does not excuse your current offenses."

"'*Offenses*'?" I was tempted to take up a fireplace iron and strike this impudent insect until he was no more than a red smear. But I held my temper with the strength of a lion. "Tell me, Bora Ali, how exactly have I offended against you, a person with whom I have never spoken or done business?"

"You have misused your position of public esteem by setting an injurious example. Your conduct with Sikandar Qazi has made it fashionable for Bigs to take Little Men as lovers."

"So a fad has taken root? How am I to blame for the conduct of other men in their bedrooms? There isn't a court on Earth or Mars which would declare me culpable for this supposed 'crime' you accuse me of."

"Culpability is not at issue here. Only the baleful outcomes matter. We Little Men are being subjugated and objectivized by the oppressive erotic imaginations of you Bigs. Your lofty gaze assaults us, whether that be a gaze of contempt or a gaze of lust. There are only two possible recourses we can seek. Either you can renounce your relationship with Sikandar Qazi, publicly repent your crime of sizeism, and implore your fellow Bigs to do the same. Or, if you refuse, there will be Schism, and you will never see Sikandar again so long as you live."

That smug little mouth. Those cruel eyes, hidden like poisonous beetles within folds of pustulant flesh. He was the minute exemplar of all the dark forces which had ever conspired against me. I wanted to obliterate him from existence. But I retained enough mental wherewithal, even thrashing about within the molten core of my rage, to suspect he was trying to provoke me — that he *wanted* me to physically attack him, because he had positioned confederates outside my windows to witness my assault upon their leader... the better to justify Schism, which I believed to be his ultimate goal.

"Get out of my home," I said, my voice barely cloaking the chaos within me. To restrain my hands, I forced my thumbs through my belt loops, all the while imagining I was forcing them through his eye sockets. "I will never renounce Sikandar, and he will never leave me. We are one, he and I, until the end of time and all things. Do not seek to disrupt what you cannot comprehend, dwarf."

He smiled, and I realized with dawning horror that I had said precisely what he had wished me to. "Then you make Schism inevitable," he crowed.

No! Never! "Under the rules to which every man of `Ard Aljamal has pledged to follow," I said with repressed heat, "two-thirds of the community must approve any proposed Schism for it to take effect. I will speak against it, loudly and indefatigably. How can you expect your word will prevail against mine? I need only to convince one third plus one that you should stay. And even if you should manage somehow to work a feat of sorcery and win the referendum, Sikandar would choose to remain with me."

"Oh, Sikandar will accompany his clan wherever we choose to go. You have no idea how tightly he is bound to us. And do not flatter yourself, Martian, by thinking your reputation is an unassailable fortress. Any fortress wall can be breached. To take but one example, there is the matter of your Martian perfidy, often discussed in hushed whispers. Your use of Martian technological wizardry to subtly alter your signachip, so that you made yourself irresistible to Sikandar Qazi. Ensorceled the poor, innocent lad, in fact—"

"That is a base *lie!*"

"Is it?" His beetle eyes glimmered darkly. "I am sure you have heard it said: a lie can traverse the eight walls of the City before the truth has crossed the threshold of a single house. Persist in your stubbornness, Ehmet Jian, and you will bring ruin down upon your head. This I promise you."

Bora Ali, that potbellied demon-piglet, proved true to his threat. He petitioned the SchneerSons for Schism. The referendum was scheduled for one month from the day of petition. I worked tirelessly to convince my fellow citizens to deny Schism, putting aside my paying job to speechify and distribute pamphlets over a marathon stretch of eighteen hour days.

More and more, however, I had to defend myself from a flood of scurrilous rumors — that I was a Martian spy, or a closeted heterosexualist. Or, most grotesque of all, that I had sliced off Sikandar's *quadib,* placed it in preservative fluid in a pickle jar, and used my Martian technology to make him a mechanical replacement, which I would only allow him to use so long as he remained my slave.

The demonic spite of Bora Ali and his criminal gang of Little Men knew no limit. Some credulous fools believed their atrocious slanders, but most men outside their tiny circle recoiled from such hateful tactics. Yet such revulsion did not redound to my benefit. Even close confidants approached me to hesitantly voice the opinion that, given the Little Men's ruthlessness and cutthroatery, perhaps it would be better for all if they left. After all, if they were willing to so savagely attack *me*, the father of `Ard Aljamal, who next might fall victim to their tiny fangs?

Sikandar wasted away. He would not eat. Throughout the month leading to the referendum, I watched his flesh melt from his precious bones, as though he were victim to a dreadful cancer. His desire for lovemaking vanished. The angelic effervescence which had once animated his eyes dimmed like a dying flame. At night he lay in bed beside me, a bundle of sticks, his breathing barely detectable.

The dread day arrived. I had pressed my shoulder to the burden of my cause with as much vigor as man or demigod could expend, yet I knew before the first vote was cast that I had lost. Bora Ali's strategy had been equally odious and brilliant. His monstrous calumnies succeeded either in making me repugnant to the voters or making him and his Little Men repugnant; either way, he persuaded our fellow citizens to choose the option he wanted.

The SchneerSons certified the voting tallies. They announced that Schism would proceed. For the great majority of the citizens of `Ard Aljamal, this change would cause less than a vanishing ripple in their lives; the Little Men amongst us numbered fewer than sixty, and the SchneerSons could arrange matters so that their specialized skills of clock repair and mending of household engines would still remain accessible to us. But for some of us, those few who had known the paradise of Little-Big love? Our world came crashing down, then ignited into flame.

I trembled as if with fever. Approaching the desiccated wreck who was my Sikandar to ask the question I must was akin to walking across glowing coals with naked feet. "Sikandar, my dearest darling, most precious jewel in all creation... will you stay with me?"

I waited for his parched lips to move. Those lips, which only weeks ago had provided me with ecstasies unimaginable, now quivered with palsied impotence, as though they had forever lost the power of speech.

"If you stay, Sikandar... if you stay, if you will only eat and allow yourself to get well, I will be all things to you. Lover, father, husband, brother, son, uncle, clansman, worshiper... even slave."

I would have abased myself in any and all ways for him. If it would have restored him to robust healthfulness, I would have flayed off my own skin, cooked it for him until tender, and fed it to him with fleshless fingers.

Yet it was all in vain, in vain. Like trying to irrigate a desert with a thimbleful of water, or breathe the atmosphere of Mars. Bora Ali, may his black soul be thrice damned to the most sulphurous pit of Hell, had been right.

My status as a community leader of `Ard Aljamal obligated me to be present at the finalization of Schism, the ceremony at which the departing citizens of `Ard Aljamal would be granted membership in the new community of Minutia, and all administrative matters would be finalized. The SchneerSons were again represented by Mordechai the Jew. But this time, he had brought an assistant with him, a black-clad woman he did not bother to introduce to us. Lowly female factotum, she performed the monotonous yet intricate work of adjusting the Little Men's signachips and entering the newly required restrictions on the settings of `Ard Aljamal's and Minutia's eruvnets.

I watched her pale fingers tap upon the keys of her portable tuning unit. In that portion of my mind where the engineer in me held sway, I understood all too well that every tap of her fingertips represented a hammer blow on the nails of the lid of my coffin. Yet it felt too terrible to be real. Was Allah so cruel? Did love and devotion lack all potency? Was the universe nothing more than Newton's clock, oblivious to the needs and passions of men, a soulless mechanism maintained by a dwarf?

I scanned the auditorium for Sikandar. Alas, a phalanx of Little Men surrounded him, hiding him from me, denying me even a final glimpse of my eternal love.

Mordechai asked Bora Ali to certify the list of persons who would be transferring to Minutia's newly created eruvnet. Searching my soul, I realized my pride meant less to me than the vanished seas of Mars. It had been crushed out of me like oil from a bushel of olives. What was pride, compared to the unbearable reality of my heart being ripped from my breast?

I inserted myself between the Jew and Bora Ali and fell to my knees. "I have a petition to make!" I cried. "I want to renounce my citizenship in `Ard Aljamal! I want to become a citizen of Minutia!"

"Impossible," the dwarf sneered.

"I know how to adjust my signachip! I can make it so that everyone in Minutia will perceive me as a midget!"

"It would not matter. You would remain a Big. We would not have you among us."

"Please, Bora Ali! I will do anything you wish! I will clean toilets. I will collect trash from the streets — I will pick up the defecations of wandering dogs with my hands. You could savor the pleasure of humiliating me daily over the span of our remaining lives. Only... allow me to walk the same streets, smell the same aromas, hear the same music as Sikandar does. For the mercy of Allah, allow me to share his eruvnet, even if we may never touch..."

"It is a sincere petition, properly presented," Mordechai the Jew said. "Bora Ali, do you wish to confer with your fellow citizens before the list of Schismites is certified as complete and final?"

"No consultation is necessary," the dwarf said coldly. "The whole reason for the establishment of Minutia is so that we Little Men who love other Little Men can have a safe space of our own. As emir, I would be grossly remiss in my duties were I to permit our safe space to be violated. We of Minutia will permit limited contact with citizens of certain other, approved eruvnets to allow for our trade in clock and engine repairs to continue, as well as other necessary commerce. However, due to his past offenses against us, we declare that Ehmet Jian shall never again perceive the citizens of Minutia, nor shall any citizen of Minutia perceive him."

A piercing wail arose from within the circle of Little Men. I recognized my darling's voice.

I remained crumpled on the floor, listening to the unnamed woman tapping upon her keys. I looked up at her, the last person to whom I could address my silent plea, even though I knew she lacked all agency in this matter. She was merely Mordechai's tool, and thus Bora Ali's. She paused from her accursed work to meet my grief-saturated gaze. Although she was both woman and Jewess, I sensed she understood the magnitude of my torment. There was pity in her face, pity which I could not bear, but also empathy, and genuine regret at my abasement. Alas, she was as powerless as I.

She pressed a key one last time. My Sikandar vanished from my world, like a dream stripped from one's consciousness by the rising of the sun.

1.6

{Nofy in Anarako Arivo}

Anarako Arivo. Home of my heart. Home which broke my heart.

Leah and I disembark from the Burrup Avenue streetcar at the ring road surrounding Lachlan Square, the northernmost of the City's seventeen public squares. Even as a young girl, I thought it strange that my ancestral clan, upon fleeing from Madagascar, had chosen the district farthest from the sea in which to resettle; for we Betsimisaraka had always been coastal people, not highlanders like the Merina and Sihanaka clans. Perhaps my forefathers and foremothers had not wished to be reminded of the seaside home they had lost, so they had selected a neighborhood pressed against the northernmost of the City's eight walls, where the sounds of the ocean would never intrude. If that were indeed the case, I now understand their desire to put a forsaken home far from their thoughts.

It began as such a trivial matter, the Schism which made me walk away from the City. Nandrianina, mother of my best friend, Mialy, broke her ankle when she dismounted badly from a step ladder. Mialy's father insisted that his wife continue to do all of the household chores, even though she was encumbered by crutches and a cast. Nandrianina was a strong-willed woman, never one to take umbrage from either her children or the other women in our village, but until now, she had been reliably subservient to her husband. Yet the parochial injustice of his insistence that she continue with her labors as though she were uninjured shattered the restraints tradition had placed on her. She refused his demands. Flamboyantly refused them. When he handed her the filled water bucket and commanded her to water the family's quartet of sheep, she hurled the bucket in his face, bloodying his nose.

Thanks to Nandrianina's public display of righteous defiance, what began as a family quarrel quickly spread to the rest of the village, becoming an open clash between the sexes. Wives refused for the first times in their marriages to submit to their husbands' wills. I was fourteen at the time, very much in love with Hery, a boy two years my senior who barely acknowledged my presence. Mialy's and my hearts filled with dread as the conflict between the men and women of our clan raged out of control; husbands and wives competed as to who could utter the most hurtful deprecations, wives denied their husbands physical love, husbands struck faces they had hitherto adored, and we young people were pressed by our increasingly irrational elders to take sides according to what lay between our legs.

It ended in Schism. Nandrianina, still on crutches, petitioned the SchneerSons to officiate over the splitting up of our clan along the fault line of sex. I went forlornly and bitterly with the women into their new eruvnet, knowing I would likely never see Hery again, never grasp his hand in mine. I would never marry and start a family of my own, unless I abandoned my clan and succeeded in finding another eruvnet community willing to take me in. During the next three unhappy years, I often contemplated throwing my lot in with an alien community, one of the seventy thousand which I had heard resided within the City's eight walls. But the more I contemplated this escape route, the more it came to seem like fleeing the drenching downpour of a rainstorm in the depths of the sea.

After all, how had there come to be seventy thousand subcommunities in our City? Surely there had not been seventy thousand different clans, seventy thousand different combinations of skin tone and nose shape and language and religion which had fled to these shores? From what I had learned at my school, there had been fewer than two hundred separate nations when the Wars of All Against All had begun, and most of those nations would have had fewer than a dozen self-segregating ethnic and religious groups within their borders. Twelve multiplied by two hundred only came to twenty-four hundred, not seventy thousand. So from whence had this immense expansion come in the century since? From endless Schisms, repeated and repeated like a piece of paper being folded in half, then in quarters, then again and again, ever smaller, stopping only when warring couples were Schismed into isolates which drifted invisibly through the City like specks of dust.

Why subject myself to more of the same? If I were so determined to leave my sundered clan, the only clan I had ever known, why not leave this heartbreaking City entirely? And so when I left, I made the big leaving. I leaped all the way to Mars, to Bradbury, to what seemed to my seventeen year-old self to be sanity.

Yet I never did find a man to fit me. I never did start a family of my own, despite fleeing headlong through eighty million kilometers of vacuum.

I am disguised as a man once more. Only this time, the disguise does not chafe me. I cannot permit Hery or my father or my uncles to see me. It would shatter their hearts, surely. Just as seeing them for the first time in nearly seventeen years, yet being unable to embrace them, will shake the foundations of my own heart. But this is my job, this is my burden; I knew in returning to the City I would risk this.

"Leah, let us wait a moment before going into the village."

She glances at me with concern; her chiseled male features accentuate this. "Are you certain you want to talk with your kinsmen? I could pose to them the questions we've discussed. You don't need to see them again, if it is too hard."

"No, it is my responsibility... I just need a moment to... settle something in my mind. Then we can go."

What I am trying to decide is whether to press the red button on my aid-suit's left wrist. Whether to dissolve, for myself only, the invisible fence which segregates the men and women of my birth clan. For just a moment. They would not be together, yet they would be... if only in my eyes. Should I allow myself this glimpse of a paradise irretrievably lost to me? Will it be a gift to myself? Or will it be an exercise in self-flagellation?

Caught in my indecision, I peer around the corner I have sheltered behind. There is Lachlan Square. My childhood playground. Its library was my schoolhouse, its hall of justice my castle, its fountain my private lagoon. Sitting at the edge of the fountain, which is still centered around the green-hued merman I remember so well, he who holds his three-pronged trident above his wet curls, are a man... and a *woman?*

Have I already pressed the red button without realizing it? Yet I sense no weakness in my body, no palsy—

"Leah, tell me — is my eruvnet set for Anarako Arivo? Or have I fallen out of the Neuronet altogether?"

It is an absurd question. Looking down, my hands are still the heavily-veined hands of a man. Leah retains her dark Arabian beak (we Malagasy collected our features from many peoples we sojourned among). Yet — a Malagasy man and woman sitting together at the Lachlan Square fountain?

"There is nothing amiss, Nofy, nothing I can see on my tuning unit. Are the adjustments I made to your aid-suit making you ill—?"

A fantastical notion occurs to me. Fantastical, yet the only deduction which makes sense. "Leah, check this for me in your records if you can. Has Anarako Arivo been involved in a Merging during the past fourteen years?"

"Mergings are exceedingly rare..." My heart batters the bars of its bony cage while I wait for her to type in her search commands. "Hold on... why, yes. *Yes.* You're right, Nofy. How did you know? Eleven years ago, Anarako Arivo and Nouveau Tamatave jointly opted for Merging."

Nouveau Tamatave... the name Nandrianina and her followers chose for their new eruvnet seventeen years ago. The eruvnet I was dragged into by my mother and aunts, the truncated community I so reluctantly joined for three bitter years.

I was too impatient. Kala Ratsy, the headstrong, the impulsive. Merging. Reunion. My good Lord. Eleven years ago. Had I held out for just three more years...

"Nofy, we mustn't miss our appointment with the clan's headman. Are you coming? Or should I meet him on my own?"

"No... I will come..."

It is like walking at the bottom of the ocean, encased in one of those primitive deep-sea diving suits from the story books, my feet weighed down with thick soles of lead. Walking across Lachlan Square, I see faces which were once as familiar to me as my mother's voice, older now by nearly a full generation. People with names I remember, laughs I remember, whose cooking I once tasted. They stare at me with open antipathy and even a hint of fear, as though I am a stranger, an outlander, someone who might wish them harm. Is this a dream? Did I never leave Bradbury? Do I lie entombed in sleep in my windowless apartment a hundred and twenty meters beneath the red dust of Mars?

The dream intensifies. It mocks me with my inability to awaken. The headman who awaits us in his office — it is Hery.

He is furious. I have never seen him so possessed by anger. Whatever outrage Ehmet Jian has committed against Anarako Arivo must be an abomination beyond measure.

"You! SchneerSons!" he cries as soon as we have entered the room. His face, still handsome, so handsome, shines with a veneer of sweat. "You have failed us! You pledged to us generations ago that we would always be safe! That the Neuronet would forever separate our enemies from us! Yet just this morning, a wolf-jackal of the Merina clan appeared in our midst, mouthing slogans of hate we have not heard since our exodus from Madagascar. He broke inside a school. Then this devil — this creature lower than slime, worse than the most wretched and evil *kalamoro* — he threatened to throw *acid* in the faces of our *girls*! To make them unmarriageable, just as the Merina did in olden times in Madagascar! My own daughter... my own daughter Koloina, my precious girl, is now hysterical with fear..."

Leah waits for me to speak, to explain, to defend the SchneerSons' tarnished reputation. But my mind is an exhausted muscle. All it can focus on is this fact that Hery has a *daughter*. That he wears a ring of marriage on his left hand.

"How could you have let him through?" he cries. "Are there more seeking to attack us, more who will jump the fences we were assured are secure? Will the next ones carry through on their threats to exterminate us? We came here to escape the depredations of the Merina and others like them. We were promised *safety*. What has happened? Is the Neuronet no longer infallible? Or are we smaller communities no longer worth your best efforts?"

"No, no, that is not the case," Leah says. "The man who invaded your daughter's school is a villain, a criminal who has stolen Neuronet technology and committed crimes in several different eruvnet communities, including that of the SchneerSons'. We have not been remiss in our duties to the City.

We too have been victimized, as much as you have been. My companion is a criminal investigator from Bradbury on Mars. We SchneerSons have invited him to detain this criminal and return him to Bradbury, where he originally comes from, for punishment. We need your assistance, and that of the children who were terrorized, to determine where he may go next."

Hery recovers from the possession his anger had placed upon him. "Of course," he says. "If you are actively seeking him, if you will take him away — *far* away — of course we will help you, however we can..."

Leah again waits for me to interject myself into this conversation. I am the investigator, after all. But all I can see is the golden ring on Hery's finger.

"Your daughter, Mr. Vintana," I hear myself say, "how old is she?"

"She turns ten years in three weeks," he says.

"And your wife? What is her name?"

"She is called Mialy. Why do you ask?"

Why do I ask? Why do I *ask?* Because my former best friend is living the life which should have been *mine*, that is why... "No — no reason," I say. "Just — making conversation, pay it no heed..."

The remainder of the morning is a blur. I ask perfunctory questions of the frightened youngsters who were so cruelly threatened by Ehmet Jian. But I barely listen to their answers.

Instead, I dwell on the face of one nine year-old girl. Koloina. The daughter who might have been mine. I see reminders of her father in the shape of her nose and the curves of her mouth. She is most like Mialy in her eyes and the heart shape of her face.

With enough effort, I can make my mind act like Leah's tuning unit. Edit out Mialy's features from Koloina's face and replace them with my own.

And so I play this wicked game, so painful and yet so quenching of my thirsts, over and over with myself, although I am here to track a murderer. Pável Ilyich Davidov would not be happy with me. I am not happy with myself.

2.5

{Ehmet in EhmetLand}

Only one path remained for me. The hard, stony path of an isolate.

`Ard Aljamal was dead to me. I abandoned my sumptuous apartment; every scented pillow, every stick of furniture reminded me of Sikandar. But moving to a different building provided no relief. I heard his voice in the music of flutes played in the grand squares. I smelled his perfumed skin while hurrying by hookah cafés, which I slunk past like a whipped cur. My honor was gone, besmirched beyond repair. I had not been the only citizen of `Ard Aljamal present at that final Schism ceremony; word of my witheringly futile self-abasement had escaped that auditorium on perfidious lips. Soon, it was as though I had never left Salama.

I considered ending my life. Who in `Ard Aljamal would miss me? I would not, certainly. Yet I forced myself to consider the fact that Sikandar might occasionally, in the process of conducting business, speak with a member of my eruvnet. What if word of my suicide should reach him? Would it not torment him? I could not risk any chance of subjecting my truest darling to that.

Becoming an isolate was not suicide. But, short of ending my life, it was the most thorough manner in which to remove myself from the world's memory, and to remove the world from my memory.

I petitioned the SchneerSons. To service a lone man requesting isolation, there was no need for them to send even a mid-level functionary such as Mordechai. They sent a nonentity to perform the work. A nonentity I had come into contact with before, the woman assistant who had accompanied Mordechai to the Schism. This time, I learned her name. I did not care for how she pronounced it, for it was a name from the Jews' book of falsified tribal history. I called her Lya the Matriarch instead. She did not object.

I asked if she'd heard any word of Sikandar, how he was faring in Minutia. She told me she had heard nothing, but that she would inquire for me when she could. She asked if I was absolutely certain I wished to become an isolate; she warned it was an arid desert of an existence, a kind of living death, barely preferable to being exiled to Gehenna with the most abominable wretches. I told her I desired true death, but dared not plunge into that blessed oblivion while Sikandar might hear of it. So an isolate's living death would be my deficient substitute.

She told me where in the City I could hope to find sustenance once I became an isolate. Kindhearted souls donated packaged foodstuffs to the ghosts who walked among them, unknowingly echoing the traditions of the ancestor-worshiping Japanese; the SchneerSons contributed by reprogramming the tiny thingchips affixed to the packages so that these donations would be perceivable to us who had opted to walk alone. Should the donations prove insufficient, she said, I could also opt to compete with the (to me) imperceptible inmates of Gehenna by scavenging leftover food discarded in restaurants' and cafés' waste receptacles, cooked food which, removed from its original containers, became objects perceivable by all.

To her mind, however, delivering these standard instructions was not enough, apparently. "I — I've never cast a resident of the City into isolation before," she said. "I hate being made to do this."

"You act as though you are doing me evil," I said. "But all you are doing is fulfilling my wish." A voice in my head rebuked me for having such a conversation with a Jewess, one with whom I should share no intimacies. And yet, given the unspoken alliance between us, sharing such hidden thoughts felt as decent as sharing bread and hummus with members of my own clan.

"But your wish is wrong," she said. "It is harmful to you."

"But it is my wish. And you SchneerSons must serve."

She cast her gaze down at the stones at my feet. "May I... I would like to do something for you, Ehmet Jian, if it is acceptable to you. I know that, morally, you are no different from the thousands of other isolates who roam the City, no more entitled to special privilege than they are. And yet... you are *my* isolate. *I* am the one who will reprogram your signachip and cast you out from among your fellow men. All those others — I did not have to look into their eyes before they forever vanished. I — I *hate* a system such as ours, which, by its very nature, condemns some to lives of utter aloneness..."

At that moment, hearing the cry of her heart, I decided I would accept whatever gift she offered, no matter how offensive I might find it. "And yet, Matriarch, some would deem the life of an isolate Paradise."

"I cannot conceive how that could be so. Life is with people."

"Life is whatever Allah wills it to be."

"I am commanded to show no favoritism. We SchneerSons must be impartial." She said this with a note of defiance, discordant in her soft voice. "But there are commandments of the SchneerSons, and there are commandments of HaShem. And when such commandments conflict, those of HaShem take precedence. I am no rabbi, but I have a mind, and a heart, and those come from HaShem. I do not want you to ever go hungry. I could not bear the thought of you wandering between donation depots, wracked with thirst, because all donated water had been snatched away by your fellow isolates. Just as we Jews are commanded to share our Passover meals with any who are hungry, just as we set forth a cup of wine for the invisible spirit of Elijah the Prophet, I will place food and drink for you at the edge of my table, every night. The door to my home will remain unlocked. You may enter any time you wish. Seeing that the food has been taken... it will tell me that you live, and that at least you do not suffer from hunger or thirst, however much you may suffer in other ways. Will you accept this from me?"

"I will accept this. And I thank you, Matriarch."

She then completed her work. In the micro-second during which a blink hooded my eyes with thin flesh, she and all the residents of `Ard Aljamal vanished from my sight.

At first, all was peace. The raging waves which had roiled my heart for as long as I could remember were stilled for a time. I was free. Free to wander wherever I wished. I no longer had any responsibilities to anyone but myself. I had no one with whom to contend, no one whose words, gestures, and expressions I needed to decipher or oppose. No one to mock me. No one to whisper scurrilous maledictions. No one to attempt to please.

I would stand in the middle of a seemingly empty street and try to run headlong, then marvel at how my signachip compelled my muscles to slow to a relaxed walk, its aversion signals subtly steering me one way, then another, expertly piloting me around and through unseen crowds, trading electromagnetic impulses with the hundreds of invisible signachips all around me, which steered their wearers away from me, my eruvnet of one coordinating with eruvnets of hundreds or thousands or tens of thousands.

Sometimes, to test myself and the technology in which I had once claimed expertise, I consciously attempted to defy my signachip's aversion signals, willing my muscles to perform acts their electronic overseer directed them not to. I would try to purposefully collide with one of the hundreds of unseen ghosts with whom I shared the street. Initially, I would experience nausea and cold sweats. If I continued my defiance of my signachip, my muscles grew heavy, as though brakes were being applied. If I pushed even more, that heaviness quickly turned to pain — stabbing pain which increased in intensity until, like a short-circuited robot, I collapsed into a leaden heap, trapped by a crushing paralysis which took long moments to recede.

Nights were the times I looked forward to. Nights I could easily fill with visits to Lya's apartment for food, and then with sleep. The days, however, stretched into endlessness. I had nothing to do but to wander the City. I watched the streetcars, seemingly empty, make their whirring ways along the grand avenues and subsidiary connecting roads, shining toys for unseen children. I conjured faces in clouds. I splashed barefoot through fountains, then left damp footprints in the halls of libraries, workshops, and worship houses, simply to be contrary.

I explored apartment blocks both new and old, searching for unlocked doors, knowing nothing of value would be available for me to steal. Anything precious or simply usable had been branded with a thingchip and so was unperceivable to me. The only things I could see or touch in those apartments were broken pieces of furniture or worn-out household implements, objects whose thingchips had stopped working or which had never been significant enough to warrant one. Such as stained mattresses bleeding their paltry reservoirs of stuffing, my only recourse for sleeping if I cared not to slumber like a dog on the ground.

Sometimes, if I could find a scrap of paper and a writing implement, I would leave the unseen residents a note. "Beware the *shabah*." "Greetings from the tricky *djinn*." Childish, yes. But that is how I struggled to fill my days.

It was inevitable, I suppose, that I would eventually gravitate toward that neighborhood of lost ʿArd Aljamal where I had spent the happiest days and nights of my existence, my all-too-brief stretch of Paradise with Sikandar. I spent hours loitering in the narrow lane which cleaved the twin rows of storefronts where I recalled the dwarfs and midgets operated their clock and engine repair shops, wondering in which of these seemingly empty workshops my dearest darling labored. Was he within the sound of my voice, if his ears would be permitted to hear my call? Did he think of me? Yearn for me? Could he still experience moments of happiness? Or was he trapped in an emotional limbo, as I was?

Then, months after my self-imposed exile had begun, came the blackest night of all. The night when boiling pitch was poured down my throat and all the demons of the netherworld descended upon me to feast on my flesh.

I went, as I did every night just after sundown, to Lya's apartment for my evening meal. To my shock, I found Lya herself awaiting me at her table.

"Forgive me, Ehmet Jian, for intruding upon your isolation," she said. I should have been joyful, after uncountable hours of brain-numbing silence, to hear a human voice again. Yet I found the tone of her voice and the expression upon her wan face profoundly disquieting. Had she been weeping? "There is something dreadful I need to share with you," she said.

I knew the strict protocols the SchneerSons observed, the prohibitions they placed upon using their unique power to insert themselves into others' eruvnets — unless they were invited, or the direst of public crises made it imperative for them to voice an alarm. So I knew Lya had broken one of her people's most sacred rules. And I knew the only event which could compel her to do so was the one catastrophe I had never allowed myself to imagine.

"Sikandar is dead."

Had she said those words? Or had Shaytan himself emerged from the netherworld to brand those burning words onto my heart?

"... How...?"

"He drank poison. I am told he did not suffer."

I have read that the gravity within a black hole is so powerful that even light cannot escape from within the darkness. I was not a collapsed star. Yet words could barely escape my inner darkness to pass my lips.

"Did he... was any message left for me?"

"No. I think... I'm sure his death was meant as a message. For all those around him."

A paralysis more severe than any ever imposed upon me by my signachip crushed me in its vise. My ribs seemed to bend inward. I could not breathe.

"I dare not stay any longer," she said. "I — I thought you should know. I'm sorry. I'm so sorry." Unwilling to witness the consequence of her revelation, she pressed a key and vanished.

My grief was a feral thing. A wolf pitched into the fire and set ablaze. Words might struggle to escape the gravity of my inner darkness. But the howl of my burning-wolf grief erupted from my throat with the force of a comet plunging into the sun.

I could not later recall what I did that night. I entered a state where mind had been boiled out of me, where I had the self-awareness of molten rock flowing toward the sea. I only know that when I awakened, stabbing pains alerted me that I was missing fingernails from both hands, and my fingers and arms were thoroughly coated with a black, sticky residue. My blood? Or someone else's? I did not know. Judging from the iron taste in my mouth, I might have bitten off my own nails in mindless fury. Other evidence, the long, parallel traces of dried blood lining the curbside wall against which I had collapsed, suggested I had torn my fingernails off while clawing the wall's rough bricks.

Where had my fugue taken me? I knew this place, this narrow lane. I was in the alley of the Little Men's repair shops. Had my signachip hammered me into paralysis and collapse after I'd attempted to seize unseen eyes from the skulls of invisible dwarfs? Had I then bitten off my own fingertips in agonized frustration? Or had I tried to pull the brick wall down on top of me, like the Hebrew's Samson — then, in the wake of that futile exertion, plunged my shredded fingertips into my mouth to curtail their bleeding?

As best I could tell, my violence, however long it had raged, had done nothing more than paint this alleyway's wall with my own blood. None of the workshops' windows had been shattered. So far as I knew, I had harmed only myself.

But the unseen blood of Sikandar, my martyred darling, called out to me from the ground.

Avenge me.

I stared at my black blood upon the wall. I would blacken my soul for all eternity if I permitted my blood to remain the only blood shed upon this infernal street that day.

I spent hours searching through garbage heaps before I found what I needed. A carving knife. Its blade was broken at the tip, its edge dull and rusted. Yet it would suffice. I honed it as best I could between a pair of rough stones, the sound of each ear-piercing scrape making me think of the wails of the damned in Hell. Hell, where I would soon send the thrice-damned souls who had killed my Sikandar.

I returned to the street of workshops. Twenty-one Heathstone Lane. That was the address of the shop where Sikandar had told me Bora Ali worked.

I stood before the window. The inside appeared, to me, to be an empty room. The dwarfs and midgets would not see me as I entered their clock surgery. They would see the door swing open, and they would wonder why a ghost would enter if he or she could not be served. Would they see the knife in my invisible hand? Would its pitted steel be visible to them, seemingly floating through the air in its pursuit of flesh? I hoped it would. I hoped terror would consume their stunted souls during their final seconds in the world of the living.

I used my signachip's aversion signals as a kind of radar, a proximity detector I am certain the system's designers had never intended it to be. The heavier my limbs became, the more vociferous my nausea and pain, the closer I knew I was to my intended victims.

I assumed the Little Men would be carrying out their work near the rear walls of the room. Judging from my body's responses, I was right. I slashed in wide arcs, trying to be as thorough as possible, reminding myself that the torsos, throats, and faces I sought were below the height of my waist. How strange, to be doing this in profound quiet, to not hear a single cry of panic or pain. I was tempted to scream myself, if only to fill up the silence.

I nearly did cry out in surprise — my blade and fist hit an unseen, unyielding surface, possibly a work table; the impact proved hard enough to knock the knife from my grasp. It skittered across the floor before coming to rest. I ran to retrieve it. Just before I could snatch it from the floor I saw it move again, as though it had suddenly acquired life of its own.

I lunged for where I estimated a Little Man's wrist must be. My fingers closed around something I could not feel but which offered resistance to my grasp, a wrist or arm hardly bigger around than a broomstick. My hand, my arm, my entire body burned as I struggled with this unseen citizen of Minutia, this dwarf or midget my signachip insisted I must not touch. Looming paralysis threatened. I fought against it with iron will, buoyed by the knowledge that my unseen opponent suffered equivalent disability.

My efforts were rewarded. My knife met resistance. Part of it vanished from my sight as it pierced the Little Man's body. I discovered something new to me — blood, once freed from its confines within veins, arteries, and skin, no longer obeyed the dictaMy greater strength, size, and weight won out. My eyes clouded with tears as bolts of pain sizzled through me, but I did not need vision to do what I needed to do. I twisted that unseen wrist in my right hand until I was able to snatch the knife with my left. Then, not letting go of the Little Man, I clumsily, blindly slashed the space where I estimated his head and torso should be.tes a signachip imposed on the integral body. It turned visible and tactile. It stank of iron, even to an isolate such as I.

To my left, I saw the door to the street jerk open three times in rapid succession. Exhausted from my struggle against my signachip, I struggled to my feet and lurched toward the doorway. I loathed the thought that any of the Little Men would escape my vengeance. Especially that one of the escapees might be Bora Ali.

Imposing myself in front of the doorway, I resumed swinging my blade in a wide arc. A burning sensation along my right side alerted me that one of the Little Men had tried ducking beneath my arm. Following the telltale pulsing of my pain-radar, I chased him into a corner. I pinioned him in the angle between two walls.

Only my adrenaline and bloodlust allowed me to overcome the fiery leadenness spreading throughout my frame.

I gauged his size and shape with my hands, bloodied hands that seemed to press against a field of opposing force. He was broad, with a head nearly as large as his torso. No midget, he — a dwarf. Bora Ali? It did not matter. They were all my enemies. All had killed Sikandar.

I stabbed. I stabbed and sliced and thrust. I stabbed until my right shoulder and arm ached, until very tangible blood, spraying above me like a fountain's jets, doused my forehead and trickled into my eyes, until the signachip on my brain stem triggered enough kill switches inside me that I collapsed onto the dwarf, now outlined in pooling ichor and not nearly so invisible as before. That forbidden full-body contact — so akin to forbidden love — set off feedback savage enough to finally hammer me into unconsciousness.

When I awoke, I found the SchneerSons had taken me into their custody. Not wanting to dirty their own Jew hands with the rough work of justice, they turned me over to the surviving citizens of Minutia. Bora Ali was not among these; I had accomplished that much, at least.

The Little Men swiftly sentenced me to banishment in Gehenna. The thought of Gehenna sparked no fear in my breast. This was the worst punishment known in the City of a Thousand Names? Without my Sikandar, I was already in Hell.

1.7

{Nofy in the Library}

"Nofy, what was the matter with you back there? When we were interviewing that headman and the girls, you were a shadow, hardly there at all. I knew your return to Anarako Arivo would be hard for you. But this—"

"Don't badger me, Leah."

"This is 'badgering' you? I'm *concerned*, Nofy. We're pursuing a dangerous man. A killer. If you don't have your head in the job... HaShem forbid, you might lose that head."

She isn't going to leave me be. She won't let me lick my wounds. "I will have my 'head in the job'... when it counts."

"How can I be sure of that? My safety is at stake, too, you know..."

"Leah, let me *alone!*" Safety! *Safety!* That is all these risk-phobic denizens of the City care about. They have never dared live on a world where an unnoticed equipment failure can deprive one's lungs of life-giving air or expose one's body to deadly cascades of radiation. "You can't understand! I saw my life back there! The life I *could have had!* If it hadn't been for such things as Schisms, and invisible fences, and my village being ripped apart by my neighbors' silly arguments over who will water the miserable sheep..."

Damn me and my unguarded lips! Now I've said too much. I've lost Leah's confidence, and thus the confidence of the SchneerSons. I will be sent back to Bradbury an ignominious failure, my mission a victim of my uncontrolled, girlish emotions.

Leah stands silently by one of the towering book stacks here in the Lachlan Square library, in whose quiet recesses we have taken refuge in order to regroup. Showing any animus or prejudice towards the City's culture and laws is strictly *verboten*, according to Pável Ilyich Davidov. I have violated one of the most elementary prohibitions of diplomacy.

Yet, oddly enough, Leah does not appear perturbed by my outburst. Rather, she seems... intrigued. "Is that why you left the City?" she says in a hushed voice, her eyes locked on mine. "Because of a Schism?"

"... Yes."

"I have seen Schisms cause... dreadful things."

Such an admission from a SchneerSon? The guardians of the sacred Neuronet? "I thought Schisms were the City's safety valve? The mechanism through which dangerous tensions are bled off?"

"That is their intended purpose, yes. But..."

"But *what*, Leah?"

"The Schisms, the eruvnets, the whole encompassing Neuronet... these are shackles on us. Blinders which keep us focused on petty squabbles, resentments, revenge... and easy escape from anything which disturbs us. We always look down, at our feet and other's feet, taking satisfaction in the sight of mud on other's shoes, trying to avoid stepping in it ourselves. We never look up at the stars."

Dissent among the keepers of the status quo? "That doesn't sound like SchneerSon philosophy. I thought your clan was dedicated to the notion of keeping disparate things apart?"

"You speak of the commandment to avoid *shatnez*, that forbidden mixing of things which are meant to be kept separate. That is important to our thinking, yes. But there is also the mystical tradition of *tikkun olam*. The mending of the world. The gathering of the scattered Sparks. Are you familiar with this teaching?"

Her face shines with an almost childish enthusiasm, a need to draw me into her esoteric mental world. "No. I am not familiar with this *tikkun olam*."

"It was a teaching of the blessed Rabbi Isaac Luria, master of the mystic *kaballah*. He held that when HaShem created the universe, he vacated a space in the center of Himself in which it could exist. Yet this act of divine contraction, or *Tzimtzum*, resulted in a void of *Tohu*, or chaos, in which the divine light meant to form this world and others escaped from the vessels it was held within, resulting in *Shevirat HaKeilim*, the Shattering of the Vessels, and the exile of the *Nitzutzot*, the Sparks of holiness. All this was according to HaShem's divine plan, of course — He always intended that His created beings should have a shared role in the perfecting of the universe. Since the time of Adam, it has been mankind's role to mend the world by gathering the lost Sparks together."

"And what does this have to do with the Neuronet? Schisms aren't exactly the epitome of 'mending.' More like *rending*."

I expect her to argue with me, but instead she fervently agrees, grabbing my hands with childlike enthusiasm. "Yes! This is what I've been trying to tell you! Generations ago, boatloads of refugees arrived at the gates of our City torn and broken, both in body and spirit. My ancestors and others decided they weren't ready to be reknit into a diverse community, that they needed the temporary refuge of absolute separation. Yet that refuge has proven to be anything *but* temporary. Its invisible fences grow ever more intricate and extensive with each passing year, like thorny vines spreading through an untended vineyard. We have enormous problems here in the City — we are outgrowing our hemmed-in space, living literally atop one another. Yet rather than confront our dilemma head-on, rather than trying to innovate actual solutions, we hide our heads in the sand of mirages, illusions of open space and solitude provided by another few hundred eruvnets. Instead of gathering the lost Sparks of holiness and restoring the unity of mankind and the world, the whole point of our existence has become an ever more rigid purification, a sifting out of dissenting views, the banishment of anything which threatens to challenge our customs and ingrained ways of thinking, or which makes us uncomfortable or uncertain—"

Her rapturous outflow is interrupted by a buzzing alarm from the tuning unit on her wrist.

"Jian has shifted again?" I say. "Where to now?"

Her face loses its color as she reads the alert. "*Here*, Nofy! In this very library! He is one floor higher, but in a different eruvnet, ElderHaven Seven—"

"Can you take us there?"

"I am typing in the coordinates now!"

Five seconds later, the great room, filled with floor to ceiling shelves of books, subtly alters around me. The volumes left open or discarded on the rows of reading tables blink out and are replaced by different tomes. More jarring is the sudden appearance of the library's patrons from ElderHaven Seven, aged Europeans, naked apart from kilts or skirts, foreheads marked with charcoal runes, reading aloud in unison from hardbound copies of *The Song of Roland*. Several drop their books in surprise. They cry out in French as I barrel through their ranks, heading for the nearest stairs to the floor above.

This time will be different. I am in no way winded climbing these stairs, surging two steps at a time. The aid-suit works in smooth conjunction with my muscles now, abetting them rather than fighting their palsy, adding its mechanized strength to my adrenaline-fueled swiftness. I won't crawl like a dying cripple toward Jian's feet this time. I will leap upon him like a hungry leopard.

Cries and crashes reach my ears when I am only halfway to the landing above. I hurl myself through the doors, to be confronted with a most un-library-like chaos — semi-naked elders pinned beneath toppled bookshelves, screaming from the pain of broken bones, loose-fleshed limbs twisted, withered dugs crushed beneath the weight of aged paper. I would stop to help — except I see at the opposite end of the room another bookshelf being rocked from its moorings, and I know there I will find my foe.

The shelf topples before I can cover half the distance to Jian. It lands with a rending crash and scatters a tempest of books across the floor. I see him then. We lock eyes. I cannot tell if he is surprised to see me. He hasn't bothered to disguise himself — he looks the same as when I saw him at the musicians' café. He is not that big. Hand-to-hand, I will take him down and cuff him.

He raises a device strapped to his wrist close to his face and speaks something into it—

And vanishes.

"*Leah!*" I scream over my shoulder. "Send me to the next place!"

Infuriatingly long seconds pass before she joins me on this level. "He has fled to another eruvnet!" I cry. "Send me *now!*"

"I have to read the alert — he's in Punyasthāna — I'm typing in the shift address—"

"Too *slow!* Can't you use voice commands?"

"It'll take a minute to shift the command interface — I wasn't anticipating—"

"I don't *care* what you were or weren't 'anticipating'! Send me there *now!*"

Precious seconds later, the room quivers as my senses burble and spurt, shifting about me again. Now the room's edges are crowded with what appear to be Hindu monks, gesticulating wildly at the fallen bookshelves, toppled by unseen hands. The bolder among them jabber furiously at me and throw books in my direction; the more fearful or superstitious slash sigils in the air and bid me with hissed incantations to vanish.

I hear pounding steps from the floor immediately below. Jian is running for the front entrance. If I take the stairs now, I'll never catch up. It's a five meter jump to the courtyard — the exoskeleton built into my aid-suit should cushion my landing. So long as the glass of the panoramic windows overlooking the square and its fountain isn't too thick... I ram the nearest window with a reading table. Luckily for me, it shatters. Shoving aside the table, I make a running jump through the suddenly unobstructed space, praying to clear the detritus field of glass shards on the walkways below—

(Airborne... like a gull soaring down toward the fountain for a drink)

And I almost make it, almost clear the glass, but I land badly my boots skid forward on smaller chunks of glass (like ball bearings). I fall backward, breaking my fall with my unprotected hands. I feel shards tear into the skin of my palms, driven deep.

An instant after my bloodied landing, I hear running steps scattering the glass in a tinkling cascade. Jian. He's down the steps to the fountain plaza before I manage to regain my footing. Ignoring the searing pain in my palms, I sprint after him. Thanks to my aid-suit's muscle-augmenting pistons, I'm faster than he is. Halfway to the fountain, I'm gaining on him. I clutch his shoulder when he's at the fountain's edge, grab hold of his tunic, yank hard, send him flailing into the water. I leap in after him, only to see him, water streaming from his face, speak into that wrist device—

And again he vanishes. I lunge for the spot I last saw him, hoping to tackle him before he can reorient himself, but he has already moved beyond my immediate grasp.

"Leah!"

I see her just inside the shattered window on the library's second floor. I pray she's quicker this time. But then I realize I don't need to wait for her. Jian, invisible though he may be, leaves a trail of wet footprints across the plaza.

I set off after him. Leah can only control my eruvnet settings if I remain within a fifty meter radius of her. But if I allow her time to catch up, Jian will escape me. Which will I run out of first — the range of Leah's unit, or water to mark Jian's footsteps?

The footsteps continue appearing on the flagstones five meters ahead of me, materializing like the circular impacts of rain droplets in a pond — but growing fainter with each new step. [SHIFT] The air around me shimmers. New sounds echo off the plaza's stone buildings: packs of children at play, dogs barking as they chase balls. Bounce, bounce. I see Jian just ahead of me, almost in reach—

[SHIFT] Shimmering, vertigo—? *What? Another shift?

I sense it before I see it — a food cart, directly in front of me. I swerve to avoid it, bump its edge with my shoulder, then—

[SHIFT] More vertigo! A parade of purple-clad women on stilts materializes, cuts me off from the other side of the plaza. I weave between their absurdly elongated legs, heading in the same direction Jian was running—

[SHIFT] Surrounded by a rally, red flags, shouted slogans—

[SHIFT] Stumble over racing miniature cars weaving about my feet—

[SHIFT] Am hemmed in by the booths of a souk, hundreds of teeming bargainers—

*No! Not when I'm so *close!*

I press the yellow button on my wrist three times, shifting myself backward through three prior eruvnets. The maximum. Not enough — I'm back in the eruvnet which is parading its women on stilts. While Jian is in the eruvnet with the children and dogs...

And his damp footprints no longer appear.

Waiting for Leah to catch up to me, I pick slivers of glass from my palms. A palm reader, confronted with this badly torn map, would not favor me with a bright future, not now.

"Nofy, I'm so *sorry* — I was running down the steps, trying to punch in commands at the same time, and my fingers must've hit the wrong keys. Either that, or the unit's transmissions grow unstable when you're at maximum range..."

The blood is trickling down my wrists now.

He has escaped me yet again.

Things must change.

2.6

{Ehmet in Gehenna}

Until I encountered the first of my fellow inmates, my existence in Gehenna seemed little changed from my life as an isolate. The primary difference, at first, was the difficulty I found in scavenging enough food. I did not expect Lya the Matriarch to continue providing for me now that I was a condemned murderer. I had to forage. Within the City's walls, foraging meant picking through garbage, as though I were a rat or mongrel dog.

The obvious course of action was to wait outside a restaurant or café for workers to discard cooked food left on the plates of departed customers. The problem with this? Every other inmate of Gehenna had also arrived at the same conclusion, and they had the advantage of having been convicted earlier than I had. Having access to a dependable source of food meant the difference between hunger and satiation, death and life. Thus, I was hardly surprised to find restaurant after restaurant guarded by lone inmates, who, upon seeing me, brandished improvised weapons, clubs or knives or crude crossbows, with the savage tenacity of a lion driving off hyenas from the carcass of a fresh kill.

I tried bargaining with the less rabid-appearing among them. "Ho, fellow! Let me share this place with you!" I called from a safe distance, showing my empty hands in a fruitless effort to placate my more fortunately situated interlocutor.

"Why the hell should I share with *you*, you hungering cur?"

"I could help you guard this place from thieves and ravagers. You cannot stay alert and awake all hours of the day and night. Give me half the food discarded here, or even just enough of a portion for me to subsist upon, and I will guard the food and you during the night, while you sleep."

"You'll slit my throat while I sleep, is what you'll do!"

"Don't be a fool — I would also be relying upon you, to guard me and the food during daylight. We would both be more secure. We wouldn't have reason to betray one another—"

He brandished his club, warning me to keep my distance. "I'll rely upon my own lightness of sleep to warn me of invaders, thank you! Or if I want a partner, I'll find myself a dog to share my scraps! A dog don't attack you, so long as you feed him!"

I found such to be the case again and again, not merely at the dumps behind restaurants, but also at the trash receptacles just inside the City's gates, where the returning miners emptied the leftover contents of their lunch pails. Men of the sort condemned to Gehenna had never known trust. They expected their lives to be minute echoes of the Wars of All Against All, only without the backing of a clan to provide even a modicum of shelter and comradery.

I could have surrendered to hunger and death. I could have told myself there was no reason for me to cling to life, now that Sikandar had entered Paradise. Yet, having been condemned to this Gehenna by the Little Men and, by extension, all the peoples of the City, I rebelled at the thought that they could succeed in compelling my surrender. I would not grant them that victory. I would plot my survival, if only to spite the City's lawful residents' smug notions of their own superiority — notions fueled by the ease with which they could wall themselves off from any who might criticize them or damage their pride. Those weaklings had thrown me into a pit with the worst of the worst. By surviving, I would show them how a truly strong man can take the muck of cruel circumstance and mold of it a monument to himself.

I devised a strategy of lingering within those large public squares where community festivals were frequently held. Tremendous amounts of food were consumed at festivals, often procured from mobile carts. The great advantage for me in such a setting was that I found myself on equal footing with the longer-term inmates — predicting exactly where and when leftover food would be discarded was impossible, so the prize fell to the swift and the lucky.

Still, I quickly came to understand such tactics were tenuous at best. During my first full week in Gehenna, I only succeeded in snatching anything of remote semblance to a meal four times. I realized that, unless I could secure a reliable source of nourishment, I would soon grow so weak that I would be unable to compete for such food as could be recovered at festivals.

What advantage did I have over my fellow inmates? They were ignorant brutes, most of them, many quite powerful brutes, all with two forceful arms as opposed to my one. I could not outdo them in strength or savagery, as I had the dwarves. I could count only upon my superior intelligence and whatever cunning I might have accrued from my familiarity, thanks to my life in Bradbury, with a variety of cultures.

What sources of discarded food within the City would virtually none of my fellow inmates think to claim? I knew that some peoples, such as the adherents of Shinto among the Japanese, left offerings of cooked food at shrines dedicated to their ancestors. Most such shrines were maintained within private homes, but some, at least, could be found inside temples. I scoured my memory of the tremendous catalog the SchneerSons had shared with me of the tens of thousands of eruvnet communities I could select to petition to join upon my initial arrival in the City. Had there been any subcommunities of Shinto adherents listed? Had I ever seen a Shinto temple on my travels within the City?

With a tinge of despair, I realized I might have passed several Shinto temples, even dozens — but not perceived them. Virtually all worship houses within the City were used by multiple sects and faith communities, some of which, I knew, held their ceremonies simultaneously, blissfully unaware of their rivals' presence. Any distinctly Japanese architectural elements within the worship houses would likely be thingchipped, perceivable only to the residents of select eruvnets. There were no shortcuts; I would have to visit worship houses in all the major public squares, as well as smaller sanctuaries located in neighborhoods scattered all about the City, hoping that fortune and Allah would smile upon me and permit me to stumble across a shrine where worshipers had left unpackaged, cooked food.

As I began my quest, my stomach felt ominously tight, shrunken like a slug exposed to salt. I discovered that many of the smaller, neighborhood worship houses were located near cemeteries and other burial grounds. I reminded myself to search those places, too — the pagans and animists originally from African lands also left offerings of food for their dead, typically on dishes left upon their ancestors' graves.

Hunger and thirst were not my only enemies. Among my fellow inmates could be found not merely scorpions, which sting when cornered, but also cobras, slithering devils that seek human prey. Events forced me to revise my initial notion that inmates of Gehenna were unwilling to ever work together. To satisfy lusts of the flesh, I learned, they would momentarily disregard their mutual mistrust to form packs.

I saw such a pack surround and overwhelm a solitary inmate who was about my size. They beat him until he could no longer make any effort to escape. Then each thrust his *quadib* within the helpless man's orifices, driven to ever more brutal frenzies by his agonized wails of protest. I overheard those not busying themselves in this act of violation argue that he should be cooked over a fire pit they had built, since meat had been in short supply.

I would be no other man's meat. I hid within an attic until the hunting pack had dragged their forthcoming meal away. Yet not so far that I failed to hear his screams as they lit the fire beneath him.

I found what I searched for — African cemeteries and Shinto shrines from which I could steal my sustenance. I realized this thievery from the dead made me little higher than a *ghūl*, an eater of corpses. Yet I had witnessed actual *ghūlan*, monsters in human form who tortured their prey before killing and eating him, and I knew that, no matter how far I had fallen, I remained better than they.

And so I passed my days, dining within burial grounds, washing in fountains, never daring to shut my eyes for more than a fraction of a second, my club with its protruding nails in my strong hand, always cognizant of routes of escape.

Then seeming disaster struck. One by one, my sources of food were denied me. The cooked offerings I had come to rely upon stopped appearing. Apparently, my thievery had been noticed by the relatives, and either the priests or the SchneerSons had instructed the bereaved worshipers to substitute other offerings for cooked foods, perhaps packaged foods which were perceptually regulated by thingchips. In any case, I was being warded off like an unseen but bothersome vermin.

The thought of suddenly needing to compete for food with the *ghūlan*, thus exposing myself to their tortures, terrified me. I nearly despaired when I saw that the Shinto shrine on Lachlan Square was devoid of the meat dumplings, raw fish wrapped in seaweed, and rice cakes upon which I'd become accustomed to feasting. But then I saw that something else had been left upon the shrine. A handwritten note. A communique for the dead? Or for the living? Reading it, I recognized the handwriting instantly.

If this is you, Ehmet, who has been taking this food, come to my apartment. A proper meal will be left for you, as previously, and much beside.

The Matriarch. She had not forgotten me. Nor, even after the blood I'd shed, had she deemed me a pariah. Reading her note strengthened me as no amount of food could. Someone in this accursed City (a Jewess!) still considered me a human being, not as vermin they had banished from their perceptions in hopes I would be exterminated by other vermin.

She was true to her word. I found familiar foods on her table, the same she had left for me when I had been an isolate: dumpling soup, baked chicken, fried potato pancakes, and sweet cabbage stuffed with spiced rice. And there was another note, telling me of other things she had left for me, and where.

She had left me, half buried in a box within a refuse heap near the City's southeastern wall, a collection of discarded, nonworking electronic equipment — worn-out eruvnet modulators, portable tuning devices, and signachip/thingchip detectors, all with their own thingchips deactivated so that I could see and touch them. This was equipment that, in good working order, only the SchneerSons were permitted to possess.

I dragged the box, which included worn but serviceable tools I could use to repair the equipment, to a little-used warehouse I sometimes slept in. What had Lya intended? To provide me with a hobby so I would not descend into madness? Or did she mean for me to restore these devices to the point where I could escape Gehenna, then lose myself in one of the larger eruvnets?

At first, I resented the decrepitude of what she had made available to me, much of which was so degraded as to be worthless. She had obviously pursued the easiest, safest path, providing only that material intended for disposal, junk whose disappearance her superiors would never question. Why couldn't she have simply used her portable tuning device to reset my signachip? Would some automatic alarm sound within the citadel of the SchneerSons? Was she afraid of being condemned to Gehenna herself?

But the longer I labored at piecing together the workable bits, solving puzzles more daunting and fascinating than any I'd faced in Bradbury, the more I came to appreciate what she had done for me. However much she may have wanted to provide me with the key to my prison — and I still did not fully understand why she had chosen to champion me she'd opted instead to make me earn my escape. To forge my own key. By forcing me to exercise my skills and intellect to their utmost, she had also forced me to resurrect myself, from scurrying vermin to man.

Following weeks of work, my night of triumph arrived, the moment I finally sparked my cobbled-together tuning unit to life. When its screen emerged at last from blackness to brilliance, I thought I saw a glimmer of my Sikandar's bottomless blue eyes. Let there be light! Oh, would my darling have been proud of my accomplishment! Data flooded into the reborn machine, which I had augmented by pilfering the best parts from a dozen other lesser units. Accessing layers of menus, swimming through data pool after data pool, I realized all the secrets of the SchneerSons were mine, to do with what I willed. With the pressing of a single ON switch, I had gone from being a flea-ridden rat to one of the most formidable men in the entire City.

I could escape. I could change my appearance, change my voice, change even the odor of my skin. I could confiscate any valuables I might fancy, transfer them from one eruvnet to another, then barter them for whatever I might desire. I could choose from thousands of potential refuges, jumping between them whenever I pleased. But, given the power I had accrued, was escape from Gehenna all I desired?

The voice of the man I had seen violated shook the windows of my memory... his agonized pleas, ignored as half a dozen men had satisfied their lusts upon him. His dying screams as the flames of a cooking fire had roasted his flesh. That might easily have been me.

The SchneerSons could have set up Gehenna so that its inmates were prohibited from touching one another. It would have been a trivial matter. But they had instead chosen to make the weakest among the inmates the prey of the stronger. They had chosen to subject us to the Wars of All Against All. The City's foundational nightmare. The all-consuming catastrophe which had so terrified its refugees, they had configured this City of a Thousand Names as a bulwark against the Wars' passions, an endless maze in which the age-old scourge of tribal and ethnic hatred would be forever lost and forgotten, a Minotaur too terrible to confront.

But the leaders of the City, those who flattered themselves as the good and the great, had continued offering human sacrifices to the Minotaur, hadn't they? I had nearly been one of those sacrifices. Yes, it had been the Little Men, the citizens of Minutia, who had sentenced me to Gehenna. But all of the City's citizens, the members of each of the seventy thousand and more eruvnets, were complicit. By having agreed to harbor Gehenna within their eight walls, they had fed flesh to the Minotaur.

Escape Gehenna? I could do so much more than just that. I could free the Minotaur from the maze. I could give the eight million citizens of this cursed City a personal reckoning with their worst nightmare.

1.8

{Nofy on the Hunt}

The hospital which treats my hands, staffed mainly by Pakistani doctors and Filipina nurses, seems reasonably efficient, despite deploying equipment and techniques which in Bradbury would be considered medieval. I think back to what Leah said about what have come to constitute the City's central values; medical advancement obviously is not included. I can't recall the name of this particular eruvnet. It doesn't matter.

Leah has sat silently at the edge of the treatment room, appearing deeply mortified while my palms have been cleaned of glass and grit and stitched up. "Nofy, I've failed you..." she whimpers.

I am in no mood for self-pity, either hers or mine. "It wasn't your fault. I nearly had him. Luck was not with me." The nurse finishes bandaging my hands. I instruct her to leave the fingers free. "As soon as we're done here, let's go to the hospital's cafeteria for something to eat. I'm famished. We'll talk there."

The roast goat pita pocket sandwich I order turns out to be quite good, better than anything I ever ate in Bradbury. The cubes of tangy meat are garnished with a yogurt and cucumber sauce and chunks of fresh tomato. Delicious. If they were of a mind to, the SchneerSons could set up a most lucrative business within the City's walls — food tourism. Feast within two dozen eruvnets in three days. Sample bountiful Earth's cuisines without walking more than a kilometer from your hotel. Learn yoga from Tibetan monks. See parades of purple women on stilts. Have your throat slit in a sidewalk café by an invisible maniac. All for one low, all-inclusive price.

"So what do we know now that we did not know a day ago?" I ask, feeling large-spirited, ready to forgive. I suck a shred of goat meat from between my teeth and enjoy my meal all over again, feeling so much less peckish now that I have food in my stomach, not to mention the pain-relievers my aid-suit injected into my bloodstream.

"Well," she says, obviously relieved that I have not launched into a denunciation of her incompetence, "Ehmet hasn't killed anyone since your arrival. Apart from cutting that musician's throat, I mean."

"Yes. But that was a demonstration directed at me, not an attempted homicide, you know? He could easily have killed the man if he'd intended to. He has been active these last few days, certainly. Very active. But he hasn't gone on a murder spree. He did not harm a single girl in that school in Anarako Arivo. He seems content to spread terror. To incite fears that the Neuronet's invisible fences are falling down, that each clan's ancestral enemies are once more free to rampage across eruvnet borders."

I think some more on this. "But spreading terror is senseless, is it not? Unless the Neuronet's fences actually *were* to fall down. Otherwise, the effects of his depredations will quickly fade. He is only one man. There are seventy thousand eruvnet communities. Do the maths. If he were to schedule ten crimes per day, each within a different eruvnet, it would take him seven thousand days, or nearly twenty years, to complete his terror tour. And to what end? He would need a team of hundreds of acolytes, each with his own tuning unit, to appreciably degrade trust in the Neuronet and the SchneerSons' oversight. We have no evidence that he has attempted to recruit anyone to his cause."

"Maybe he has no plan at all? His first crimes were crimes of passion. Couldn't he be doing this out of derangement, or senseless malice?"

"I don't think so. I sense purposefulness behind his actions. He seems to almost invite me to give chase. Is this just a game for him? Or is he seeding the soil?"

"For what, Nofy?"

"For the eventual fall of the Neuronet. He's priming some communities to be on hair-trigger's edge. We can reasonably assume he hates the system as it is. A Schism robbed him of his lover. Then the system banished him to Gehenna. Perhaps his ultimate goal is to watch the system crashing down? All the invisible fences toppling, trampled into the dirt by thousands upon thousands of opposed, outraged mobs, all squeezed inside a walled City far too small for them?"

She turns her face away from me. "That's... that's a nightmarish scenario. Do you really think people would just... *attack* one another, as soon as the fences were gone? That they'd throw aside civil society so easily?"

"What 'civil society,' Leah? Your eight million inhabitants have never *learned* how to exist and thrive in a civil society — all they've known are *clans*, sheltered clans. If Jian were to make the

Neuronet fail, how would he do it? Where would he begin? Could he make it crash by sabotaging the City's power stations?"

"No. The Neuronet doesn't rely on any central power stations. Each individual signachip and thingchip is independently powered — solar power, sunlight on receptors or skin — and any excess power is fed to the Neuronet as a whole."

"All right. So bombing power stations is out. How would Jian do it, then?"

"I am no expert on the Neuronet's architecture," she says, meeting my eyes once more. "None of us SchneerSons are. But I know some things..."

"Then tell me just enough so that I can pose semi-informed questions to the system engineers in Bradbury."

"All right. This much I know. The Neuronet has tremendous redundancies built in to protect against system corruption or failure. I am told it has the capacity to act much like a biological brain, transferring processes from a damaged sector to a redundant, less used, undamaged sector. But damaging more than forty percent of the eruvbands simultaneously will overwhelm the Neuronet's capacity for rerouting vital processes. That would lead to a cascading, catastrophic system failure."

"Forty percent — that would mean about 28,000 eruvbands would have to be simultaneously corrupted in order to cause cascading systemic failure. From what I know of the Neuronet, any viruses and corruption would be firewalled off within individual eruvnets. There's no pathway for viruses to travel between eruvbands, aside from being physically carried from eruvnet to eruvnet. Again, Jian is just one man. Before he would have a chance to corrupt even a tiny fraction of those 28,000, either you SchneerSons or the system administrators in Bradbury would detect the damage and correct it. I think we can safely rule that out. What else could he try?"

She ponders this for several moments. "There is, oh, one vulnerability I can think of," she says. "But Ehmet would need access to Segregatronics's most heavily secured files to exploit it. Even we SchneerSons have never been given access. Again, I'm no expert, but this is what I've heard. The Neuronet depends upon just thirty-six keynodes to maintain its architectural cohesion—"

"'Keynodes'?"

"Eruvbands which act as the Neuronet's temporal lobes, so to speak. The coordinating nexuses which give logical order to what otherwise would be the chaos of 70,000 independent bands. The keynodes' locales aren't permanent; in the interest of security, all thirty-six keynodes randomly shift among the 70,000 eruvbands every twenty-eight days, at the new moon. No combination is ever repeated."

"Why thirty-six?"

"All Hebrew letters have numeric equivalents. The word *chai*, meaning 'life', is spelled with a Het and a Yud, which equate to eighteen, a lucky number. Thirty-six is twice eighteen, double life."

Double life. Thirty-six keynodes. Thirty-six eruvnets. If that is what Jian is seeking to disrupt, my field of search is narrowed by orders of magnitude. "So from the beginning of a cycle, Jian would have twenty-eight days to invade these thirty-six random keynode eruvnets and corrupt them? And at the end of those four weeks, if has run out of time, he would have to begin all over again with a an entirely different set of keynodes?"

"Yes, that's right, so far as I understand."

"When is the next new moon?" I haven't paid the slightest attention to the moon since my arrival in the City. The City itself, this chameleon metropolis, has fully absorbed my vision. "New moons are festive occasions for you SchneerSons, aren't they?"

"Yes. The next new moon is tomorrow night."

A pattern — I've been searching for his pattern ever since I first saw him at that café near the gate. My rising excitement disperses the lassitude induced by a full stomach and plentiful pain killers. "Leah, do you know if a record is retained of expired groupings of keynodes?"

"You'd have to ask the Neuronet administrators at Segregatronics."

Oh, I will. And if they won't answer me, they will surely answer Pável Ilyich Davidov, without whom their lucrative trade agreements would not exist.

Leah and I make good use of the two days spent waiting for the bosses at Segregatronics to agree to send us the file listing the just-expired keynodes. I squelch my impulse to go chasing after Jian each time Leah's wrist alarm alerts us that he has shifted to another eruvnet. Although my stomach roils with the thought of the offenses he is committing, the horror, fear, and distrust he spreads, I know my time is best spent ensuring that my future pursuits of him are not futile exercises. I have Leah work under the remote guidance of a tutor from Segregatronics to upgrade the modifications she made to my aid-suit. She suggested the idea, and it is a good one: the next time I am able to achieve close proximity to Jian, my aid-suit will lock onto his tuning unit, ensuring that wherever he shifts, I will shift, too. No more chasing after wet footprints.

At last, the file, heavily encrypted, arrives from Segregatronics.

"Leah, here's our chance to see if your suspicion that Jian's working with a confederate at Segregatronics is accurate. Match your list of his travels during the past moon cycle against Segregatronics's list of last month's keynodes."

I breathe shallow breaths waiting for her to complete her comparison. "Let me see what you're looking at, Leah."

"It — it wouldn't make much sense to you. Just rows of numbers, like geospatial coordinates. I'll only take a few more minutes."

It doesn't take her even that long. She looks up at me from her screen with an expression of vindication. "Starting a little over a week ago, they match, right down the line," she says.

"How close did he come to hitting them all?"

"He only visited eleven of the thirty-six keynode eruvnets, but his earliest visit wasn't until the twenty-first day of the last lunar cycle. I assume he didn't receive the list until then."

He's getting closer to his goal. But with this fresh knowledge of his plans, so am I. "Do we know for certain whether those eleven eruvnets were disrupted by some form of virus or sabotage?"

"That information isn't available through my portable unit. But he must have some sort of disabling virus or device available, or else he'd have no reason to seek out the keynodes, instead of eruvnets chosen at random. He was able to visit nearly a third of the keynodes in the fourth week of the last lunar cycle. He spent an average of fifteen point three hours in each. We should assume he'll be more efficient this cycle, should he have access to the new list."

"We would be more than foolhardy to believe he doesn't." Part of me is appalled that Jian is in partnership with a mole dug within the innermost vitals of Segregatronics. Yet another part of me is elated, for I now know where he will be, if not when. Which means I can finally get ahead of him. "If he manages to perfect whatever form of sabotage he's engaged in, his on-target time within each keynode could be reduced to a few hours. Or minutes, for all we know. We may not have much time left at all."

She shoots me a penetrating look. "You're certain he means to bring the Neuronet down? You're *certain?*"

"Oh, yes. The evidence points at nothing else." I feel like a hunting hawk perched anxiously on my master's padded glove, yearning for that glorious moment when my hood is lifted from my eyes and I can take flight. "I have to get hold of that keynode list myself. If I can't, I might as well board my ship now and leave the City to its fate."

William Shakespeare had one of his characters propose, *Let's kill all the lawyers.* He forgot to include the bureaucrats.

"Mr. Sandoval," I say into my ship's interplanetary radio, "I must have that list of current keynodes as soon as possible."

Any sort of conversation between Earth and Mars is exasperating, due to the communication delays of anywhere between three and twenty-one minutes. Currently, the lag stands at twelve minutes and forty-three seconds. Given that Jian is progressing through the keynodes at an unknown rate — but progressing, nonetheless, leaving me with Damocles' Sword hanging above my scalp, suspended by a fraying cord — 'exasperating' is not the word I would use. *Infuriating* is more on point.

"Ms. Rabemananjara," he replies after the nearly quarter-hour delay, "I don't have the authority to share that level of extremely sensitive security information with anyone outside of Segregatronics. Even within our company, only the uppermost tier of technicians and administrators would be granted access, and then only after multiple justification forms have been filed. Your request is unprecedented. I understand you are a law enforcement officer, and you have your responsibilities, but the liability my company would face should information of that level of sensitivity fall into the wrong hands... it is almost incomprehensible. I'm sorry."

[... 12min 43 sec...]

"Mr. Sandoval, you don't seem to understand. Your extremely sensitive list of Neuronet keynodes has *already* fallen into the wrong hands — the wrongest hands *imaginable*. Someone in your company has leaked the file to a murderer named Ehmet Jian who used to work for your firm before he emigrated to the City of a Thousand Names. He is in the process of bringing down the City's Neuronet. *Right now*. Unless I obtain that list of keynodes myself, I have virtually no chance of catching him before he causes a catastrophic systemic failure."

[... 12min 43 sec...]

"You've made a very serious allegation, Ms. Rabemananjara. Most serious. We will need to initiate an internal investigation."

[... 12min 43 sec...]

"I have proof that such a violation has occurred. I have *proof.* But that doesn't *matter,* not now. Do your investigation *after* you have sent me the file. Pável Ilyich Davidov of the Directorate of Trade will vouch for me, for my security clearances and the urgency of my mission. I cannot afford to waste time. If you lack authority to grant me that file, put me immediately in communication with whomever *has* the authority."

[... 12min 43 sec...]

"That would have to be Ninotchka Sen Davidovich, the president of Segregatronics. But Ms. Davidovich is unavailable until the end of this week, at the earliest. I will make the required inquiries, and I will certainly add your urgency, but my hands are tied until Ms. Davidovich's return."

[... 12min 43 sec...]

"I suggest for the sake of your career at Segregatronics and the continued viability of the company that you immediately *untie* your hands and deliver to Ms. Davidovich this message. How long would it take for other Segregatronics client cities to abrogate their support contracts once it becomes common knowledge that the Neuronet's flagship city, the place where the technology was invented, was brought down by sabotage that your company could have prevented — and that the saboteur was a *former employee of Segregatronics?*"

I get my file.

Thirty-six keynodes. Thirty-six eruvnets. I work fervidly to map the geospatial centers of each, those neighborhoods or districts where the majority of each eruvnet's population congregates. In formulating my one-woman dragnet, I make the assumption that

Jian will choose to continue his campaign of incitement and terror, even as he methodically spreads his corrupting virus or sabotage from keynode to keynode.

I plot the keynodes on an electronic map of the City and its seventeen public squares, unable to collaborate on this with Leah, since Segregatronics would only provide me with the list of keynodes if I swore to not share it with anyone, not even trusted SchneerSons. Beginning with the southernmost square, the one closest to the sea, two of the keynodes are roughly centered around Yoting Square; moving clockwise around the eight-sided wall's inside perimeter, I see between one and three keynodes are centered around each of the other seven outermost squares. A roughly similar distribution exists among the eight squares which punctuate the Middle Ring Road. But the heaviest concentration of keynodes, five of them, are centered upon the City's center, Queen Elizabeth Square and its iconic Gladstone Clock Tower, with its eight giant time pieces each facing a different point on the compass.

My technical contact at Segregatronics (so much more responsive than that loathsome Mr. Sandoval — the engineers are always to be preferred over the bureaucrats) assists me with transferring the list of keynode addresses into my aid-suit in such fashion that I will be able to cycle through geographically co-located keynode clusters without having to call upon Leah's assistance. I could wait for Jian to jump first. I could wait for him to strike a keynode (why hasn't he yet this month?), then head for the public square closest to the geographic center of the eruvnet he has invaded. Yet I fear falling into the trap of fruitlessly chasing him around the City. The logical way for him to attack the keynodes would be for him to invade them geo-cluster by geo-cluster, keeping his physical travels to a minimum, yet he may not opt for the logical, easiest path. He may be following some internal map I am not privy to, a deranged psychological map of remembered resentments and furies.

Am I not following a similar map of my own? I need to move. Every muscle in my palsy-free body is primed for action, immediate, decisive action. I cannot bear another minute of waiting. And this is because I cannot bear another minute of *thinking*. About the family which might have been mine. About that girl. About Hery.

I swallow the dregs of coffee at the bottom of my cup. Before the bitter sludge hits my stomach, the single sound I anticipate more than any other buzzes from Leah's wrist — the alarm that Jian has shifted again. "Where is he now, Leah?"

She flips open the screen on her wrist and reads. So slow. Always so slow — *too* slow. "He just entered the Concordia eruvnet. In the Giraween District, near the intersection of Balarang Avenue and Bellingham Road with the Maningrida Square ring road. I have the precise coordinates, but he won't stay in one spot for long."

Concordia. It's not on the list of keynodes. "What is he *waiting* for?" I stare out the window at the giant timepiece glowing like a moon above us, one of the Gladstone Clock Tower's eight omniscient eyes in the night. "Is he so confident in his virus that he can afford to dribble away precious time, invading eruvnets not on the list?"

She offers no answer.

"All right," I say, slamming my empty mug down on the table. "I cannot control his actions. I can only control mine. If he won't move first, *I* will. Let's head for Maningrida Square, the closest one to Concordia's population center." The population cores of three keynode eruvnets intersect there. "Maybe he needs to accomplish something in Concordia before he begins invading the keynodes. Or maybe he's giving in to an impulse to cause random mayhem. In either case, there's a decent enough chance he'll begin his trail of keynode degradation with those eruvnets centering on Maningrida Square. And I can't stand sitting here another moment."

I command my aid-suit to randomly cycle me through the three keynode eruvnets geo-centered on Maningrida Square, depositing me in each for fifteen minute intervals. Chance, blind chance, that's what I'm counting on. But informed chance.

I don't remain stationary. For just over two hours I crisscross the square and the surrounding neighborhoods, shifting eight times among three keynode eruvnets in the interim.

Nothing. No sign of Jian. No mayhem in progress for me to break in upon.

I receive a radio call from Leah. "Ehmet must've taken the Balarang Avenue streetcar. He just shifted to a new eruvnet, Ningjing, just south of Barham Square."

Another eruvnet not on my list. But I cannot discount the possibility that he will begin his march towards Neuronet collapse in one of the two keynodes centered on Barham Square.

Again, nothing. Again, he flees, or simply progresses, this time to the next square clockwise on the Middle Ring Road, Malaya Square.

I begin to detect his pattern. He moves in a consistently clockwise pattern, from one square on the Middle Ring Road to the next, then out along a connecting avenue to a square on one of the segments of the Outer Ring Road, there to invade an eruvnet in or near one of the outer public squares. Never a keynode. In and out he moves, like the hands of an accordion player, consistently clockwise.

Is his intention to exhaust me before he begins his primary assault on the Neuronet? Eighteen hours have passed since I first arrived at Maningrida Square. I am now in Rodney Square, the eleventh of seventeen, shifting between the keynodes of Kubu, Chrokkaon, and Pinan, watching for him. Waiting.

It is not fair — he can sleep, while I must remain vigilant. He can rest, while I waste my energy. Thoughts of fairness are absurd, of course. At least Leah has procured us a motorized cart, so we do not need to rely upon streetcars. But the cart travels even more infuriatingly slowly than do the streetcars, automatically pausing for invisible road-crossers, sluggishly weaving around other carts and pedestrians, both seen and unseen.

Is Jian circling the City like a carrion bird, waiting to taste flesh until the moment I drop?

Twenty-nine hours now. I am in Warspite Square, sixteenth out of seventeen. Leah sleeps on a bench by the square's central fountain. She has been catching cat-naps between alarms. I've commanded my aid-suit to periodically infuse me with stimulants; they jab at me like fiendish monkeys with sticks. But even fiendish monkeys must in the end surrender to exhaustion.

The moon has risen. Still hardly more than a sliver. It is upstaged by the luminous clock faces of the Gladstone Tower, two kilometers distant. They are never less than full in shape, for time never stops. Time never sleeps.

Jian will start his destruction in Queen Elizabeth Square. That is all that makes sense now. It is not the seventeenth of the City's squares; it is the first. The City's center, its ever-ticking heart — that is where he will first inject his poison. Five keynodes. For me, the final five of thirty-six; for him, the first. Refugio Dios, Thī hlb Phay, Bei Naan So, Sanctuaire Placide, and Schuilplaats.

Three minutes after I shift into the last of these, my radio squawks. Leah. "He's shifted into the Schuilplaats eruvnet," she says. *At last.* At last he has begun his invasion of the keynodes! "He's at — this is *strange*, Nofy. He's up on the observation deck of the Gladstone Clock Tower. One of the most congested spaces in the entire City. Why would he go *there?* You can only get up or down by way of two sets of stairs. I don't understand…"

Oh, but I do. Having led me on a merry chase all around the City, he now wishes to face me. Now that I am thoroughly exhausted, or so he presumes. Now that he can taunt me and perhaps attack me, figuring he will have the upper hand because I will feel constrained by the encroaching crowds.

But he doesn't know about my tasers. They do not depend upon my level of alertness to be effective. I will have him yet.

I double up on my stimulant infusion and head for the clock tower's stairs. Fifteen flights to the observation level. One-hundred-eighty steps. I remember from my girlhood that there are resting places and drinks vendors every five flights. I won't be taking advantage of those amenities tonight.

1.9

{Nofy at the Clock Tower}

The observation deck only looks uncrowded. In actuality, it is thickly congested with sightseers who come to see the inner workings of the eight giant clocks, their rear mechanisms exposed by glass covers, and to peer out the viewing ports at the City's carpet of lights.

The sound here! I'd forgotten. That ponderous ticking, amplified by the eight tremendous mechanisms evenly spaced around this octagonal hallway; their ticks, even if perfectly synchronized, reach my ears in staggered succession because of the varying distances the sounds must travel.

I pause at the edge of each inner corner of this eight-sided floor, extending my aid-suit's tiny remote camera slightly around the corner to see who is standing in the next segment. I find Jian casually slouching against the glass housing of the clock which faces Warspite Square, like a spider adhered to a window pane. He hasn't bothered to disguise himself.

I press the button on my wrist which irrevocably locks me onto whatever eruvnet he occupies, so long as I remain within half a kilometer of him. When he shifts, I will shift, too, no action required on my part.

If he runs? I will depend upon the greater speed my aid-suit provides. If he fights? I have my training and determination. As a last resort, should he wield a projectile weapon, there are my aid-suit's auto-tasers.

Now go.

I turn the corner sprinting. He sees me.

[SHIFT02]

A Hindi family, mother and father and four children, appear between us. He runs.

[SHIFT03]

The family is gone. They are replaced by a pair of youthful romancers, staring out a viewport, startled by my sudden clamorous appearance. He's only ten meters away, weaving. I'm locked on him. This will go differently than our fountain encounter.

[SHIFT04]

If he's trying to shake me, he's failing badly. Five meters ahead. I pirouette to avoid a gaudily dressed man selling chocolate-covered pretzels; he screams Dutch deprecations at me. Like a billiard ball striking invisible bumpers, I rebound off unseen civilians, stumbling over their flailing limbs, wincing from the internal electroshocks my signachip peppers me with in its futile effort to make me avoid them.

[SHIFT05]

Jian's stumbling, too. Worse than me. My aid-suit helps keep me upright. He benefits from no such balancer...

[SHIFT06]

A mass of children dressed in sailor-like school uniforms scatter like pigeons in a courtyard. Almost there. Almost in reach. I can nearly grasp his shoulder—

[SHIFT07]

I have him! I swing my arm around his neck, apply a choke hold, lunge forward, and use my momentum to smash his face against the wall. A woman screams. Jian grunts as we slide to the floor.

[SHIFT08]

He's writhing like a beached eel. Got to get those arms constrained. He twists so that I'm now atop his stomach, not his back. Good. I want his face in front of me.

[SHIFT09]

"You're under detention!" I scream down at him, feeling for the cuffs on my belt. "I'm a Bradburian law enforcement officer!"

"But I'm no Bradburian, you brown beast," he says, grinning. And spits in my face.

[SHIFT10]

Rage sets fire to my bloodstream. I lose control. Punch his face with all the force my aid-suit augmented right arm can muster. I hear his nose break.

[SHIFT11]

"Beast," he says, slurring the word. "But a *useful* beast, certainly..." His spittle drips from my chin onto my breast. I hit him again, aiming for the nose. I feel the stitches in my palm tear asunder, sense fresh blood seep into the leather of my glove. But my pain is rewarded with his, far worse than mine.

"I surrender," he says, slurring through a minute red waterfall that crests his upper lip and dribbles into his mouth. "*Capituler, aistislam, teslim, tóuxiáng*... are those languages too advanced? Should I translate it into clicks, or try some form of primitive sign language?" [SHIFT12] "*Oook oook?* 'Me give up'? You can take the girl out of the jungle, but you can't take the jungle out of the girl. By the way, is there a law against police brutality in Bradbury? I'm sure you'll be kind enough to provide a complaint form for me to fill out, and the proper orifice through which to insert it." [SHIFT13] "If you manage to get me back to Mars. And you won't."

"Why not? Because I'll eject you through the air lock into open space, along with the garbage?" I struggle to unhook the tri-cuffs from my belt. Not easy when I'm pinning his arms with my knees; the cuffs' clasp became bent in our struggle.

"Bad guess. Keep trying."

[SHIFT14]

I manage to work the cuffs loose. I grab his right hand first, cuff it, then his left. The third cuff I fasten to a hard mount circling my left wrist.

"Oh, yes, handcuff me," he says. "Follow procedure, by all means." [SHIFT15] His eyes narrow as they lock on mine. Cold orbs, cold as the rocky moons of Mars. "Togetherness," he hisses, "no man is an island, after all..."

"Expect solitary confinement in Bradbury," I say, adjusting the cuffs.

"I think I've had enough of solitude," he says. "You and I, we're about to have a lot of" [SHIFT16] "fresh company. More than you can imagine. Delightful folks, all of them."

What is he babbling about? Does he delude himself that he's still bringing down the Neuronet? "You can't escape me. Your plans are over with, you anarchist."

He smiles, showing red teeth. "Not at all, not at all."

[SHIFT17]

His satisfied tone chills me. "What do you mean?"

"*I'm* not crashing the Neuronet. *You* are."

I shove my forearm against his windpipe. "*What—?*"

[SHIFT18]

He coughs as delicately as a fawn. "Let — let me *speak*, woman, and I'll happily tell you. I never had the list of keynodes. Not last month's. Not this month's. Not until you gave it to me."

"But Leah said — she told me that the final week of the last lunar month, you visited eleven of that cycle's keynodes—"

[SHIFT19]

"Lya *lied* to you. Jews have gotten pretty good at that, what with four thousand years to practice."

"This is a *trick—*"

"No trick. This is truth. I've *already* tricked you. I don't need to repeat that modest feat. I created" [SHIFT20] "a virus. Lya uploaded it into your cripple-suit while you thought she was providing you with upgrades. The virus is written so that it only injects itself into an eruvnet's base code when you and I are frequency-locked, both within the eruvnet simultaneously — I could've written it so that it would launch when just you entered an eruvnet, searching for me" [SHIFT21] "but there was a chance some SchneerSon or Segregatronics tech would discover the damage too early and stop you from plunging so heedlessly through the keynodes. I captured your precious list simply by tracking your shifts as we went round and round the ring roads. Then I programmed the list" [SHIFT22] "into my kit. Beating me up more won't do you a bit of good. We're on autopilot. By my count, you've already fatally infected twenty-two keynodes."

There's still time — I can terminate my lock on him. Plant myself in this one eruvnet until I can determine the truth and figure out a way to get back to Eruv Rav. If Jian continues shifting through the keynodes, it won't matter; he'll still be chained to my wrist.

[SHIFT23]

I press the button Leah installed. Nothing changes. Press it again. Again. It won't turn *off.* I can't break my harmonization with Jian...

"Can't shut it off, can you? That handy-dandy little upgrade you figured would let you hound me across an infinity of eruvnets?" He laughs, a gurgle choked with phlegm. "I *told* you Lya wasn't working your corner. She hates the injustice of this City's Schisms and invisible fences" [SHIFT24] "nearly as much as I do. Do you believe me now?"

"I believe I can shut *you* off!" I grab his left forearm — skeletally thin, a third shorter than his right — and smash his portable tuning unit against the floor, harder and harder, until mangled components scurry across the hallway like roaches fleeing light.

"Oh, but *can* you?" he says.

[SHIFT25]

It hasn't stopped...

"Those of us not bred in the jungle have developed this little skill called 'thinking three steps ahead'," he says. "I told you, we're on autopilot. You'd need to butcher me like a beef cow to find and destroy the tiny component you're so desperately looking for. Do you have the stones for that?"

I have to get away from him — half a kilometer away. These damned cuffs... of *course* he grinned like a hyena when I chained us together! Get them unlocked—

[SHIFT26]

He snarls and bludgeons my hand with his knee, sending the key sliding across the floor. "Not that easy," he says. I struggle to rise, hampered by his passive resistance. The key comes to a halt, then shoots forward again, kicked by an unseen foot or feet. I drag Jian behind me, relying on the extra strength provided by my aid-suit, focusing only on the key.

It continues skittering across the floor as it is kicked again, like a half-dead mouse intermittently remembering it is alive. I'm barely keeping pace. [SHIFT27] Then I watch in horror as it levitates from the floor. Someone — a child? — has noticed it and picked it up. I see it drop again, but only a few centimeters — into a pocket?

"*No!*" I cry. I know they cannot hear me. But logic has fled. "Do not *take* it! Come *back!*"

I watch my precious key float through the air and vanish around a corner.

"Isn't it a bother how the little things always seem to get away from one?" Jian says from the floor. "No stepping off the merry-go-round until it comes to a complete stop."

[SHIFT28]

I'm not beaten yet. The cord connecting us — it's stronger than steel, but it's *plastic*. Which can be melted by my aid-suit's utility laser. Low-wattage, but it should suffice...

He wiggles the cord, preventing me from focusing the laser on a single spot. "Keep doing that," I say, "and" [SHIFT29] "I'll cut through your *wrist*, instead." An empty threat — bone won't melt, at least not for this modest a laser. But he appears to believe me — the cord remains stationary.

It melts. I stretch the softened plastic until it is the thickness of a hair and pull my wrist free. Shame about that key walking away — I could've chained Jian to a guard rail. Can't have him following me. I'll have to stoop to more brutal tactics...

"Forgive me, anarchist," I say. [SHIFT30] I kick him hard in the stones so he won't resist what I must do next. While he groans, half-curled into a ball, I pull his leg straight, twist it so I can step on the side of his knee, then grab his foot and yank upward with all my augmented strength.

His scream and a wet crunching sound confirm that I have dislocated his knee.

Surrounded by deafening mechanical ticking again. It never went away. Just impossible to ignore now. Seconds, flowing away from me like lifeblood.

[SHIFT31]

I'm running through the eight-sided hall towards the down staircase, knocking unseen sightseers aside, ignoring jolts both external and internal. Fifteen flights down, 180 steps. Even at the bottom, I still won't be clear.

I count on aversion signals to help me weave around invisible descenders, praying my aid-suit's gyroscopes will sustain my footing. My feet slap the stairs like I'm a dervish tap dancer. But even with my aid-suit's balancing corrections, I still must grab frantically for the guard railing whenever I strike unseeable flesh.

Down to floor eleven now [SHIFT32] and a gaggle of hunched-over ladies in shawls block the steps half a flight below. "Look out!" I cry. "Police emergency! *Clear a path!*" The ones that can hear look up. Pressing my way through them is like fording a river of mud.

Jump between landings? Land right, my aid-suit keeps me from shattering my legs. But I can't see who's below. Land wrong, break bones, and it's all over. All lost.

All lost.

[SHIFT33]

Two more shifts bedevil my senses before I reach the bottom stair. How many do I have left? How many more before the Neuronet collapses in on itself like a burgeoning black hole, sucking all the invisible fences into nothingness?

The night air is thick, humid. The plaza appears deserted. The only sound I hear is the serene tinkling of the fountain's waters. Serenity. I have not known it since childhood.

Run. What direction is best? Doesn't matter. Away. Away from the tower. Run like the young, willful Kala Ratsy once ran, the ugly girl who never knew her place. Who was always running. Who grew strong and swift, crazy-swift, almost fast enough to outrace disaster...

[SHIFT36]

1.10

{Nofy in Hell}

A second ago, Warrengo Avenue just beyond Queen Elizabeth Square was empty as the red Martian desert. Suddenly, not. My view of the avenue is obscured by an instant flood of people, and I know I have failed.

Evening shift workers, late diners, club hoppers, gangsters, mystics, insomniacs from a crushing multitude of eruvnets, all waking up from parallel dreams to the hideous reality that they have been sharing the same space. Screams rain down from the windows of the apartment blocks fronting both sides of the avenue. All those thousands upon thousands of surreptitiously shared living arrangements, multiple families crowding the same rooms without ever knowing it, never seeing or hearing one another's presence, apart from the opening or closing of a faucet or the flushing of a toilet... now they cannot avoid one another.

I have failed.

Astonished cries, warnings, deprecations in more languages than I can count. Everyone is pressed by walls of flesh. Everyone, horrified.

Shoves. Shouts. Blows exchanged. The small minority of hotheads sets the mood on the street. It begins.

I am powerless to prevent it. And I grow more powerless by the second — Neuronet gone, my palsy creeps back. The aid-suit does what it can to steady me, but it will take time for it to recalibrate to my weakening condition. Will the mob grant me that time? I'm in the City's center — do I have a chance of reaching a gate? Of fleeing across the scrub flats to my ship?

Something crashes through a third-story window, showering the street and the crowds with shards of glass. A man. Hurled through the window, or forced to jump. He lands brutally atop a woman and her child. They both scream. The man emits no sound, other than the thwack his torso makes against their bodies.

Four men lift him from atop his inadvertent victims. They begin tearing at his flesh in inarticulate fury, as though he were to blame for the collapse of the invisible fences.

A flower vendor's cart is set on fire. Then a storefront. Other stores' windows are smashed with stones or clubs or skulls being bludgeoned against glass. The panicked crowd grows ultra-panicked — but there is no room to run. They're all cattle squeezed onto the slaughter line. The weaker and the smaller are ground under, trampled.

The rot accelerates, the City's heart putrefying like organ meat tossed into a fly-infested bin steaming in the sun. Less than two minutes have passed.

Move, Nofy. Don't be overwhelmed. Where to shelter? My clan's neighborhood is as out of reach as the inner wastes of Mongolia. It's night. One of the big municipal buildings back in the square might remain empty, with a maze of rooms in which to hide—

A crash above me. Rain of glass. Then something pounds me into the ground like a giant's fist. Can't *breathe* — wind knocked out of me, abdomen squeezed in a vise. A bureau landed on me. Stuffed full of suits of iron, or lead bricks... books, more likely. Aid-suit's servos aren't all on-line — can't get the legs to respond, don't have the leverage to shove the damned bureau off me with only my arms. My palsied legs, unsteadied, twitch like the tail of a speared fish.

Can't tell if bones are broken. Feels like they are — ribs merely cracked, if I'm lucky. Bile burns my throat. There is a man dancing in the middle of the street, pirouetting around and around. His partner is the upper half of a mannequin, which trails the muddied, bloodied shrouds of a wedding gown.

I hear distant gunfire. Volleys which seem to come from several points. The soldiers have entered the gates. Guardians meant to keep invaders out. But now they are the invaders — no resident of the City, apart from some of the SchneerSons, has ever seen a member of the Defense Force before. To the panicked, feral mobs, those unrecognized protectors are a new and deadly threat.

The soldiers will kill more than they are killed, at least until they become overwhelmed by sheer numbers. And then, after hacking the downed soldiers to pieces, the victorious mob will take up the guns from the corpses' hands.

And so the City eats itself.

The eastern sky, already tinted a lurid orange thanks to uncontrolled fires, adds the pink rosiness of a struggling dawn to its palette. My aid-suit, not fully functional, now possibly no more rational than the mob itself, has been pumping me with alternating sedatives and stimulants. Snatches of drugged sleep are broken by adrenal surges and dry heavings.

I hear a voice behind me. A hatefully familiar voice. "So there you are, Kala Ratsy. Do you know how difficult it is to descend twelve flights of stairs with a dislocated knee? A lucky break, though, so to speak... I spent the worst hours of the violence sheltered in the clock tower's stairwell. I see you didn't get very far."

Were it not for the sedatives in my bloodstream, I might break my own back with my effusion of outrage. As it is, I can barely muster a groan of contempt.

"Not very talkative, are you?" Jian says. "Well, given the magnitude of your failure, I can't imagine you have much to say." I turn my head just enough to see him. He peers at the devastation surrounding us with what might be wistfulness. "If only Sikandar could have lived to see this... ah, well. Wherever his spirit now resides, it cannot be ignorant of what has transpired here. They have all paid for what they have done. Best of all, they have extracted that payment themselves."

"Monster..."

"No, not quite. A 'monster' would leave you to be violated and to eventually die of thirst. Excruciatingly. I, on the other hand, will show you mercy worthy of the Prophet by swiftly lopping off your folly-filled head. Consider this thanks for your invaluable if unwilling assistance."

He lightly touches my neck with the curved edge of a scimitar, calibrating his aim, then raises it above my head. Unwise of him, to physically threaten me — taser wires spring out from my aid-suit's shoulders like a spider's silken filaments. Their barbed ends cling to his clothes and skin; fifty-thousand volts carry .12 amps throughout his nervous system. He drops like a coconut dislodged from its branch by a storm gust.

To my surprise, but not my dismay, my suit's wires fail to retract. Instead, additional taser wires spring forth, shooting more amperage into Jian's prone body, like bees' stingers which continue pumping venom into the object of the hive's fury even after being sundered from the insects' hindquarters.

Twitching uncontrollably by my side, he begins to cook. I do not find the aroma entirely unpleasant.

Gulls circle overhead, keen eyes searching for choice morsels. No shortage of those around here. The crows are less shy about their appetites; two of them have already begun pecking burnt flesh from Jian's arms and face.

A bearded man approaches. I feign death. Until one of the crows delivers an exploratory peck to my cheek — then I can't help but jerk my head away.

"Nofy? You're alive?"

Only three people in the City knew my name. At least one of those is dead. I open my eyes. "Baruch? Baruch Emmanuel?" He isn't wearing his black coat and black hat, nor the prayer shawl with which all male SchneerSons wrap themselves. His loose-fitting shirt (borrowed from a corpse?) is patterned with bright purple and pink crescents, cheerfully incongruent with stains of dried blood. Three parallel slashes mar his face, leaving his nose a torn and listing lump.

"Thank HaShem you've survived," he says.

"Baruch... were you... mauled by a tiger?"

"I would have preferred a tiger, I think," he says. "Let me see if I can get this furniture off of you."

He has the leverage I've lacked. After a moment's struggle, we manage to dislodge the bureau. Baruch helps me to my feet.

The bastard. He would have to lift a thousand bureaus from off my back for me to feel anything other than contempt for him... and his treacherous protégée. "Leah betrayed me."

"I know. She told me, moments after the Neuronet collapsed."

"Where is she now?"

"Dead."

"Where did it happen?"

"Just outside our offices. I've learned pogroms do not require much in the way of organization. Merely ample hate. A contingent of the mob sought out us SchneerSons. They blamed us for what had happened, as I'd known they would. And thanks to Leah, they were not entirely mistaken."

"Why did she do it, Baruch? Did she tell you?"

"A surfeit of idealism. A malady to which the young are prone. She wanted to mend the world."

Mend the world? The world is beyond mending. I've witnessed the world. The world is shit. Should the Neuronet ever be restored,

I will become an isolate. I never want to see another human being, so long as I live.

"She saved my life, Nofy. The mob intended to tear us apart, me and all my coworkers. Like Lot in Sodom, Leah offered herself to the marauders so that the rest of us might be spared violation. Better than Lot — he offered his daughters, not himself. Some of us managed to escape. I was injured by other attackers before I managed to discard my telltale clothing, but matters would have been far worse for me, had it not been for Leah."

"Had it not been for Leah, tens of thousands of people might still remain alive."

His face turns ashen. "True. She will face judgment. Yet HaShem's judgment will be tempered by her inarguably sincere repentance. I have my own repentance to make. In my excess of caution, I denied you the help which might have enabled you to capture Jian. Part of this catastrophe rests upon my shoulders."

He stares expectantly into my face. What does he want of me? Absolution? I have none to give.

"The violence cannot last much longer," he says, glancing at the black smoke smudging the horizon. "I feel the palsy gathering in my muscles. Those younger and stronger than I may resist the deterioration longer than I can. But soon, even they will be forced by palsy to abandon their mayhem. Then the hunger will set in. And pestilence."

Does he expect me to weep for them? After what I have seen? "May they all die in torment," I whisper. "I hate them all."

"No — you must not say that, Nofy."

I whirl on him, nearly falling forward in my unbalanced vehemence. "I cannot say that I hate them? That I hate *you?* Would you deny me even *that?*"

He stares at the blood-soaked ground. "Hatred in itself is not a sin. HaShem commands us to hate evil. And there is much evil here to hate. But hatred without discernment...? Eight million people resided in this City, Nofy. One million of them children who had not yet reached double digits in years. Does your hatred extend to them?"

I do not answer. I will not give him the satisfaction of cheap absolution through acknowledging his rebuke of *my* shortcomings. I did my best...

"Is your help-suit capable of self-repair?"

Why should he ask that? "To a limited extent, yes."

"In the land of the blind, the one-eyed woman is queen." He offers a tentative smile. "Soon, you will be the most able-bodied person within the City's walls."

"So? As soon as I am able, I will return to my ship. I will leave this accursed place."

"What will you return to on Mars? Official censure? Disgrace?"

"Thanks to you and your wild-eyed idealist protégée, yes."

"Stay with us. Help us. You will have the power to choose who will eat. Who will live."

"Out of millions? You expect me to *choose?*"

"You must. To refuse to choose is also to choose. There is a saying among my people... 'To save a single life is to save an entire world.' You have seen a world — multitudes of worlds — destroyed. Which worlds will you choose to save?"

Which worlds?

If my *nenibe* was right, soon this City will fill up with lemurs, those scuttling creatures who house the souls of the dead. In Anarako Arivo, we allowed ourselves to remember the deceased, but we convinced ourselves to forget those who disappeared, those we could no longer see. Now we cannot fail to see; the moon's brilliance can no longer blot out the existence of millions of lesser lights.

"Will you stay and choose?" asks Baruch the SchneerSon.

In Malagasy, the language of my birth, there are two words for 'we.' There is *izahay*, which means 'us but not you.' And there is *isika*, which means 'all of us'.

I give the City of a Thousand Names a thousandth-and-first, the only name by which it can live.

"I choose Isika."

About the Author

ANDREW Fox has been a fan of science fiction and horror since he saw *Destroy All Monsters* at the drive-in theater at the age of three. His books include *Fat White Vampire Blues*, winner of the Ruthven Award for Best Vampire Fiction of 2003; *Bride of the Fat White Vampire*; *Fat White Vampire Otaku*; *Fire on Iron*, a Civil War dark fantasy; and *The Good Humor Man, or, Calorie 3501*, selected by Booklist as one of the Ten Best SF/Fantasy Novels of the Year for 2009. In 2006, he won the *Moment* Magazine-Karma Foundation Short Fiction Award. His stories have appeared in *Scifi.com* and *Nightmare.com*, and his essays have been published in *Moment* and *Tablet* Magazine. He edited a companion volume to *Hazardous Imaginings*, the international anthology *Again, Hazardous Imaginings: More Politically Incorrect Science Fiction*, which will be available from MonstraCity Press in December 2020. His next novel, *The Bad Luck Spirits' Social Aid and Pleasure Club*, revolves around an alternate Hurricane Katrina and will be published in February 2021. He lives in Northern Virginia with his family, where he works for a federal law enforcement agency. He can be reached at http://www.fantasticalandrewfox.com.